Sigrid Estrada

Ehud Havazelet is the award-winning author of two story collec-
tions, *What Is It Then Between Us?* and *Like Never Before,* which was
a *New York Times* Notable Book and a *Los Angeles Times* Best Book.
He has been awarded fellowships from the Guggenheim, Whiting,
and Rockefeller foundations. He teaches in the Creative Writing
Program at the University of Oregon, and at the Warren Wilson
MFA Program for Writers. He lives in Corvallis, Oregon.

BEARING THE BODY

EHUD HAVAZELET

PICADOR

FARRAR, STRAUS AND GIROUX

NEW YORK

www.picadorusa.com

Picador® is a U.S. registered trademark and is used by
Farrar, Straus and Giroux under license from Pan Books Limited.

For information on Picador Reading Group Guides, please contact Picador.
E-mail: readinggroupguides@picadorusa.com

Designed by Jonathan D. Lippincott

ISBN-13: 978-0-312-42750-4
ISBN-10: 0-312-42750-6

First published in the United States by Farrar, Straus and Giroux

First Picador Edition: December 2008

10 9 8 7 6 5 4 3 2 1

For Molly,
beyond words

Without forgetting it is quite impossible to live at all.

—Nietzsche, *On the Advantage and
Disadvantage of History for Life*

Even in heaven eternal bliss would be possible only by the grace of a criminal loss of memory. Should the blessed not be punished with hell for this?

—Harry Mulisch, *The Discovery of Heaven*

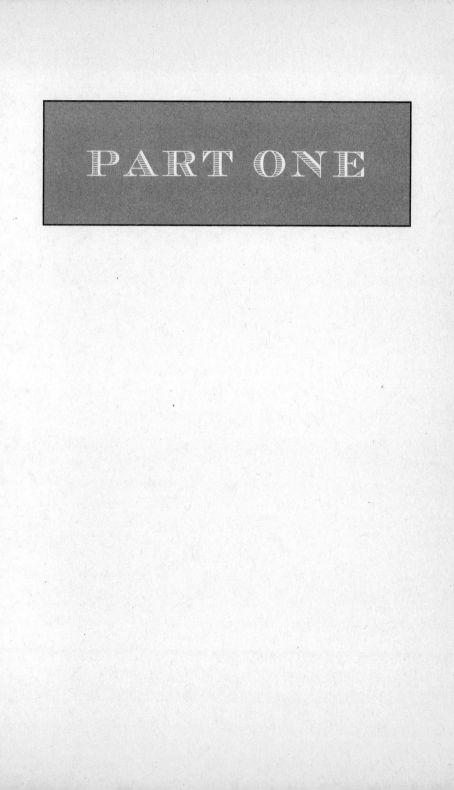

PART ONE

PROLOGUE, 1968

It was a spring evening and he had come in too soon. Beyond the dining room window the catalpa tossed heavily, leaves grown huge this week, trailing seedpods comically like tassels. The light over the houses was a charged blue, not as in winter when it drained abruptly into night, but softer, a presence, almost liquid, an invitation, a tease. In the street, a car circled a second time, its radio up, and he leaned in to hear but caught only the thin edge of a melody before it turned the corner and faded.

Nathan was fourteen and after two hours of basketball had run the mile home, could have run another. He sat in his damp clothes with his body humming. A plate of food was in front of him, chicken, potatoes, beans boiled until their skin came loose, but he wasn't eating. The sweatshirt against his neck just beginning to cool, his calves, the area between his shoulders throbbing an agreeable ache. He watched his mother cut small pieces of chicken with a knife, her eyes fixed on the news across the room. His father, the *Post* beside his plate, also not eating, glancing from time to time at his food as if surprised to find it there, stabbing something without looking and bringing it to his mouth. Nathan reached past his father for the carton of milk, looked at his parents, at the newscaster a blank moment, then back out the window.

Long ago—he couldn't even remember when—he had developed the art of segregating himself. So while part of him hovered nearby, made sure he answered questions, chewed some food, the other part—the essential part, he knew—was able to split off entirely. He was back on the cement court behind the school, the warm, nubbly ball in his hands, waiting at the top of the key for Larry Cohen to lunge, as he knew he would, so he could put a shoulder into him, glide by and float the ball from his fingertips into the basket, while all Cohen could do was gape, flabbergasted, as if it were all choreographed, inevitable.

At the same time he was behind the chain-link fence where some girls, including Shari Rosenheim, paused on their way from the library to watch, books squeezed to their sweatered breasts, in among the smells and laughter and quiet sarcastic appraisals. And he was upstairs, where he had gone straight from coming in, on his bed with the lights out, with the towel he had bought himself and which he really needed to replace, Shari Rosenheim in her plaid skirt, the green sweater gone now, hair falling into her face as all his blood gathered and he closed his eyes and she reached down to touch him.

His mother had said something. Nathan had missed it and so had his father. His father looked up, eyes batting as they did when he worked to be patient, but his mother was alarmed as she said it again, "Daniel," and they all looked at the set. The six o'clock news, Walter Cronkite's dull, reassuring baritone, the same every night, guaranteeing that even if something happened nothing ever changed. Columbia. The demonstrations. Cameras zooming in and out, kids hanging from windows, banners, students facing off with cops on the library steps. A red-haired guy shouting into a megaphone. Just after he'd made that move, split the defenders and left Cohen holding his dick, he'd looked back at Shari Rosenheim, who had smiled as she walked away. She'd seen it. He knew she had.

On the television a camera was jostled, everything slurrying, and when it steadied, the building came into focus, steps, white columns, second-story windows where students called down and threw papers, one huge sheaf catching wind and scattering. A reporter was saying, "Walter, this may be growing serious here." Kids were barricaded in the building, had trashed offices. Now rumors a fire was set, chaos, many students had fled, concern for those remaining inside. The camera pulled in to three kids on the ledge, holding the sill behind them, cops below on the ground scrambling at their legs. There he was. His mother said it again, "Daniel." Though the breeze whipped his hair they could see the green army jacket, the black hat, the thin face, the complacent half-grin, the eyes. Daniel. His mother made a noise. Now two cops had him by the feet, hauling him down. But first he straightened, looked at the crowd. He moved hair off his face with two hands, put his arms out to the sides, as if he was on the board at the lake at camp, as if he was about to take off right over their heads. And before he was dragged down, two cops in face shields, another red-faced and cursing, they saw him look at the camera and smile.

The car passed a third time, its radio blasting. Some neighborhood kids out riding, circling the streets. Nathan could see their faces, their elbows on the door frames, the cigarettes in their mouths. They were cruising, they could drive into the city, upstate, anywhere. The same song. Was it? He leaned into the sound, made out a guitar, a drumbeat, and he leaned harder, determined this time to catch it.

1

1995

The letter sat before him, unopened, propped against a coffee mug. He had known it was there, somehow, even before he found it among the wad of junk mail, bills, and offers of credit cards he neither wanted nor could afford that plugged the brass box in the lobby. He had paused with the tiny key in his hand but then opened the box and reached in, not because suspicions were silly—the opposite, if anything, was true—but because whatever was there had arrived, was already unavoidable. There was a letter for Janet also, from her mother, and he placed it on the bench by the door where they left each other's mail before discarding the rest under the sink and filling the pot for coffee. He hadn't slept in thirty hours and he didn't want more coffee, he wanted a drink. But he didn't want a drink, either.

He had two cups, making repeated circuits from the kitchen, where the letter lay on the table, to the living room that sloped east toward Mass. Ave., to their bedroom in back, where the sheets were still twisted and hanging to the floor. He thought of lying on the bed, pulling the stale warm darkness of the room over his head with the blankets, but returned to the kitchen with the dull resignation he had felt opening the mailbox, nothing else to do.

The lamp with its weighted cord shifted in the draft of the floor heater, marking circles of pale light on the table. Across the street a man came out of his house, looked around him, zipped a bright blue parka over his stomach, and began walking toward the avenue. Idly, Nathan leaned in his chair to see which direction he turned at the corner.

The letter, in the emphatic, slashing hand that could only be Daniel's, was addressed to His Holiness Msgr. Nathaniel Mirsky, SJ, DDS, LSD, and had been mailed six days ago from San Francisco. The postmark was smudged, off kilter, but he could make out the city and date. There was no return address.

He was still at the table when Janet arrived. He heard her kick off her shoes, heard her open her letter and sit on the bench in the hall, and over the next few minutes heard her laugh and exclaim to herself. His head felt exactly as if two hands pressed hard behind the temples, something in his chest darted and clenched, a pulled muscle, heartburn, early signs of infarction. A brief hope had flared when she came in; now he was even more alone. Across the street the man had returned, wearing a *Hogan's Heroes* hat, fleece-lined with flaps that could be pulled down over the ears. He was a portly gentleman in a blue parka, which also looked new, and he stopped at the top of the stairs before going inside, looking around with a pleased expression as if all his prospects were improved, now he'd gotten a warm new hat.

Nathan made a sound. In the hall Janet heard him and said, "Nate? Are you here, honey?"

She came into the kitchen holding her letter, a bag of groceries in which he could see a baguette and a bottle of wine. She was in her stockings, and she walked with feet slightly splayed, flat-footed, which always made Nathan think, for some reason, of a small child, and which, for some reason, he found quite sexy. She put the bag on the table in front of the letter, leaned against the sink and said, "Listen to this. It's about Dana." She picked up a foot and began massaging the toes, one by one, through the sheer stocking. Dana was eleven, her sister back in Cleveland, and Nathan liked hearing about her, more, anyway, than about Janet's parents, who even over the phone—the mother flirty and solicitous, the father bluffly man-to-man, always with some home-improvement project he wanted to discuss—seemed to be asking for something Nathan didn't have in him to give. Janet read from the letter.

" 'Yesterday, after dinner, she was on the phone with Carrie, one of her friends. Oh, it's the thing now, talking on the phone. If you come into the room she stops and stares until you leave, and if you stay she says huffily, "I can't talk right now. I'll have to call you back." ' "

Janet paused, looked up at him with a pleasure-filled, disarming smile that ratcheted the pain in his chest. Please, he found himself thinking. And then, Please what? "Let me find the good part," Janet said.

She came to the table and sat, the angle of the lamp illuminating the slope of her breasts in the white dress shirt, the slight pucker of the material when she leaned forward. She put a foot onto Nathan's shoe and continued reading. Two months ago she had moved out, gone to her mother's for a week. Things were bad between them. Nathan had agreed to counseling, Janet had returned, and since they had moved around each other with a studied gaiety and hopefulness that filled Nathan with a queasy despair.

" 'So, later, I just couldn't help myself. I said, "Honey, who were you and Carrie talking about?" She's in bed, reading *Narnia* (again), she's brushed and put up her hair and put on moisturizer, but still in her bunny pajamas, of course. "Amanda Vukovich," she said. "She's a ho." "A what?" I said. "A hoe?" "A *ho*, Mom. *You* know—she'd have sex with like anybody who asked her." ' "

Janet put the letter down and looked at him. She laughed. "My God," she said, "my pigtailed, Wonder Bread, Episcopalian sister. Ho ho ho. I blame MTV."

Janet began unloading groceries, filling a pot for pasta. When she handed Nathan a corkscrew for the wine, she took the shopping bag from the table and saw the letter against the coffee mug.

"Oh," she said, said it again, and sat. She reached over for his hand but he moved to scratch something on his face. She let her hand drop to his knee. "Oh, Nathan," Janet said. "Have you read it?" He knew she was looking at him. When he didn't answer, she kissed him lightly on the hair, left him to open the wine, and began heating the marinara. Nathan wondered what the man in the new hat was doing, was he wearing it inside? He'd like to knock on his door, find out. He felt the urge to run, to cry, to scream. He saw how the night would unfold and closed his eyes against it.

They drank the wine, and when the bottle was finished opened another, and after that Nathan got the scotch from the cupboard and the weed from the freezer. In the periphery of his awareness he could see Janet moving carefully, trying, in the way she arranged their dinner, the pretty salad with the carrot shavings and cherry tomatoes, the nice sweater she changed into, the way she accepted the joint from him a few times though she rarely enjoyed getting high, and never in the middle of the week, when she was tired from work. He was aware of all this, the way she let her hands or lips linger on him just long enough to have him know she was available, and as he poured his second scotch he resolved not to look at her anymore.

Later they made love, and she left him dozing heavily while she went to shower. He woke, hearing her cleaning the dishes, watering plants, opening the bills she had retrieved from the trash. From Mass. Ave. he could faintly hear music starting up at the Plough. He wondered if Robin was there, or Nicki. Or Eleanor. He lay in the dark, listening, until, much later, Janet came in.

She sat on the edge of the bed and began brushing her hair. He moved over and put a hand under her T-shirt, holding a breast from below.

"Hello," she said. "Somebody want dessert?"

He pulled her into bed, slid her T-shirt over her head, her sweatpants and underwear off. He was like a man running too long, knowing only that he had to finish before he could stop. Janet lay under him, looking at him with her bright, kindly eyes. "C'mere,"

she said, putting her arms behind his head to draw his face to her.
Nathan took her by the shoulders and turned her, and when she lay
on her stomach he put his hands under her hips and lifted. With his
palms, trying to be gentle, he eased her cheeks apart and positioned
himself.

"Honey," she said, her voice muffled by the pillow. "Sweetheart,
no, not now, okay? Not right now. Maybe later we could."

He ignored her, began pressing against her.

"Nathan," she said. "Let me do you, okay? I'm really in the
mood."

He was nearly ready. He rocked back and forth, pressing against
her until he was hard. He pulled away a moment, saw her long
white back, the silken hair covering her averted face. Outside Irish
music surged when someone opened the door to the Plough. Somebody called somebody's name.

He moved in hard, once, twice. Janet let out a short scream,
pressing her face into the pillow, reaching back to clench one of his
hands. He kept moving, steadying himself against her. Soon she let
go of his hand, was silent and didn't stir in front of him. He couldn't
even hear her breathing. He prayed for it to be over and prayed she
wouldn't turn and look at him, this woman who on his best days, his
naïve hopeful lighter days, he tried to love. He closed his eyes and
finished.

In the morning, Nathan waited until Janet was gone, pretending to
sleep, trying to. Despite himself he attempted to gauge her mood,
listening for her voice in the shower, whether she put things down
more heavily than usual as she moved in the bathroom and kitchen.
He couldn't tell. She closed the door behind her, and, though that
was what he had been waiting for, he lay in bed a while longer, determined not to think about anything. When he did get up he
called Dr. Ammons' secretary at the hospital, who was completely
mystified by what he told her.

"You'll be missing rounds, then, Dr. Mirsky? And your shift?"

He had said he was leaving for a few weeks, maybe longer, of course he'd be missing goddamn rounds. "Just give him the message, please," Nathan said, and after a moment, as if she was giving him time to take it all back, she hung up.

He packed, unwilling to decide what he might need, sweaters or T-shirts or maybe even a tie, tossing in whatever his hands found until the old Samsonite he'd inherited from Daniel when he went off to college was nearly full. He topped it with a handful of underwear and socks from the dirty clothes hamper at the bottom of their closet. He sat at the table in the kitchen, trying to compose a note. "Hey," he began, "I gotta take care of some stuff . . ." He tore the paper from the pad and began again. "I'll call from New York . . . ," the next note said, and the next, "J, I need . . . ," and the last, "Janet, I'm sorry." He left this one, threw the others in the trash, and went through the apartment one more time to see if he'd forgotten anything. In their bedroom he paused at the dresser, looking at the dish she kept her rings in, the assortment of clips for her hair. He stood before her part of the closet a moment, then kneeled to put the clothes he'd scattered back in the basket. He thought of making the bed, but the inadequacy of the gesture struck him as obscene. So did the note he had left for her on the table, which he stuffed in his pocket along with the still unopened letter, before taking his suitcase and locking the door behind him.

ᘡ ᘡ ᘡ

"Fucking old men," Mirsky thought, looking balefully around the locker room. They had a smell that even chlorine couldn't hide — fish about to go bad, or a day-old sandwich left in the sun. He couldn't help himself as he scanned the truly astonishing array before him — hairy backs and ears, speckled bald pates, scrotums dangling like watch fobs, skin withered and flaked and rumpled like canvas. Disgusting. He forced himself to look away, to avoid seeing himself in the row of mirrors opposite the lockers. Not that he held illusions he was any different.

At the other end of the locker benches, Melamed was dressing, talking with someone Mirsky recognized, but whose name he had forgotten. Melamed was an importer, retired, a snappy dresser with pressed pants and jackets with handkerchiefs in the pockets. He wore goggles to do his laps, a silly tight cap with a boomerang on the side. Sometimes they talked about medicine. Melamed asked about Nathan up in Boston, and Mirsky saw the man was offering him the opportunity to be proud, which he accepted, if grudgingly. Melamed had no children of his own.

"Tell him," the other man was saying to Melamed, gesturing over at Mirsky while pulling on a spotted yellow undershirt. "Ask him if police brutality's the biggest problem we got." As he sat on the bench to pull off his shorts, Mirsky caught a glimpse of the man's left forearm, the black numbers faded to green but still visible, like those on Mirsky's own arm under his shirt. Maybe years ago they might have sat somewhere, he and this man, and talked about it, where they had lived, their experiences. Not now. Mirsky turned his back and hung his pants by a belt loop in the locker.

"I didn't say it was our biggest problem," Melamed said, quietly. They had been discussing the case in the Bronx, two police emptying their guns into a black grandmother. The man was defending the police, saying you could ride the subway now without risking your life. He shrugged impatiently at both Melamed and Mirsky and shuffled off to put his head under the hand drier.

"How is it?" Melamed said to Mirsky. "The shoulder." He had seen it the day before.

"Fine," Mirsky said, though at that moment he was taking off his shirt, which caused him to wince. He saw Melamed staring at the wide bandage, the bruised skin, yellow and blue, leaking around it.

The two men continued in silence a few moments, Mirsky pulling on his baggy trunks, Melamed folding his towel, loading the little shoulder bag that had the same boomerang as his cap. When he was dressed he walked over and stood before Mirsky.

"I just heard," he said, "about your boy." Then he added Mirsky's first name. "Sol. I wanted to tell you I'm sorry."

Mirsky nodded in acknowledgment, but Melamed didn't move. Mirsky looked up at him, the creased face and berserk eyebrows, the patient gaze of a man used to soliciting complaint, offering comfort. Mirsky realized distantly it would be nice, were the circumstances entirely different, to speak with him. But they weren't. He had nothing to say, to him or to anybody. At least with Melamed he didn't have to try. They stayed there another moment, then Melamed gently touched him on the arm and left.

The pool was half full, aged men and women, the only ones at the Y in the middle of the day, struggling through the lime-blue water, bobbing like seals by the tiled rim, talking. The high opaque windows let in a diffuse sunlight, and the air was saturated with the oppressive humidity and odor of the place, chemical, human, old masonry and pipes. Years ago Mirsky would rush right in, welcoming the bracing shock the cold gave his system. Now he had to wait while two *alter kockers* stood arguing on the steps into the water. For ten cents he'd drown them both.

His stroke was makeshift, inefficient, a spastic forward plunging that filled his mouth with water and every few feet left him submerged, goggling at the legs of the other swimmers until he was forced to surface, gasping, half blind. But here he was every morning, as he had been over forty years now, doing his twenty laps, chuffing and splashing and clearing a wide berth, slowly forgetting himself in the movement and the sounds of his own labored breathing, his world constricted finally into blank walls and ceiling, the cracked blue bottom of the pool and the shimmering expanse of green water before and around him.

He swam a lap, two more. His left arm was nearly useless, but he kept going, an occasional sharper sting telling him he'd torn away another piece of bandage, using this as a goad to swim harder. When he stopped to get his wind he saw three women by the steps looking at him. One looked away, embarrassed, another smiled compassionately. He lunged back in.

It was six days ago. He'd hung up the phone, some stranger, a girl, telling him the news. He had walked around the apartment, waiting for an impulse, a clue about what he was to do next. He had called Nathan in Boston but found he couldn't utter any words once the machine picked up. He called again, this time forced himself to leave a brief message, then, as if it were any other Tuesday morning, got his ratty Mets gym bag from the floor of the bathroom, the dank towel and trunks and shampoo still wadded inside, and left for the Y.

Except it wasn't any other day. The colors of cars and buses were too bright, the sounds of horns and voices out of sync, as if dubbed onto the action. His head was filled with roaring and everything seemed far off. When the boy turned the corner and made directly for him, Mirsky had to remind himself to look down, deflect what he could of the menace. But the boy came right up and grabbed him with one hand, then his bag with the other. Too startled to let go, Mirsky hung on, feeling his cap sliding off his head, catching at the boy's jacket, then putting both hands on the strap of the gym bag. The boy dragged him up the sidewalk.

"I'll fuck you up, old man," the boy said. "Let go." He was dark-skinned and thin and astonishingly young. He kept looking around him. Mirsky said nothing, but held on.

Inside the bag were just his wet clothing and shampoo, no money, nothing of value. He could have told the boy this, but he didn't. He held on grimly and the boy hauled him toward the street.

"Let go," the boy said, through gritted teeth, then whispered it. "Let go." His bright brown eyes were focused on Mirsky now, scared as badly as the old man. He couldn't be more than thirteen.

"No," Mirsky said.

The boy shoved him and he stumbled, landing hard and awkwardly on the curb's stone edge, flashing streaks of light in his head and a searing pain down his arm, but he held on.

"Tell me," Mirsky said, half gasping, his body in the street. "Tell me. Why you need it."

This enraged the boy. With a violent tug he pulled the bag from Mirsky's hands and stood glowering. "Don't fuckin' need nothin', old man," the boy said, aiming a sharp kick near Mirsky's head but stopping short of contact before running up the street toward the subway.

The shoulder was sprained but not dislocated, he was bruised and badly scraped but nothing was broken. The nurse who put on the dressing at the emergency room looked at the already impressive contusion and told him he was lucky. He would have laughed in her face if he could have found the energy.

Mirsky realized he had stopped counting laps. He was in the deep end and suddenly exhausted, stomach cramping, shoulder throbbing hot pain, breath impossible to coax into his lungs. He held his injured arm to his chest and paddled to the wall, where he waited for his bearings to return. He didn't know how long he waited. Nearby, an ancient white-haired man who seemed to be here always, no matter what time you arrived, stood with a confused look on his face, which slowly relaxed. "Fucking old men," Mirsky muttered, pulling himself toward the steps, not needing to look to see the spreading oily cloud about the man's legs.

∾ ∾ ∾

The letter began full force, no greeting or introduction, as if Nathan were joining the middle of a conversation. All Daniel's letters were this way.

There was this girl—I don't think you knew her, two years behind me, in ninth grade. New girl, pretty, very thin . . .

Nathan had pulled off at a rest stop on 84, two hours out of Boston, when weariness came crashing over him in great waves that left him wrenching awake, once with his right wheels on the shoulder. The rest stop was long, dingy block washrooms and gated candy machines on an island between the parking spaces. Nathan drove to the far end, to the area set aside for buses, took one of the last spots under a bare sycamore, and didn't remember shutting off the engine before dropping into sleep.

He was unsure how long he had been out when he was roused by voices. A school bus parked a few spaces over, kids lining up for a trip to the restroom. He was groggy, unsure for a moment where he was, a sensation strengthened by the vague impression something was wrong with these kids. He sat up and rubbed a hand across his face. He looked closer. Down syndrome kids—Special Needs Children nowadays, "retarded," or things less kind, when he was young. They stood in a shambling queue by the front of the bus, a dozen or so; more, those who didn't need the restroom, were visible through the windows. There was an air of gleeful hilarity, laughter, calling, someone Nathan couldn't see chanting. They were dressed like typical teenagers, floppy pants and tees, printed designer sweatshirts and backward baseball caps. But the clothing hung awkwardly, half tucked, pulled sideways. Nathan rubbed his mouth and the back of his neck and reached over to start the engine.

A new voice cut through the clamor, crisp, authoritative. "Children," it called out. "Children." And this, too, seemed oddly off—they were adults, nearly. A teacher stepped from the bus and instructed them to place a hand on the shoulder of the person before them; she herself took the first girl by the hand and they trooped by Nathan's car, smiling, craning their heads about, talking to one another. A girl with glasses so thick her eyes floated behind them looked at Nathan and smiled. A boy, tapering head lolling on his already man-sized neck, was last in line. When he saw Nathan in the car he let go of the boy in front of him, looked over, and shot

out a finger, an uncanny, uncannily graceful rendering of the hip-
ster greeting Nathan saw kids perform on the street, or in movies.
"Yo," the boy mouthed, and gave him a thumbs-up. Nathan barely
managed to wait until they had passed by, were in the restrooms or
mingling by the candy machines. He opened his door, leaned out,
and was sick on the littered asphalt, the force of it making him gasp
and close his eyes. As soon as he was able he drove off, fast, trying
not to gun the engine. In the rearview he saw himself, eyes rimmed
gray, deadened, staring back.

He hadn't been to his parents' apartment in Queens since his
mother's funeral a year ago. He remembered the limousine could
barely negotiate the small circular drive, his father thin-lipped,
silent, far over at one end of the seat, Daniel, stoned, trying maybe
to hide it behind dark glasses, up front with the immobile driver.

When he pulled up, the doorman told him his father was not at
home and Nathan said he would wait. The entryway, lavish and
arty—mirrored walls, a two-foot gilded giraffe, a framed close-up of
Picasso—was overwarm, and the only seats, a row of thin-cushioned
benches on a slightly raised floor, were remarkably uncomfortable.

He took the farthest one, dropped his bag at his feet, and got the
letter from his pocket.

*There was this girl—I don't think you knew her, two years be-
hind me, in ninth grade. New girl, pretty, very thin, Corey
Petaluma. Not Petaluma, of course, but that's what I remember. Corey Petaluma. New, pretty—you know how that is,
everyone checking her out, jesus, high school—remember?
Everybody noticing everything, everybody measured every minute. Who's in, who's out, who's dating, who's got acne or hali-
tosis or tits, who seems to be getting laid. Who seems ready to
blow at every seam. Why invent hell when you've got high
school.*

So Corey Petaluma, she's beautiful. Not knock you out, in

*your face, Who are you kidding you'll never get a taste of this
beautiful, but quiet, a slow song. Cool green eyes, pale skin,
delicate energy, sylph-like in the way she moved, airy and still,
like she was aware of herself. Not vain, not like that, more
watchful, you know? Measured. Like she knew something and
the rest of us hadn't got a fucking clue.*

*Corey Petaluma, and me heartbroken, sore in love. (I was
with Rita Daeger then, remember Rita? All sex all the time.
They called her RotoRita, remember?) So I sidle over and talk
to her in lunch line one day, lameass stuff like How's the new
school, watch out for Moskowitz, he holds grudges. Me, big
shot, student council, growing my hair, hippie socialist
swishdick. Couldn't stop looking at her eyes, her hands, beyond pale, floating up to move her hair, brushing my arm a
minute to reach over and grab a milk. Couldn't take my eyes
off her. Only spoke to her two, three times. What I wanted was
to dazzle her, make elaborate proclamations, I mean it, de-
scribe our future together. Shy out of the blue, didn't say a
word to her. Nada. Nada fucking word.*

*Later, a month, maybe more. I've stopped talking to her,
having embarrassed even myself—tongue-tied by a freshman.
Maybe you heard about this. Typical crap lunch, macaroni-
cheese compost, I'm sitting with Tobin and Lewis and we're
about to go to the synagogue stairs and get high when there's
this commotion on the other side of the room. Somebody
screams and drops a tray, we get up and see girls standing
with hands over their mouths, teachers running. Weiss, our
dandy/fascist assistant principal, shouting into the phone. I
make my way through the crowd and there's Corey Petaluma
on her back, legs under the table, one shoe off. A teacher's got
a towel from the kitchen up against her face and I can see red
and I'm thinking, Some fuck knocked her down. Then she
coughs, and I see where the blood's coming from. She rolls*

*over and spits into a dish. I move closer till I can see her eyes
and they amaze me. Not scared, sweet jesus—fucking patient.
Unsurprised. I hear myself wishing it was me. Don't believe
that, do you? I did. They get a stretcher from somewhere and
carry her out. She looks in my direction and I do something
with my hand, who knows, peace, hang in there. But she
doesn't see anything and they carry her to the elevator.*

*How's the doctoring trade, Brother Nathan? I do sorely,
time to time, wish you were here. Some brotherly ministration
might be just the thing.*

*Out this window you can't see the bay, not really, but the
sensation, the way light changes over the far buildings, the
way space opens up. Can't see it but you know it's there.*

*I looked it up, I still remember. Emia, of the blood, leuko,
like lux, from light. Light in the blood. You believe it? How's
that for comedy? You don't die from light in the blood at fifteen years old, it's too fucking ridiculous.*

*Gotta go, some things can be put off no longer. Hang in
there, save some lives. Remember Santayana: Beauty is a
pledge of the possible.*

The doorman was talking with a man in overalls and a watch
cap. They stood between the inner and outer entry doors, backs to
Nathan, outlined in glare off the glass. Something the man in overalls said made the doorman laugh.

Nathan, too, knew the synagogue stairs, had lost everything but
his virginity there, after school, between classes, he and Elise Davis
exchanging a coded glance and meeting by the door to the rooftop,
she with her breasts in her hands when he reached her, breathless,
on the fourth floor.

Another memory, sophomore year, 1970. Nathan was shy, not
situationally like Daniel, but all the time, especially in a new
school, younger brother of a celebrity, founder of Students Against

the War. It was spring, Nixon was bombing Cambodia, there were rallies at the bandshell in Central Park, music, speeches, petitions circulating in the crowd. Daniel was up there with the organizers, laughing, raising his fist, speaking into the megaphones. "Mr. Dick doesn't get it," Nathan remembered him saying. "This is *our* world he's fucking with."

He had invited Nathan up once but Nathan had declined. He stood toward the back, near the trees, watching the people, the pretty, wild-looking women in long skirts and headbands, feeling young and awkward and emotionally adrift, debating whether to accept any of the joints being passed through the crowd. He decided he would, if any of the women talked to him. None did.

One day he's in study hall, sitting in the library trying to read about the Peloponnesian Wars. This girl he doesn't know runs in and tells him to come quick. Out in the hall they hear voices, lots of them, they run downstairs to the front entrance. The doddering security guard has his nightstick drawn, the trembly secretary is chasing someone toward the door. "Animal!" she's shouting. "Leave this instant!" Just before he hits the street Nathan sees his brother, down from Columbia, hair across his back, barefoot, the black cowboy hat with the leather tassels. He's almost laughing too hard to move but he lets the secretary chase him through the hallway and out the door.

The girl, a freshman, just looks at Nathan—everybody knows who his brother is—with amazement. Nathan shrugs, smiles a little, and heads back to study hall while the security guard helps the secretary onto a chair and someone brings her water. Spray-painted on the glass front doors are two peace symbols, hugely white, still dripping. Nathan climbs the steps to the library, feeling many things, worry he'll be blamed by association, envy at his brother running barefoot through New York on a school morning, vague annoyance at Daniel's unceasing, attention-demanding performance, and, under the rest, small and warm, delight, prideful affection.

Nathan looked back at the letter, folded it and put it in his bag before leaning against the wall to sleep. Corey Petaluma. Was there ever even such a person? Fucking Daniel, he thought. Fucking Daniel Chaim Mirsky, reaching out from the grave to make him laugh and remember and flood with regret.

∾ ∾ ∾

They moved through the rooms like strangers, unsure what to do. But not quite like strangers, Nathan thought. Strangers can make small talk, or ignore each other. So much was unspoken between them it weighted, like an awkward pause in an unbearable conversation. After a few minutes his father insisted he would make tea, put together some sandwiches, and though he wasn't hungry, Nathan offered to help. His father told him he didn't need any help. "Sit," he said, reaching into the bread drawer, not looking at his son. "Relax. You must be tired."

While his father busied himself in the kitchen, Nathan walked through the apartment, surprised yet pleased to find it not in total disarray. It was different, no doubt, since his mother's death, a man's dwelling now. There were newspapers and magazines on the couch and floor, which she never would have allowed, and the plants she patiently cared for were either desiccated in their pots or wildly overgrown, as if Sol had decided only a few were worth the bother. There was a small pile of shoes by the front door, and the bathrooms, while not spotless, were serviceable, obviously tended. Wedged under the sink was the plastic Key Food bag Sol had carried with him when he came from the pool, the dank clothes inside giving off an odor of warm chlorine and sweat. Nathan smiled. Freda had always bought Sol new trunks for his birthday, insisted he carry his clothes in a gym bag. Now Sol made his own choices.

He had been concerned he'd find the place a wreck, his father's life in tatters, one more worry to add to his pile. A foolish concern, he now realized. If Sol was anything in his life, at home or in the factory, he was a manager. Managing was what he did best.

The bed was unmade, which Nathan found strangely comforting, a mess of Band-Aids and gauze on the turned-back quilt. The old man was clumsy, constantly nicking himself at home or the pool. Her bedside table was still cluttered with tissues and eyedrops and a stack of paperbacks. A bottle of lotion, her reading glasses in their case.

After they had returned from his mother's grave site, it had been the three of them together—the last time, Nathan now realized. Daniel and Nathan sat on the small wooden stools the synagogue provided, Sol sat at the end of the couch. No ritual for him. He hadn't been inside a synagogue in decades, considered it a concession that he let Freda take the boys a few times a year. When the rabbi, a ruefully pleased little man who was his best at deaths and sickbeds, approached Sol with a knife to cut the lapel of his jacket, Nathan had thought he might strike him. Daniel stepped in, offering the collar of his own shirt instead. The rabbi, a professional consoler, smiled in understanding. They sat, no one saying a word. Soon the ladies were coming out of the kitchen with plates of food for the table, cups and saucers for coffee, and the men, cars parked, were filling the chairs around them. Daniel had gone into the bathroom and locked the door.

It didn't trouble Nathan to look at the items on Freda's nightstand, the clothes in the open closet. They were there even with her gone. He could not imagine anything in their place, and he thought he understood his father's reasoning. You don't fill an absence by taking more away.

For a moment Nathan sat on her side of the bed, the mattress hard and unyielding (Sol's back needed a firm support), thinking of Freda lying here, reading her Mickey Spillane and Ellery Queen paperbacks, waking to the oddly truncated reflections in the parallel mirrors over their dresser, outside the pale sky over Forest Hills and the old tennis stadium. How many days, right here? Thousands, he figured. An unexpected gripping sensation in his stomach, tightness behind the eyes. Janet, in bed last night, pretending to sleep. Nathan, the anger long gone, awake and also unmoving beside her, desolate, shamed, hating himself most of all for needing her to forgive him.

In the living room, Freda's needlepoints lining the walls, along with Israeli batiks, the framed enlarged photograph of Sol and Freda Mirsky on the square before the Wailing Wall in Jerusalem. The boys had had it made up for their fiftieth. It was slightly blurred, a flaw not readily apparent in the original three-by-five snapshot. Daniel was furious with the people at the photography store, who had not mentioned the imperfection and charged them full price. Nathan, too, had been annoyed. But now, like the sight of his mother's belongings in their place, the picture seemed right, the two of them on the white plaza with the famous stones behind them: Sol, squinting through the glare, large and untidy in a floppy Gilligan hat, Freda, smaller and more stylish in sunglasses and a white visor, both slightly out of focus, as if the camera had been jostled at the last moment, or they had started to move.

On the round side table the dense thicket of family photographs in every conceivable style of frame, fluted chipped wood to silver to transparent plastic. Stiff, posed wedding shots from the Old Country, wan-faced brides and grooms in local Jewish costume, Hasids in striped coats and flowing beards, city folk in long woolen coats and thick brocade. Sol and Freda's wedding picture, the two of them impossibly young; Daniel holding a baseball bat; Nathan imitating a Pete Maravich poster he had in his room, looking in one direction while holding the ball in the other; graduation shots from Columbia and Stanford—the American dream arrayed before him. On the wall above, more relatives—an uncle, at three or four, on a carved wooden horse that had fascinated Nathan as a child; a trim, ascetic-looking young man in pince-nez; a woman in a photograph so washed out it had turned yellow and parts of her dress and face had disappeared; two children, a boy and a girl, grimly posing before a photographer's backdrop of a mountain scene, lakes, waterfalls, a picturesque castle in ruins. Along with most from the table below, they had not survived the war. They held Nathan, they always had—strangers whose names he didn't even know.

As the kettle began whistling and his father called him to the kitchen, Nathan glanced into Sol's study at the rear of the apartment. It was at once fastidious and disheveled, much, Nathan thought, like Sol himself. The desk meticulously clean, pencils and pens in separate holders, stapler and box of clips and tape dispenser aligned by the blotter. On shelves, built into the walls on three sides, were masses of albums and boxes, rolled-up sheaths of maps, and the marbled green file holders Sol bought by the case, labeled and numbered according to an obscure system of his own design. Here Sol would be working every night, compiling data, writing letters, organizing notes. This was his sanctum. If you came in, you did so in silence; if Freda sent you here for being impossible, you sat in the one extra chair, doing nothing. Sol's immobile, wordless concentration was rebuke and punishment enough. But sometimes, unable to sleep, Nathan would drag in a blanket, certain to find Sol working under the heavy desk lamp he'd brought home from the factory. Even Sol's imperviousness was company of a sort. Nathan would climb onto the springless, worn easy chair and listen to his father breathing, the scratch of pencils and scissors on paper, and soon he would close his eyes.

Sol had made a salad, cucumber and tomato and green pepper in tiny cubes, oil and strong vinegar. He had bagels and cream cheese and a strip or two of lox, which he insisted Nathan take. The coffee was black and so strong it tasted like cinder. Nathan went to the refrigerator for milk, which his father watched him pour with an impassive interest. Nathan found he was hungrier than he had realized.

"The hospital?" Sol asked.

"Fine," Nathan said. "Busy."

"They still have you rotating?"

"Yes, still doing my rotations. I'm in the ER now."

"No," Sol said flatly. "You're not." He shook his head, annoyed. Nathan reached for the second piece of lox and for several minutes they ate in silence.

"I saw Sylvia Grossman downstairs," Nathan said. A neighbor, a lively woman in her sixties. She and her husband had been friendly with Sol and Freda. Nathan wondered occasionally if Sol and Sylvia, now a widow, might not somehow drift together.

"Good," Sol said. "Was she walking?"

"Yes," Nathan said. "She looked good."

"Last summer she fell. They thought she broke a hip."

"She looked okay to me."

"Lucky. For an old woman, breaking a hip can be the end."

"Dad." Nathan laughed. "She's probably ten years younger than you are." Sol glanced up, not smiling.

"So, if I'm old that makes her young?"

He waited, as if to let the logic of this descend on his son, then went to the stove for more coffee. Nathan accepted half a cup, feeling the caffeine race through his veins, accelerating the weariness that had settled into his eyes, his neck and shoulders. Janet would be home by now, he realized, looking at the wall clock and seeing it was after five. When they had finished eating, his father began clearing the table. Nathan stood to help.

"The doctors," Sol said from the refrigerator. "They let you leave?"

"I got someone to cover for me," Nathan answered, preferring this lie, however inadequate, to anything he might say closer to the truth. "It happens all the time."

Sol stacked plates and ran the water, spooned the remainder of the salad into an empty cottage cheese container. He was shaking his head again, his entrepreneurial sensibility offended—how could

these doctors expect to run a business this way? Nathan came up
behind him with the coffee cups and Sol turned too quickly at his
approach. Sol gasped, put both hands on the lip of the sink.

"What?" Nathan said. "What is it?"

Sol took the cups from him, put them under the water. "Nothing," he said. "You don't sneak up on people."

When he had opened his eyes in the lobby downstairs his father
had been standing there, grimy cap askew, mildewy shopping bag in
his hand. He was looking at Nathan with resignation, as if his being
in New York confirmed something Sol neither desired nor resisted,
but whose arrival confounded him nonetheless. It had taken Nathan
a moment to be able to speak. Now he felt that way again, a familiar
if unnameable rebuff in his father's stiff-backed slouch. He left the
kitchen and the remainder of the dishes to his father, went to the
couch in the living room, and closed his eyes.

∽ ∽ ∽

For the third time that day, Nathan was unsure where he was. He
had been dreaming of the busload of children. Now he was the
teacher, leading the first girl by the hand toward the bathrooms, but
he couldn't remember where they were. They walked up and down
the rest stop, searching, the children treading obediently behind
him in their chain, as Nathan led them toward the trees.

The light outside the windows had thinned, casting shadows
about the room. It was evening now. Nathan couldn't tell if he had
been asleep a few minutes or over an hour. The desire to close his
eyes again, stretch out full on the couch and sleep, was nearly over-
powering. Then he heard the water.

He dragged himself upright and into the kitchen. His father was
as he had left him, at the sink, water streaming from the tap. Even
in the dimmed light Nathan could make out the steam rising.

Something in Sol's posture alarmed Nathan. He moved quickly

toward his father. Was he alright? Was he crying? Unkindly, perhaps, Nathan hoped he was. It would make things easier, somehow, if he was crying. Something this day had to be easy.

But Sol was not crying, just standing by the sink with his hands in the water, as if that was all he intended to do for the time being. His fingers, motionless in the steamy flow, were raw, painfully red. Nathan looked into his father's face a moment, then reached across him to shut off the faucet. He found a towel and offered it to his father, who did not take it and did not turn from the wall over the sink.

"Dad?" Nathan said, his voice loud in his ears after the sound of the water. "Dad, come sit down."

The old man ignored him. Nathan looked at him again for a clue, but all he saw was Sol's habitual expression, stolid, impenetrable. Anything could be happening behind it, or nothing at all.

"Dad," he said again.

"He was weak," Sol said, nearly whispering, causing Nathan to lean closer to hear. "Weak. Irresponsible."

"Dad," Nathan said quietly. "We don't know . . ."

"Burned up, a pile of ashes. I hope he meets his mother and has to explain."

"Dad, please. He was sick. You know he was having problems."

"Problems," Sol said. He turned toward his son now. "You don't die from problems. Problems you look in the face."

"I know, Dad." Nathan put a hand briefly on his arm. His father winced. "I'm sorry," Nathan said. "Please. Let's go in and sit down."

Sol was looking away again, at the sink filled with brimming soiled cups and plates, a piece of bread, a few bits of vegetable floating in the water. His father wouldn't move, and Nathan backed off a step.

"He was in pain," Nathan said. "I think about that. What I might have done." He leaned against the wall. He thought he might collapse from exhaustion. He had to call Janet before he fell asleep, and what would he say?

His father looked at him. Something in his eyes fastened on Nathan, as if he were far off and had just come into view. Nathan fought the urge to look away.

"You think forgiveness is that easy?" his father asked. A new tone, deliberate, ugly, had come into his voice. "Is that the world you live in?"

Nathan knew his father was proud he was becoming a doctor. He knew this from the money Sol sent when asked, from the expressive if gruff approval that slipped through their brief, interrogatory conversations. And Nathan himself was proud, thought he might have found, finally, what he needed to do. But now it didn't matter to Sol, who wouldn't even let Nathan help him to the couch. "You're right," Nathan said. "I don't know." Before either of them could say anything more, he left his father in the kitchen again.

His writing was elegant, a bit elaborate in its cursive loopings and generous letters, but very clear and easy to read. As a boy in Dubossar, Sol had been vain about it. His grandmother, the one who died before he could remember much else about her, had bought him a set of pens and creamy paper in its own box. He looked again at the letter before him, the two photographs, and began to write.

My Dear Mrs. Selmanowicz,

Thank you for the donation of photographs for the archiv. I do not have to say to you how seeing them has moved my heart.

On the other issue I'm afraid I don't have news. About your Samuel I have not been able to locate more information than which I have already given to you.

He was taken on Transport number ### from ### to ### on ###. Records indicate after Mauthausen he was shipped to ###, and from there perhaps to ###. I have been unable to locate any record of Mr. Theo. Rozack, who you say was the last to mention, by letter of 1946, Samuel's whereabouts. I am very sorry. Be assured I will keep looking.

I know from myself how difficult. But your little Tommy is a delightful boy, just from the photograph I can see. Mrs. Selmanowicz, look at him.

As I have told you it is my intention to publish the work, including, with your kind permission, data of you and Samuel and your family. Alas I cannot say at this time when such a date may arrive as the labor of years is still far from completion.

With salutations of health and good fortune,

Solomon I. Mirsky

The photographs were of boys. One, bright-colored, almost wet-looking, was Tommy, her grandson, in a striped shirt holding a Sesame Street doll. He was looking off camera at something and smiling. The other was wallet-sized, a copy of an old photograph with a torn edge. In it, Samuel, the only picture the poor woman still had, a serious scholarly boy in a white shirt and black tie, his hand resting ostentatiously on a thick volume.

Sol folded the letter back into its envelope. From the shelf behind the desk he removed a thick folder marked "Mauthausen 1943, July–Sept.," and inserted the letter. The photographs he put in an old shoe box with a Gimbels label. There were several such boxes, marked "Photographs, A–C, D–F," and so on, along with the inscription TO BE SORTED. He had already cross-referenced the letter and photographs in his logbook.

At his desk he looked at a list on a piece of paper. From another shelf he got a similar folder and sat down to read a letter. He took a piece of fresh stationery from the pile and began to write.

My Dear Mr. Twirsky,

Thank you for the correspondence.

The news I have is not good, although there is comfort in knowing, at least, the facts. This I know from myself.

Your mother Raisa, your father Joseph Lieb, your two sisters Magda and Irene and your brother Levi-Hersh were shipped on transport number ### on ### . . .

2

Sol dropped immediately into sleep, before the plane had even left the gate. Nathan was relieved. When he had risen in the middle of the night to use the bathroom, then to stand by the window and look toward LaGuardia, he had seen light under the study door. He had not approached, had stood watching the occasional plane take off. He had thought of calling Janet again. In the end he lay back on the sofa and sometime later, listening, drifted restlessly to sleep.

In the morning he opened his eyes to see his father dressed, to the smells of tea and eggs burning. A suitcase by the bedroom door.

Sol stuck his head into the living room. "I'm going with you," he said, which struck Nathan as so heedless, unfeeling, misguided, and most of all as so typical of his father's headlong stubbornness, that he rose without a word and went into the bathroom to shower.

The conversation with Janet had gone badly. She had become frantic when he wasn't home by eleven and she couldn't find him at the hospital. She had knocked on neighbors' doors and nearly called the police. She wasn't blind. She knew he was upset. Then she'd seen the suitcase was missing, the half-empty hamper, and that was even worse. He was a fucking selfish prick. Whatever he was going through, he obviously didn't want her help or involvement. Again. As usual. "You know what, Nathan?" she had concluded. "Do it alone. That's what you're good at, right? Do it all fucking alone and don't expect me to be interested. It has nothing to do with me. And you know what, Nathan? I don't give a . . . ," she said, her voice catching at the beginning of tears. "You stupid selfish . . . ," she said, and hung up. He didn't interrupt once. He had some things he wanted to say, things he needed to say. But he didn't get the chance.

Slumped at the window beside him, Sol was a vaguely disturbing sight. At home, he rarely slept. But put him down outside— anywhere, a park bench, a lawn, somebody's front porch—and he'd be out cold, happily oblivious to whatever went on without him. His face, loosened in sleep, looked older, neck flaccid, jaw sunken, eyes behind the glasses fluttering in pale gray pockets. He looked to Nathan somehow alien, bearing no relation to the tense, animated face he knew, yet at the same time eerily familiar, carrying the in- herited hallmarks of the Mirskys—high forehead, ripe, wide mouth, the concentration of expression about the eyes, proclaimed even louder in sleep. Nathan waited until the drinks cart reached him, then ordered two scotches. One thing he liked about flying was he could have a drink, even at eight in the morning. And they were never surprised when you did. He poured the small bottles into his glass, drank quickly. He sat back, tried to take stock.

These were the facts: Daniel dead at forty-three, cremated, ap- parently according to his prescribed wish—who even thought of such things at forty-three?—before any of the family had been noti- fied. About his brother's death all they had been told—first Sol, then Nathan, who called the police in San Francisco—was that it was a homicide, something preposterous about gang activity. None of this, from his death to its circumstances to the handling of his body, made even the slightest shred of sense. To top it off he had written Nathan a letter, typically chatty, entertaining, the same day. Probably dropped it in the mailbox on the way to being shot.

Nathan himself wasn't in much better shape (though he flinched even making the comparison: not dead yet). To leave a residency without notice was no cunning career move for any doctor, let alone one thirty-nine, oldest by far in his class, with by no means a stellar or unblemished record behind him. He had come to medicine in hesitating forays, long pauses and detours—as an organic pizza maker, EMT, substitute bio teacher, a year scuffling through the Southwest with a backpack full of Huxley, Merton, Kerouac— broken by short bursts of enthusiastic application. It had taken him six years to sign up for the MCATs, three more to apply. Since enrolling he had considered specialties in psychiatry, pediatrics, radiology, family practice. Until a few days ago he had thought his present clerkship, in emergency medicine, might be the answer. Until he had left it. Had he? There were moments when he was not poleaxed from sleep deprivation that it had felt right, his first good choice.

And now he really had ruined things with Janet. The other night—all the other nights—she was wrong about the need to hurt. Wasn't she? That wasn't what he wanted, it couldn't be. It frightened Nathan, made him want to be sick, as he had been in the car at the rest stop. And something else, though it did nothing to clear the confusion. At dinner, in bed, Janet had been gentle, loving. Kind. And somehow that was what pushed him over the edge. Explain that.

He knew some things. It was juvenile, regressive, he thought, as if knowing the big diagnostic words made it any easier to figure out or to stop. The night after Eleanor, Nathan had slept in the bathtub, even after Janet had relented, called him to bed. Some mornings he woke up on the floor, didn't remember moving there. Don't look at me, he'd warned her in bed—had he said it out loud? Please. Don't fucking look at me.

He drained the scotch, looked around for the steward.

Was it over? Did he want it to be? When she'd gone to her mother's two months ago he had felt she was right to go, justified. She was right about Nathan, and had finally acted. But after a few days he had missed her too much, had called about seeing a coun-

selor, had told her he'd flushed the pot down the toilet and hadn't
been inside the Plough or had a drink since she'd left. Hadn't spoken to a soul, not man or woman. Hadn't bathed. He made her
laugh about his disastrous attempts to replicate her tamale pie, her
potato-and-leek soup. Even the fat tabby who lived in the hallway
wouldn't touch them. Three days later she was back. And along
with genuine relief at seeing her came the confusion, the tinge of
deception underlying the quiet celebratory reunion at their favorite
Italian place, the considerate lovemaking after, the well-mannered
solicitude around the apartment. As they accepted their roles again,
Nathan felt the return of the bewilderment, the dull continuous
alarm, the familiar emotional mayhem that left him wanting, more
than anything, to run.

Where was the damn steward? Nathan hit the call button, causing Sol to purse his lips in annoyance. Certainly, sir, the man said,
widening his eyes in sham pleasure. Will that be the two again?
Nathan gave him a delighted smile. Make it an even half dozen, he
felt like saying. Sol unhooked his seatbelt and awkwardly climbed
past Nathan to the aisle. When he came back a few moments later
he squeezed by without a word, and in another minute was again
asleep. As Nathan waited impatiently for the scotch to take hold
(the first two hadn't made a dent), he tried not looking at the
old man.

Janet. Sweet, pliant, funny Janet, who traded everything—her
playful, surprising sexiness, her endless (well, apparently not quite
endless) optimism, a home, interesting friends, a full cultural and
social calendar, forbearance with his sudden rages and betrayals—
traded it all for the promise he would someday, if not quite yet,
come to his senses, land on his feet, wake up finally and look toward
a future together with her. "I believe in you, Nathan." How many
times had she said this, reading his need to be told, "You're a good
man," holding his hand or his head, offering her faith and patience
and hope as warrant against his own lack.

Maybe she did—believe in him. And for this—his secret, irreducible, gemlike truth—for this Nathan despised her.

He stirred the melting ice into the scotch, took a big swallow, sloshing some on his shirt. Aside from their mother's funeral, he had not seen his brother in four years. Daniel. Janet. Another door closing. Nathan finished the drink.

Somehow Sol slept, though his posture was twisted, his shoulder held at what must be an uncomfortable angle away from the wall. Was he cold? Should Nathan ask his new buddy for a blanket?

In the months following his mother's death Nathan worried. How would Sol, after fifty years of companionship, how would he take to being alone? He needn't have worried. Sol kept at his archive, went to the Y, took in a movie (which one he could never recall, even when Nathan asked him by phone the same night), attended an occasional lecture at the Senior Center ("I could do a better job. A trained monkey could"). For months Nathan thought of bringing Freda up, asking was it hard now for the old man. But Sol, in his clipped responses to questions, equally clipped inquiries about Nathan's residency, made Nathan know somehow he was fine. And more. It was none of Nathan's business.

Surprisingly, it was Nathan who struggled. With his mother gone, the long-buried fantasy that somehow he and Sol would discover a common ground for the first time had seeped back to the surface. The look on Sol's face when Nathan had opened his eyes in the lobby was all he needed to know how ridiculous it was.

Nathan reached for the plastic glass, stirred the melted ice with a finger, and remembered what he had been dreaming when he awoke last night.

Those kids again, he couldn't shake them. They had encamped in his head. It was becoming a parody of something. He was leading them, hapless Nathan still looking for the toilets. He led them down a corridor and through some curtains that rustled as he pulled them back, ushering the children inside. He motioned for them to gather around the bed, indicating with a look that he expected them to re-member what they'd been told. Silence. Respect.

He recognized the room in the dream immediately. His last year of med school, his pediatric stint in the ER. The rescue team had medevacked in a dead boy, three months old. He was dead when he reached them. They were on the way home from somewhere, the boy and his parents and the grandmother. He was fussing, had an earache earlier that week, the antibiotics should have worked by now. The parents were tired. The grandmother thought she'd share some of the peanut brittle she was chewing with the baby, he could suck on the sweet candy and maybe that would help. It was only when they got home, under the garage light, that they saw he had stopped breathing.

The EMTs in their small town had intubated the boy and called for the helicopter. Someone in haste had inserted the breathing tube not into the boy's lungs but past them into his stomach, grossly distended when he arrived. The kid never had a chance.

The parents and grandmother reached the hospital by car a few minutes after they called the time of death, the grandmother, terri-fied, holding shaking hands in front of her open mouth, unable to lower them. The attending spoke to them, leaving out, for the time being, any mention of the mistake with the breathing tube.

He was a portly Italian guy, De Stefano, and Nathan liked him. They used to watch the Celtics on the fuzzy black-and-white at the nurses' station and De Stefano was full of stories about the Bird/McHale/Parish era, full of contempt for the present team. De Ste-fano had to leave the room twice while talking to the parents. He told Nathan later he didn't know what to do—strangle the old lady for murdering her grandson, call the police on the moron who had screwed up the intubation, or just shut up and let them grieve. He sat at the small desk in the nurses' station, furiously making notes in the boy's chart, ripping pages and starting over. Finally he took his frustration out on the operator in the coroner's office, who told him

it would be several hours before the boy could be signed out and released to his family. "Hold on a minute," he had shouted into the
phone. "*You* tell them, okay? I'll put them on the goddamn line and
you tell them." A nurse had come in and closed the door, quietly
taken the phone.

In the dream the children are around the bed. The baby, on his
back, is in a restful pose, could possibly be sleeping, except rigor has
begun, lividity pooling fluids downward, the lower parts of his body
a dappling of purple spots on red. They have removed the tube
from his mouth. First, the girl with the glasses. She's frightened,
which Nathan understands. It's alright, he whispers. Nothing to be
scared of. Gently, he urges her forward. The other kids watch,
silent, respectful. The girl puts out her hand.

As if privy to his son's dream and exasperated by it, Sol shifted
position, made a smacking sound with his lips, and turned farther
toward the window. Nathan looked at his jaw, two days' worth of
grizzled white matted unevenly across his cheeks, and nearly
nudged him awake. No one invited you, remember? But as he
would if he were awake and Nathan had actually spoken, Sol ignored him, and Nathan blankly returned his attention to his empty
glass.

∾ ∾ ∾

Although the flight lasted six hours, it was barely midday when they
touched down in San Francisco. Outside the terminal it was summer in October, tanned people in shorts and tropical shirts and
odd-shaped sunglasses that made them look, to Sol, like insects.
This was California. How many years had his son lived here, without once inviting him? And Nathan, no better, skipping his own
graduation to run and play in Mexico. It was appropriate, then, Sol
thought, the startling colorful bustle and noise, people dressed for
the stage, unloading giant baggage in the shape of wings, kissing in

the street, running toward the glass revolving doors. The sky was unmoving, an absolute blue, not a cloud or even the hint of one, nothing to indicate it was real and not painted over the rooftops and
brown hills. Eighty degrees in October. Sol felt like he had again
just arrived from Europe, foolish, agape, incongruous in his heavy
winter coat and cap, watching a spectacle he had no hope of understanding or making his way into. The light, though he could not locate the sun, was dazzling, it hurt the eyes. Nathan risked his life by
walking into traffic and hailing a taxi. Perfect, Sol thought. What
did you expect?

The driver, a middle-aged Indian in a turban, loaded their luggage hastily in the trunk, without a word, as if they had kept him
waiting long enough. Inside, his cab was some kind of shrine, a museum on wheels. There were figurines, including a jeweled ele-
phant on the dashboard, color photographs of Indian gods, a trim of
red fringe with furry tassels along the windows and backseat. The
radio was loud, tuned to a talk show on which some lady, constantly
referring to herself as a doctor, ridiculed her callers—who by calling in the first place deserved it, Sol thought—for their misery and
weakness. She laughed without pleasure, as though she and the
callers were enjoying each other, which obviously wasn't the case.
Her words said one thing, her voice another. Like the cabdriver, Sol
thought, like himself, like everyone these days, forced to a task that
was baffling and distasteful and unavoidable.

Beyond the airport was a massive construction zone—Sol had
expected that red bridge or the island with the prison on it. Huge
concrete platforms swung into the air and abruptly stopped, suspended over small cities of cranes and girders and yellow earth-
moving machines, piles of rubble and supplies, restricted areas with
warning signs strung along their gates. "It's big," Sol said, meaning
the highway being built, the airport, maybe even his immense
adopted country, which he had taken fifty years to traverse. "I didn't
know." Both Nathan and, in the mirror, the driver looked at him as

if he must have something more to say, but he didn't, and they moved slowly through traffic, listening to the angry doctor.

Off the freeway they entered a maze of streets over which buildings crowded, like in New York, but the streets were on hills that made you queasy to look at—the driver never pausing at the crests wasn't helping—and the houses were startling colors, like from a box of crayons, with elaborate wooden scrollwork over deep porches. Some of the street signs weren't in English.

The cab pulled up before a dowdy, rust-colored building several stories high, with BROADMOOR chiseled in the stone pediment and a handwritten sign on the door that read "Rooms To Let See Manager." Nathan paid the driver and carried their luggage up the two steps as Sol watched a hand pull aside the dingy shade in a lower window, then a grizzled face peer out. Nathan came up beside him, the shade was dropped in place, and a moment later the door opened.

An Oriental man, old, in white shirt and brown pants hitched high on his belly, stood in the entry.

"You the Mirsky?" he said.

Nathan nodded, putting down the bags.

"I wonder you'd show," the man said, pulling out a ring of keys from his pocket and turning without another word, leaving the door open behind him and starting up a narrow flight of stairs.

They followed. Nathan left the bags in the tiny lobby, under the brass mailboxes, and first he, then Sol, who was nursing a bewildered weariness smoldering into anger, climbed the stairs.

At the head of the second landing, and again at the fourth, the manager sat in chrome-legged kitchen chairs that seemed to have been put there for the purpose. He breathed heavily, his shoulders and chest moving, and looked at Nathan and Sol without expression. On the fifth floor he stopped before one of the metallic green doors.

"I no she in there," he said, or something equally impenetrable, Sol thought, and with the keys from his ring turned three locks on the door and pushed it open.

He stood there a moment, until Nathan took a step into the darkened hallway. He looked at Sol. "You go?" he said.

Inside the apartment dim light came from the end of the long hall. A window by a tub and shower were the only objects Sol could make out. There were odd shapes on the wall — clothing, coats, and a general impression, without more detail, of shabby disarray, even squalor. There was a smell, which might have been food, but Sol couldn't tell. A draft of overheated air carried it to him and he had the momentary, unreasonable urge to grab his son by the shoulder and pull him back onto the landing.

Nathan moved up the corridor, looked into one room, went a few steps farther and looked into another, where he stopped. The manager poked Sol with the keys. "You go," he said.

Sol walked in, his footing unsteady, afraid he would slip on something he couldn't see. At the end of the hall Nathan stood before a large room, unbelievably cluttered. His eyes adjusting somewhat, Sol saw a table and chairs, a refrigerator, a stove with pots on it, overloaded bookcases, and vague piles on the floor. A sofa bed, open, bedding scattered. Sol nearly jumped backward when he saw movement in it, and his breath was already stopped when a figure emerged. A young woman, dressed only in white underwear, her long hair wildly disheveled, took a few steps forward. She turned around once, as if confused. Then she saw Nathan and Sol in the doorway. "What time is it?" she asked, without a hint of surprise, rubbing her head with both hands and waiting for an answer.

∾ ∾ ∾

The hotel wasn't bad. Nathan would have preferred separate rooms, but Sol had signed without asking, still fuming, and Nathan was in no mood to argue. His father was in the shower now, had been nearly a half hour.

How stupid had they been just to get on a plane, fly across the country, traipse up the dingy stairwell, and burst through the door.

What the hell had they come out expecting to find? As he had for days, Nathan felt he was sleepwalking, experience and sensation reaching him at a lag, diffused, unreliable. Much of it, he knew, was his schedule these last months—twenty-four hours on, twenty-four off, the twenty-four on sometimes stretching to thirty or longer if the caseload was complicated, or if he got too far behind with the charts; sleeping through the days, eating doughnuts and cold pizza and whatever crap they had in the machines; drinking enough coffee that he could sit and watch his little finger, sometimes the whole left hand, in an alien microscopic jitter. Sometimes it happened in his left eye, too.

The nights, especially in the ER, were usually frenzied, overwhelming, it was a challenge just to remember which case was which. Starting Thursday when the bars closed were the gunshots, stabbings, ODs, and lately a rash of people cut with broken bottles. But even on a slow Monday there were abdominal pains and chest pains, migraines and STDs and ectopic pregnancies. The construction worker who had drunk almost a fifth of Hiram Walker on the way over (what remained sloshing in the bottle he held around the shoulder of one of the friends who helped him in, gray-faced while he was laughing), a two-foot spike of rebar going from the sole of his boot right through the instep. Before he fainted he had said, "Hurry, Doc. I gotta get this back before the crew chief notices it's missing."

Last week the little girl who brought in a toy fireman because maybe he could help Nathan put out the fire in her ear. The homeless people frozen nearly solid in doorways on their cardboard pallets, one with an inflamed boil, oddly clouded, on the side of his neck. When they lanced it, hundreds of baby spiders scattering over the blue surgical drape.

Worse: kids with cancer, old people with so many problems you didn't know where to start (if they were cars you'd give up and sell them for scrap), girls not out of grade school performing abortions on themselves with coat hangers, corkscrews, once an ice pick. Then the DOAs, almost welcome on the busiest nights because here, finally, was a straightforward case, nothing to do but fill in the forms and hand them over to the ME.

But when you're done—this is the thing, the precious thing— you are done. You brief the next doc, take a long shower, maybe sit in the cafeteria over some dry bacon and coffee. You go home, and no matter what you've accomplished, whether you succeeded or failed, usually you've done some good, most days the best you could have managed, and it's like miles walked behind you, finished. There was that in medicine for Nathan: it was defined, circumscribed. Even at its craziest, it had boundaries and it kept to them. It was clean. It made him clean. You've helped some people. Now rest. Nowhere else, nothing else in life gave him that.

So maybe that's what he had hoped for, sticking his head into the musty darkened room. A situation, problematic but limited. Answers. Closure. He would do what he had to, and then, as he was trained, leave it behind.

Her name was Abby. She had excused herself, walked between them to the bathroom, where they heard the toilet, then the water running. She came out in a striped kimono, loosely tied, turned on the light in the main room, and, without apologizing for anything—the place looked like a bomb had gone off—moved books and plastic horses and a wicker basket full of laundry off a sofa along the near wall. Nathan, then, after a pause, his father, sat down.

"I only have instant," she said, filling a kettle and running water over three mugs she retrieved from the sink.

If the apartment was oppressive, even vaguely menacing, in the dark, it was shocking in the light. It looked like a storage shed, or somebody's garage. Nathan could now see the pots on the stove, dried pasta snaking along the side of one, a crust of red sauce rimming the other. There were plates on the table, on one a congealed mound of leftover spaghetti and the browned quarters of a pear.

There were magazines and a pile of letters and, in a Folgers can, a sheaf of markers, colored pencils, paste tubes and glue. There were books everywhere: on the sagging shelves, in stacks on the headboard over the bed, on the floor, the windowsills, on top of the refrigerator, which was plastered with white sheets of paper covered in bright paint. One showed a stick-figure man and a dog with a black tongue hanging. "TOME," it read in thick blue letters. Past the bed was a closet, its open door revealing clothes spilling from drawers and hangers, and on the littered night tables were bottles of wine — empty, from what Nathan could tell.

On the walls, where there was no shelving, were Daniel's things. Some Nathan recognized from college — Che smoking a cigar, John Lennon in front of the Statue of Liberty. There was a photograph of Martin Luther King Jr. leaning in to talk with Ralph Abernathy and John Lewis, in the background a remarkably thin and young-looking Jesse Jackson in an afro. A march, Daniel in the first group holding a banner, walking behind two black men in army jackets and sunglasses, fists raised in salute. Jerry Garcia, wild-haired in a striped sweater, playing on a flatbed in the Haight. A birthday present Daniel had gotten when they were kids, a photo of Joe DiMaggio with his arm around the neck of an adolescent Mickey Mantle, the Mick grinning, shy, everything ahead of him. The old Soviet flag, a tear below the yellow stars.

The woman put the plates in the sink, cleared some room on the coffee table, and set out the mugs. One had Nixon and Agnew waving at the Republican Convention. One had the queen of England, and one, chipped at the handle, was a cartoon of two bears holding balloons. The smaller one, a startled look on its face, was being lifted into the air. The other was staring straight ahead.

"I don't have milk," she said, set out the jar of coffee, spoons, and poured hot water into the mugs. She put two spoons of coffee in hers, stirred it, and took several swallows with her eyes closed.

Nathan, who didn't want any coffee, fixed a mug for himself and one for his father. When she opened her eyes, he said, "I'm Nathan, Daniel's brother. This is Sol."

She looked at him. "I know who you are." There was neither malice nor curiosity in her voice. It was a statement, a matter of fact; if there was anything at all to detect in her voice it was resignation.

"We didn't know," Nathan said, trying for friendliness. "Daniel never mentioned . . . " He never did, all the years, all the women. She closed her eyes and took another sip. "We would have called first," Nathan said.

"Yeah." She put down the coffee and brought a pack of cigarettes from the pocket of her kimono. She lit one with a match from a box on the table and said, "I wondered if you'd show up."

She smoked and Nathan drank some coffee, tasting the gritty crystal residue he had not stirred enough. The same thing, nearly, the manager had said. Had they talked about them? No reason not to. He was searching for something to say when Sol, to whom he had handed the queen-of-England coffee mug, abruptly put it back on the table, spilling some, stood, and walked out of the room. They heard the heavy front door open and shut.

Nathan sat in silence with the woman. He finished the nearly scalding coffee. Sentences occurred to him, flashed through his mind like words projected on a screen, then faded. "He's tired. We both are." "A hard week. For everyone." Then single words: "Sudden." "Unexpected." "Unprepared." He watched them dissolve. Behind her head, on the wall across the room, snapshots curled away from the wall at angles. What he wanted to say was "I make no apologies." And "Who are you? What can you tell me about him?"

He said nothing.

The hotel was near Union Square, a few blocks from the apartment, north of Market. It was fine. The room was too small, the twin beds separated only by a narrow table. Nathan wished he still smoked so he could have an excuse to take a walk. In the bathroom the water was still going—the old man would use up the whole building's supply, he sourly thought—and Nathan turned on the TV, flipped through all the channels without really looking, then stood by the window, staring at the street. Workers were digging a trench. One manning a jackhammer had taken his orange safety vest off, and his shirt. His broad belly danced over the handle and he took a hand away to wipe sweat from his eyes. Eventually Sol came out, skin flayed-looking from the hot water, rubbing his hair with a towel, in a clean shirt, same pants. Nathan nodded at him, went past him into the bathroom, which was in steamy fog, undressed, and stepped into the tub. There, unexpectedly, on the shelf for soap and shampoo, were his father's glasses. Sol was blind without them, and Nathan stepped out and put them on the edge of the sink for the old man to locate when he realized they were missing. There was still some hot water left.

Abby, she said her name was. They had lived together—she, Daniel, and her son—for two years (two years!). Before that she and Daniel were together, on and off, for a couple more. She had a job to get to, they had agreed to meet at the restaurant for dinner. She hadn't risen when he'd said goodbye.

When Nathan had come out the front door, he had looked over his shoulder and there, as expected, was the manager at his window. He looked at Nathan a long, impassive moment, then let the shade drop in place. Nathan stepped off the small stoop, searching for Sol, exasperated when he couldn't find him. He picked up the suitcases and moved out toward the street. There, on the corner, buttoned into his winter coat though it was a bright hot afternoon, was Sol. Turning the map over in his hands, looking up and down the avenue, he was plotting their route to the hotel.

You don't remember this, I bet—how could you, they never told us a thing. Aunt Rachel, you barely knew her, we called her Tante. She lived up the street from the house in Brooklyn, you were what, six when we moved? There was a cherry tree we used to climb. We made believe pirates lived in the garage. I'd go to her place after school till Mom came to get me. Old lady's house, furniture by the ton, a whole front room for plants. She had a black-and-white in the living room and glass jars filled with cookies she spent all day making. Prune and apricot and chocolate filling. Really damn good—you remember any of this? We'd stay over. She had little Mott's apple juice cans, just for us, which we thought were some kind of treasure. She loved old movies, Bob Hope, Bing Crosby. One time she laughed so hard her teeth fell right out of her mouth. Nothing has ever astonished me so much again.

So one day she goes away, Tante, and I ask Mom where and she tells me Don't worry, Tante's just tired, she needs a rest. They're going to do some tests. So next day I ask, How did Tante do on those tests? and Mom says Good, she did good. When's she coming home then? Did she get some rest? Soon, she says. Maybe tomorrow.

A day or two later I wake up and Mom is getting you out

of bed. We were in that big room with the trains on the wall-paper, this you should remember, four trains repeated every two feet but you insisted each was different, which would make like 500 different trains. You'd stand there pointing at these identical trains, and say, See?, like you'd won a case in court. Obsessive little shit even then.

So I wake up and Mom's getting your sleepy Doctor Den-toned ass out of bed and you drag over, rubbing your eyes. Her eyes are swollen. She sits you on my bed and says, Boys, I have something to tell you but I don't want you to be sad. Tante Rachel has gone to heaven to be with Uncle Joe. She holds our hands. I don't want you to be sad, she says, but good luck, you know?, you're fucking terrified—heaven's no consolation to a four-year-old, and I'm sad, but I'm something else, also. What about the tests, I say. You said she did good. She did, Mom says. She was just very tired.

What I am is angry. Maybe I didn't know it then, but I was. I've just woken up and you're crying, even though she said not to, and so is she, which kind of leaves me out. I've got to piss, have one of those little-kid piss hard-ons, the ones that hurt, but before I go I give her a long look. They could have said something. I liked the old lady, when she could keep her teeth in her head. I liked the cookies and the apple juice and that she let us stay up late as we wanted without even bargain-ing, let us sleep on blankets on the floor in front of the TV. She was something to me too, this old lady. Maybe I would have liked to know she was in trouble. Why? What difference would it have made? Fuck knows. I could have prayed—we prayed then, remember? together every night before bed—I don't know. I could have said goodbye.

But the grief wasn't supposed to be ours. Remember? You must fucking remember this, Nathan. No funerals, no graves, no death, all time we were kids. Kept it from us, never told us a thing. Protecting us, I guess that's what they thought, out of love.

Well, who's really protected, when you get right down to it? That's what I'd like to know.

Flash forward ten years. This you remember. The bad times, the strike, the day at the factory. Everything gathering momentum after all those dormant years, straight for the cliff, and I'm thinking, Good, let it come.

I'm in college, you're still thinking you'll be the Jewish Walt Frazier. Clyde Mirsky. (Never could go to your left.) Anyway, Dad slips on the ice out front, what was it, a Sunday? I helped Mom carry him in, lay him on the couch. Later that night the pain's so bad they call an ambulance, and he's in the hospital two weeks. You would come straight from school.

Turns out it's a bruised kidney, or some such, turns out he's got some kind of abnormality in there to begin with, something from the war—remember? Something never healed. And the stress, probably. He was fine, built like a pit bull, but it was scary, you know? Touch and go for a few days, or at least it seemed that way to me. You and I talked about it. For a few days, before the tests were done, we were preparing for the worst. And I felt particularly bad, we were at each other's throats, me and Sol—What if he kicked while we hated each other?—high noon of our mutual disgust, my hair, my politics, my friends on his side of the ledger. On mine, to be honest, every damn thing about him. It wasn't like I knew the guy, any more than you did. But even I wasn't ready to lose him yet.

Still, he's Solomon the Adamant, the Aggrieved, the Last Angry Man. I don't know what you expected but I thought, Look out, here it comes. Line up for the big show. Tough as this may be on him, the pain, even the dying, maybe, just watch what he'll make it for the rest of us.

Well, wrong.

(Need I mention, of course, the bracing jolt of guilt: the Mirsky family crest—two bloody sticks over some sorry shmuck with his hand to his mouth. Our motto: Paeniteat omnium—look it up, Doctor.)

They put him in this room with big windows overlooking the Grand Central. His roommate, in for a hernia, a plumber from Rego Park, big guy, amazing hair on the neck and arms. I don't mean ethnic here, I mean simian. Some kind of evolutionary roadblock. Maybe I'm prejudiced because he always managed to talk about Wallace and LeMay when I was in the room. Every fucking day he asks me if I know Goldwater is Jewish.

So, we're expecting fireworks—Dad's not exactly in the mood for more encounters with the working class, right? And here it is, the big D, the final affront, after all he's been through, with one son who thinks he's black and another who's a scoundrel. Now some plumber. Poor Mom. Poor nurses. Look out, God.

Mirabile dictu, not that at all. Transformed. Sol the Mild. Evolved (maybe he borrowed chromosomes the plumber wasn't using). They'd sit in their beds and look out at the highway like they were on a cruise ship, talking baseball. (Baseball!!) He was nice.

At ease, our haunted, livid dad, all of a sudden at the glowing center of a world he—for all any of us knew—might in a few days be leaving. With the nurses he's funny, gracious, he and Lou Albano are like they grew up together. He's grateful, diffident with his doctors, he knows how busy they are. Introduced me to Captain Lou, this is my boy, the older one, he's at Columbia, wet eyes turning on me. Tore me into pieces.

Where was the world he had brought me into, taught me to live in? (your world, too.) Where the violence, the betrayal?

Where was God, cynical, patient, holding all the cards, with eternity to watch our failures unfold? This world, his world, suddenly gone, banished as he chats with his roomie about the Mets' chances.

Most amazing with Mom, gentle, quietly consoling her. When's the last time you saw that?

Me, I'm suspicious, of course. Was this some kind of show? A newfound forbearance? A last and desperate scam (and for these, maybe even more laudable), cover-up for his fears and regrets? The man had me utterly spooked.

What could I do? I responded, felt the wet eyes and shy smile drawing from me the free affection I hadn't felt in years. Daddy redux. Oh, my papa. We talked about baseball, me, Sol, Captain Lou. Our father knew who Eddie Kranepool was. Tom Seaver. We made plans to catch the Mets at Shea, a doubleheader later in the season.

Stunning. Unbelievable. I don't know what was happening, who was fucking with who, but, jesus, I loved it, my doting, gentle father, me the aspirant—eager, dutiful boychik. Who would have guessed. We enjoyed being together, in that room with the plumber. He was proud of me.

So go figure. One person kicks and, with all the secrecy and protection and hoarding of grief, it's like she never was here to begin with. Zap, no more. Then Sol, who has only managed to take—I don't deny justification, to a point—suddenly giving something that, even when he got the news and we packed him up and brought him home (the arguing, I remember, started up in the cab), even then, could not be taken away. My father— our father—granite man, pillar of salt, rage and suspicion and resentment his very humor and blood, what kept him standing all those years, now looking at me and saying, Daniel, it will be alright, don't worry. Everything will be alright.

Weird fucking world.

3

How they could build a city in such a place was beyond him. Just looking up was enough to make Sol dizzy, and when cars came barreling over the hills, or that cockamamie trolley with the bells and people hanging off the sides, he had to stop and stare, resist the urge to reach out and hold on to something. Walking, when he trusted his feet enough to look, he saw at the base of the long declining avenues an opening up of light, sails, gray water. Nathan had suggested a cab, but Sol had said, "I can walk." Now he regretted it.

Though it was dusk, none of the stores seemed ready to close. An old Chinese man poured hot water from a pot in front of his store, a young girl sweeping after with a plastic broom. To her side an ancient woman fanning herself with a paper. At the park with the palm trees and big column, a black man in a white suit and bowler hat singing and smiling and waving a cane. Young people posing like movie actors before glass storefronts, talking on little phones, a radio squawking about the temperature, unseasonably high. Crowded coffee shops spilling tables onto the sidewalk, a whole street given over to restaurants, tables on the cobblestone, waiters balancing small trays in the air, Italian music.

It was warm, especially for October, but Sol was glad to have his coat with the deep pockets, and his snug cap. He walked beside Nathan and didn't talk, peered from under the short brim, and if anybody glanced at him quickly looked away. The black man in the suit had fastened wide eyes on Sol mid-song and approached with a hand out, as if they knew each other, and it took Sol a wild moment to realize he was a street performer, this was part of the act. Nathan, a few steps ahead, didn't notice. Sol took the man's rough warm hand, briefly (the man smiled even larger, turned to somebody else), and repressing a mild curse, struggled to keep pace. He was lonely, and he was afraid. He didn't know this place.

He wasn't straight off the boat, after all. He'd been in this country since 1946, and Forest Hills wasn't Dubossar, some backwater hamlet. He had traveled, also, to Israel and Canada and Mexico. For the Alliance of Footwear Manufacturers he had been all over — Texas, Miami, Detroit. He wasn't some bumpkin with shit on his shoes — he lived in the biggest city in the world. Still. He couldn't express it, would never try, how wrong all this was, every single thing about it, wrong.

How many times had he thought what he would do if his parents were to visit, how he'd take them to the city on the subway (the biggest in the world), to the top of the Empire State Building and the Statue of Liberty. Along the way he'd point things out, talk to cabbies, shopkeepers, cops — see? he knew the lingo here, the people. He'd show off, indulge in a little proprietary boasting, as if he himself had a hand in making New York what it was — which was true, in its own small way, wasn't it? He'd take them to the factory in Jersey City, show them the whole setup, from the loading bay where trucks delivered the leather and chemicals and dyes to the cutters' tables and the machines that treated the leather and stitched the shoes. It wasn't that big an operation, he'd seen what big operations were, had sold out to one in Chicago just four years ago. But to them, to his mother and father for whom Bauman's milk farm was an empire, Kleinot's dusty warehouse for flour, pickles, and herring in barrels of salt a major enterprise, he'd seem like Henry Ford. And what would be the harm in that? He would give them the grand tour and then take them to Radio City, and after, to a meal where they could eat until their heads dropped. That's what he would do, he often dreamed, in welcome. If he could.

Not like this. A father shouldn't have to come all the way across a continent, three thousand miles, without someone to greet him. Shouldn't worry if he was wanted (if there was someone to want), why he wasn't asked years ago. Sol's shoulder throbbed—he'd stood too long, even as it ached, in the hot water. He slipped a hand into the coat, searched for the warm, sorest spot, pressed gently. Come, after all, under circumstances like these. Come, after all, too late.

Where was Nathan taking him? At the hotel, when Nathan had said they were meeting the half-naked girl from Daniel's apartment for dinner, Sol had nearly begged off, willing to plead weariness (the truth—he was exhausted, flushed) or say nothing at all—did he really need to explain not wanting to spend more time in that person's company?—lie on one of the beds and watch the news channel until he drifted off. But in Nathan's pause, his encouraging smile, Sol could read this was exactly what Nathan was offering, expecting him to do. Ready, Sol told him. I'm ready to go.

Now they had walked maybe twenty minutes, out of Chinatown, through the business district, past dozens of restaurants of all types, any one of which would have suited Sol. And still Nathan walked on. By the windows of an adult bookstore a *schnorer* on a cardboard pallet sat holding a filthy paper cup and a written sign. Beside him, an even sorrier-looking dog slept on the cement. "Disabeld," the sign read. "Homeles. Need $ for medcine."

The man stared ahead at the legs of passersby like someone in a trance, didn't flinch even when a woman dropped two coins, which missed the cup and rolled off the cardboard onto the sidewalk. The dog, too, didn't move. There was a time when Sol might have stopped and given the man a friendly lecture about initiative, responsibility, how in this country no one had to go hungry if he would stand on his own two feet. What was his training, Sol might have asked—this was his specialty as a manager: everyone had train-

ing in something, it was just a matter of bringing it out. Maybe he'd
have offered a job at the factory, something menial at first, sure, but
there was always room in his shop for someone who appreciated
hard work. He might even—though this would have been years
back—have sized the man up and asked about his history, ventured
a few hopeful words in Yiddish. *"Gegessen heint? Ret Yiddish?"*

Ahead, Nathan had turned the corner, and Sol didn't want him
to come back after him. He retrieved the coins that had fallen near
the man's foul sneakers, he could see the chafed skin of his ankles,
added whatever he found in his pocket to the paper cup, and hurried to catch his son.

Around the corner, Nathan had stopped. Sol could see a poorly
lit restaurant, too-small tables, walls crowded with bookshelves and
fliers. People read, ate, stood around talking. For this they had to
walk across the city? Nathan waited by the door, looking in, the
weak light of the entryway holding him. As Sol approached and saw
Nathan's tense, nervous posture, he felt suddenly the weight of the
long walk in his legs, in his wounded shoulder, as if standing there
he were sifting full of sand. He shouldn't have come. One mistake
led to another—better simply to stop. He looked up again, but that
made the dizziness return. Whatever he found inside that restaurant, Sol was abruptly certain, would make nothing easier.

Could he find his way to the hotel? There were cabs on the busy
streets, he could hail one. Good to sit down. However foolish, or
cowardly—they could call it what they wanted—better to sit at the
hotel until he could return to the airport, maybe tonight, if they
could change his ticket back to New York. An image of his kitchen
table, by the windows in the still morning light, filled his brain.

Nathan looked over at him one more time, moved his head, a
gesture of impatience, and entered the restaurant. Sol commanded
his feet to carry him.

Back in Dubossar there was a *schnorer*—Yitzik, the village idiot,
though Sol never learned the term till years later. Yitzik slept in a
storeroom behind the shul, which the *gabai* allowed in exchange

for his unofficial, and largely illusory, position (he was a wanderer) as watchman after dark. Yitzik was of an age impossible to tell, somewhere between fifty and eighty, with green eyes and a worn felt coat some rich Jew from Kishinev had sent in a charity trunk. It was too big and hung off him like drapery. He had extraordinary brown teeth, long and erratically spaced, an odor of unwashed flesh and decayed food you only had to smell once to remember forever. Yitzik would walk the streets, grinning, muttering prayers, reprimanding dogs, giving advice to whoever passed. He would beg a few kopecks, even from the smallest children, who had none, pulling from his pockets old bones and various unidentifiable scraps to demonstrate his need. Warm afternoons he would sit in the market and stare at an old newspaper, though rumor was he couldn't read a word, until he dozed off.

The boys enjoyed imitating him and would occasionally run behind him to knock off his hat. The wags would stop and confer with him about the latest gossip, asking would the price of grain hold steady, what about war with the Chinese? Feet spread and hands behind his back, an expression of mordant attention on his face, Yitzik would listen, occasionally pulling his beard with two fingers. His invariable response, after deliberation, would be, "Big doings, children. Certainly one must proceed with caution."

The cruelest taunt the girls could extend toward one another was that their parents had been to the *shadchen* to arrange a betrothal to Yitzik. He would join in, laughing along with everyone (save the furious, embarrassed target of the joke), his amazing brown teeth glistening with spit. "*Shaynkeit,*" he would mutter to her with tender affection. "Beauty." Or if he sensed, as he somehow did out of the blue, you were having fun at his expense, he would turn away, exclaiming single words: "Bedbug!" "Nevertheless!" "Commissar!"

Someone told Yitzik the czar had sent a conscription order. He was to report to Petersburg within the fortnight and was responsible

for supplying his own horse and sidearms. For a week the old imbecile cried in his storage shed, would not be consoled, even by the
rabbi's wife with a hot plate of food, reminding him there were no
czars anymore. Some older boys, maybe Chaim among them, had
found a picture of a dead Polish countess, a brocaded harridan with
a face like a dray horse, and told him she had twelve children and
was moving to the village to marry him next spring. Standing in the
road he would pull the frayed paper from a pocket and kiss it with
wet smacking sounds.

Sol hadn't thought about crazy Yitzik in years. They used to tell
the seasons by him, depending on whether he was roving the streets
before dawn—warm weather coming—or walking all day wrapped
in a stable blanket—nights were growing colder. On holidays he
would go from house to house—no one turned him away—eating
and drinking his fill until he was found asleep in the street somewhere and had to be carried home. Sol had no idea what happened
to Yitzik in the war. It was absurd, but he had an image of him in
Dubossar still, whatever it was now, a whole new civilization sprung
up around him, still begging from vendors' carts, dispensing advice,
hovering in the square till someone left a newspaper on a bench.

Sol retreated a few steps to see what had become of the man on
the cardboard mat, and was surprised to see he was gone, his sign
and scrofulous dog with him. Beyond his vacated spot, down the
long street, taillights streamed toward the water, dark now, a dull
shimmer in the waning light. Of course he was gone, Sol thought.
Ridiculous place. Any minute the whole damn city could slide right
into the ocean. He tugged the lapels of his coat closer and headed
to the restaurant.

∾ ∾ ∾

He should have come alone, Nathan thought. He had been feeling—since they got off the plane, since last night on the phone with

Janet (even longer?)—an unpleasant sensation of being stuck, alter-
nating lassitude and anxiety, moving without purpose or any logic
he could discern. He felt he was forgetting or overlooking important
things, which should have been obvious, which would tell him
what needed to be done. He'd call it jet lag if it didn't seem so familiar. And now, having to look back every two minutes to see if Sol
had gotten lost (the one time he slowed, the old man, of course, had
picked up speed, moving ahead though he had no idea where they
were going), was just enough to put him over the edge. When the
guy doing Louis Armstrong had extended a meaty hand, Sol looked
like he would pass out right at his feet—assaulted by a giant
shvartzer in a white tuxedo! The expression on his father's face had
been something to see. But Nathan had enough on his mind without worrying if the old man would wander off into traffic, bundled
up like some Ellis Island refugee, goggling at every person who
passed, stopping every five steps to stare into a store window or at
some poor shmuck sitting on the sidewalk begging for change. He
had looked at the guy on the cardboard so long that Nathan had
nearly shouted back at him, but then Sol had dropped something
on the sidewalk and clumsily bent to pick it up. Nathan, exasperated, had turned the corner and left him.

He stood by the entrance, looking uncertainly inside. It was a
crowded place, a hangout for students and people with time on
their hands. Bookshelves sagged with books and odd knickknacks,
with leftover plates and cups and saucers. There were fliers stuck to
the walls and windows: NARAL, Rainforest Action Network, ska
band looking for a bass player, Poetry Slam: every Friday at ten. Directly ahead of him, a group of kids sat arguing and drinking coffee
while two of them, a girl in black and a boy in long, checkered
shorts and chains, kissed languorously, mouths and tongues searching, she pausing to adjust her gum and look around the room, once
right through the glass door at Nathan, who stood there like a fool.
He took a last glance at his father, suddenly wishing the old bull
were here to lead the way in, but Sol was . . . heading backwards! . . .

toward the corner again, and Nathan gave up on him and pulled open the door.

He saw her immediately, at a table toward the rear. Though there were No Smoking signs posted, the air teemed, maybe with steam from the espresso maker, the dull roar of so many people talking. She sat reading a magazine, her long hair pulled back chastely (what a word—but he had last seen her nearly naked) in a ponytail. Nathan paused again, realized he had no idea how old she was. Young, clearly, but here in public she looked different, even younger somehow. He was jostled as three people moved to an empty table, and she looked up and he waved, as if he had just walked in, as if they were friends, and made his way through the crowd.

He stopped again when he saw sitting next to her, on a chair by the wall, a small boy drawing on the paper tablecloth. Nathan remembered the stick figures in black on the refrigerator at her apartment ("TOME"), and then, through the din of dishes and talk, he heard the door close, and there, stock-still, blocking the entrance, was Sol, glaring furiously around. Nathan turned and, apologizing as he wove through the crowd, went to collect his father.

He took hold of Sol's sleeve—the old man looked poleaxed standing there—but was ungently shaken off, and turned again to lead the way to the table. There had been studies, dozens, of how stress could endanger your life. What about rage? Nathan thought, shaking his head. Fifty years of pure, unabated rage, rock hard, glowing inside—what kept the old man even walking around? The little boy was finishing a blue and yellow house, was starting something complicated nearby, red, maybe a car.

"Hello," Nathan said.

Sol approached and she said to the boy, "This is Mr. Mirsky and his son."

"Nathan," Nathan said, and indicated his father. They both looked. "Sol."

"This is Ben," the girl said.

The boy leaned from his chair, offered his hand to Nathan. "Or Benjamin," he said. "But not Benny. And not Benjy. I hate those." His hand felt hot, tiny, in Nathan's. He squeezed it once and let go.

"Why don't you sit?" Abby said, and fished in a large purse she took from the floor. She wanted a cigarette, Nathan could tell. She pulled out matches, a juice box, sunglasses, finally a roll of spearmint candy, which she undid as they sat.

"His idea," she told Nathan, putting a piece in her mouth. The boy's? But then he understood. "To help me stop smoking. Another great scheme. Now I've got two addictions."

Sol was sitting, still in his cap and wool coat, staring at the boy. Luckily, the boy didn't find Sol nearly so interesting. He had returned to his picture, making breathy sounds as he drew.

He was black. Not actually black, light copper, the color of one of the crayons in his ragged box of sixty-four. He was about six, you could see Abby in the lustrous hair and eyes, something about the mouth. Back in the apartment Nathan had seen the drawings, the basket of horses, and had prepared himself for learning he was an uncle. He realized now he wasn't, in the off-kilter, dissonant way he was realizing everything these days.

Benjamin paused from his drawing and looked at Nathan. "You Danny's brother?"

"Yes."

"Danny died."

"Honey, let me talk with these people," Abby said, and the boy leaned over the drawing again.

"If you want something you'd better get their attention," she said. "They'll never find you on their own."

"Can I get you anything?" Nathan said.

"We're fine," she said, at which the boy opened his eyes wider. Nathan went to the counter and ordered a chicken sandwich and a tuna sandwich (Sol could choose which he wanted), three coffees (no, not mochas or latte frescos, just coffee), and a hot chocolate

and cookie for the boy. When he returned to the table he could tell
they had not spoken a word. Ben was humming, working on the
steering wheel of the car. Both Sol and the girl watched him
silently, as if he were some anthropological demonstration.

"How's the food here?" Nathan asked. For the second time today
he wished he were still smoking, could bum one and stand outside
with the rest of the banished.

"It's okay, probably won't kill you," she said, which made
Nathan look at his father first, then at the boy.

"What are you drawing?" he said.

"Our house," Ben said, not looking up. Whose house? Nathan
wondered. The generic Cape Cod with the tree out front bore not
even the most fanciful resemblance to their gritty brick apartment.
Ben pointed at the car. "That's Danny's," he said, and Nathan recognized the attempt at rendering Daniel's Alfa Romeo. He was surprised it was still around.

"Looks good," Nathan said.

"What color's your car?" the boy said.

"Green."

"Red's the best color for cars. Then blue. Yellow's the worst."

His mother sat looking at him kindly, Nathan thought, but
distantly, as if she were too tired or wrung out to register fully
what he said. Nathan regretted not ordering a sandwich for her, or
one of the murky soups in the huge cauldrons he had seen the
waitress ladle. He wondered again what the past weeks had been
like for her. Had she loved him? Had Daniel loved her? He tried to
picture his brother, all energy and sly insinuation, the world's great
ironist, with this quiet, pretty woman. Would she ever have been his
wife?

As the waiter brought the food, Sol still had not removed his
coat. He sat there looking at the three of them, the table, like someone waiting for his name to be called so he could get up and leave.

"Dad," Nathan said. "It's hot in here. You'll have a stroke."

His father looked at him as if he had spoken a foreign language. "Your coat, Dad. Take it off."

And, as if suddenly grown feeble, Sol had trouble getting the coat removed, half standing and pulling at it with one arm without using the other, getting nowhere until Nathan, embarrassed for him, got up to help.

"I didn't know what you wanted," Nathan said to him when he was seated again. What was wrong with him? Maybe he *had* stroked out, one of the silent ones. Sol stared at the sandwiches as if he had never seen anything like them before. "Chicken or tuna? Dad?" Nathan said, raising his voice to be heard. When Sol didn't respond he slid the plate with the tuna before him.

"This is for you," Nathan said to the boy, "if it's okay with your mom." The boy looked at her and she nodded, and he took first the platter-sized raisin cookie and then the mug of chocolate in his hands.

"Blow on it," she said, and he did.

The last thing Nathan wanted to do was eat. The chicken salad was browned at the edges and his first bite was gristly and elastic. Maybe Sol's would be better. He forced himself to swallow, took another bite and some coffee.

Abby let them eat a few moments. She broke the boy's cookie into pieces, gave him a napkin and reminded him to use it. She took the band from her hair and redid it, tugging the hair back over her ears firmly, as if preparing herself.

"Sorry about this place," she said. "It's mostly for coffee. I work here and it's near Ben's school. We come here a lot."

"It's fine," Nathan said. "Good chicken salad." Sol had not touched his.

"And about this morning," she continued. "Also. I didn't mean to sound like that. I don't know you at all, I shouldn't have said anything. It was, it was just waking up and seeing you there—I hadn't heard the door . . ." She blew on her coffee and took a sip. "I don't know why Mr. Li thought he had to let you in."

"Please." Nathan stopped her. "We should have made him knock. We didn't mean to barge in like that."

He turned to Sol for confirmation of this remark but Sol was looking at the boy drawing.

"Well, anyway," she said, taking the napkin to the boy's smeared cheeks, "I'm sorry."

"What's your child's name?" Sol said.

Nathan smiled, panic surging upward. "Ben," Nathan said. He put a hand out on his father's, felt the warm, papery-thin skin move under his. "Dad, Abby introduced us. It's Ben. Or Benjamin. But not Benny, right?" he said, smiling at the boy.

"How old is the child?" Sol said, not moving his hand from under Nathan's.

"He's six," Abby told him, her expression alert but calm. Did she notice something about the old man's condition, too? He tried feeling for Sol's pulse through the skin.

"Ben is six years old," Abby said again, as if giving Sol another chance to take in the information. She looked over at Nathan.

"Dad?" he said. "You feeling okay?"

But Sol gave him that look, as if he were some creature from another planet who insisted on making conversational sounds when it was clear Sol understood not a single word. Little beads of perspiration had gathered on his lip and forehead. He looked at Nathan a full moment, then away. He said nothing, moved his hand out from under Nathan's and put it in his lap.

"It's been a long day," Nathan said, looking to Abby and then at Sol, examining him for slurred speech, any signs of palsy or disorientation. But Sol's gaze wasn't unfocused, just empty. "Feels good to eat," Nathan said, and lifted the sandwich for another bite, but he gave up and dropped it back on the plate. "Maybe we should . . . ," he started to say.

"What time is it here?" Sol said, and moved his arm oddly out to the side to check his watch. He grimaced as he did this, and a sound which scared Nathan, half breath and half cry, escaped the old man's lips. He leaned strangely forward and gasped.

"Dad?" Nathan said. "Dad, what is it?"

The boy had stopped drawing and was looking at Sol. Abby put a hand on his shoulder.

"Dad, talk to me. I can't do anything until you tell me what it is."

Sol turned to him a moment, and Nathan was shocked by the look in his eyes, the anger flaring, as if, no matter what was torment-ing him, Nathan, sitting right there, was its cause. Nathan put a hand out to his father's shoulder, which released another strangled cry and Nathan recoiled, then gathered himself to feel his father's forehead.

"He's got a fever," he said.

"He doesn't look good," Abby said, and the boy, alarmed now, moved from his chair to her lap. "You better take him back."

"Yeah," Nathan said, reaching for his father's coat and help-ing him rise. His striped shirt was dripping wet and there was a tremor in one of his hands. As gently as he was able, Nathan put his jacket on.

"Here," Abby said, handing him a torn section of the tablecloth. "Call me tomorrow."

Nathan took the paper and guided Sol from the table. He looked back once and saw the boy questioning his mother with widened eyes. What had she said, he was six? What had this boy seen the last few weeks, Nathan wondered. The nearby tables had grown silent, a kid moved his chair so they could maneuver through. The boy in the chains and checkered shorts called out, "I'll get you a cab," and the girl he had been kissing held the door open for them as they passed.

∾　∾　∾

He wouldn't answer questions, hardly said a word. Did he feel fever-ish or dizzy, was there any specific pain, had anything happened that might help Nathan understand? Nothing. He sat in his corner of the cab in his coat and slouch cap, the area over the brim sweat-stained, a dark lip—from now? Nathan wondered, from earlier? Freda would have tossed it in the trash before allowing Sol into the street wearing it. After a few blocks, the cab moving in brief, frantic bursts through traffic, then sitting, waiting for the lights, he tried one last time.

"Dad," he said. "Let me help."

Back in their room, Nathan, without asking, got his father out of his coat. In Sol's suitcase, clothing and shoes crammed in, a mild rankness wafting—had he also just grabbed clothing from the hamper?—Nathan found pajamas and left him to change while he went to locate some Advil in his kit. When he came out with the pills and a glass of water, Sol was sitting on the bed, hadn't made a move. Nathan gave him the pills, offered the water and watched him swallow. He lifted off the cap and suppressed the urge to fling it in the corner, and, thankful for his training with recalcitrant patients, began undressing the old man.

The shirt, unbuttoned and off one arm, wouldn't come loose. He gave a soft tug, which brought a wince from his father and filled Nathan's nose with an acrid, unmistakable odor. He leaned around his father's shoulder and saw a moist area in the shirt fabric, darker at the center.

"Dad," he said, no longer trying to contain his impatience. "What is this?"

When Sol made no response, Nathan moved around the far side of the bed, behind his father. "Sorry," he said. "This will hurt. I need to take a look."

He peeled back the cloth and the undershirt beneath was soaked with lap lines of perspiration, dried exudate, and, where he'd just removed the shirt, a bright, dark pooling of blood. A stained and stinking bandage, the adhesive long torn away, was held in place by the wound itself, green and yellow streaked now by red. An inflamed border an inch wide surrounded the gauze.

"Jesus," Nathan said.

He went into the bathroom, filled the ice bucket with warm water, took the two washcloths and dropped them in. He moved Sol to the small table, sat him down, and turned on the lamp. Sol squinted, as if the light hurt his eyes.

For a moment Nathan stood in front of him. "You couldn't say anything. It would kill you to just open your mouth? Did you fall, Dad? Were you shot, knifed, mugged? Why bother saying anything, right?"

As Sol lifted his eyes to Nathan, perhaps to answer, Nathan moved behind him, put the bucket on the table, lifted off the undershirt, and, daubing the edges of the bandage with the warm compress, began peeling it slowly away. The original wound was unidentifiable, badly infected now, suppurative and hot to the touch. The smell was awful. What the hell had happened? He began cleaning it as best he could.

"Ever hear of septicemia, Dad? Blood poisoning? Shock?" He tried channeling his annoyance into the words, moving his hands as softly as he was able. The wound was possibly a week old, though that didn't explain how bad it looked. It would need debriding, IV antibiotics. "Didn't they tell you the dressing needed to be changed? Who did you go to, your barber?"

"They told," Sol said quietly. "I couldn't reach."

Nathan dropped the soiled washcloth on the tabletop. He came around to Sol's front and stood there. He let loose an angry laugh and raised both hands, palms up, to either side of his father. "So you did . . . what? Nothing?"

His father looked at him, the heavy sweat on his face showing the strain of the cleaning. His eyes were brimming with sweat also and his stare was removed, shocky, withdrawn to wherever it is we all go when we need to focus on our body's pain, Nathan thought. Nathan remembered the mess of bandages and tape on his father's bed yesterday. He lowered his hands, unsure what to do with them. "Just sit here, alright? Let me get you some water."

∿ ∿ ∿

The hospital room was small, but Sol had the side with the window. The other bed was empty. Sol was dozing, less fitfully now, it seemed he might sleep awhile. Nathan had asked about the free bed and the charge nurse told him he could use it, unless they had a late admission. Maybe he would. The thought of returning to the hotel alone wasn't appealing, and he doubted he could sleep, anyway. Might as well stay awake here. He sat by the window and looked out at the hospital buildings. Down the street, a lit avenue, he could see kids walking.

It had gone well enough, he supposed. The LPN in the ER hadn't listened when he told her he was a doc, began suggesting treatment (Nathan was offended, didn't say another word), but they'd taken Sol in quickly. The resident, though, Gonsalves, with the wired efficiency of someone on his second twenty-four hours, was more than happy to listen. He had three gunshot wounds, gang bangers, a baby who wouldn't stop seizing, a migraine not responding to Imitrex. And the cops wanted to talk to the youngest GSW, a kid about eleven. Looked like he started it. Did Nathan want to put on some scrubs?

As Nathan described Sol's symptoms, Gonsalves deftly examined the old man, who seemed more comfortable under a stranger's touch. Nathan suggested a blood workup, CBC, differential, a culture, maybe a tox screen. At this last, Gonsalves perked up.

"A tox screen? Has he taken anything?"

"Doctor, I have no idea," Nathan said. "He won't, or can't, tell me. I'm a little worried about his disorientation."

"Mr. Mirsky," Gonsalves said. "Did you hear your son? Have you taken any medication today?"

Sol glanced at him, then, as if too tired, closed his eyes.

"We'll do a chemistry panel," Gonsalves said, writing on the chart. When he had finished he told Nathan, "The wound needs debriding. I'll start an IV and call surgery." He put a hand on Sol's arm (again Nathan noted how easily his father accepted the touch) and said to Nathan, "It's not gonna be fun. How does he tolerate morphine?"

"I don't know," Nathan said. "I don't know that he's ever had it."

Gonsalves made another notation as a nurse came in to tell him he was needed. "Gotta watch for allergy, then." Nathan watched him pull back the shade and follow the nurse, obscurely envying him the gunshot wounds and seizures and traumas, all the focused and delimited intimacy—you helped these people, and maybe they remembered you for it, maybe not, but they were strangers, first and last, and when they left, trussed, medicated, healing, or taken upstairs and admitted, either the wide world or the greater intricate machinery of the hospital closed over them, and they were gone. Sol, on the raised bed, was trying to doze, lying so as not to put pressure on his shoulder, looking at the wall. Nathan pulled the shade shut, moved the molded plastic chair nearer his father, and waited.

The surgical resident had offered to let Nathan observe the procedure and Nathan had thanked him. But once in the room, with the needles and ampules and scalpels set out, and Sol made more comfortable by the morphine (no allergic reaction), Nathan declined. He didn't want to be in the room after all. Like a simple family member, he paced the waiting area, thumbed the outdated and dog-eared magazines, looked up every time the automatic doors to the OR swung open.

It took longer than he expected. The resident came out and Nathan rose to meet him.

"He's fine. Had a bad time of it, I'm afraid. We had to give him another dose of morphine, which I don't like doing with the older ones." He worked his head slowly to one side, stretching. "Pretty loopy, is what I'm saying. How long has he been diabetic?"

"Diabetic?"

"You're a doc, right?" Why was this guy losing patience with *him*, Nathan thought. "You don't get that level of necrosis and ab-

scessing from a simple fall, or whatever happened. Has he been taking his insulin?"

The resident was dour, slim, with the slightly irked reticence
Nathan found infuriating in surgeons as a type.

"Yes," Nathan lied. He had no idea. "I'm sure he has."

"Well, he's got a galloping cellulitis. Something's helping it
along. Let's wait for the blood work." He stretched his neck the
other way, put on a clipped, reassuring smile—unmistakable signal
the conversation was over. "He'll be fine, Dr. Mirsky. I've got another procedure. I'll see you upstairs." He offered a hand, red and
roughened from scrubbing, and Nathan took it and thanked him.

And loopy Sol was. Twice he tried to get out of bed, though the
rail was in his way. He looked around the room and spoke in Yiddish, and Nathan couldn't make out a word. The first time Nathan
held him back, but the second time they had to put restraints on
him. He needed antibiotics and fluids, he could rip the IVs out if
they weren't careful. Plus, he could fall. The nurse explained all
this to Nathan, looking apologetically at Sol as she bound his wrists.
Nathan had seen this done before, of course, but watching Sol laid
out flat, his arms pinned at his sides, was surprisingly hard. He
pulled at the restraints—odd how even dreaming patients knew they
were tied down—mentioned Chaim, his older brother, somebody
named Yitzik, and at one point was talking to someone, Nathan's
mother maybe, or his own, mixing Yiddish and English. "I know,"
he said, comically, even through his delirium managing a sneer.
"*Ich vays.* You don't have to tell *me.*"

He was calmer now, and Nathan, looking out the tinted window, remembered how tired he was. If he didn't stop soon, he knew
from the hospital, he risked a full collapse. Maybe he would lie
down on the empty bed, for a while, anyway. He checked his watch
again, wondering if he should call Janet, partly relieved to realize it
was too late in Boston, after four a.m. In another hour she'd be getting ready for work. He could phone then, tell her about his father,

how he couldn't sleep—though he'd feel craven and a little sick, asking her for reassurance. Anyway, he wouldn't phone then. It was—had been—a joke between them, Janet's morning surliness. She would stumble around the apartment in her robe, drinking coffee, literally unable to speak or answer a question until she had her second cup and a long, steamy shower. He used to watch her and laugh.

He thought of Abby and the boy. He'd thought he might call her, also, just to tell her Sol was okay, apologize (again) for them both. He had an oddly vivid image of the dingy, scattered apartment, Abby in the disheveled bed, the boy in his room, under the basketball and animal posters. Red's the best color for cars, the boy had said, as if he'd made a study of the subject. Jesus, he was tired. The cool window against his forehead was soothing, and he realized he was thinking about the dark, overheated apartment because for some reason he felt there he might sleep. Maybe he'd ask the nurse for a pill. One thing he wouldn't do was stand by the window till morning. Behind him Sol murmured in his sleep, the intonation of a question, and Nathan turned to check on him.

∿ ∿ ∿

The dream had the placidity of memory—not to say memory wasn't painful, Sol would be the last, ever, to claim that. But it was contained, bounded by event, and, most of the time, recollection was a matter of choice. Not like dreams, which knew where to find you, how to get in.

First the hot dizziness of fever, the dull, aching accompaniment of his shoulder, like a maimed part he had to drag along. Then the hospital, Nathan's joking and nervous appeal with the doctors just about more than Sol could stand. He loved his son, of course, but his way of talking, of approaching the world, as if a straight line had never been invented, was something Sol could not understand, tolerated only with stiff restraint. It seemed a kind of cowardice to him (Freda had seen it otherwise). Now some cat-and-mouse game with the hospital people, half the time he's a doctor, knows what he's saying, half the time an impostor, looking down with guilty eyes. Who was this person? It was easier for Sol to close his own eyes and concentrate on the pain.

Then the medicine, chill in his arm, the tumbling, which he expected would frighten him, but he didn't fight it and it wasn't so bad. Sometimes he was falling through a cloud he couldn't see but could feel, sometimes he balanced on top of the cloud, a funny, joyous sensation. And sometimes he was pulled from it, flying fast toward some fixed point, again, one he could feel but not see, and at the end of it were Nathan and the doctor moving behind him, and searing bright knots of pain that were somehow the purpose (cause?) of all this movement. At these times he could hear the doctor, he could see the room, and, shamed by it, he could hear himself.

Then a deeper sleep, and dreams. Back in Dubossar, back in Forest Hills, on the streets of some far city, walking with Nathan. When they were boys he used to take them on long walks Friday nights. This was when they were young and taking a walk with their father was still something to want. Sol was young then, could carry one, the smaller one anyway, if he got tired. They would walk toward the city, counting bridges, or into the park with the sprawling empty plazas of the World's Fair grounds, the glistening steel globe, some robot's dream of earth, and three high platforms, like huge flattened trees to Sol, but to the boys a landing area for aliens, headquarters for a confederation of superheroes. There was a restaurant up there once, he had taken Freda . . .

Then another room suddenly, and Nathan, other people behind him—Freda? He should wave and smile at her, she was so given to worry (her real talent, not to be unkind). Not to fret, just taking a little rest. Finkel, from the factory, him he could ignore, with his charts and projections and sour, anxious face. Others he couldn't see, looking, despite himself, for Daniel, for Chaim—what was he expecting? People in the room's dark corners, he couldn't make them out . . . really, this was quite annoying—you don't come into somebody's house and stand in the shadows like a gang of thieves.

Then—from where?—a calm, the whole body letting go, even the non-body parts, your dreaming, your memory, opening up, like what? like a flower, but bigger, softer, like light. Buried deep in his cells he remembered sleep like this, seventy years ago, and he remembered when the boys were small and, rarely sleeping himself, he would go to their room and sit watching, listening to them in their beds.

And then, last, the dream that was a memory. What is this now? he asked. He watched it like a movie, passive, grateful, unafraid.

There are long days after the rains when the body finally believes it is summer. Free from helping at the shop, from the endless smoky drone of school, they have promised their mother they will stay nearby. But as soon as they set out, without a word, they know where they are heading, and this, the secret of it, plus the very fact of his brother's company an entire day (in public Chaim has become one of the serious older boys, with little time for him), has Sol nearly skipping with eagerness (he'd do it, too, if he weren't watching himself).

The pond is not so distant by foot but they must pass through two neighboring villages and their mother does not have to put words to her anxiety. But neither does she have to tell them how to do it, every Jewish boy knows how to pass through a strange neighborhood, how to keep your eyes ahead, focusing on where you are going, how to walk, not slow enough to become engaged by someone's glance or conversation, but not fast enough to seem frightened or as if you yourself question why you are here. And anyway, in between the villages are the fields, rye and sugar beet and oats, each in its own green, rows of linden and beech, and finally the forest, with its own smells and light and cool, earthy enclosure.

There's a pond outside Dubossar, but its banks are eroded, wide dirt lanes where farmers bring their cattle to water, and there's always someone washing. This pond is in a clearing, there are only a couple of lanes to reach it, the rest reeds and impenetrable bramble. No one is here today and the brothers jump off an overhanging limb, splash in the thick, green water, float on their backs and look at the sky. Sol likes walking on the muddy bottom, squeezing his toes, until the water, warm at the edges, surprisingly cold and clear near the middle, closes over his head, and he tries to stay under as long as he can, his eyes peering through green swirl at the dim slanting sunlight above.

A nap on the bank, a last dip in the pond, Sol getting mud on his trousers as he dresses, which Chaim points out will anger their mother (Sol knows) and betray where they have been. Some pouting, a brief fight with pinecones, but both boys are tired and happy and have no real energy for malice. Then the walk home.

Small birds dart along the fence lines, bigger ones circle or land in the trees. At a bridge they stop and look for perch, aim stones at a boulder midstream. When they reach the first village they grow quiet, move determined, as if they are on some business that both explains their presence and will not wait for them long.

It's between the second village and home, at a roadside clearing, that they encounter the peasants. They stop before they see them, when they can only hear, and look for another path around but the tree line is overgrown with nettles and berry canes, and there is only the one road, and it is getting late, they will already be scolded even if they hurry. Looking at each other, they walk, as close to the far side as they can, and approach the clearing.

Two men are fighting. Both Chaim and Sol (who wants to take his brother's hand but isn't certain if this is the emergency that warrants a show of weakness, maybe it's still coming and he had better save it) try to walk briskly, not running, but looking up the road, nothing of their concern here.

But no need to look away, the men are too involved to care

about them, and the fight, in its quiet, concentrated ferocity, is something new, and they risk glances, then openly look, and finally, a little past the clearing from behind a wide oak, they stop and watch.

There is hardly any sound. A cart with some provisions is up ahead, maybe the source of the argument, but it clearly doesn't matter now. This is no fight like the boys have seen before. In the square at Dubossar most fights are limited to shouted insults, an occasional darting slap. There was a pogrom, and the students tore up the synagogue and several stores, and six villagers were killed, but that's different, war, a visitation, fate, too huge and devastating to comprehend—this is right here.

One man is older, his beard flecked with gray. He is smaller, too, but wirier than the younger, larger man, and seems a better fighter, with quicker instincts. He is covered with dust and mud. His pants are torn up one leg, and he is bleeding terribly from an ear, its lower half dangling. The other man, though stronger and able to take each blow with less trouble, is moving oddly, as if a leg doesn't work as it should, and his breathing comes with a whistle from his lungs. There is blood on him, too, though it's impossible to tell from where.

Worst is the silence. They fight slowly, methodically, as if they've been at it hours, maybe days. No screaming, no cursing, just the grunting of blows given and received, the sound fists make on flesh and bone, the strain of bodies grappling. They come together in a clinch, their fists and legs, sometimes their teeth moving almost deliberately, as if there's a ritual to it, every move a step in some terrifying preordained dance.

At one point the younger man loses energy. The other has him against a tree and is hitting him with a fist lowered from behind his head like a hammer, the younger man too tired or indifferent to raise his hands in defense. Two, maybe three blows to the face and his left eye is pooling blood which spills down his face and flies in small spurts on his breathing. Sol has long ago seen enough but is too afraid now to even move. He looks over and Chaim is whispering, he can't make out what. He is holding Chaim's hand, can't remember when that happened.

Then, slowly, almost regretfully, the younger man wakens. He reaches out, still absorbing the other man's blows, somehow gets his hands around the man's head and pulls him inward in a slow embrace. The smaller, older man is still fighting, lands a hit or two to the body but something is seeping from him in the trembling clinch, pressed into the other man's chest, his face darkening, his eyes looking in the boys' direction, though it's impossible to tell what he sees. When the younger man releases him he drops to one knee and stays there, as if trying to remember what is next for him to do, and the younger man, with a huge muddied boot, kicks him to the ground, and this is when the boys leave, suddenly running fast as they can up the road toward home, Sol unable to keep pace, Chaim reaching back to pull him, the slow smacking rhythm of the prone man's skull against a stone not fading, it seemed, until Sol could hear the words of Chaim's praying and they reached Dubossar's first scattered outbuildings.

Then it is memory, entirely. Sol is awake, in a hospital bed, Nathan asleep in a chair by the window. They had never talked about it, the two brothers, not even to each other. What was the fight about—drink, betrayal, revenge? What made them keep on, even after whatever it was, the cause, could hardly have mattered any longer? Their faces were full of blood, moving with the exertion of the fight but otherwise blank, almost distant. What was in their minds? It was too awful to think about, somehow both boys knew this, and nothing was ever said, as far as Sol knew, to anyone. Sol thought, later, they had witnessed evil that day, not in the two men, but in their savage, methodical, implacable rage. Here was the limit of human aggression, he had thought, without the words or courage to formulate the idea in his mind. He had seen the limit and come away, and he had learned something from it. Later, he saw how wrong he was, that to some things there is no limit, and that he had learned nothing at all.

He was in a hospital bed, and though he could not remember much of the preceding hours, the place had the familiar feel of a room he had been in awhile. The pain in his shoulder was there, but less acute, less urgent, and he could sense the distant retreating hum of both his fever and the medicines they no doubt had him on. He lay facing his son and the window behind him, where thin, early light was brightening the curtains. He was curiously and welcomely empty, not so much floating or buoyant but weightless, emptied of everything, unable, unwilling, to move. That morning, too, he had been this way, lying in the bunk unmoving, watching the door which had to remain open, sounds of roll call drifting in.

They had let him sleep, though it could mean the worst for any of them, for him, as well. He didn't care, and, perhaps, after that night, none of them did, either. He had lain there until the drone of the roll turned to shouting and the air swelled with running and angry calls, even the emphatic tattoo of the machine gun overhead not causing Sol to move. He had kept still, watching the door slowly fill with daylight, and he knew that nothing, whatever this day or any other would bring, would touch him ever again.

It seemed to Nathan the trouble had always been there, though he'd not seen it this way until recently, and only still more recently acknowledged it as trouble.

Dr. Pendergast, soft-spoken, gentle-eyed, with grooming and manners so meticulous it seemed a discourtesy even to think he might not have all the answers, told Nathan the main measure of addiction was an adverse effect on life. Would Nathan say, Dr. Pendergast mildly wanted to know, this was having such an effect?

The Psychiatric Services building was several blocks from the hospital, on a tree-shaded street, a family home that had been taken over and remodeled. It was easy to see why the choice had been made—Nathan knew from his psych rotation the importance of making the patient (odd, applying that word to himself) feel at ease. This place looked like a set from a comfortable sixties sitcom, the American Ur-home, wide yard, deep porch, a tire swing still hanging from one of the trees. Who wouldn't come here and talk?

"Dr. Mirsky?"

It was a courtesy, Nathan knew, the "Dr." Still, it jarred, as much as this man calling him Nathan might have.

"We were discussing costs," Pendergast said.

"Costs?"

"The damage you think might have been brought on by your problem."

Dr. Pendergast was trim, in his forties, one of those men who would never lose his hair, have trouble with his weight. He had a way, after asking a question, of inclining his head as if he was really looking forward to your response, which was nice, except he did it every time, whether he was asking about your next appointment or whether you felt it was time to reveal where you'd stashed the body. He was competent, unflappable, and, to Nathan, utterly maddening. ("The man smokes an actual fucking pipe," he had pleaded with Janet, who remained unmoved. "What is this, 1952?") He brought his focus back to Pendergast and shifted on the red leather couch, which registered every move he made with a petulant squeak. "What kind of costs do you mean?"

Pendergast smiled. "That's for you to say."

"Well, are we talking material costs, psychic, social? I've never been in jail, if that's what you mean, never lost a job or hurt anybody." But this last, he immediately realized, was not true, and he added, "I mean, badly. Permanently, anyway."

As if on cue, Pendergast reached for the pouch of tobacco, the pipe in the ceramic tray. Finally Nathan had said something absorbing.

"Alright," he said. "Give me an example of impermanent hurt."

"You know, life's bumps and bruises," Nathan said. "The necessary spurs to an adaptive mechanism." This was exhausting. "Evolution."

Pendergast nodded, as if any of this made sense. "Example," he said.

"Fine. Bring that match too close to your face and you light your head on fire. You learn not to do it again. You remember the pain, but that's not the essential part of the memory. What you learn is."

"I see," Pendergast said. He held the flame over the pipe a moment, drew it in, and shook out the match. "I take your point." He paused to suck the stem twice. "Of course, you avoid the issue of agency. If I burned myself, in this case, it would be an accident, no matter what benefits or costs came of it." He loosed two coils of aromatic smoke into the air.

"Meaning it would be a different lesson if I was holding the match," Nathan said.

Pendergast smiled around the pipe stem. "Perhaps."

The man was amazing, in his own way, Nathan had to concede. Here they were, a month into these sessions, and he had never once pressed Nathan to talk about Janet, Eleanor, the fight, what had brought him here in the first place. Even when they did talk about it, it was in the vaguest, most oblique terms. "Problem." "Difficulty." What they had were literate sparring matches, some form of drawing room joust. It's a scam, Nathan had first thought, he'll talk about anything, take his two hundred dollars, and laugh. But Nathan found himself, too often uncomfortably, entered into obscure areas of revelation, the eerie feeling he was saying more than he really wanted to ever say to someone like Pendergast. It occurred to Nathan, as it had before, to just tell him the truth. Which was what, exactly? That he had a compulsion to sleep with almost any woman he met? That it had nearly gotten him killed, did kill off more than one relationship? That even in the woman's bed he was never satisfied, or quiet, had to drink himself into a stupor so as not to get up and run?

"So cost cuts both ways," Nathan said.

Another puff. "Usually."

"Isn't smoking bad for you?" Nathan said, louder than he'd meant to.

Pendergast nodded, as if this was welcome, a sign of progress. "Does it bother you?"

"No," Nathan lied. "Isn't it illegal in a doctor's office?"

"Private property. I could stop if you like."

Nathan looked around. He knew there was no clock but searched anyway. In his psych rotation there was a clock mounted on the wall, prominently displayed. It's their time, his supervisor had said. Let them see what they're paying for. But the only clock in Pendergast's office was small, in an elegant marble casing; it sat on the table between them with its back toward Nathan.

"Feel like some association?" Pendergast asked.

Christ, Nathan thought. Must be more time left than he realized.
"Why not," he said.

"Care to try closing your eyes?"

Without answering, Nathan did as he was told. He saw himself
gently lecturing Janet about why he had stopped coming here, how he
had gone along with everything Pendergast asked of him, even these
silly, useless games.

"Cost," Pendergast said around the pipe.

Nathan sighed. "Payment."

"Harm."

"Damage."

"Memory."

"Loss."

"Sorrow."

"Sadness."

A pause to relight the pipe. "Guilt," Pendergast said.

"Memory."

"Guilt."

"Anger," Nathan said.

"Guilt."

"Theft." Nathan opened his eyes, suddenly furious. Pendergast
was looking away, toward the bay window and the house next door.
Nathan forced his eyes closed again.

He knew the drill. When Pendergast stopped he was to talk about
whatever came into his head first. It was exasperating, one more annoying thing about the man, and most often what first came into
Nathan's head was the sight of Pendergast, finally surprised, as he
watched Nathan slam the door behind him. But the effort of express-
ing his annoyance without opening himself to an eager riposte ("Interesting. Why would you say that?") had proved greater than just
going along, describing literally whatever appeared in his head. And
talking covered the intimate sounds of Pendergast filling his pipe, the
urgent soft sucking, the flare and sharp odor of the match. For a tense

moment Nathan was silent, nothing at all to offer. Somewhere a door shut, and he could hear muffled voices from the hallway. He opened his eyes and this time Pendergast was looking at him.

"There was this kid," Nathan began, turning away, no idea where he was going. "Marshall. He lived across the street from us in Brooklyn, we played stickball."

Pendergast looked at him with clear, untroubled eyes. Nathan continued.

"He was Jewish, Lichtenstein or Edelstein originally, I don't know. They'd changed it to Stone, but they were Jews just like the Cohens and Mirskys and Adlers up and down the block, all part of the melting pot, the great Jewish American experiment."

Nathan heard Pendergast tap the bowl on the ceramic tray. He waited until the match caught and continued.

"Except they were better at it, the experiment, more American. With them it didn't look like acting. Nobody spoke with an accent, even the grandparents, who lived somewhere on the Island and drove a blue Lincoln. Nobody hung underwear on a clothesline across the driveway, or rugs out of windows to beat with brooms. The older boy, Steve, had friends who didn't look Jewish, and they worked on cars, rolling around underneath them, the radio blasting. Sometimes girls came over to watch and they had water fights with the hose."

Nathan paused, feeling both the spread of memory before him and his reluctance to allow it.

"Marshall's mom was different, too. Looked younger, though probably she wasn't. You could see her as somebody's girlfriend. She changed clothes when her husband came home, and they would sit together on the porch. She was pretty, always had her hair done up. We all had dreams about her, every kid on the block. They'd sit together and have a cocktail, something else no one did, and Mr. Stone, big guy, always tired, would look around at his yard, his kids, his pretty wife, like he owned everything in sight. He'd made it. I don't know how to explain it, that was the most American thing about him.

He had what everyone else on Forty-eighth Street wanted, my father working sixteen-hour days at the factory, my mother taking us to Gimbels and Alexander's every fall so we would know how to look. It was like there was a line down the middle of the street that read 'Old Country' on one side and 'America' on the other."

Nathan paused again, giving Pendergast a chance to comment, redirect. The only way this worked, Nathan had learned, was to speak, as completely as possible, by association, let whatever words lined up in his head tumble from his mouth, with a minimum of thought or investment. If Pendergast wanted him to go on, fine, he would. If he wanted to change the subject, drop it, fine, too. The point was, whatever Pendergast thought they were accomplishing, it didn't matter to Nathan. It was Pendergast's show. When Pendergast didn't interrupt his contemplative gaze out the window, Nathan continued.

"We weren't that close, me and Marshall. He didn't go to Hebrew school, which my father approved of. At synagogue for High Holidays, he looked embarrassed wearing a borrowed yarmulke. I was shy and defensive, probably not too friendly myself. Then one year we started playing stickball and ended up with a makeshift league, our block against the others. Marshall was an athlete, could go three sewers every time. Soon we were hanging out. They were the only people on the block with a barbecue, and I remember some awkward talk between his mother and mine—my mother drew the line at shellfish, bacon—before they could invite me over for dinner. They had a Shabbos candelabra over the refrigerator, which was a great surprise to me, and a prayer book or two on the shelves, though I never saw anyone open one."

Pendergast spoke around the pipe. "You had these things? Candles? Books?"

"Concession to my mom. Like synagogue on the holidays."

"And your father?"

"The most unreligious man I know."

"Really?"

"No. I'm lying." If only Janet could see this guy.

"How do you mean unreligious?" Pendergast lifted the tobacco from the table, a folded pouch embroidered with some American Indian–looking design. He dug around in it with the pipe. For some reason Nathan could never avoid watching this pointless, repetitive procedure.

"The war," he said, as Pendergast brought the pipe up and tamped it with a manicured thumb. "His family was religious, when he was a kid. Not him. Not after."

"Ah."

Ah? What the hell had that revealed? The match, the interminable puffing and sucking, the man's wet lips nursing the stem. Panic began rooting low in Nathan's stomach. Finally it was lit.

"You were what age?" the doctor said.

"What?"

He looked at Nathan over the pipe. "Your story. Please go on."

"Ten. I don't know, eleven, maybe."

"And your friend?"

"The same. Maybe a year older. As I said, I didn't know him that well."

Pendergast said nothing more, and Nathan had the irritating sensation they were engaged in two separate conversations.

"So I started going over. They had a basement with a Ping-Pong table and color TV, and his mother was always doing amazing things like appearing all of a sudden with a plate of cookies and punch. We'd lie on the floor and watch football with his dad and Steve. These were very intense events, no one spoke except to cheer or curse. Mr. Stone drank beer like he hated it, moving from one can to the next, Mrs. Stone bringing in fresh ones on a round tray. It was, looking back, weird as hell, but I loved it. I couldn't get enough. I'd hang around to help, doing things I never offered to do at home, rake the yard, wash the car, whatever."

It occurred to Nathan that he could go on endlessly, delete or fabricate, and Pendergast would never object. Around then the alien abduction happened, right before we were all murdered in our sleep.

Whatever it was about the man, docile imbecility or deep cunning, it was absolutely infuriating. The sound of that pipe. Somehow it made his hands itch.

"Anyway. Marshall had comics and board games in his room, and occasionally some Playboys he'd steal from Steve. It was my least favorite place, actually. I preferred the kitchen table or being outside, but we stayed in his room a lot, watching TV, talking sports. He had a bank in there, a huge plastic coin, brown, shaped like a penny. Had it since he was a little kid and it was full and he never bothered with it anymore. It was heavy, I lifted it one day to check.

"Marshall was somewhere—bathroom, setting the table, I don't know—and I went over to the bank. At the back was a little plastic tab you punched out when you wanted to empty it. I pushed at the tab but it wouldn't budge, so I took a penknife from his desk and pried away a couple of the little prongs that held it in place. I shook out a couple of coins and lay on the floor with a Spiderman *until* Marshall came back."

This would be an obvious spot for comment, so Pendergast, naturally, was mute, even the pipe still for once. Nathan leaned forward on the couch, looking directly at him, and plowed toward the end.

"It took about three weeks to empty. I never took much at once, didn't want to get caught. Also I wasn't sure why I was doing it, and it must have made me feel better to take only a little at a time. And maybe I realized things would have to change once I was finished. I never spent any, not then, anyway. I put whatever I had taken in my underwear drawer and left it there. Later, I must have mixed it with my own money. I really can't remember.

"Marshall and I didn't see each other as much. It was the start of fall and I was back in school. We had our own friends and interests and it wasn't so easy to get together. I stopped by to see if anyone was going to watch the Yankees one Sunday and Mrs. Stone let me in, asked how I was, sat me down, and gave me a glass of U-Bet and milk, like she always did. I could hear voices from the back of the house, not screaming exactly, but not happy either. Mrs. Stone just *raised her eyebrows once, like we were enjoying some private joke, and she asked me about school, my parents and brother. I wondered what was going on but I was in love with Mrs. Stone and I used to imagine somehow she'd see something in me that would make her fall in love, too. We'd wait till I got a little older and she would leave her husband and we'd have a kitchen of our own someplace. She asked if I wanted more U-Bet and I said, Thanks. Anyway, you can guess the rest."*

Pendergast, staring at something above Nathan's head, looked incapable of guessing anything.

"They came into the kitchen eventually and Mr. Stone was holding the empty bank, the back tab completely removed. Marshall was red in the face and fighting back tears. He'd been hit, I could tell, and it was embarrassing in front of me. He was staring daggers at Steve, who was keeping an eye on his father and otherwise made believe he couldn't care less. Mr. Stone threw the bank on the table and said, 'Little cocksucker won't even admit it.' He went heavily down the stairs, and we heard the TV go on. I was in some kind of shock, not thinking very clearly. Right there was the evidence of what I'd done, but no one was even looking at me. I'd never heard that word before, never heard anyone curse like that—we were big on silence in my house. I had a crazy confused idea Mrs. Stone would have to leave Mr. Stone now that he had said such a thing, and we could be together. I didn't look at the bank. From the basement we heard the announcers doing the game. Frank Messer and Bill White. We sat there I don't know how many minutes and then Marshall lunged for Steve, knocked him off his chair. Steve just laughed and held him off, but Marshall was nuts, flailing with hands and feet until they were both on the floor, and then Mr. Stone came back in and started whaling on both of them, using his fists, I could hear them landing. Mrs. Stone showed me to the door like nothing at all was happening, like it was just time for me to go home for dinner. She was still pretty and smiling, somehow, and she said Marshall would see me tomorrow, have a good day in school."

When Pendergast was not actively smoking, the air took on a pleasant quality, not musty exactly, but no longer overwhelming, a background smell Nathan didn't mind. He wondered what the girl whose room this had been would make of it if she ever came back to visit.

"Anyway, a couple of years later Steve had some kind of stroke. There were rumors about drugs, an OD, but no one ever knew. Marshall and I barely said hello to each other anymore, but everyone heard about it, of course. When they brought Steve home they had to help him up the steps. We went over, the whole family, the only time we were all there together. We brought fruit."

Nathan stopped, looked around for something in the room to fix on. He was done. He looked down at his hands, raw from where he'd been scratching them.

"And you felt responsible?" Pendergast hadn't spoken in so long Nathan was startled, as if he'd been interrupted.

"About the stroke, you mean? No. Why would I?"

Pendergast shrugged, lifted both hands in a questioning gesture.

"You don't cause strokes. Anyway, who knows what the kid was up to, what went on in that house? Are you saying I should feel it was my fault, because of a few dollars in change?"

Pendergast still had his arms raised, a gesture somehow accomplished without moving any other part of his body, like a diagram of a man with a question. "I'm not saying anything. I'm asking how you feel."

They sat a moment longer, Pendergast making no move at all, looking at Nathan, Nathan wanting just to get out of the room. A soft knock came at the door and a voice said, "Doctor? Overtime."

Nathan was out the door before the receptionist had reached the top of the stairs. He was halfway down them before he remembered his jacket, still on Pendergast's couch. Pendergast was in the hall waiting for him, the jacket in his hands.

Downstairs, a frightened young woman with lank blond hair looked at him as he passed.

The receptionist, absolutely composed behind her desk, greeted him with friendly delight. "Next week?"

Nathan ignored her, then turned back from the door. "The family that used to live here, you know anything about them?"

"Pardon?"

"Before it was turned into offices. The family who owned this place, I wondered if you knew where they went or anything."

She looked at him as if her job description included smiling at lunatics. Probably did.

"I'm not sure what you mean," she said. "This was Dr. Middlefield's and Dr. Horowitz's offices, and they were here, my goodness, maybe forty years. I'm not certain what family you mean."

Nathan nodded, and she smiled apologetically. He went through the door, across the porch, and down the steps. Over his shoulder was the window where the girl's room had been. He paused. Something came into his head, something he might have (never would have) told Pendergast. A summer afternoon, coming back from the park, he and Daniel started running. One would cuff or jostle the other, then dart ahead to be caught and cuffed himself. Soon they were running flat out, crossing people's lawns, dashing across streets using moving cars as shields, ducking behind sycamores and pelting each other with their fallen pincushion balls, laughing and thoughtless and overjoyed. Nathan could still recall the feeling—his breath coming loud, his small curses and grunts as Daniel was almost in reach, then escaped again, the way he could actually feel the blood in his veins, his heart in his chest—a moment shared, the kind you never had past a certain age, never with anyone but your brother. "Oh, close one," Daniel said, and Nathan lunged at him even harder.

At last, exhausted but reluctant to stop, they reach home. On the porch, Sol and Freda and a glass pitcher of iced tea. Nathan hates the stuff, sweet and bitter at the same time, but he's reckless and elated, takes a sip right from the chilled, dripping rim—Daniel's got Freda's glass—turns to splutter about how far they'd run, how he'd *been ahead part of the time, they should have seen it, one more block and he would have beat him. He hears his heavy breath echoing in the glass pitcher, that's fun, too, but when he lowers it to continue talking Daniel hasn't moved, Nathan's not sure why, and their father is looking at Daniel. Nathan, his guard let down, has missed the moment's change. Their mother hasn't, she fills her glass with fresh tea, holds it out to Daniel, who takes it but doesn't drink. Sol remembers himself, picks up the newspaper and flicks it in front of his face, but before he manages it, Nathan's seen the look he'd given his brother— he's seen it himself—and suddenly the iced drink is cold in his bowels and he's sick, angry, and afraid. There's a small explosion and Daniel has thrown his glass down, Nathan feels the wet spray and Daniel has slammed the door inside, a hand up to his cheek. Nathan stands one more minute looking at the paper behind which his father has disappeared. He goes inside, too, turns on the TV, sitting right on the couch in his sweaty clothes, watches some show he can't remember, wanting to shout, wanting to break something, now, thirty years later, that look on Sol's face as vivid to him as it was then, sweating on Freda's couch that afternoon—as if his own son was some evil thing sprung up before him. Upstairs Nathan can hear Daniel throwing things in their room.*

As dusk imperceptibly deepens, Nathan, who will be late for his shift at the hospital, stares up at the window of the girl's room. Memory. Theft. Guilt. What was taken, exactly, that summer day all those years ago? A good question for a psychiatrist.

4

Sylvia was surprised to hear from him, hadn't even realized he was out of town. Sol could tell from her tone she was hurt. "Such a hurry. I'm sure you were too busy to call."

She had been upset with him since the news about Daniel and Sol's offhand pronouncement there would be no shivah, not this time, not in his house. No blue-faced rabbis and weepy maiden aunts tramping around his rooms, not again. Sylvia had blinked, opened and closed her mouth several times, but let it go. She was a silly old woman—Sol still held this opinion of her, but softly. He enjoyed watching her negotiate her invariable stages of shock, disapproval, bafflement, before settling back into the solicitous affection she was most comfortable with. "They cover the mirrors, the busybodies." He couldn't stop himself. "For what? Spirits? Believe me, it's not the mirrors you should worry about." When the kettle had whistled for tea, Sol let her fetch it, it was nice having someone tend him, and for all his bluster, nice having someone here. And knowing that Sylvia, old habits dying hard, was happy to do it for him.

"Yes. It was kind of a rush."

A sniff. Sol could see her, the handkerchief in the sleeve always at the ready, the sagging old face, charming really, a gentle and pretty face, ready to come apart.

"Right now I'm calling you," he said. "From the hospital."

It really was unfair, this toying with her. But she must enjoy it, too, somewhere. You don't bury two husbands without learning where to take your pleasure. But this was too far, even for Sol. He heard her breathing harder on the phone line and said quietly, "Sylvia, it's nothing. I'm fine now. Just an infection."

"Where?"

The blood, he wanted to say. Everywhere. "The shoulder."

"Which shoulder?"

Annoying old woman. What difference which shoulder? "The left."

"The one you were holding so stiffly? The one you said was just a cramp?"

He said nothing.

"Are they giving you antibiotics?"

"Both arms. A few legs, too."

"Are you running a fever?"

"Not anymore."

"Sleeping?"

"Oh yes. Many interesting dreams."

Sol could honestly say he had not noticed Sylvia Grossman until maybe a year ago. He knew her, of course, recognized her from the elevator and the street, a neatly dressed lady with a bright and too-ready smile and hello, someone he instinctively shied from, in recognition of a vague but urgent need circling and ready to fasten on him. Freda had mentioned her once or twice: Nice woman. Terrible, the way she lost her husband. Sol had nodded abstractedly, his role in their conversations, the way he did when she told him Feinberg the dentist was retiring to North Carolina or the new restaurant on Austin with the tables outside and the fancy waiters wasn't as good as everyone had hoped.

All that happened was they passed each other in the lobby a few times, Sol on the way to the Y, Sylvia to her shopping or what she

called, absurdly, her constitutional. He helped her carry some bags
to the elevator, and once on a hot day they both sat on the torturous
bench down there, catching their breath. She asked if he ever
walked in the afternoons and something kept him from telling her
he wasn't one of those old farts who wandered up and down Queens
Boulevard all day like potted plants on legs. And then they were
walking together and it wasn't so bad, she didn't talk much, or, at
least, mind when he didn't, and in spring the pathetic little trees
bloomed even in the middle of the cement and a breeze sometimes
came up the avenue.

Then she was making dinner once in a while and he was doing
some shopping for her, her leg never coming back all the way from
her fall. And that was it. No big deal. A couple of nights a week they
ate together, walked slowly down the street. In her apartment she
would put piano music on, Mozart, whom Sol couldn't stand, in his
the TV played CNN, but turned low so they could talk. Mostly,
they were quiet. Once, watching some teary old Cary Grant movie
which made him want to sleep, she reached over and held his hand
and he allowed it, what was the harm, and another time he woke up
with his head on her shoulder. When he had the flu last winter he
stayed with him, sleeping on the couch, and before Yom Kippur
they both visited Beth David, her idea, where they laid flowers and
she prayed in front of her Hank's and his Freda's gravestones (Sol
standing behind, looking at the sky, the grass medians and graves,
which could stand a little mowing), and he put together a little
meal for her to break her fast after her long day in shul.

Truth be told, he was fond of her. He liked calling her Baba and
Old Girl and warning her not to get too excited because at her age
anything might carry her off. He felt their twice-a-week routine was
entirely sufficient, but there was a pleasurable loneliness now, an
absence, small but piercing, pleasurable because it could be recti-
fied, when he was alone in his rooms, and though it was the last
thing he'd ever admit to her (or to nosy Nathan, whose business it

couldn't be less of), he looked forward to their evenings together and missed her when she was gone. He enjoyed the way she worried over him, triggered her concern whenever he could. He was moved by and a little vain about the way she did her hair up, wore nice dresses for their outings. A few times he had felt the impulse to kiss her, and he did, once or twice, chastely, on the cheek. From time to time, a more urgent longing, or the memory of one, a warm dull insistence which told him he was alive yet, and which he pacified by special purchases in among her groceries, the Little Schoolboy cookies she liked, some French vanilla ice cream, or flowers, the white or yellow, expressive of fondness without showing off about it.

That day last week, hearing her making tea in the kitchen, the soft, tuneless humming she lapsed into when she was upset, he, too, had been glad of the distraction. No shivah in my house, he had said, not again, no lecturing rabbis and fussy old ladies with their whispering and sloppy grief. And he had meant as much, it was the truth. But not the only truth. He sat looking out the windows, Sylvia humming and filling the teapot. He couldn't tell her, couldn't say a word. In misery and rage and helpless regret he blamed the rabbis and the ladies from the Sisterhood and the Neighbors' Watch, all of whom had descended, eager to animate his suffering, share it, as if they possibly could. Idiots, all of them. Let us gather now and mourn and tell stories of the boy he was (how would they know?), the man he would have (should have) been. Let us remember and by remembering ease ourselves, let the healing begin. Well, bullshit, thought Sol. All of it. All of them, vultures come out of the trees. Sylvia was filling the cups, and Sol turned before she could call. He stood up and went to the window but didn't look out. He realized his hands were in fists and put them in his pockets.

There wasn't even a body to put in the ground.

Now Sylvia was telling him about a treatment she had read about, involving teas and Korean massage. It restored the body's endocrine balances. She had magazines all over her house, *Women's Health*, *Nature's Remedies*, and Sol's personal favorite, *Prevention* (who were they kidding?). He let her talk herself out and told her, again, he was fine, Nathan was looking after him. Had she heard his son was a doctor? Finally she was done.

"You think I'm a silly old fool, Sol, but I worry about you."

"Baba," he said. "You're not so silly."

"I don't know why, believe me, but I care. It's been hard for you, I know, dreadfully hard . . ."

"*Shah. Shah* now, *shtil*. It's alright."

"And you haven't been yourself lately, you know."

"I know." So who had he been?

"Not that I should mind," her voice softening.

"No."

Then she was quiet and he was, too, for a time, and he asked her how her leg was feeling and told her she should get out and exercise while he was away. He told her to take care of herself and he would see her soon, and felt he wanted to say more but couldn't determine what, so he said goodbye and hung up the phone. The remote for the TV was on the bed, and he found his glasses and picked them up. From the hallway came sounds of footsteps, the clatter of plastic and rubber wheels that meant lunch, or medication, was on the way. He sat holding the control but didn't push any buttons. Outside, the heavy cart advanced room by room up the corridor.

ര ര ര

In high school once, his class went to a TV studio to see how they made the shows. They walked onto the set of a hospital soap Nathan vaguely recognized from bored afternoons home with the flu. He was amazed to see the entire hospital reduced to a nurses' station, a single patient room, an elevator (he remembered now how many scenes took place in an elevator); the chief of staff's professorial office was a shabby mock-up, painted books on painted shelves, the lab just a table with two ridiculous-looking beakers (denoting science). In the background window a painted New York landscape so flat and lacking in detail he could have done it himself in ten minutes. Remarkable, people's gullibility. And even these bare surfaces weren't genuine; if you peeked around the walls you saw dusty studs and drywall, a sandwich wrapper and a crushed Pepsi can. The sets were stacked together, the elevator a step away from the chief's office—the whole thing could fit inside a big garage.

The actors who came out to talk with them, coiffed and sun-baked and flirtatious, were no more real than the set. One quoted Shakespeare (incorrectly, Nathan suspected, but he couldn't be certain). Another, fifty if she was a day, lacquered ringlets piled high like Cleopatra from a Hercules movie, leaned forward, her powdery brown cleavage puckering, troubling Nathan's haughty adolescent notion of sexual beauty (not a wrinkle anywhere on Elise Davis). She asked him, "Do you act?"

On the subway uptown the kids were raucous, sarcastic about what a fraud it all was, the more confident deriding the others for not knowing all along. Nathan came away with a different feeling, an inversion of what he had expected to feel. Not that it was all fake, but rather it was *all* real, a parallel reality like the one in the *Superman* comics he had read until recently. The sets believed they were a hospital in the same way those mannequins believed they were actors. At home they brushed their teeth before two-dimensional sinks slapped up against drywall, then sat in cartoon living rooms drinking sherry (colored water), reading from books with blank pages. They ate and made love and conversed with scripted ease, aware of their blocking and the position of the camera. They laughed a little too loud, with their heads back, and cried picturesquely. Don't try telling any of them it wasn't real.

Here's what wasn't real: his classmates, hooting and shouting across the subway car, swaggering in their midday freedom, earnestly showing off for the girls. What wasn't real was him, his own turbid teenage life, the fumbling, urgent, often unbearable desire with Elise on the synagogue steps, the preposterous dreams he lulled himself with every night (the point guard fantasy replaced with one equally extravagant: Dr. Nathan Mirsky-Schweitzer dispensing sober and rescuing counsel to the afflicted). Or least real of all, home, his silent mother moving through her days in wordless, dignified acquiescence to everything—illness, age, disappointment—as if none of it could ultimately matter. And his brother, hair down his back, braided sometimes with flowers, dressed like a character from a Robert Louis Stevenson novel and speaking like one half the time, dreamy pronouncements about the Establishment and the Doors of Perception, a new girl on his arm every time Nathan saw him. On his belt, a conjurer's leather pouch from which he drew an intricate little machine for rolling his joints, and pills, pyramids and ovals and barrels in candy colors which he said Nathan was too young for.

Or Sol, night after sleepless night in his dusty, half-lit cave, buried in paper, charts, letters, photographs, his private inviolable domain while his family slept, or tried to. Nathan used to sneak in (it felt like sneaking) when his father wasn't around, just to look. He remembered thinking, So this is where he lives.

Once—he was nine or ten—he'd taken a thick file from the shelves. What he found inside was incomprehensible—timetables, lists of names and numbers, foreign place names so full of consonants they hurt the eyes. When Sol came in, stood near the door, Nathan had no idea what to do; the urge to run, so common in him, rose. Inside, the familiar queasy moil of feelings he had whenever his father looked at him—regret, a spreading shame. As they watched each other, before Nathan walked to the bookshelf and returned the folder, he heard himself thinking, Other kids play catch. Other fathers speak. Sol's immobile face unwatchable, severe, and hardest of all to see, a little wild in the eyes, as if with fright. What could Nathan have possibly found out? Nobody said a word as he replaced the folder and walked past his father into the living room.

Who was Nathan to say what real was? Least of all he.

So as he pushed open the wide glass doors to the Hall of Justice, Nathan knew immediately where he was.

The vast marble lobby, the inscriptions and the air of municipal authority, another imitation, an elaborate set for a bunch of actors, Nathan among them. Beyond the inner glass wall, Angie Dickinson, playing a lawyer, laughed at something Tony Danza said, showing off her still-dazzling smile. The guy from *Welcome Back, Kotter*, the teacher, escorting a perp, hands cuffed before him, to a special elevator marked RESTRICTED. Extras milling about, a cop and two hookers, straight from central casting, moving through a gray door to what must be the holding cell, the lockup, the pokey.

Ahead of Nathan in line, a thin man in torn jeans and a leather jacket set off the metal detector. He stood under it a moment, looking around as if trying to decipher the association between the blaring noise and himself. Nathan recognized him, too, from work, he'd stumble in late, hoping for pain meds, maybe even a nap in the waiting area while whatever he was on wore off. Finally he shuffled back through the gray metal frame and began emptying his pockets. Nathan looked through the glass wall beside them for Sipowicz, Jimmy Smits, the guys from *Law and Order*.

Behind the desk by the detector, a huge cop, sweating already in the thin morning light, sat watching as the man produced cigarettes, coins, a pink long-toothed comb, Life Savers, a five-inch hunting knife in a leather sheath. The man continued dutifully, working the pants now, as the officer stared at him in bland amazement, tapping a gold-ringed finger on the desk. Lottery tickets, keys, sunglasses, half a dozen toothpicks in paper wraps. When the man was done he said to the cop, apologizing, "That's all I got."

The cop nodded, said thoughtfully, "C'mere. Lemme ask you somethin'." He moved a big hand through the articles on his desk. "Where the fuck you at?"

The man opened his mouth, then closed it, unsure if this was a trick question. He was bone thin, most users were, Nathan could see the muscles in his neck, a vein fingering across his forehead.

"Courthouse?" he said. "Jail?"

The man checked, looking all around him. His face swept Nathan's as he turned back, a twitch working one eye. Nathan looked behind him—was anyone else seeing this? An older couple, Vietnamese maybe, stared impassively. The woman held a dog-eared manila envelope, the man wore a straw hat and chewed something slowly.

"Here's my question," the cop was saying. "Here's what I need to know." He had a hand on the little man's shoulder, seemed to be slowly driving him into the marble floor. "You bring a fuckin' knife into a courthouse?"

Nathan watched the man gather his belongings, stuff them into his pockets. At the exit doors, he carefully put on his sunglasses, put one candy, then another, in his mouth before leaving.

"You," Nathan heard. He moved forward and began emptying his pockets.

In the Homicide Office, he sat in a waiting area with three chairs and a coatrack before a crowded desk. The secretary was out. Behind the desk, a poster, drawn by a child, showed a woman walking through slashing raindrops, black clouds overhead. She wore a yellow raincoat, and you couldn't see her face. The caption read: "These black clouds have a silver lining. California Cares." On the front of the desk was a bumper sticker. "Remember: We work for God."

Nathan shook his head as if to clear it, rubbed both sides of his face. He was giddy, he was exhausted, he found everything he saw arch and humorous and connected in some mysterious and utterly

trivial way. Through one door with a sign that read LIEUTENANT, another crowded desk under a bulletin board covered with snapshots,
grandchildren at camp, skiing, a pileup on the lawn. From time to
time a detective—he guessed they were detectives—came in, asked
politely if he'd been helped, and disappeared inside the office,
where Nathan could see desks, filing cabinets, where two men
joked with a woman about a fishing trip. "He was sick from the time
we left the pier, green as a dollar bill," one said. The woman was
laughing. "Yeah," a second voice said. "Who caught the only fucking fish?" "Yeah," the first voice said, "but who ate it?" Nathan
found this exchange oddly humorous, as did the woman, who
laughed the entire time the men spoke, and was laughing now,
waiting for them to continue. Nathan slouched forward in the
chair. He rubbed his face again.

This giddiness, the careening sense of hilarity, was obviously
troublesome. Inappropriate affect. He put his legs out before him,
wedged himself more firmly into the seat. Why this? Of all the
possible ways to feel, why this? He was light, taut and elastic like
a balloon that would bob against the ceiling if he didn't watch
himself.

He stood and looked into the lieutenant's office, got a paper cup
from the dispenser and water from the cooler. What was that thing
Daniel used to say, one of his name-dropping, I've-read-more-than-
you-ever-will quotes, about knowledge being an obstacle to (the opposite of? the end of?) understanding? Only experience led to
wisdom. Nathan couldn't remember. He dropped the paper cup
into the overflowing trash basket below.

"Dr. Mirsky?"

The room was crowded with desks, each with a computer and a
wooden chair beside it. Over the desks were fliers, charts, photos—
police in ranks, shaking hands with dignitaries, signed pictures of
Dusty Baker, Jerry Rice. The two men and the woman detective
were typing or on the phone. No one looked up. The man who had
introduced himself as Inspector Rivera led Nathan across the room

to a desk in the corner. Over Rivera's desk the walls were bare. He stood until Nathan reached him, a hand out toward the chair, inviting him. Nathan sat. Rivera sat as well, turned his chair toward Nathan, smiled, waited for him to speak. What was he supposed to say? I'm here to identify the remains. Or would that be collect? A joke Daniel used to tell: How many Jews can you fit in a Volkswagen? A thousand: two up front, two in the back, the rest in the ashtray. A thousand and one now, room for one more. Begin with that? Maybe the inspector liked jokes, jokes were always good icebreakers. Rivera, a trim man, muscular, good-looking, waited patiently.

It wasn't giddiness, after all, Nathan realized, but hostility. Why bring a knife to a courthouse? What better fucking place?

For one thing, Rivera was too young. Neatly dressed in a shirt and tie, hair fashionably cut and combed. He looked like one of the smart young interns at the hospital, the ones who should have M.B.A.'s, not M.D.'s. Nathan would have preferred Sipowicz.

Rivera flinched first. "Sorry to keep you," he said, sounding just like a junior executive.

"It's alright," Nathan said quietly.

"How's your father?" Nathan had called yesterday, postponing their meeting.

"Better. He'll be out of the hospital tomorrow."

"That's good news," Rivera said. Nathan said nothing.

Rivera opened a file on his desk and turned a few pages. The phone rang and he told somebody, "Right. Thanks for checking." He gave Nathan a look when he hung up and made a notation in the folder. When he was done, he smiled briefly.

"Again, Dr. Mirsky, I want to tell you how sorry I am for your loss."

The tight, rueful smile, the subtle lean in his upper body, all very convincing. No wonder he'd gotten the part. "Yes," Nathan said. "Thanks." On a wall over the desk near Rivera's was an antidrug poster, "D.A.R.E." written in slashing blood-red letters, like the title of a horror movie.

"As I told you on the phone," Rivera said, "we're treating this as a homicide."

Nathan looked back at him.

"All our information seems to indicate this. There are a few remaining facts to ascertain."

"What facts?"

Rivera looked at him, sizing him up. Clearly, Nathan wasn't going to make this easy for him. Nathan had a similar role in his job—the families always started out wanting to know everything. At least that's what they said. Nathan could help by a receptive expression, a leading question. Not that he was about to. He took a pencil from Rivera's desk and squeezed it in one hand, passed it to the other. Rivera returned to the file.

"Okay. I can tell you this. Your brother, Daniel." He paused. "*Chaim?*" he said, looking at Nathan apologetically. He had pronounced it wrong, knew he had, was offering politely to be corrected. Guy should be a social worker, Nathan thought. He said nothing.

"Daniel Chaim Mirsky," Rivera continued, "found on the morning of October third, deceased. Cause of death, gunshot. Locale and disposition of body indicate foul play. Investigation ongoing."

"I know all that," Nathan said. "You told me all that on the phone. The *San Francisco Chronicle* told me that."

Something hard came into Rivera's face, the shadow of a change in expression. He was too poised, too good-looking, to disclose anger. He said quietly, "I'm aware of what I told you, Dr. Mirsky." He folded his hands on the open file. "As I said to you yesterday, and, I believe, when you first arrived, I cannot disclose details of an ongoing investigation. I'm telling you again. So what can I do to help you today?"

"You can start by not reading to me out of some fucking report, Inspector. My brother's dead. All I get is a bunch of jargon and polite double-talk. 'Evidence of foul play.' 'Disposition of body.' How are we supposed . . ."

The pencil snapped in his hand, one end hitting him below the jaw. He picked it up from his lap, looked at the other half, his fingers white around the yellow wood. He put both pieces on the edge of Rivera's desk. Rivera ignored them.

"All I'm asking," Nathan said, the words coming harder. "What does any of that mean?"

He stopped again. Rivera was looking right at him, undisturbed. He continued. "Look, Inspector. I'm sorry. I shouldn't talk to you that way. It's been a lousy week, you know? I'm sorry." He shook his head, rubbed the spot where the pencil had nicked him. He picked up the broken ends and made a gesture of futility with them. With a tilt of his head, Rivera indicated a wastebasket by the side of the desk. Nathan tossed the pieces in.

"Alright," Nathan said. "We've established I can be an asshole. That's some sort of progress, right?" Rivera didn't contradict him. He sat back in the wooden chair.

"Inspector, we don't know what happened, we don't understand. My brother and I, at the end, we weren't very close, kind of lost touch. My father and I. We'd like to know . . ." He gave up. "I just want to understand."

Finally, Rivera moved. He looked a moment at Nathan, as if about to speak, then minutely shook his head. Nathan, needing something to do with his hands, held them together in his lap, thumbs locked behind the fingers.

"Alright," Rivera said. "Listen. I'll tell you what I can, Dr. Mirsky, and that's *all* I can tell you. I realize how—part of how—you must feel. But you must realize investigations have been destroyed because of wrong or leaked information. Let us do our job."

Nathan nodded.

Rivera closed the file and put it on the desk. "Your brother was found dead in an alley not near his home. I can't tell you where. He was shot, that's all I can say. We're looking into what he might have been doing there."

"Okay," Nathan said, keeping his hands locked. It seemed vitally

important he keep them still. Now he appreciated how families felt
when he gave them the news. He concentrated on being respectful,
speaking slowly and clearly, modulating his tone to their expres-
sions, their body language. They listened with meek attention—all
that was left them to do—nodding, as Nathan was now. "I see," they
said, when what they were feeling was a clenching in the gut, the
kind only getting sick would relieve, your whole body swelling with
it. What he was feeling now.

"What was he . . . Was he looking for . . . ?"

"We're not sure. Those are the 'facts' I mentioned before." He
reached into a drawer for a box of tissues and slid them to Nathan.
Nathan was surprised—was he crying? "Did your brother ever have
a pistol permit? He had a gun on him, a .22."

Nathan felt his face for tears. Nothing.

"I don't follow," he said quietly.

Rivera shook his head slowly, not impatiently, but as if to indicate this was exactly what his reticence earlier was about, what he
had meant to avoid. Look what you're making me do. "Dr. Mirsky,"
he said. "Your brother was killed in a neighborhood run by gangs,
disputed territory, several of them constantly at war. This is their
borderline, their battle zone." He raised a hand, palm open, in front
of him. "Look. You just don't go in there, waving a gun around. He
wasn't a beginner, your brother. He was a user, longtime. He knew
how to get his fix somewhere else, in his own neighborhood." He
shook his head, brought the hand down. "Without doing this.
Putting himself in absolute danger."

"So he went down there to . . ." Nathan let the sentence drop,
not knowing how to finish it.

Now Rivera was speaking without being asked. "That's where we
are. And you know what I will tell you—it's not going to be easy, a
user, a man clearly distraught—who knows what was going on." He
waited until Nathan's eyes came back. Nathan opened his mouth to
speak, maybe to tell him he had heard enough, he wasn't certain,

but Rivera continued. "What I'm saying . . ." Rivera spoke quietly, looking tired himself suddenly, a pale net of wrinkles under the eyes, dark thumbprints in his otherwise tan, robust skin. Too many unsolved murders? Belligerent family members? "He knew. You don't go to a place like that without knowing the consequences." He rubbed the side of his face with two fingers. "With some little popgun. He wasn't that stupid. He knew."

∾ ∾ ∾

The nurses were polite, competent. But some treated him like an infant needing to be coaxed and wheedled, and they talked funny — "Don't we like the rice pudding?" (We who?)—and others were brusquely efficient, moving him around like he was in the way, popping thermometers in his ear (where next?) before even saying a word. "Doctor will be in soon," they announced, already on their way out the door.

But one Sol liked. The name on her white tag with the hospital symbol was Clara. She came in the evenings, was older, slower-moving, did everything deliberately, as if deciding first whether it needed doing, though she could turn a patient (not that Sol needed help) or hand out medicine as quick as any of them. She knocked. She stuck her head in to see if you were awake and before putting hands on you asked how you were feeling (you, not we). And when Sol merely stared at her, not understanding the question, or its motive, she just smiled and said it again. She couldn't really want to know—even Sol understood enough about hospitals to know they weren't movies—but she apparently wanted an answer. She would wait until she got one. So he told her. Fine. Better now. This one he liked.

The first time Sol saw her, or recognized her, he was stupid from the drugs they were pouring into him. He was dozing, off and on, dreams whose vividness in sleep was mitigated only by the furry unfocus the drugs left him in when he opened his eyes. He woke this time gasping, moving jaws and lips in spasms as if to empty his mouth — this dream he knew — reaching blindly around for water. And there she was, Clara, giving him water, a paper cup with a straw and one steadying hand on his unhurt shoulder. "Slowly," she said. "Slowly."

Where was his son, he asked, after he'd managed to get some water down. She'd sent him to the cafeteria for dinner. He'd been here all night, all day. More water? No, he told her, subsiding against the raised pillows. "I need to change that dressing," she said, her dry, light hand on his arm. She had an accent, one he couldn't trace. "Okay," Sol said, and he let her move him forward on the bed.

In the two days since, they had become friends, Sol thought. He had, without admitting as much to himself, begun looking forward to the evenings, when Clara's shift began (he always had women tending him, all his life, and depended on it, without admitting it to himself). He asked about her grandchildren, a girl and boy whose photos were pinned to her uniform in small oval frames. The girl was in glasses, maybe seven years old, her adult teeth crowding her child's mouth in a grin so exuberant it made Sol smile, too. "She's going to be trouble," he told Clara. She bent both frames toward her face and looked at them affectionately. "That one trouble already," she said, smiling back.

He found he could joke with her, and complain, her broad, dark face retaining its expression of tolerant, amused exasperation no matter what he said. She was a big-boned, heavy-moving woman, and though Sol as a rule preferred women petite (Freda was small; so, for that matter, was Sylvia), he liked the way Clara could hold him with one arm while checking the dressing with the other, the way she placed her hands on him matter-of-factly. When he told her the hospital food was poison, she said poison (she pronounced it "*pie*-zun") might spice it up some, and when he complained of his neighbor, who with his equally loud and obnoxious family watched and commented on every imbecile talk show there was on the television, she went around the shade and turned down the set without a word, and none of them, not the foul-mouthed patient or his deaf, belligerent son, made a sound. She asked him was he in California for vacation and Sol surprised himself by telling her about Daniel (not the guns, not the girl), and she shook her head slowly, her face registering what he said without shock or automatic (and fraudulent, Sol was always certain) sympathy. Sol recognized for the first time the reaction he had been seeking, the only one he could trust. All she said was, "Your oldest?" and Sol told her, "Yes, my oldest boy."

This morning they had wheeled in a new patient (the curser must have left during the night), and Sol had watched groggily. He assumed they were silent because they were trying not to disturb him, but as the day shift came on they were oddly muted around the adjacent bed, less talkative with him. He asked a nurse in a whisper what was wrong with his neighbor, but she just made a sound with her tongue and shook her head. He decided he would wait and ask Clara.

After checking that he was sleeping (Sol had tiptoed over during the afternoon and seen it was a teenage boy), Clara went to the far side of Sol's bed, also shaking her head, as the day-shift nurse had done. It was a boy they all knew, who had been coming in for years, a boy born all wrong, mother on drugs, alcohol—who could even say? Because the family was rich they put him in a care facility, but there were flare-ups, problems, then they brought him here. What was wrong now? Sol asked. Lungs, Clara said.

"They never been right. They fill up with fluid, child can't breathe. They drain it, they try all sort thing, but it don't matter now. Nothing help now."

"Is he dying?" Sol asked.

Clara shook her head, not meaning no, he wasn't, meaning maybe, nothing to do but wait.

He was fourteen, fifteen. Sol had peeked around the shade, dragging his IV pole on its three wheels. He was prepared to duck out of sight if spotted, or, if he had to, put out a hand and introduce himself. But when he saw the boy sleeping, he pushed the pole before him and followed it closer to the bed.

He was surprised later when Clara told him how sick the boy was. He had looked alright to Sol. Not hale, not as full-fleshed and heedlessly tossed into sleep as a teenage boy should be. Sol remembered Daniel and Nathan from this age, how they collapsed anywhere, like a spell had been put on them: the couch, the floor right in front of those trunk-sized speakers with their headphones on. There was something impressive, even wonderful, in their animal heat and abandon (and they were hot, if you touched them), in their commitment to their body's headlong requirements. This boy slept differently, tentatively, as if he anticipated being woken any minute (his boys had always woken shocked, as if in disbelief that they were expected ever to rise). But he looked okay, overall. He had a breathing mask on, and he made a ratchety, congested sound, maybe from the chest, but Sol had figured bronchitis (he had had it himself), maybe pneumonia. They'd pump him full of something and send him back to school. It would never occur to Sol the boy was dying.

"I haven't seen his family," Sol said.

This triggered something in Clara, something in her eyes. She began tidying up around his bed, removing used water cups and tissues, checking the IV bag, reaching for the chart to make notations. "They be here when they find the time," she said.

Years ago, returning from a week in Florida, Sol was driving a two-lane road from the beach to the highway. Freda dozed beside him. The boys were in the back of the station wagon among their sleeping bags, shoes, books, knocked out by long days in the water and sun. It was not quite night yet, the blue summer dusk expanding, taking its time. Sol was tired, grateful for the silence after the boys' constant noise and complaints. He would have preferred leaving that morning, or at least after lunch, but the boys had been so insistent, and they looked so good, strong and healthy in their summer tans, that he and Freda had relented. This meant they were all collapsed now as he drove, leaving him with no one to help should he get drowsy, but he was alert, just tired, and he would stop somewhere for an hour or two when he needed a rest. This was before the interstate connected everything in one identical road. He drove through small towns, stretches with nothing but orange trees and fruit stands in pale, sandy soil, an occasional home far back, its lights visible through the trees. He forgot himself, relaxing into the drive.

After a few miles there was something in the road ahead. He slowed and saw a cardboard box, its top open, directly in his lane. He had the quick urge to smash it, send it flying over the top of his car or into the trees (what idiot leaves a box in the middle of the road?), but this might be dangerous, and he braked, preparing to curve around it. Then something (he never knew what) made him stop the car. It was past twilight as he pulled onto the shoulder, turned on his hazard lights, and got out. Ahead was a pale blue band over the trees, still light somewhere, but here it was dark, his headlights garishly illuminating the square brown box, red lettering along its side. He walked over.

As he neared it and prepared to look in he heard a laugh, a throaty, triumphant hoot, and a boy in a striped T-shirt with blond hair cut short suddenly stood up from the box and laughed in his face. He was about Daniel's age, nine, ten. "Ha!" he said. "Ha-ha!" And still grinning, he jumped from the box, a specter running into the trees.

Sol moved the box to the side of the road. When he got back to the car Freda was just opening her eyes. She hadn't seen it, she asked why they were stopped. Sol didn't know what to tell her, didn't know if he should try to drive while his arms and hands were still shaking.

"Sol?"

"I thought I saw something," he said.

Freda yawned, stretched her arms sideways, then covered her mouth. She looked over the backseat at the boys. "Did you?"

"No," Sol said, "I guess not," and she rubbed his face with a hand, yawned again, and rearranged herself for sleep against the side door. "Well, wake me if you do," she said.

Sol had decided he would tell her later, back in New York, when they were safely home and far from this place which had been so warm and full of relaxed invitation but which now seemed to him ominous, alien, teeming with indeterminate threat. He decided he would tell her in the morning. But he never did.

Somehow, for reasons he couldn't locate, the boy in the next bed recalled to him that night on the Florida road. When the grinning blond imp had popped up triumphantly, insolently beaming, as if he'd bested Sol at some game Sol hadn't realized they'd been playing, Sol had been too surprised to move. If it had been one of his boys, Nathan or Daniel, he would have moved quick enough, slapped him till his head rang, but he did nothing, just stood still as the boy gave his victorious call and disappeared into the woods. Now, watching this other boy, understanding no more thirty years later and three thousand miles across the continent in a hospital room, something of what he might have said to the boy in the Florida night came to him. What are you thinking? he might have said. What world is this?

He thought these things late at night, after Clara had come in for her last check and asked if he'd like a pill to sleep, after Nathan had arrived, flustered and agitated, wanting to talk about some policeman he'd been speaking with, stoke whatever anger he was brooding over into full flame. But Sol had pleaded weariness. He was too tired to hear about it now, he had a headache. Tomorrow. Nathan could tell him tomorrow, when they let him leave.

Then, when he was alone, he pulled himself slowly from bed — the fever was gone, and some of the pain, though his entire left side was stiff, and his shoulder, if possible, as sore as when he had first come into the hospital. They had taken the IV from his arm after dinner and, feeling oddly untethered, Sol walked around the curtain and over to the sleeping boy. Clara had told him the boy, his name was Brandon, had had a good day, though he'd been awake only an hour or so, hadn't said much—it hurt, apparently, to talk—and though his parents still hadn't been to see him. They expected he would be taken to Continuing Care, Clara said, maybe tomorrow, maybe the next day, when things got worse.

Sol approached and took a good look. He was normal-looking, pale and wavy-haired, his head turned, his mouth slightly open below the clear green oxygen mask. His eyes fluttered every few seconds, and his breathing, which Sol knew now was the location of the trouble, was more unsteady (or was Sol listening better?) than it had been even this afternoon. But still he didn't look too bad, surely not so sick? He looked like he might wake up any minute and ask for some water, something to eat, ask Sol to turn on the television, which Sol would be happy to do.

What was it like, Sol stood there wondering, to know from the day you were born that you wouldn't last? Did he know? He was on borrowed time, Clara had said (and Sol had stifled his smart response—who isn't?), lucky to have lasted this long. What was it like to wake every day with this knowing, this knowing that you couldn't share with anyone, no matter how close they were or how much they tried to understand? Had anyone tried? What are you thinking, he wanted to ask the boy. What world is this.

Somebody should be here, somebody who knew what to do. Somebody should push the hair back from his forehead, feel him to see if he was warm enough, or too warm, just by touching him to let him know he was cared for, someone was paying attention. Freda could do it, Sylvia could. Maybe Clara had. She was a good woman, and she wouldn't have neglected what was clearly a duty somebody had to recognize. All day again, no family. Sol stood watching the boy, measuring the breaths he took from the sound, the rise and fall of the thin blanket, the peculiar eye movement which seemed to be connected to the pattern of his breathing. Brandon reached a rough moment, something lodging wetly in his throat, and he nearly woke, maybe, rolling his head. But it passed before he was fully roused, before Sol could move to the red call button in the wall. He stood another moment or two to make sure the crisis was over, then pulled aside the curtain between the beds and, quietly as he was able, returned to his own bed and got back in.

∾ ∾ ∾

Drunk in a new city. The summer before freshman year, Nathan and a friend had traveled through Europe, eight countries in less than a month, and had formed their lasting impression of each city their first night, when they could see it drunk. London was a good town, they thought, at least inside the smoky, mirrored pubs. Paris was beautiful, with the river and the lights on Notre Dame, toward morning, searching for the hostel. Madrid in the sun, drinking Rioja. Zurich was fine, until in a loud workmen's bar by the river a man sat across from them at a round table and repeatedly stuck a coin to his forehead, smiling at them, only at them, till it fell off and he did it again. A thick-faced man, with veined blue eyes and a mustache that held foam from the beer. Probably nothing in that smile but what was in theirs, jovial emptiness—his friend had found it hilarious, couldn't get a coin to stick to his own head—but it spoiled Zurich for Nathan, had stayed with him the rest of the trip. Amsterdam was best: they'd bought some hash from a guy in the train station, and when they stumbled out of a jazz bar long after midnight no one had gone home, absolutely everyone was on the streets, as high as they were, there was music and noise and action. Amsterdam was the best city to be drunk in. Nathan had written that on a card to Daniel.

Drunk in San Francisco, then. That, in any case, had been the plan. Hadn't quite worked. What skills we lose, Nathan thought, lighting a cigarette, walking up Grant toward Chinatown. Used to get high, enjoyed that, until all it did was make him anxious and so recessed in his coiled thoughts that he was unable to climb out. Used to enjoy classical music, could sit still an hour enjoying it. Not anymore. Used to read, loved movies, any movie, nearly.

Used to get drunk. Nothing had cheered him so much as a bar, the half-lit bustling intimacy, the faces in smoke, conversation clipped by laughter and the chime of glasses, bottles. He would look around and feel it in the air above them: sex, celebration, something tribal and festive. They had all left their cramped and disappointing lives to come here, this night, this is where they brought their hopes. What was as good, as alive, as that? And when he'd meet the woman, spot her at a table or down the bar, when he'd first say hello, when they'd walk out holding hands, the feel of their bodies together already becoming familiar, he knew what was coming—every ritual has its culmination—the new bed, the quiet talk, he was always at his wittiest and most relaxed. Then sex, hours of it, if it turned out they liked each other alright. But there was always a hesitation in the beginning, while getting their coats, when he was reluctant to leave, realized this was the moment he would remember. Here, in this place, warmly drunk, he'd found what he came for and was grateful, a sense of benediction in the steeped dark of the room.

That, too, gone, apparently.

How long had he even been in the bar? And before that, how long in the other bar, near the bookstore? He looked at his watch. After two. He knew that. That's when they closed, at two. That's why he'd left. He wasn't getting drunk, just stupid. Nathan realized he had forgotten to check the street sign at the corner. He looked around, Chinese restaurants, guys dragging black garbage bags out to the curb, an old lady in a sweater and felt hat smoking while her dog, some little lap rat, took a trembling shit. No idea what street. He kept walking.

That woman in the bar. Could be with her now. A student

maybe, or a young professional, he could be hearing all about it. Some little apartment he could wander through after she was asleep. Framed Impressionists on the wall, flowers in a vase on a table. He could look at her books, the cereal she ate. Usually a window to sit at, maybe a blanket around him, to look at the street. When he heard her moving, early, he'd make coffee.

Ahead, the woman bent with a plastic bag, working the round, slack turds into her hand. Nathan walked over to ask her the time.

Goddamn Rivera. Inspector. What did that mean? Didn't they even have detectives in this town? Nathan stumbled, didn't look back, righted himself. Have to watch that. Daniel would know, would most definitely, infuriatingly, know. Inspector. Speculate. Spectacle. Speculum. Trim and mustached and nothing got to this guy. Even the ashes, giving them to Abby—they'd fucked that one up, hadn't they? So cool. Not a ripple of bother. Made somebody proud.

Then Sol. Nathan had news. He'd run up the stairs, four flights, to tell him, but the old man had altered course again, why didn't Nathan anticipate it by now? Tired, too tired to talk, though he didn't look tired, he looked wide awake, he looked pretty good, to Nathan. Some new kid in the bed next to him, the nurses had forgotten to draw the shade between the beds. Nathan did and pulled up a chair. To talk. But Sol wanted to wait until tomorrow. Tomorrow. Talk in the morning. Fine with him. Whole new city out there to be drunk in.

Under a streetlamp Nathan stopped and took a cigarette from his shirt pocket. He'd borrowed so many from the guy at the next table in the last bar he'd just left him the pack, the lighter, a red plastic tube with the Golden Gate monogrammed along the side. Good guy. Tax accountant from Minnesota. Montana. Looking for Carol Doda, seen her when he was in the navy, twenty years ago. Never forgotten. Couldn't believe she was no longer dancing. Nathan focused on the street sign—Beckett—meant nothing to him. Ahead more restaurants and larger buildings, lights still on in some windows. The woman carried the dog in one hand, the bag in the other, somehow managed to unlock an apartment-house door and enter. Nathan lit the cigarette and walked on.

She was a nice girl. Lonely, wary, optimistic. There was a balcony in the bar; out the windows you could see people in the bookstore across the alley, walking up the crowded avenue. Buses, taxis, lights, neon, and flashing bulbs. Inside you could look down into the room, movie posters and odd, witty signs on the walls, pictures of James Joyce and other Irish luminaries he didn't recognize. He was about to leave, find another place, when he noticed her alone at the bar, ordering some kind of highball. She laughed at something the bartender said and tipped well, with bills. She had long fingers and nice hair, rolling dark past the shoulders, and she put her head back to blow smoke away from the other people at the bar. She was mid-twenties, on the plump side, the kind who would go to fat or become a workout fanatic. She had on a brown sweater and black skirt and bright lipstick, and she was lonely and hopeful and looking around as if this would be the night her life would change. He could tell all this right away. A predatory sense, Pendergast once called it, the way predators instinctively size up their prey, the odds, the risk.

Fucking Pendergast.

Janet had not been home all day. He tried her after leaving the Hall of Justice and again after reaching the hospital. It was a Saturday, and she could be out, but he had tried several more times, and at last he must have filled the tape on the machine, because the phone just kept on ringing. So on a hunch he had called information and gotten the number for Shelby, Janet's friend from work. There was music in the background, throbbing oceanic strings — Shelby was a connoisseur of healing. Nathan listened as she paused before answering.

"Yes," Shelby said. "She's here." Again a pause, as if she was looking away from the phone. "Nathan. I'm not sure she wants to talk right now."

"I've been calling the apartment."

"Yes," Shelby said. "She's had quite an upset."

He could see Shelby in her cluttered rooms, the pillows and throw rugs and silkscreen drapes, gesturing with the hand not holding the phone, the beads and scarves and bangles, her alert, sensitive face mirroring the world's pain. A genuine nut. How could Janet stand her? Nathan always wondered. The instant, torrential commiseration, the flamboyant concern for everything, everyone, all God's children. She had read his stars (or his tarot—which was which?) one time they were over at her place, charts and wheels and lists of numbers all over the living room floor. When he told her he didn't know his birth hour, she had smiled in disbelief, cocking her head quizzically, as if the world had yet again offered up something unfathomable. Really, she said.

"It was morning, I think," he remembered saying.

"You think?" Shelby had said, tilting her head farther, still smiling. Then she had winked at Janet (when was the last time you saw that? Nathan thought, an adult actually winking), and Nathan had gone into the kitchen for more wine.

"Well, I've been worried about her, Shelby," he said now, pressing the receiver harder into his ear. "I've been calling all day."

"Yes," Shelby said. "She's been here. With me. She's concerned about you, too. Nathan."

This, on top of everything else, was too much. With me. Nathan was in a coffee shop across from the hospital. He looked up and down each of the booths, at the guy scraping the grill, before turning back to the half-enclosure of the telephone with its Plexiglas fenders and metal shelf. And what was this way she had of saying his name like that, all alone—Nathan—as if it might soil the other words it bumped up against.

"Yeah. Well. Look, Shelby, thanks." Ridiculous, to have to get through her to talk to his own—his what? Lover. Partner. To Janet. "Can I just talk to her? I just want to see if she's okay, it'll take one minute, alright? One minute."

Another pause, the chugging languor of the music while he waited. He could see Janet on the tapestry-covered couch, some awful mug of tea in her hand. It was his own fault she was over there. They just needed to talk.

"Nathan," Shelby came back to say. "Call in forty-five minutes."

He had nearly laughed. Not an hour. Not half an hour. Forty-five minutes, in Shelby's precise, self-important lisp. Too fucking much. From now? he wanted to say. Shall we synchronize watches?

So he had run up the four flights to talk to Sol, who was too tired, though he didn't look it, who acted like Nathan couldn't leave soon enough, so he had done just that, gone back to the coffee shop, which sold Miller in bottles, and he'd had two or three, waiting the allotted time. He called back in forty minutes, exactly, daring Shelby to mention it. He asked if it was alright to speak with Janet now. Shelby put her on.

Nathan was smiling, warmed by the beers. The phone was at the far end of the narrow restaurant. He could see the hospital across the street, a loading dock where men in blue uniforms piled boxes onto dollies. In the street, taxis, pedestrians, bicycle messengers zooming in and out of sight in bright racing jerseys, yellow and purple and black. He was still smiling. Jesus, he would say. Sweetheart, if I knew you'd end up with Shelby, I never would have left. I swear.

But Janet spoke first, before Nathan had a chance to say a word. She spoke quickly, deliberately, as if she had been thinking what she was going to say also, even rehearsed it. Nathan tried breaking in a time or two, a joke, something to ease the tension, then gave up when she silenced him. "I need to say this, alright? All of it." As he listened he watched the street. He loved cities, the constant vivid tableau, always changing. A taxi pulled up before the coffee shop, and the driver got out and opened the back door. He leaned against the hood, smoking, big guy in a knit shirt and plaid shorts. Nathan signaled the man behind the counter for another beer.

She was moving out. Had moved out, begun anyway, the rest of her stuff would be gone by the weekend. Two years was a long time, it was hard to see it thrown away, but she had thought about this. She had thought about it and talked to people (Shelby, her mother, maybe—not him), and they were concerned for her, the people who cared about her were concerned, they had been for a long time.

"Janet," he said. "I'm one of those people."

"No," she said, and, relieved to hear it, he detected a quaver in her voice. "You listen. I'm talking now."

"I am," he said quietly. "I'm listening."

You know what killed her? She had thought love was enough. Stupid, huh? It used to keep her up nights thinking, did he love her, would he grow to love her, maybe he already did, in his own way. People were different, right? Who was she to say what love was for somebody else. She loved him, Janet loves Nathan, a slurring, sarcastic emphasis on the verb. Congratulations to her. Probably still did, even now—how sick could you get? Well fuck all that, Janet said.

She paused, crying openly. He could hear Shelby in the background, hovering, murmuring support. There had been several times as she spoke when he would have liked to jump in, defend himself, point of order, redirect. All they really needed to do was talk. That's what couples did, talk. But now, when he had the chance to speak, he said nothing. He picked up the beer and drained half of it.

"I thought . . . ," she said. "And do you know how fucking *stupid* it was, thickhead stupid—Shelby, I'm al*right*, goddammit. Go sit down." The cabby leaned back over the hood, blowing smoke rings. From here Nathan couldn't see them, not even the smoke. "I used to think we'd be together a long time, Nathan. Forever, believe it or not.

It's not that you were perfect, I was never that blind, it just seemed we would be, you know? I don't even know why. Together. So we'd work it out, you know? Whatever happened, we'd work it out."

She broke off to blow her nose, crying again. Despite himself he was glad. If that was the only way to get a word in, get her to listen, he was glad. With effort he turned from the window and forced himself to speak.

"Honey, don't," he said. "Sweetheart. I'm sorry. It's been a bad time. Really bad. You don't know what's been going on out here."

She didn't say anything.

"Look, everything you said was right. Two years, that is a long time. And I do love you, I don't know how well, that's what Pender-gast is helping me with, right? You wanted that, right? And I'm do-ing it, every week." He paused, but not long enough to let her speak now. His turn. Someone had scratched something into the Plexiglas of the mini-wall beside him. He couldn't read it from this side. "I'm sorry," he went on, quickly. It seemed important, vital, to hurry. "You know that, don't you? Don't you, Janet? I just want us to think about what we're doing." He heard her thick breathing, clotted with tears. He reached for the beer, surprised to see it empty. "Listen, J, listen to me. I need you. It's crazy out here, you won't believe what's going on. Sol's in the hospital with sepsis, there's this girl, with a kid, she was living with him, nobody knows how long, and the cops, they just handed him over, the cops are fucking ridiculous. She walked in, this friend of his, and signed some papers and you won't believe . . ."

"I was in the hospital, too," Janet said.

He'd been on a roll, the start of one, he could feel the rhythm of his words building their own momentum. He was moving his free hand, emphasizing, accompanying. Words were good, one thing he'd learned from Daniel. Words could put some space between you and the world, give you room to breathe. He was doing that. The more he talked, the more she listened, the farther they were from things they had said and never meant to, things they had done. If she'd just let him talk to her. He felt his hand drop to his side.

"What?" he said.

"I didn't stay, don't worry. It was the day you left and I was still bleeding. That hasn't happened before. I got scared, so I went after work. I didn't stay, I couldn't, it was just too embarrassing. And it seemed to be stopping by then, on its own."

She wasn't whispering, leaning into the phone. Shelby was listening, must have heard all the details by now. That was somehow the worst thing about it. Janet had stopped, giving him a chance, he supposed, to say something.

"Are you alright?"

"Yes," she said. "I'm fine." Suddenly no one was speaking. Janet breathed out, a long slow expiration that seemed to draw off some of the tension between them. A minute ago Nathan would have seen this as his chance. Now it felt different.

"I didn't," he said. "You don't think I meant to . . ."

"No, I don't," she said, gathering herself. "Look, Nathan, you'd better call Dr. Ammons' office. They're freaked. That secretary, what's her name, she keeps calling, very angry, giving ultimatums. Don't give them to me, I told her. I finally unhooked the phone."

"Janet," he said.

"I took the kitchen stuff, it was mostly mine anyway, I left you most of the books. I tried to sort the CDs. I may have gotten some wrong, I'm sorry, it was late and I was tired. I don't really care, Nathan, you can have them. Anything you want, just call Shelby."

"Shelby? Will you be over there?"

The cab was still outside the coffee shop, the driver reading a paper now. How long had he been waiting? At one of the front tables a woman in a leopard-print jacket and black hat stood, put on her sunglasses. She embraced first one then the other woman she had been eating with, took her shopping bags and walked out the door. The cabby folded his paper and met her at the open rear door of the cab. When she got in he took a cloth from his pocket and wiped his neck, and before he drove off Nathan saw him turn back to the lady and smile.

"She'll know where I am," Janet was saying.

"But Janet. Please."

"Shelby will know. I don't want to see you, and I don't want you to call."

The other ladies, similarly dressed, were finishing their coffee, getting ready to leave. There were no cabs waiting out front. "Janet, you just can't—"

"I am, Nathan. I already did. I told you to listen to me."

"Look," he said. He was finally getting angry. The ladies stood, gathered their bags. "Just listen to me. This is ridiculous, okay? Let's not be fucking stupid, alright, Janet? Both of us. Let's watch what's happening here. Just slow down, okay? Can we do that?" The ladies, the guy at the grill, were looking at him. He realized he'd raised his voice. He turned his back on them. "Janet, I'm sorry. God knows, I'm sorry as I can be. But take a minute, okay? Can we at least do that?"

A voice from behind him, indignant, one of the ladies, no doubt. The bell over the front door jingled as it opened and closed. Nathan looked at the thick scratch marks again, letters, a word. *C*, *h*, *o*. Or *a*. He couldn't make it out. Janet was saying something.

"You take a minute," she said. "And don't you yell at me. You don't get to do that anymore, alright?" Something on the other end of the line fell heavily to the floor. He heard it roll. "Shit," Janet said, and "I've got it." He heard the phone being dropped a moment, then picked up again. "Nathan," she said. "You hurt me, you sonofabitch. You hurt me and I tried to tell you and it didn't matter and it wasn't the first time. And when *I* was in pain and I needed *you*, where the fuck were you? Fucking gone, Nathan. You take a minute."

He opened his mouth to say something. The ladies had left, the cook was chopping meat on the grill. Other tables were occupied but people were just eating, talking. No one was looking at him. He felt sick, with the beer, maybe, his stomach roiling and his pulse hot in his head and fingers. The restaurant swooned a moment, shifted, but not less clear, clearer, luridly distinct, everything too defined in color and size and shape. The whole room came at him. He closed his eyes.

"I'm done," he heard from the phone. "Nathan, are you listening to me?"

It was better outside. It was city air, it carried exhaust and soot and noise, the exhalations of a million mouths and noses and throats, but even on a stale warm breeze it came up the avenue and cooled his face, and he leaned against the glass wall of the coffee shop to breathe it in. He was alright. He had had a bad minute or so, but he was alright. He checked his wallet, his pants pocket for money. He had said goodbye, he must have, he had paid and he was out here now. He looked up at the blank windows of the hospital. He was alright. After a while he moved away from the wall, staring up and down the avenue until he picked a direction and started to walk.

Now it was hours later, half a day later. Back east it was already morning. In the hospital, Sol was getting his sleep. Nathan reached the street he was looking for, Market, slanting through the office buildings and running the streetcars. Here he would orient himself. He walked over to an empty bus shelter and sat on the bench. Across the street, in the partly lit alcove of a department store, a group of men stood smoking, passing a bottle. Absurdly, Nathan raised a hand. None of them saw.

He pulled Daniel's letter from his jacket. He had taken it from his bag this morning, thinking he would show it to the police, if it helped, thinking, if it was no help, he'd get rid of it, toss it in the nearest trash bin. Years of letters, every few weeks, long after Nathan had stopped writing back; witty, self-deprecating dispatches from

Daniel's life, stuffed with poetry, history, philosophy, baseball, all affectionately condescending, as if to say, his own life a steaming wreck all around him, Daniel was still the big brother. After his own last letter Nathan hadn't opened Daniel's, even threw one or two out. But he did want to know if Daniel was okay, after all, and he always could make him laugh. Nathan looked at the white envelope, scuffed from being carried in his pocket, at Daniel's urgent, headlong script. Pay attention, the characters themselves seemed to say. Pay attention, you don't want to miss this.

His own last letter, two years ago. He had told Daniel not to be in touch any longer. He had met Janet, was finishing his third year of classes, seemed, against all probability, to be getting his shit together. He didn't have any more money to send. Or patience. Or love. Some pompous, nasty, self-serving crap about needing to get his own life in order, and Daniel had run out of chances. We need to move on, he remembered writing, both of us. As if he had. As if you could. About three months of silence, then a letter about Rilke, Barry Bonds, Proposition 280, as if Nathan had never said a thing, had wired the money when asked, as if they would see each other next week for dinner or a beer, as if everything, as it was meant to be all along, was going just according to Daniel's plan. Insufferable. Exhausting.

Monica. Monique. What was her name, the girl in the bar. She had laughed so freely, looking at him with bright eager eyes, throwing her hair over a shoulder and matching him drink for drink. She worked in a bank, or an office. She had a dog and a roommate, she liked one, hated the other. Even then, hours ago, he could barely bring himself to listen. He had let himself stare at her neck, her tits, and when he moved past her to the bathroom had put a hand on her thigh, halfway up, and she hadn't moved aside. It was too fucking easy.

Maybe afterwards he could sleep, on a sofa, or in a chair by the window. Just being in someone else's apartment often did the trick.

He would have to focus his attention, he really should try to listen. In the bathroom, rocking ever so slightly at the urinal, he saw the evening stretch out before him as if he was already past it, remembering. Another drink, some offhand funny line about how late it was, a shame to bring such a nice evening to an end. A cab to her place, kissing, his hands moving on her. Then bed, close enough in so he could stop seeing her eyes on him, her expression stupid with hope; when she would be, finally, breasts, neckline, rib, leg, everything reduced at last to its essence — sensation and sound, breathing and heat and motion and no thoughts in his head. Then maybe he could sleep.

Another vision, as he zipped himself up. What about taking her out into the alley, back behind the bar, right there, skirt over her hips, hands under her clothes, not having to see anything as he thrust her against the brick, not having to talk or look at her eyes looking at him, not have to remember her name.

Janet.

Eleanor.

Nathan went right past drunk to sick, the small, harshly lit room tilting on its axis. He was somehow urgently aware he couldn't be sick here, making for the door, slamming his shoulder heavily into the wall beside it. Monique at the bar, hair brushed, turned expectantly, about to say something, smile. Nathan pulled out a twenty, another, lay it on the bar, not looking at her face. Sorry. Must have drunk. Have to. Sorry.

Nathan looked around the shelter for a trash bin. Even in New York they had them near bus shelters. None here. He stuffed the letter back in his pocket, stood and searched for the Transamerica building, his designated compass point to find the hotel. He turned in the street twice, then gave up.

No matter. How lost could he be? He walked toward a group of men by the storefront. In the windows, headless mannequins in bathing suits and bikinis. Surfboards, sandy floors, starfish. As he approached the men, first two turned toward him, then another. The fourth, standing behind them, was covered in shadow, though Nathan could see his feet, filthy tennis shoes, no socks. They formed a line, half in the light, half behind it, in the far end of the alcove, and stared at him without moving as he came near. In the corner a dog slept on a cardboard mat. They were homeless, he realized now, had realized before, without thinking about it. Their faces, in the store's slanting light, were obscure. What the hell was he doing? He considered fishing in his pants for some money to offer, then one man, second from the front, took a step forward and Nathan, again, idiotically, put up a hand in some weak, meaningless gesture. He backed away and walked up the avenue.

The doorbell didn't work, at least it didn't feel like it could, not giving at all, no matter how hard he pressed. He had moved from the building, was walking away when the intercom buzzed at him. "Who is it?" an indistinct voice said, and he rushed over and spoke into the dented voice plate. As the door buzzed open he saw movement in the curtains to the right of the entryway.

The door was unlocked and he let himself in. The hallway was entirely dark, though he could see, ahead, a night-light on the wall of the bathroom, and, after his eyes adjusted, another small light under the door of the bedroom off the hall. He moved forward. Even in the darkness he could tell the place had changed, there were no clothes on the hallway floor, the table and couch had been cleared, the bed made up. She sat there, in her robe, her hair wild again around her shoulders, smoking a cigarette in the far reach of the street's dim light. She had an ashtray in her lap. She stubbed out the cigarette and looked at something in the room, then down at her lap. She didn't move or say a word as Nathan stood, reeling in the hall, waiting for her to look up again and see him there.

PART TWO

PROLOGUE, 1995

He had not dreamed of her in years, had barely thought of her (he
barely knew her), yet now he dreamed of her every night, the dope's
varied lulling fog lifting near morning, every morning, on the same
scene.

Corey Perlman. Junior year of high school. Later he realized it
was illness that gave her the pallor, the delicate motion, the hesitant, or just exhausted, smile. He felt—and this was unique—
hesitant approaching her (all it took with Rita Daeger was the wave
of a joint at a party and they were up in the parents' bedroom, she
climbing all over him), as if—and this was too weird—too much
was at stake. He spoke to her meaninglessly a few times, and even
felt bad about it, as though he might easily intrude on the very quiet
that drew him. She was a freshman, sat at the freshman tables at
lunch, laughing at the right times, eager to blend in, dispel any notion of her apartness, her singularity. He could have walked right up
to her and said hi. She would know who he was, hotshot insurgent,
antiwar organizer, sent home weekly for hair too long, or braided,
suspended for showing up barefoot, for sewing a yarmulke embroidered with a peace sign onto the ass of his jeans. She would probably be delighted, flattered, but he never got the nerve.

That day, when she fell under the table, when they carried her
out to the hospital, coughing carefully into a handkerchief already

seeping red, he had been shocked. The world had lain behind an open door, golden, waiting, all he had to do was step through. And this moment stunned him, brought something freewheeling inside him to a full stop. He had never seen anyone so sick before, so suddenly naked and damaged and exposed. He thought, just as suddenly, that he was in love, dismissed this, in the days that followed, as moony teenage posturing.

But now, thirty years later? Why now?

They'd been studying Yeats in senior English, and one day he read a poem and just got up from the classroom and went to find her (this was how unbalanced he was). He couldn't summon the lines now, though he used to know them. He was too high (the point, after all) to remember. Bees. Noon glowing purple. Yes, one line, "peace comes dropping slow." He hadn't found her, maybe she was out sick. He had imagined sitting with her and reading it. He wouldn't ask anything of her, wouldn't touch her. He'd say, I thought maybe you'd like this poem.

His kit lay on the table—syringe, rubber tube, bent spoon. Enough for one last boost, a small one, and he'd need it. Medium sleeping, would be out for hours if he was lucky. Daniel had left fifty-four dollars, enough for two weeks' rent. He'd have to get more if he came back. Every available surface in the tiny studio, except for the corner of the table Daniel had cleared to write his letter, was covered in soda cans, fast-food wrappers, magazines. Daniel listened for the skittering, familiar now, in the trash spilling over the plastic bin. Nothing. Even the mice were asleep. Again he looked out the window, at the sooty brick and fire escapes identical to this building. One night, too high to fuck around like this, Medium had made the leap from their rusted metal cage to the one opposite, barely catching hold, deranged, giggling, poking his head into window frames and waving. Above the neighboring wall, roof capstones grimy and chipped, Ionic capitals incongruously pointing to a time when people lived in these buildings by choice, long gray light took

on tinges of blue and pale yellow, and Daniel knew if he kept looking the day would break. He could smell the bay.

Medium slept under a filthy sleeping bag he must have had
since Cub Scouts. Cowboys lassoing steers, sunset over a fence stile.
His head was covered but his feet showed, his left middle toe poking through a hole in the sock like a curled stubby fuck-you to the
world. Daniel had been amazed that anyone could live this way.
His first night, small rustlings woke him. Investigating under the
sink, pushing aside the trash, he saw hundreds of tiny black turds,
what he thought was a used teabag, actually the denuded body of a
dead mouse, and by its side in a mess of stuffing from Medium's
lone armchair, a nest of blind, nakedly pink babies, their piercing
needley cries hardly audible. In two weeks he hadn't seen Medium
shower down the hall or change clothes. Half-emptied buckets of
KFC, some with wings or gnawed legs protruding, sat on the
counter, piled in the sink. One morning something bigger perched
there, working a piece of meat, long tail draped leisurely down the
sink front. Maybe a dream, maybe a nightmare. All Daniel remembered for certain was reaching for his stash.

Now the room didn't amuse or dismay or even irritate him. It
was where he was, where he would be, unless he did something. In
the old days he thought he knew the future and how wrong he had
been. Now again he knew it, and he wasn't wrong this time. This
time no brakes, nothing to grab hold of. He saw himself spilling
down a chute, over and over and over, landing right where he was,
waiting for the mice to stir, the morning, Medium's soft anxious
whimpers groping toward wakefulness, so they could begin the day's
desultory plan to cop. Here he'd been coming for years, ever since
the first panicky gleeful jolt mainlining in an alley behind the
Warfield, a slamming from the base of his spine so powerful he
thought he would pass out, to his neck, his shoulders, the back of
his skull, finally both hands, which he looked at, one then the
other, in vague, awed amusement, until he looked past them at

nothing at all. This is it, Daniel knew. No manifesto, no boys' adventure book, no thrilling dream, no creed, his or someone else's: this. And with the faraway thrum in his veins and head, with the furtive complacent joy of the purest high he'd ever known, came something he'd never felt before: relief, the lightening of escape.

He'd tried. Abby, Ben, eight months clean, three months twice, six months, a meeting now and then, writing his brother like flinging a lifeline three thousand miles out to sea and never feeling it land. Abby said not this time, said I don't want you, don't want you back, this time is the last. Can't rely, can't wait, can't afford to trust someone who won't be there. Live your fate, an old voice told him: an addict's dream is to be an addict. On his pallet fretful Medium grabbed a handful of cowboy and pulled it close.

End of thinking. It led backwards or led forwards and Daniel had made his choice. He would, at last, choose the present, no past insistently hovering, no future holding out its spurious soft lies. Carpe diem. Always liked that. Horace. Ovid? Carpe diem, quam minimum credula postero. Grab hold, fuckers! How easy it had seemed—today, tomorrow, forever! More bullshit. Another lie that wouldn't hold. Lesko dead. Rudd teaching high school, Jerry Rubin, entrepreneur, wiped out by a minivan in Los Angeles. Someone told him when Ted Gold exploded himself all they found was a hand severed at the wrist, blown through a window—even that probably a lie. The rest, like him, disappearing, each into his own cowardly sinkhole. What had Daniel, Aquarian golden boy, worldshaker, accomplished? Absolutely nothing.

Carpe what? For now, not even the whole day. One moment, enough. A moment.

Clawing fingers now, sweat, herald of the shakes, soon flesh would try peeling itself from his bones: you can't do this, you're not the man for the job, we know you—fixing with sick cold fear on the works on the table, bringing from his pocket the plastic lighter, the baggie, brown, raisin-sized nub all he had left. No. Not yet, and then someone said it. Not yet. Not time. Clouds heating in the still, blind sun, tumbling over the rooftop, piling into each other.

Ramon Ortiz, the kid's name. Shorter than most, awake, some- times a trace of the boy in his forgetful wide-open attention. Couldn't quite pull off the rock-hard glare, the casual sneer, the shambling strut they all pathetically thought made them look like thugs but made them — ten-, eleven-year-olds in too-big clothes and mashed caps and do-rags — look even more like children, playing a game they'd always lose. Come to Daniel one day, nervous, not wanting to say why, checking the empty door in case someone should see him talking to the enemy. Rubbing palms on his floppy jeans, tracing something over and over on Daniel's desk. A kid. Five minutes and it was out, the rigid stare dissolved, the voice whispery, threatened by tears. The Mission boys, older ones, they'd been com- ing around. Hey, quinto, I like your mommy's tetas. You got a cell phone yet, pendejo? What's your shoe size? Carry this, take it to this cleaners, this bodega. Don't fuck up, we're watching. The words nonstop from Ramon's side-turned, smeared face, fingers kneading the lace of his new Raiders hoody. One kid said no, he said quietly, got two fingers broke.

Daniel began the distracted, careful inspection of his body, which was the last signal he needed to fix, touching his upper lip, pressing gingerly at the side of his neck, an odd burrowing pain in the bone behind an ear. The pressure in his back was massing and he twisted away from it, though it made no difference at all. There was another kind of waiting he remembered. A cup of instant and a book, the small lamp by the window while at the end of the room Abby slept without stirring, anticipating sounds from across the hall, the boy's private, breathy exclamations, the quiet lecturing of his toys, then, almost too late, the thud of his feet on the wooden floor, the sprint to the bathroom, and Daniel would try to find the Cheer- ios or pancake batter without turning on the light and waking her any sooner than he had to. Outside, white streaks in the streaming fog, a blue tinge in the shredding sky. He would be awake now, Ben, playing in his room. Daniel stuffed the baggie and lighter back in his pants, sat at the table, immediately stood and returned to the window.

Recently this idea, proposition alluring and resonant and useless, one more anchor thrown with no line attached: life made not of design—what they'd been taught—not of history and narrative, but simply, for the lucky, a succession of pleasing, culminated moments, a string of happy events that took on a story's consoling shape. "From the beginning I knew . . . Everything led right here." For the others, the unlucky, one moment only—a night, a year, a terrible mistaken instant, never ending, its term never elapsed—and they, trapped inside like insects in amber. This, where you brought your life, is where it stays. For Sol, a lifetime looking back in grim resolute silence. Freda, even more unreadable, halted by the past, stricken dumb. Maybe by averted gazes and devout silence they felt they could deny the past, hold it at bay, sequestered. Not true. Now Daniel understood. For Sol and Freda there was no past, no present, one eternal Now erasing all that came before, making all that came after a lie. At last, maybe Daniel understood.

Quam minimum credula postero. Can't lose what you never had.

Was this what he saw in Corey Perlman? God, a lovely girl. Green eyes come alive when she laughed, then drew back, the body's soft admonition, summons to the real—the hum in her blood, illness on its efficient march. Her time.

Lesko in the dirt behind the bandshell. Daniel's.

He sees his brother, Freda had told Daniel once, trying to explain. A boy crying, room littered with thrown books, lamp overturned, window broken. Do you see the way he looks at me? he had asked. The old man never come inside after him, back to the factory on a Sunday, nearly evening. Do you see it? Freda had tried wiping the blood where the glass had cut but he'd thrown her off, her hand on his now, unmoving. Quietly, as if she'd said this many times, she told him, his brother, Daniel. When he looks at you he sees his brother. From then. Daniel squirmed under this idea, some primal call to resist what he, never hearing it, had long understood—How do you know that? There's no pictures, Freda, how do you know? And when she said nothing, tried again to touch his face, he allowed it but turned away, coming loose from himself, looking at a place on the wall as if a dark tunnel had opened. Another history, not his, not one he'd ever know, sifted its weight over him like ash.

Before the shaking made it impossible, Daniel tapped the tarry bit into the spoon, on the third try got the lighter to catch, praying his friend Medium wouldn't sit up and want some. Skin-pop, missed the fucking vein, too late to argue now, didn't feel the needle slide . . .

Fragments. Shards refracting no more than their miserable incompleteness.

Abby, pulling off her top and throwing it behind her, smiling her secret smile. Reading by two lamps in the quiet room, Ben asleep, Daniel in the green chair by the window, Abby on the couch, working her toes under his thigh. Coltrane first, the Dead, Evans, Kimock, a few times music itself offering to open up and take him in. Scotland dawn a hundred years ago, night just a deeper blue radiance, and Daniel standing, unable to breathe, as a massive gray-orange sun seethed behind a string of misty islands and there simply were no words for what he felt, a peeling back of layers, a nakedness not fearsome, a drawing into something else, like the first time on acid or smack, that same sublime evaporating, immanence of calm and surety he'd pursued, receding always farther, ever since.

The beach, Ben's face stretched in absolute wonder as a red kite snaps higher, a hundred feet, two hundred, in the rocketing winds, the whistling twine Daniel's let him hold changing notes, the boy's almost hysteric laughter. Younger Ben toddling backwards to flop in Daniel's lap, not even turning to see was anyone there to catch him, knowing Daniel was. These are the moments, look at them all—

Daniel heaving breath slowly, trying to fill his chest—Nathan, a baby in his crib, staring. Why weren't they enough?

Brooklyn summer, lifetimes ago, evening. Sol and Freda on the front porch, iced tea in tall glasses with yellow sun designs, Sunday paper spread around. They've run from somewhere, Daniel and Nathan, running just to run, for the pleasure of breathing loud, of muscles pumping, blood sound in the ears. Up the brick steps gasping happily, quick sip from Freda's glass, bitter but wonderfully cold and wet, some typical Freda remark, Rest now, Don't overdo it. I could run ten miles, Ma. I'm not even tired. Look at me, Dad, do I even look tired? Sol, glasses pushed to his forehead, paper slowly coming down.

And there, if blood could freeze it would: Sol's mouth open, the pink inside. Drops of sweat over wide eyes, yellowed teeth showing feral, lips fighting to hold still. Expression unmistakable—shock, detestation, a terrible fear. His wind suddenly gone, all Daniel can do is retreat, throw the glass hard on the porch floor, glad among everything else to feel the small piercing shard in his cheek.

It had come as a canny vengeance, the grimmest of jokes. That day at the factory his father said, I'm telling you, I wish they'd left me there. Burned me up, too. So Daniel told Abby, Do it. If I die, just do it and send the fucker my ashes. She thought he was fooling, of course, thought he was high. He wasn't. A gesture, all he had left to give. Do you see the way he looks at me? Offering to his father: Expiation. Allegiance. Futility.

He forces himself clumsily to his feet, Medium stirring, hairy toe flipping off the world, Daniel stumbling to tug the fallen sleeping bag over him. He'll need words. Hey, you guys, I know some of you from school. Mr. Mirsky, remember? How's it going? Listen, look what one of them brought to school, these are little kids, man, can we talk?

Downstairs, outside, clouds boiled off, morning. A dirty yellow mist coming apart, then fixed blast of the sun. In his pocket, the gun he'd taken from Ramon Ortiz, who'd paid forty dollars for it on Sixteenth, who'd said, Nobody's breaking my fingers, Mr. Mirsky. Come-apart newspapers thrash up the sidewalk, people in doorways look emptily at the street. If he turns his head he could see a span of the bridge, but he doesn't turn his head. Abby. Ben.

Enough now. Movement. The mind seals. The body takes over. Attend. First Howard, then Folsom, west till the highway overpass. Don't run. Don't think. Walk.

That poem. Something about an island. The island of . . . I will arise and go now, something about a cabin, a beehive, and noon glowing purple. The sound of water in a lake. Peace dropping slow.

5

There were thirty-five dogs. There used to be thirty-six but Ben didn't like thinking about it. Two or three times a day he'd look around, between the wall and his bed, under the shelves, behind the cushions of the couch in his mother's room. He did this even though he'd done it a million times, him, his mother and him together, since he'd lost the dog last week. Sometimes he'd still imagine, though, that the dog was stuck someplace or hurt, or just patiently waiting for Ben to find him and bring him back. So he kept looking. He knew it was silly, just as he knew counting them over and over would not change the number (thirty-five every time) and that he was happier not thinking about it. He counted the dogs first thing in the morning and last thing before getting into bed at night.

He was cold. He had on his pajamas, the ones with the balls and bats and the orange SF in circles. He'd gotten them for Christmas, and already they were too small. His mom said he grew like a weed. Ben liked that, he didn't know why. His feet stuck out and his stomach wouldn't stay covered unless he pulled the shirt down all the time. But he liked them. They were his favorites, and his mom had said she'd buy him a bigger size but she hadn't yet. He kept thinking to remind her, but not the way things were the last few days.

He'd gone out into the hall, crossed to her room, thought he might get into bed with her. It was amazing how much heat grown-ups had in their bodies. In his bed, under the covers, he was usually pretty warm. But there was always a spot, down in a corner somewhere, or if he rolled over in the middle of the night, where it was cold, and it was a surprise every time, and he had to lie there in that place between asleep and awake and decide if it was too cold, did he need to wake up and do something, or was it just a little cold, maybe it was warming up already and he could keep sleeping.

His mother's bed was always warm. Sometimes she and Danny slept late, sometimes they even forgot to take him to school, and when he crawled up between them on the bed and then down in the space under the covers, he felt like an animal in a den, like the foxes he'd seen on a TV show, or the baby rats in the store, all toasty warm in a heap. Last week his mom, though she was usually saying how he had to be a big kid and do for himself and not be asking for little-kid things all the time, had let him sleep in her bed every night, had held him, which wasn't as comfortable as lying next to her—he liked to move around—but he tolerated it, since he knew some of the time she was crying.

From the hall he had seen the man on the couch. The way he was lying you could tell he was asleep, so Ben had walked in and looked at him. Danny's brother. He looked like him, sort of—younger, his hair was lighter and he wasn't so skinny. Ben tried to remember his name but couldn't. He had bought him a cookie.

Somehow getting into bed with his mom when there was a man lying on the couch did seem like a little-kid thing to do, so he took his coat from the peg in the hall—he had to be quiet moving the stool—and went back into his room. The coat helped, though his feet still stuck out. He should put on some socks, he told himself.

The dogs were in a circle on the floor before him. Sometimes he talked to them as a unit, when they were an army and he was the general, or when they were about to head off on an expedition and he was the commander, like now. He scolded the Dalmatian, who never paid attention, and his friend, the wooly white one with his tongue hanging out, who did whatever the Dalmatian did. This will be a hard mission, he lectured the dogs, looking at the Dalmatian. Not all will survive intact.

Often he separated them into groups to compete against each other in games he devised, and sometimes, when he was bored, he threw them around the room and then went to find them. He felt guilty doing this, and a little excited when their small rubber bodies hit the wall, and he always gathered them back with delight and apologies, especially since what happened with number thirty-six.

He wished it was the one he held now that was lost. He turned it over and tried to read the name. When his mother and Danny had bought the dogs, each had a string around its neck with a gold tag which said its name and what country it was from. Ben liked to pull on the strings, and a few broke off, so he and Danny spent one morning writing all the names on the bottoms with a black pen. Ben had lots of letters, for instance A, B, E, D, M, V and C and R and Y and some others. He knew words, too, like CAT or STOP, or his name. This one had a Y and an R, and T began a second word, but he'd taken a few dogs in the bath with him one night, though his mother had said not to, and now some of them made a sound when you shook them and some of the letters were hard to see.

He didn't hate any of the dogs, but he did wish this one was number thirty-six. It was the only dog with a ribbon in its hair, and it had a long yellow beard, like a lion but tiny, and held a paw up in the air like it wanted to shake, which you had to admit was pretty cute, but you couldn't like all of them the same, it wasn't even possible, and maybe this one would have been okay, a top one like the retriever and the husky, if it didn't have that stupid ribbon, but it did, and Ben threw it behind his head without looking and tried not to hear where it landed.

When they were trying to find number thirty-six, his mom had asked him what it looked like. He started to tell her, then realized he couldn't remember. He went back into his room, where the dogs were on his bed and he lined them up in four rows (one only had eight in it) and looked at the dogs and the empty space in the last line expecting the missing dog to appear in his head. When it didn't was when he started to cry and his mom came in and sat with him and kept saying, I know, honey, I know, which was ridiculous because she didn't even like his dogs all that much, and then she was crying too and he had to sit and wait until they could start looking again.

Later, when they couldn't find it anywhere, and he was in the bath with his whale and his sharks and his diver, she was washing his hair and she said, Honey, why did you throw your dogs around like that? Don't you love them? And he'd said, Yes, and, I don't know. Which was the truth but also felt like a lie, which he didn't understand.

He just did it, that's all.

He thought of the old man in the funny hat at his mom's restaurant last night. When his mother told him he would be meeting Danny's father he was interested, and he wanted to take a good look and ask some questions, but every time he tried the old man was staring at him, which made him uncomfortable, so he tried humming and concentrating on his drawing. He didn't look anything like Danny, anyway. He wasn't skinny like Danny and he had no hair except around his ears, and he was big and had shiny old-man skin and stupid glasses and he kept looking at Ben and his mom like they'd done something to him, which was impossible since they hadn't ever seen him before, at least Ben hadn't. And if he didn't like them that was okay with Ben anyway, who had talked about this kind of thing with Danny when some kids were mean at school. Not everyone is going to be nice, Danny said. Remember, you get to choose who you like, too, and Ben did remember.

He started throwing more dogs over his shoulder and this was kind of fun, but one knocked something off the table near his bed and he heard a voice outside his door, not his mom's. Was this a school day? He never knew until his mom came to get him, sometimes all rushed and upset, like he hadn't been awake a long time already, waiting for her. He threw another dog, aiming for the bed, and tried to listen and not listen at the same time, the way he used

to with his mom and Danny, to hear the way the words sounded—
happy, angry, sad—but not the words themselves, which sometimes
just made him scared. His mother said something now, and then
the bathroom door closed and he could hear the kettle being filled.
He could almost smell his mother's first cigarette.

His feet were still cold, but instead of finding socks he pulled his
blanket from the bed and over himself and the remaining dogs. He
lay down and arranged them in front of his face. This was the dangerous part of the mission, he told them (they were spying on the
enemy), and he lined the dogs up in size order, listening and not
listening. The sounds that came in were normal, the toilet, the sink,
coffee cups and spoons. The Dalmatian was joking around again,
he and the big wooly one moving to the edge of the blanket to have
a peek. Ben knocked them both over with a finger and they got
back in line.

Now he was thinking about it again. Stop it, he told himself. But
that didn't work and he was angry, and he thought he might give
himself a pinch, the skin behind his hand, hard, or the place under
his ear. But he was angry, also, at the part of him that was angry.
There was number thirty-six, and there was Danny, and what would
happen to him and his mom now, and would she ever get through
one day without crying? There was even his dad, who he usually
managed not to think about pretty well, but that was harder now,
too. Okay? he said to the stupid dog with the black tongue and orange fur. Okay? Okay, the dog said, okay, I'm sorry, and Ben pulled
him over and lay down listening to the sounds from the other room,
the shower running now, keeping an eye on the Dalmatian and his
friend to see what they were up to.

∾ ∾ ∾

The water came out of the showerhead with a pounding noise that
both soothed and amplified the hammering in his skull. Nathan let
it hit his back and shoulders, then the top of his head, then he

turned and let the water, hot as he could stand it, run off his face. When he opened his eyes—he didn't want to use all the hot water—the only soap he could find was in a Winnie-the-Pooh bottle. He twisted the head and poured pink soap into his hands, rubbed it over his body and into his hair. The shower was clean but badly worn, the baseplate for the pipe pulled away from the wall and a small conical mound of plaster directly below it on the tub. The bath itself was scrubbed, a series of hairline cracks converging in a yellow stain toward the drain. Cold water dripped from the lower faucet. On the wall a mesh bag hanging from a hook, fish and turtles and a diver in scuba gear. Chubby foam letters. Empty shampoo and conditioner bottles, the ones you got in hotels, a blue disposable razor. He worked the soap into his hair, closing his eyes again and feeling the water. When he opened them, he saw something above the rim of the tile enclosure, just over his head. He reached up and took it, knowing what it was. He turned the hot water down until the shower was cold enough to numb him where it struck, and forced his head under.

∽ ∽ ∽

Now that he was in the shower, Abby felt she could get out of bed, move around the room. The order of the place, its bare tidiness, contributed to her disorientation. It had been the other way so long that each clean surface, each dish in the drainer and knife in the block and offensively cheery potholder over the stove—a blue checked pattern with yellow suns and red tractors she'd let Ben choose in a weary moment at the Goodwill—seemed a silent call to action, a demand that someone get moving and be useful. She thought she could manage coffee.

There were some things she missed from being on the stuff. Not enough to go back (she swore), never enough to forget what it cost them, but some things she missed. The way it brought your needs to a precise, limited focus, when it didn't obliterate them altogether—

Ben, food, sleep. Sometimes just Ben. That was all she could manage and she knew it, and there was comfort, on the days she did
manage, in doing all she had expected of herself. Daniel somewhere on the perimeter, fending for himself.

Another was the way you could go hours, whole days it seemed
sometimes, without a real thought. Not that your brain was still, just
passive, languorous, all day on the luxurious margin of sleep (until
the panic returned). You were on permanent receive mode—if you
had to pee or get dinner or remember to pick the boy up at school,
the message would arrive and you'd say, Yes, coming. But thoughts
of your own, generated by memory or a need to understand or plan
for tomorrow—gone, their absence a furry maze of blank hours to
wander in. Full of being empty. That she would always miss.

She got the jar of coffee from the cupboard, two mugs. What
was she supposed to do with him? Yes, they were grieving, and yes,
they had rights, and yes, even, there were some things she could tell
them, things they could take back with them to New York. About
Daniel. Danny. Son. Brother. Lover, she'd thought, friend, she'd
also thought, companion. Selfish lousy fuckup. Traitor.

She spooned the glassy brown powder into two mugs. The way
the boy said it, the slightest soft emphasis on the first syllable,
Dahnny, it sounded like Daddy. Daniel heard it, she knew he did,
the way he'd scoop the boy into his lap to tickle him, or put a quiet
hand on his head. She heard it, too, saw it in the boy's eyes, when
she could stand to look. Not often. Even in the best of times she
knew better than to trust.

She filled the kettle just partway, not wanting to scald him in
there. Went across to check on Ben, on the floor with his blanket
and dogs, one in his chubby hand. Thick, regular breathing. Warm
enough? She thought to check but she might wake him—God
knew how long he'd been up already—and he was probably okay,
he had the blanket. Dogs scattered around the room. What he'd put
her through with number thirty-six.

So was she supposed to make breakfast, play hostess? Croissants, maybe. Quiche. Not fucking likely. She lit a cigarette and walked to the far side of the bed, dropped her kimono, pulled on a pair of jeans, a sweatshirt. Went to the dresser in the corner and got underwear, socks, not looking, really, T-shirt, chamois shirt from the closet, laid them on the couch. What else? Watched the kettle, a spot of water sizzling on the reddening electric coil. Waited.

When he came out, rubbing his hair with a towel, in just his pants, she felt it again. She stood and looked away as if he was naked.

"Clean clothes," she said. "If you want them." She gestured at the couch.

He saw them, the socks and shorts on the folded shirt. He continued rubbing his hair. "Okay," he said after a few seconds, "thanks."

When he came out of the bathroom again he wore the T-shirt and chamois—he'd left the underwear and socks on the couch—and his hair was combed. He smiled, toweling the back of his neck. Abby was at the stove. "What about a big breakfast? You and Ben. Omelette? Pancakes? He likes pancakes, doesn't he?" Still rubbing his neck. "Thought I'd take you out, if that's okay."

In Daniel's gray shirt, a little big around the shoulders, he was too hard to look at. Fool—what did she expect? Hair lighter, skin, too. Younger, not just in age but in wear, in better shape, that was part of it, but without the faded, scuffed look Daniel had around the eyes and cheeks, the little cracks and seams in the skin. All those years on the shit. Trying not to, she remembered Daniel just a few years ago, how he could make her stop whatever she was doing when he walked into a room.

He stood there, the brother, smiling, nervous, unsteady—what was she supposed to do? What did he want from her? She turned back to the stove, half expected him to clap his hands, loud, the way Daniel did when he had a plan for them—the Exploratorium (he'd

loved to hear Ben mangle the word), kite-flying on Baker Beach—
and she closed her eyes against the sound. "Ben's asleep."

"Oh," he said, voice dropping. "Sorry."

"I only have . . . ," she started to say, and held up the jar of
Folgers.

"I could," he said, pointing both index fingers—another familiar
gesture—at the door. "I could get. Unless you don't want." His
hands fell to his sides. "I could go get some coffee."

Why not. She told him where the coffee shop was on Post. He
smiled again, shaking his head, a cryptic half-apologetic grin that
she knew could grow to annoy her very quickly. He walked past her
to the couch, got his wallet from the floor, and put on his shoes.
Then he was gone.

She was still holding the plastic jar. The kettle began to shriek
and she moved it, turned off the stove. She stood there, leaning over
the concentric rings, watching them cool from flaming orange to
red flaked with gray. Something inside her rose quickly and she had
the urge to press her hands, hard as she could, on the still-bright
coil. She didn't. She emptied the kettle in the sink, and went back
to the bed and sat, just where she'd been the night before.

She gave in now, let it come.

It had begun when he'd buzzed from downstairs. She'd been
asleep and sleepily asked who it was and sleepily hit the button.
She'd unlocked the door and sat on the bed, and when he stumbled
up the hall she'd looked at him as he stood there while his eyes got
used to the dark. She could smell the liquor from across the room.

Whatever it was, she had thought, furious now, she was ready.
Middle of the night. First his angry, unfriendly father, couldn't even
spare a smile for the boy, now this reeking stranger weaving in her
doorway. Fine. Whatever he was bringing, fine. She was worn out,
with worrying and coping and figuring out how to make it from one
day—fuck that, one hour—to the next. So whatever this brother,
who'd come all the way across the country to claim it, whatever he
figured he was here for, she was ready. Bring it, you asshole.

Fuck or fight, Daniel used to joke, holding her arms down in bed and smiling over her. Both, she'd say, and lean up to kiss him.

But he did nothing, just swayed, fumbling for something in his jacket, breathing clotted and wet. And when he didn't move after a few moments she thought he might be sick, right there in the hall. Instead he tripped forward, somehow found the couch, pulled off his jacket and lay down. Just what she needed, she thought, another stoned-out cripple. She found a blanket and covered him, got back into bed, listening for Ben, if the man on the couch was breathing, half hoping he wasn't.

But when she lay down herself, forced her eyes closed, the anger emptied away and she was left with the feeling, the one she'd had in a confused moment when she heard the voice on the intercom, a terrible sweet instant when he came into the room. Just an outline in the doorway, before she could see clearly, before she smelled him and heard whatever it was he mumbled before he fell onto the couch. Danny, she had thought, just one sweet, lying instant. You've come back to me.

∾ ∾ ∾

He carried the bag in one hand and the tray with the drinks in the other and he tried to balance them on the rusted metal railing to reach the buzzer, but it didn't work, so he put both the tray and bag on the cement step, splashing coffee onto his shoe. The heavy door opened, the manager—Mr. Li, had she said?—shuffling backward in his slippers to make room. He had on the same pale striped shirt as yesterday, the same lumpy buttoned sweater. Low across the belly a gray smudge in the worn golden weave, like the ones on Sol's shirts at home, the ones he insisted on wearing until Freda threw them all out together, replacing them, despite Sol's annoyed insistence they were perfectly fine. Nathan gathered the tray and bag from the stoop.

"Thank you," he said. "I was just about to ring." But the old man had turned and moved toward his apartment without a word. Nathan caught the door with a foot and walked in. When he was at the bottom of the stairs he looked back and there was Mr. Li standing outside his door, a large white napkin in his hand.

"You father," he said. "Sick?"

"No," Nathan said. "He's okay now. Better."

But as if this were the bad news he had expected to hear, Mr. Li waved the napkin, shook his head, and went inside.

She had put away the blanket and the clothing he hadn't used, brushed and tied back her hair. Plates and silverware on the table. Nathan busied himself emptying the bag, taking the paper cups from the tray.

"I didn't know what you liked," he said, laying out biscotti, three muffins—corn, cranberry, and peach—a sesame bagel, a chocolate croissant for the boy. "They only had the one bagel," he explained, though she was looking at him, not the food. She sat down across from him and lit a cigarette, and he draped his jacket over a chair and sat as well. She inhaled and moved the cigarette to the side of her face. He wanted one, and at the same time, the sick residue of tar in his mouth made his head reel.

"You want one?" Abby said, pushing over the pack.

"No," Nathan said. "Thanks, I just quit again."

She looked as if she might say something, but only averted her head to blow smoke away from him. He needed to get something in his stomach, something to do with his hands.

"Bagel?" he said. He turned the plate. "Muffin? What do they call these—biscotti?"

She took a corn muffin and broke off a piece. He took the cranberry and did the same. He moved one of the coffees toward her.

"Is he still asleep?" Nathan said.

She nodded. Smoked. She looked right at him, some small expression—patience, resignation, indifference—on her face. He, meanwhile, could barely look at her.

He ate another piece. The muffin was terrible, crusted with sugar, the cranberries like dried maraschinos. He wiped his hands on a napkin. "So listen," he said. "I feel like I should explain. About last night."

She took the plastic lid off the coffee and blew on it.

"I'd had a couple of drinks."

She looked at him again.

"Right. I know. That's not the part I have to explain." He smiled, held it a moment, hoping she'd respond. She blew on the coffee again and took a sip. He thought of the props he had when he saw patients: stethoscope, prescription pad, examining light, pen. He envied her the cigarette. "It was late. I was kind of a mess. I couldn't . . . I got lost. Ended up downstairs."

A lie. He hadn't intended to lie, but she wasn't helping any just sitting there, and it was easier to say than trying to approach telling her what he'd been feeling last night.

"Anyway," he went on. "I'm sorry." A wave of nausea rolled through him. Sorry. How many times, already, had he said that to her? To Janet, Sol, Rivera. Should have it tattooed on his forehead. He finished the muffin in a big bite and took the bagel, since she didn't seem interested. He tore off a piece. "I appreciate your letting me stay here. And I thought maybe we could talk. Alone."

"How's your father?" The first words she'd said. It helped, a little. She stood, went to the refrigerator, came back with a tub of butter substitute.

Nathan drank some coffee, too quickly, scalding his tongue. "Okay, now. He hurt his shoulder, I've got no idea how. He's not the most forthcoming of people, you might have noticed." Another try, he gave her a minute to smile. She didn't. "He's diabetic, also news to me. That made it worse."

"He'll be alright?"

"Yeah. He's got to take care of the wound. I mean, we have to. I have to help him. And be careful about his meds. He'll be okay."

She ate another piece of muffin, pressed a few crumbs from the wooden tabletop together with her fingers. "That's good," she said.

"Yeah. That's good."

They drank the coffee, he ate the bagel, first spreading it with some of the alarmingly yellow not-butter. The room was entirely different from yesterday; it must have taken hours to clean. He looked around, at the overfilled shelves, the Soviet flag, the group of snapshots, some familiar even from a distance, on the wall. Tried to imagine his brother sitting here, day after day, at this table, draped over the easy chair, reading, nodding off on the couch. Home.

He finished the coffee, crumpled the paper from the muffin and dropped it inside. He waited until she'd lit another cigarette.

"I wanted to tell you. I started to say this yesterday." She was looking at him now, whatever it was in her face—tension or hostility or, accept it, simple annoyance—finally gone. Still, no easier to look at her. She was pretty—he'd seen that right off—with her hair pulled back and her sweatshirt just a little too large (Daniel's?), falling over her wrists. In her rounded face, something about the eyes—one a bit higher? lighter?—gave her expression an animation even when she was still, her mouth open, not stupidly, but as if she were about to respond, criticize or approve. When she wasn't smoking or drinking she laid her hands out on the table, the fingers curled toward the palms. No nail polish. He saw, for an instant, her sitting in bed when he'd walked in last night, shoulders and neck in the dim light, felt again the blind demand that had driven him here—not lost for a moment—and turned from the sight. Talk. Now.

"I feel bad. I mean, look, I feel ridiculous that I didn't know who you were. And that might have made it seem I was, I don't know, jumping to conclusions. To be honest, I probably was. I'm sorry if it seemed that way." He watched her for a sign of acknowledgment. There was none, he had to go on.

"We used to be close, did you know? Me and Daniel. Closer

than most brothers. Tight." She was looking at him at last with some interest. He really could use one of those cigarettes.

"He was my hero." Nathan laughed quickly—where had that come from? "Sounds stupid, doesn't it? The oldest cliché. But he was. My whole childhood, my whole growing up, I looked up to Daniel. Envied him, you know?" Some change in her expression, a nod? "Not what he had. Well, yeah. Everything he had. But not only that. I envied *him. Being* him." Her hands again, bringing the cigarette to and from her mouth, small, knuckles raw and nails bitten, the fingers of her left hand moving to some slow rhythm, as if she were humming to herself silently as he talked. He decided to look only at her hands, his own beginning to burn, an ache in the soft spot between his thumb and forefinger. "We fought, too. Drifted apart. You probably know that." He glanced at her face, then away. "Those last years. I don't know if what I did was right." He raised the aching hand, palm open, let it drop. "How right could it have been, you know?" He looked around the room again. "I mean, considering."

He stopped.

Considering what? He didn't know. Considering Daniel had a life out here that somehow Nathan never managed to learn about? Considering he was gone—dead, not just gone—and what did right or wrong matter now, too late to do anything about it? Considering Nathan himself, and Sol, who were they to judge anybody, after all? He didn't know. If she said to him, What do you mean by that, he'd try, maybe he could figure it out. But she was quiet, smoking and moving crumbs around the table.

He got up, carried his plate to the sink, walked over to one of the bookcases. Marx, Reich, Marcuse, Castaneda—he'd kept all the old books—mixed with Carver, Amy Tan. Babar and Curious George. He lifted a corner of the Soviet flag and brought it to his nose. Patchouli and dope, just as it had always been. He remembered dropping in to see Daniel at Columbia, a woman (Nina, he still remembered her name) barely covered by the thin red fabric, answering the door with a hand to her lips, Daniel asleep in the bed behind her.

He looked at the photographs thumbtacked to the wall. The three of them, Daniel, Abby, Ben, in front of a sequoia, both holding the boy's hands. Ben as a yellow pumpkin a year or two back. Abby, in front of the window in this room, looking up from a book. The family shot, the same one Nathan had somewhere, the four Mirskys in a boat on the lake at camp, laughing. And one he didn't remember ever seeing, him and Daniel, somewhere, must be '74, '75, from the clothes and hair, Daniel a little behind him, both of them looking at something out of the frame.

"May I?" Nathan said, holding the edge of the photo in his hand. Abby nodded and he carefully pulled out the tack that held this photo and the one of the family from the wall, brought them to the table.

"He was the best liar I ever saw," Nathan said. "Amazing. Could lie about anything. To anyone." Abby had finished her coffee, gathered the muffin paper into a ball and dropped it inside her cup, as he had. She leaned back in her chair.

"We used to go to this camp, a Jewish camp, in the Poconos. My father wouldn't allow much Jewish stuff in the house—the most unreligious man I know—but my mother, she remembered things from growing up, in the Old Country, and it was a constant tug-of-war. This camp, where we learned about Israel, and some Hebrew, was one of his concessions."

He lifted the picture of the four of them, he and Freda in front, Daniel and Sol on the rear bench of a rowboat, all of them, even Sol, laughing. No wonder he'd kept it.

"He was twelve, thirteen. Had a girlfriend. Big thing was to sneak out at night and see your girlfriend. Or try. They were strict at this camp. Two things they were strict about were sneaking around at night and being alone with girls. Hardly anyone made it. Counselors patrolled with flashlights, and the caretaker, he lived with his family by the entrance, had a golf cart he used to drive. He was harmless, probably nice enough, but we were city kids, Jewish, and he was country, a goy. Different species entirely. That's what we thought."

He looked at her to see if she knew what the word meant, if it offended. Neither, both, he couldn't tell.

"He raised turkeys, I remember this huge pen, silliest sounds you ever heard. His son had a motorcycle, you could hear it all night through the camp. We made up stories about the caretaker, not very friendly, and he probably knew it, which accounted for his being less than friendly to us. Stupid, ugly stories to scare ourselves with. He'd whip you if he caught you, had threatened kids so they wouldn't talk. He beat his wife, shot stray cats, stuffed them and had them all over his house. Had a retarded kid locked in the attic. No wonder he hated us.

"So Daniel announces one night he's going to the girls' side. This other kid joins him, they dress in black, take flashlights, water, like they'll be gone for days. After the counselors pass on patrol they sneak out.

"I was younger, didn't get the details till later. They get maybe a thousand yards, past the boys' bunks, when the caretaker rumbles up in his cart. They duck behind some trees, scared now, they're kids, too, after all. They run into the woods. Immediately they're lost and it takes a good hour to find their way back to the bunk where now they'll be humiliated. Not only didn't they make it to the girls, they got lost, their clothing's a mess, hair full of twigs and leaves. Near the bunk Daniel says to the kid, 'Let me do the talking.'"

She got up from the table, and for a moment Nathan thought she was done listening. But when she got to the sink with the remaining plates and turned on the water, she looked back at him over a shoulder, if not encouraging, clearly expecting him to continue.

"So. They're inside the bunk and all of a sudden—the other kid told his brother this, who told me—all of a sudden Daniel's out of breath, his eyes are wild, he can barely get a word out. The other kid is flabbergasted, but this is the hand they're playing so he goes along, breathing hard, working up a sweat, waiting for what's next. They gasp for water. They ask someone to see if they're being followed, someone to post a guard. Once or twice Daniel, then this other kid, hear something and say, 'What was that?' all terrified, and soon all the kids are scared, too, which is just what he wanted."

She finished rinsing the dishes and turned now, her back to the sink and the towel in her hand, a smile—reluctant maybe, but a smile nonetheless—on her face.

"So Daniel tells them the story. They were almost there, they could see the girls' bunks, hear them laughing, when they hear this weird sound from behind them. Singing. Chanting. Some kind of music. They decide to investigate. Head deeper into the woods. They hike and hike, following the sound. They're scared, but curiosity keeps them going. Then, in a clearing in the woods, they see it."

Nathan paused, on purpose. If she didn't talk here he would simply stop. She had to give a little. And she did. She said, "What. What did they see?"

"An altar. Strange music and lights. The caretaker and his family, some counselors and other people, singing a song in a language they'd never heard. Sacrificing a goat."

"A goat?" She laughed, a sudden ringing sound in the room. Nathan smiled.

"They're dressed in robes and they have knives, some of them, and when they're done with the goat they throw its blood on the altar and—this is where you can tell it's Daniel's story—then they stop what they're doing, all at once, synchronized, and stare into the woods, right at where the boys are hiding. They scream for their lives and run to the bunk, certain they're being chased."

She came back to the table and sat. She was smiling now, shaking her head. She tugged at the band holding her hair, pushed the sleeves of her sweatshirt up over her arms, then pushed them quickly down again. Her face changed. Nathan went on anyway.

"Of course they can't tell anyone. Counselors, any adult, they're all in on it. Apparently a couple of kids in the bunk get too scared, they want to go home or tell someone, so Daniel takes back the stuff about the blood. Says he made that part up—only that part—for dramatic effect. The rest is real. This, of course, makes them believe him even more."

She picked up the cigarette pack, tapped it on her palm but didn't bring one out.

"Best part. Next day—and this I saw—there's Daniel and this kid, leading an expedition, maybe twenty boys, into the woods to locate the altar, verify their story for the skeptics. Never found it, of course, so Daniel said they must have figured they were found out and dismantled it, covered their traces. Everyone was sworn to silence, for their own safety. The stories about the poor caretaker got even more gruesome, and some kids probably had a miserable, scared few weeks, but the point was this: nobody ever mentioned to Daniel that he'd never made it to the girls' side."

She put the cigarette pack on the table, having just picked it up, and Nathan, not wanting to, glanced at her hands for signs of tremor. Only the left one moved, the same slow rhythm in the fingers.

"That was Daniel," he said, aware suddenly of the tense, how naturally it came to him. Hardly a week. Under the table, he rubbed one hand against the back of the other.

Now she did take a cigarette out, lit it, inhaled. When she blew the smoke out it was over his head, she didn't try to turn away. He looked at her.

"Did he really hate you?"

"Who?"

"The caretaker. The goy. 'No wonder he hated us,' you said."

Nathan sat back in his chair. "I don't know. Probably not."

"Why would he hate you?"

"I don't . . . Probably didn't. I don't know."

"What happened to him?" Abby said.

"Sorry? The caretaker?" He was confused, felt himself growing agitated.

She smoked, looking at him, that expression fully back in her face.

"I don't know. You mean did he get in trouble? Did he get fired?"

She didn't answer.

"This was all a joke. It was over in a few days. Nothing happened." He was mystified. What did she care about the caretaker for? He really didn't know what happened to the guy. He was there the next year, the year after, maybe. Then he was gone. Somebody got sick. Somebody died. What did that have to do with it? She stood, gathered the napkins and the sugar and the tub of margarine.

"I don't remember anyone getting in trouble," he said, putting both hands flat on the table. "It was just a story about Daniel." He couldn't even remember why he'd told it.

She was at the refrigerator, her back to him. Though she'd put the margarine away she stood there without closing the door.

"Abby," Nathan said, standing. He realized he'd never said her name before. He realized, too, that he hadn't explained why he was here last night. Not to her or to himself. "Abby. I said I was sorry."

She let the door swing closed. It made a small clatter as glass moved inside. "Yeah," she said, laughing, a different laugh, part exhalation, part sneer. Who did she sound like, Nathan wondered, then realized. She sounded like Sol. "Yeah, you did."

He had it wrong, so much of it wrong, always did. Never a clue Abby loved him for this most of all—how wrong Daniel had nearly everything.

He was a man used to being noticed, admired. Hard to say how, over the years, that changed a person, but it did. A smile that was all things to all people—wide open and friendly if that was what you wanted, insinuating and gently full of intrigue (I don't smile like this for just anybody) if that was it. That long wonderful hair, jet black in pictures, elegantly graying later on. When he spoke he looked at you, which you didn't realize was rare until you met someone who actually did it. You could sense his eyes on your eyes, your face, even sometimes your lips, and there was no way to explain how good that could make you feel. He'd read nearly everything. He liked to laugh. He made love slowly, paying attention. Once in a while, still, he spoke as if the world would become better, it would just have to, and she could see him, younger, fresher, up on a stage, stirring people with his words. He moved that way all these years later, as if the world itself couldn't help but give him anything he wanted. She'd asked once, surprising herself, how many women he'd had. He tried to shrug her off, but when she persisted he leaned back on their sofa and looked at the window. You mean a number? he asked.

After she'd dropped out of college she'd been with a boy a little *like Daniel. Dale, self-appointed rock manager, full-time dealer when he could swing it, which wasn't often. Another beautiful boy, languorous in it, generous, as if he knew all about his incredible good luck and was more than happy to share it with you.*

But nothing stuck to Dale. When things fucked up, and they always did, it was somebody else's fault, the friends he'd trusted, "the man," Abby, and all he needed to recover was a good dreamy high, some vigorous, restorative sex, some tunes. It had seemed—christ, it really had—the perfect way to live for about six months. Dale the Teflon Man. Like some movie star who emerges at the end of the film attractively bruised, covered in dirt, clothing sexily in tatters. The one you had paid to see, would pay to see again. Didn't like this? he would suggest. Don't worry, next will be better, I promise. I'm the one thing you can count on, the only real thing here.

But you couldn't, of course, count on anything. Dale wasn't selfish, really, not insensitive or unaware or self-absorbed. If anything he was the opposite, too aware, preternaturally aware of what you, of what everyone around him, really wanted. And he tried, within his powers, to give it to you. If he failed, the failing—and you felt this way, too—was somehow yours. If patient, prodigal, seductive Dale, if even he couldn't give you what you wanted, maybe you wanted the wrong thing. Maybe, as you'd suspected all along, the trouble was with you.

Sometimes Abby wondered where Dale was. He'd be nearly forty, astounding to consider. She could apply any of several scenarios to his life. She could see him reformed, sliding from a life where drugs and music had been the fulcrum to one where cars and money were; kids, a toned, lovely wife, a house on a sunny cul-de-sac. Or maybe he'd finally found a band with the talent and dedication to deserve him. Maybe he was in L.A., with fancy hair and new drugs. Maybe he sold cars in Fresno, real estate in Walnut Creek, was up in Montana or Alaska, homesteading. Maybe he'd found Jesus or Lao Tsu. She had no idea. That was the point about Dale. When she'd known him he'd had no history, never spoke of parents or the past or life growing up except to gently deride Abby's own sorrows, regrets. He carried nothing he didn't need. Lithe, lovely, obvious Dale. Somewhere he was smiling, of that she was sure, and making somebody ache for the need to please him. Somebody like her.

Abby herself had a past, not interesting or original or in any way appealing. It was such a cliché that at times she could forget it had happened, that for twenty years almost, it had been her life.

She'd told Daniel about it, and the word she found herself using over and over was "actually," as if it was all hard to believe. Her father was a successful lawyer, kindly in a distant, ineffectual way. He actually bought a new car every fall, actually played golf twice a week at the Club, wore actual tuxedos to take her mother to the Holiday Gala and to his annual college fraternity reunion. He loved buying people things—when she was seventeen he'd actually taken her to Paris to buy clothes—and this wasn't, as far as she could tell, to flaunt his love, or coerce love in others. It was, if anything, to celebrate his fortune—in life, in family, in his ability to make everyone he cared for, if they had the simple sense to accept it, happy. She told Daniel she'd had an actual coming-out party at a yacht club in the marina, an actual taffeta-and-lace dress, antique. First dance with Dad. Tears in his eyes.

Her mother was locally famous, not just for her husband, not just for the charities and functions she chairpersoned, or for her regular appearances in the fashion pages. She was famous for her house, a tiered Spanish-style villa in the hills over the city, famous for its views and gardens and landscaping, but most famous for her "hobby," as she called it, of decorating. She did a room a year, starting in the kitchen downstairs and moving through the dining and living rooms and parlor, the solarium and Henry's den, upstairs to the bedrooms and her study, the children's rooms, now for guests, the ballroom cum banquet hall cum legendary spot for parties and get-togethers that she had made of the converted attic. When she was done, it was time to start over. She and her house had been in Architectural Digest, House & Garden, on the cover of San Diego Today. She told a feature writer she felt she did not simply live "in" her house, but "with" it. They changed and grew together.

Mrs. Henry Morris. Louisa. Trim, even in her fifties. She did yoga and walked every afternoon in the hills with friends. She was on the board of a dozen local charities and once, for their church, had gone personally to deliver a check—twenty thousand dollars, no chump change—to a sister village in Venezuela after an earthquake. She'd brought Abby a pair of handmade sandals. Her dearest cause was Save the Children. Each Christmas they adopted another child from impoverished lands like Nicaragua, Sudan, Bangladesh. Christmas afternoons Abby wrote letters, dutifully, ambivalently—there were dolls she had barely played with, dresses to try on again. Dear Brother or Sister. My name is Abigail Morris. I am seven, I am nine, I am twelve. I live in Chula Vista, which is in California, in the U.S. Maybe you could come visit. I have a big room, there's lots to do here.

"You're kidding," Daniel had said from across the wooden table.

"No," Abby said. "I'm not."

" 'I have a big room'? 'There's lots to do'?"

"I did. There was."

She'd kept in touch with a couple of them, Abby told Daniel. One, Esteban, came to Buffalo to be a pharmacist. They wrote but never met. A girl named Tamila was killed. Her family said it was an illness, but Abby didn't believe it, somehow. Their words, their anger—they never said what disease. They talked instead about the army, how they'd had to move. How she'd kept all Abby's letters.

This night was barely a month ago, the last time Daniel was straight. Well, straight for him. When he was off the stuff they agreed to get stoned, as if by tacit consent. Daniel nervously talked, rolling joints with his long connoisseur's fingers, licking the perfect white tubes and lining them up on the table. He drank steadily, beers Abby got from the fridge, occasionally the cheap scotch they kept under the *sink for nights like this, twisting his head sharply to the side as he downed a shot like it was medicine.*

"Where was this?" he asked.

"Tamila? Sri Lanka, I think. It was years ago."

He shook his head once, in confirmation, not denial. He looked over at the hall leading to Ben's room, lit a joint, took a long drag, then three short puffs of smoke coming off the lit end, and passed it to her. He always checked to see if Ben was around, never would smoke, not even have more than a beer or two, if he was around. It was so Daniel—stubborn, endearing, and useless. As if the boy hadn't seen him nodded out on the couch, the floor, his scaly arms flung outward like evidence, as if he hadn't been there when Daniel was too out of it to talk, to do anything but stare from behind his cipher's empty grin. Ben was no fool, there wasn't much he didn't understand. What exactly was Daniel protecting him from?

Still.

With the joint in her lips she went to the refrigerator for two beers. Daniel immediately started peeling the label from his.

He was getting wired again. All that talking had scared her. She couldn't get him to stop. After the first joint he had quieted, let her talk, had seemed to will her to continue with his eyes, calm, looking at her with that absolute, still attention that could make her fall in love with him all over again. Now she could see it passing. His body vibrated minutely and she could tell, under the table, his leg was shaking.

"What were you like?" he said, rumpling the label with a thumb.

"Me? When?"

"At home. High school."

"Angry. Wild."

"What about?" Daniel said. "Wait, this was 19—what, 85?" He ran his thumbnail up through the red-and-white label, began peeling back both sides.

"Earlier—'82, '83."

"Reagan." He shook his head again, reaching for the joint. "And San Diego. Wow." He performed his ritual with the joint, little kisses off the lit end. "So you had, like, huge hair?"

"Not so huge. Permed, though. Even went through a Lycra stage."

"Headbands?"

"Briefly."

"Chains?"

They laughed together.

"You must have been hot."

"I was alright."

"Boys go crazy?"

"A few jousts."

"Well, love is a battlefield," Daniel said, rolling the beer label into a ball in his fingers and flicking it, near her, on the table. He stood.

It was late, after two. She had to be at the restaurant by nine, get Ben up and off to school first. The last thing she'd wanted tonight was beer and pot. No, the last thing she wanted was what had happened earlier, the scene that had led to this, that made this seem an antidote, the easy sleep after the fever breaks. And it was. Oddly enough, it was. The two of them at the table, Daniel's old Allman Brothers album for rolling his meticulous joints, the bottles, the hunk of Gouda they occasionally—mostly Abby—pared a slice from. Ben asleep— she hoped—in his room. Just talking, laughing. She thought, as she had before, if she could freeze time she would. If she could keep this, have it to fall back on when the shit hit the fan, as it would, she knew, how nice that would be. Soon maybe they could sleep. She would go over to him, put out a hand and take him to their bed, she'd pull off his shirt and kiss him, let him watch as she took off her clothes. They'd slide under the sheets and kiss some more, their fingers and lips exploring, the old sweet surprises. Sometimes, when she came, she reached out and grabbed his hair, pulled him into her harder, as if she could hold him like that, as if, if she did, he'd finally get it. Danny, she'd whisper. Danny.

He went to use the john, and involuntarily she shook her head.
What could she say? Don't pee? He saw it, came over and kissed her
hair, ran his hand under her shirt, over her neck and the tops of her
breasts. He went for another beer and then past her into the hall,
humming "Hit Me With Your Best Shot." She heard him quietly
open the door to Ben's room as he did a few times a night, to see if
he'd tossed off his blanket. Then he went into the bathroom and
closed the door.

What a long night. What had gotten into him, made him talk to
her like that? Why now?

You never could tell with Daniel. He acted not hastily, not dra-
matically, but suddenly, like a hillside giving way from water pressure
you didn't even know was there. Lesko, was that the name? Pat Lesko.
Daniel had done a bad thing. It was bad, she wouldn't deny it. She
could see Daniel needed her to accept it for what it was, that was why
he was telling her. Don't minimize this, his eyes demanded. Don't
console me, don't give me context, mitigation. Don't take this away.
And she hadn't, though it was hard, watching him suffer. Why
couldn't she say what she felt?

And why tonight? That was the question that kept repeating in
her head. She got up from the table and went to her side of the
bed, got the industrial-sized bottle of hand lotion she bought at
Walgreens, brought it to the table. This was her one guilty pleasure
(okay, sex, too) when she was high, guilty because she didn't want to
be high anymore, or, more accurately, she wanted not wanting to be
high, she was training herself for the denial. But lotion, when she was
stoned, was delicious, the warm melting glide on her skin, making her
warm. And high, her hands, almost as if they were detached, felt like
someone else's, patient, ministering, the skin both hers and not hers,
pleasure in the feel of it from two sides, giving gladly, gladly taking.

Poor fucking Daniel. He'd been carrying this around how long?
Twenty years? What could you even begin to say? She finished her
arms. She pulled off her T-shirt and rubbed lotion on her shoulders,
as far as she could reach. What could you say? Maybe what she told

Ben when he couldn't sleep. When he was upset, crying and thrashing around, Abby would go in and get him to lie still, thumb his eyebrows the way he liked. Baby, she'd say. Listen, baby. Remember? We've got two things going on here, she told her son, not really sure if he could understand, not really sure she believed or understood herself. First, we've got the problem that you can't sleep. Okay. That's a problem. But then this whole second thing, you being upset, you crying and being all scared and worried and worked up. That's a second problem, problem number two, maybe a whole different problem from number one, maybe even bigger than number one. You see what I'm saying? How about we focus on number two and see what happens?

And it worked, usually. Something in her voice, or the odd experience of her whispering abstractions while he was in bed, or simply her sitting there, her thumb pressing his pretty, dark eyebrow just the way he liked, whatever it was, Ben was usually snoring by the time she'd finished explaining the concept.

Anyway, that's what she would have liked to say to Daniel. It was a bad thing. I see that. I have no argument. But now we've got two problems, Daniel. There's the event itself, the deed, whatever you want to call it, the treachery, and yes, that was rough. Bad shit. But do you see there's this other thing, this thing you've made of it to carry all these years? I'm not talking about then. I'm talking about everything since then. About now. Could he see that? Could he try? What had this second thing done to him, to his life, his future? To his chances—not of forgetting, of forgiveness—of simply moving on. What about what it had done to them?

But she had no words for a thought this tenuous, complex, certainly not to Daniel, who used words like a magician used scarves, he always had more than you, and better, and he could bring them out to surprise or delight or hurt you. And anyway, he didn't want her to talk. He wanted her to listen. The words, the story slid out of him and his face was dark with the ugly taste of it, and he looked at her as if saying, Here it is, finally, the real me. What do you think now?

She hadn't said a word.

Then the evening shifted to their ritual dance, Daniel looking in his stash, Daniel lying to her face, saying he needed some air, maybe a quick beer at Ruby's, even that he'd go get her some cigarettes. And Abby standing in the hallway, her body between him and the door. I don't want any fucking cigarettes. We have beer here. No, Daniel. Please. Stay with me. Stay here, with me. We'll talk.

And the desperation in his face, the old serene beauty completely worn off, the handsome face about to come apart. Please. Holding him by two hands to lead him back inside. Kissing him, rubbing his neck. Cracking a beer. Reaching behind their bed for the rolling board and pot, trying with exaggerated clumsiness to roll a joint, knowing, hoping he'd laugh, get distracted enough to take the whole thing from her and do it himself. Talking all of a sudden, sounding in her ears just like her mother, cheerful, breakneck sentences, needing to fill every bit of air between them so he couldn't drop in a casual lie, pinning him in his seat. About what? About anything. About her family, her mother and father, christ, about the debutante ball and her mother's house and those idiot articles. About Dale. Anything to keep him there.

And now she was high. Now it was nearly three and she'd had four beers (was it four?) and she was high and she had to get up in a couple of hours to get everyone started on their day. She was exhausted and angry and she rubbed the lotion on her arms and neck and chest and poured out some more and rubbed that onto her stomach.

How would she have lived with a thing like that? Would she do better? Not wanting it, she finished her beer.

Was this it, then? Pat Lesko, twenty years ago? Before Reagan, even. Fucking Brezhnev and Jimmy Carter, Nixon still skulking around. Disco. Gilda Radner. Newsreel stuff. She'd been eleven years old. Was that it, all this time, the part of Daniel she never understood, the part held back, or missing—history? What was she supposed to do with fucking history?

Daniel told her one time he had no idea where his family came

from. Literally. They'd disappeared, all of them, in the camps, except
one aunt and an uncle who'd died before he was born. His parents
had met in Bruges, after the war. All they had of their past was some
photos—his mother's, his father had nothing—she had managed to
keep. Weddings, graduation shots. She wasn't even sure who some of
the people in them were, his mother had told Daniel. Family, probably. All she had from then. About where they had come from, what
town, was there anyone left there who might remember, who could tell
them what life was like before—nothing. His father absolutely for-
bade any talk about it. The day I got off the boat, he told them, I said
my last word in Russian. Everyone was up front, looking at the statue,
crying. I was at the back, looking where we came from, and I spit on
that time, that life. I remember no Russian now, not a single word. It
took years.

How much could Abby say about her past? She still had grandparents back in Nebraska, she'd had a great-grandmother until she
was twelve. She knew one ancestor owned a mine in Colorado in the
1800s, another was a politician in Lincoln and a friend of William
Jennings Bryan. Her parents could trace their roots to Holland and
the Ruhr Valley and Yorkshire. Her father would talk of them happily, all she had to do was ask. Her history was there, intricate, lay-
ered, preserved in family records, but it had nothing to do with her.

They'd never been angry with her, not when she dropped out of
UCSB, not when she bounced around the Coast for a year, not when
she hooked up with Dale, not when she demanded that they stop asking where she was, how she was living, when she might come home.
When she threatened never to call again if they did ask, they were
hurt, subdued, never what you would call angry. It became difficult
for her father to talk on the phone the occasional times she did call,
and her mother inevitably fell into tears, but it was something different from anger, even from disappointment. They were stoic people, in
their own way. They had seen the life they wanted, worked hard to
achieve it, accepted its joys and difficulties without complaint. That

was the American Dream, wasn't it? To see clearly what you wanted, to go out and get it, to spend the rest of your life living it? Her father's questions were well-meant, stiffly supportive: Was she staying fit? Were there any prospects where she was, for employment, investment? How were the schools? Just say the word, he told her, I'll wire the funds—there was, in this bright Fatherspeak, in her mother's breezy recitation of marriages and decorating and church events, not anger, not resentment, not even the embarrassment Abby was certain was theirs among the smart set at the Club. What there was, instead, was quiet dismay, something you didn't talk about, a small but insistent and recurring shock that wouldn't go away, like fear. Which was why talking with them was impossible, even thinking about them so diffi-cult. Look at what we've done here, it said, even without the words. Look at what we've made. For you, Abby. All of it, for you, everything we ever did, this life, its sun and plenitude, its endless opportunity. We're not angry with you, Abigail. We love you. How could you not want all this?

They'd never seen their grandson, didn't even know he existed.

She did have that to carry.

Another thing she hated about being stoned, the way your thoughts became a funhouse maze, a labyrinth leading from one turn to another, and you never knew, even when you shook your head and looked up, if your thoughts were true, deep insights, or just open-mouthed, stoned window-shopping. Pot made you introspective and stupid at the same time, a useless combination, which was why you wanted music and sex, when neither of these mattered.

Before she could begin following this thought with another, Abby rose and put the lotion back on the bed. The air as she moved through it felt good, her skin and nipples tensing. She should put on her shirt, close the blinds, check on Ben, get into bed.

She brought the bottles over to the counter, the plate with the cheese. She began rinsing the bottles for recycling.

She envied him, she suddenly realized. How totally perverse. She envied Daniel his past, a terrible thing even to think, monstrous even through the thudding haze of the pot. All those poor slaughtered people, this Pat Lesko he dragged around all these years like a stone on his back.

But that was it. He carried it, though before tonight he'd hardly spoken a word. He carried it on him, all of it, but it told him, unmercifully, by its crushing weight, who he was. While she, who probably should have married Dale, was weightless. Like Dale, she could end up anywhere, doing, or not doing, anything. What was her past, when she allowed herself to think about it? A dazzling emptiness, each day coming into place by erasing the one before it.

Now she was crying, fighting not to. The water overran the beer bottle in her hand, had begun filling the sink, lapping the leftover wedge of Gouda on the plate, half a joint spinning a slow circle.

If they were different people, Abby thought, tonight could have turned out another way. Other people, after a night like this, would come closer together, would see this as a missing piece — a terrible, painful piece — but now no longer missing. What did he think, that he would repel her, now she would run away? If he had let her take him to bed she would have told him she wasn't going anywhere. She would have loved him and fucked him and held him and told him what he, so damn smart and elusive and complicated, couldn't see for himself. We all do bad things, Daniel. How else could we learn what matters?

She picked up the Gouda, slick with its own oils and the chill water, and held it, not knowing what to do. As if you could explain anything to Daniel, who saw everything exactly backwards, who had flushed the toilet before opening the window and climbing onto the fire escape, as if she wouldn't hear it, as if Ben wouldn't wake and wonder, again, what the hell was going on. If he had just come back, blasted, cursing, crying, wanting to take a swing at her, anything, it could have been different. But not Daniel. What could he do but get it wrong?

6

When they offered the sleeping pill Sol should have taken it. Instead he'd said no, rattling the little pink lozenge in the paper cup the nurse held out, writing, little numbers or letters he couldn't begin to read, on its side. He wouldn't need it.

"Where's Clara?" he said.

"Midnight to eight," the nurse told him, noting his temperature on a pad she returned to her pocket. "Her grandson's in the school play."

Had she mentioned it? Maybe she had. This nurse, probably right out of school herself, was Clara's opposite. Young, brisk, and where Clara moved with the almost sedate efficiency of someone who had performed these tasks for years, this nurse grabbed you by the arm or jabbed the automatic button to raise the bed as if she thought you'd argue about it, answered questions over her shoulder as she was walking away, looked at the dials and bags and monitors all around you, but never at you, if she could help it. Courtney, her badge said, a name Sol didn't know and wouldn't look silly trying to pronounce, but which seemed to suit her, he thought, distant, bristling, anonymous.

Still, she was young, a kid. The smocks she wore looked better suited for pediatrics, colorful birds on pieces of floating branch. Her hair was in braids. The first day, when she not so gently turned his wrist to measure his pulse, he'd seen her stop at the numbers just above her fingers. She stopped, looked at him for the first (nearly the last) time, and he softened a bit. She had no idea. So he tried, especially now he was feeling better, talking.

"I've been having dreams," he said. "I worry."

"This will help," Courtney said, one hand moving to her hip, looking at the pill in the cup like it was right there, proof.

"It hasn't so far."

"No?" She looked at him a moment, her face gone puzzled, still, and he realized that maybe she wasn't this way all the time, with everybody. Maybe she was uncomfortable with him. If this was true he was sorry, but what was he supposed to do about it?

"No," Sol said, handing back the cup.

Courtney, in one motion, took it, swiveled on her legs and moved toward the cart, where paper cups were lined up in little military rows. Her braids swung into place behind her.

"Well, call us if you need us," she said brightly, as if they'd just been laughing together, and was out the door.

Now he did need them. Not Courtney, though, whom he wouldn't call.

The dreams left him breathless, frightened, like the assault in front of his building. But something here was different, something even harder, as if he—who else?—brought them on himself, each night summoned these febrile, careening, hurtful visitations.

At home he rarely dreamed, though Freda had claimed the contrary. When things got so bad at the factory, with Daniel—how many years already?—Freda had dragged him to some doctor who only wanted to talk about dreams. Do you dream in color, he had wanted to know. Pictures only, or sound? Any dreams that recur? I don't have any dreams, Sol told him. Everyone has dreams, the learned doctor said, taking off his glasses to rub them with his tie. Everyone. Good, Sol told him. Ask them.

Like an organized nightmare where you walk from one crazy

terrible room to the next, the dreams came in succession, and Sol
could remember, almost as if he had watched himself, trying to stop
them, to force his eyes open, to waken. None made any sense.

Some house, none he'd ever been to, a mansion from the old
days, run-down, rooms stripped bare as if they'd moved out, whoever lived here, except one he found by accident, behind a door,
walls covered in red cloth, plush couches long enough for two people to lie down on, books, the museum kind with leather straps, lying open. The feeling he had come here to see someone who had
just stepped out, was about to return, Sol frozen on his feet, telling
himself to get out.

Then some wet place, pools of water in green fields, moss hanging from trees, tremendous birds, gray with red spots, yellow with
feathers coming from their heads, quietly walking.

Then the basement of his own factory—what's wrong now?
where's Finkel and exactly what *is* his job? Sol needs to check the
furnaces, huge shuddering chambers in the back of the dark arched
tunnel. You feel their heat long before you turn the corner and see
them. The little boy is with him, the *shvartzer* son of that woman,
and slowly they move into the first window where you can see the
flames dancing.

Then the dream he knew, the one he'd lied to Freda about, the
fat little doctor with all the questions, the one he'd had for years,
since the camp. A pocket watch. Sol is eating it. It's in his mouth,
and he grinds metal and breaks it, so hungry, mouth full of gears
and springs and glass, shards rasp the teeth, cutting him, taste of
metal and blood, he's gagging and trying to spit but also chewing
harder, more pieces filling his mouth. Spit, he begs, Swallow, Stop,
Please stop, and then he is flailing, he can feel it from inside the
dream, reaching for the water pitcher and then the cold that finally
woke him and opened his eyes to this still room, nowhere he knew,
alone, and wet now, and scared.

He had to do something. Forcing his legs to move, he went

around to unplug the IV. In the bathroom he wiped himself down, on a shelf found a blanket which he put across his shoulders and another he spread on the bed in place of the soggy sheet which he threw in the corner. His head throbbed palpably, he could feel it if he put hands to its sides, and his shoulder, which had been giving him some peace, was awake now also, sending small, hot signals of pain when he moved his arm. He welcomed them, welcomed the headache, the chill gown that clung to his back, anything that would push the dreams deeper, away. Moving, the simple act of it, doing something, helped as always, and, pulling the IV pole along beside him, he shuffled around the curtain to see who was there.

Brandon. They hadn't moved him. Sol feared he might have woken whoever was in the other bed—certainly he'd made sounds—but Brandon lay sleeping, if anything, more restfully than earlier. He was a sick boy, dying, they said. Now, at whatever late time it was, whatever hour on whatever day, Sol could accept this. He didn't doubt the message in Clara's face when he had asked, but had resisted it, had, for all the time he'd sat today and last night by the boy's bed, refused to look at it directly, or, he now realized, at the boy's face directly, in the same way the young nurse refused to look at him.

Dying, then. Sol dragged the single chair closer, arranged the blue blanket around himself, and sat. He was warmer. Getting up had helped. Coming over here had helped. In the bed the boy slept undisturbed, though even Sol could see the way he worked at each breath, his eyes making that odd, tense flutter, two veins, or tendons—how was Sol to know?—pulling in his neck.

How long had Sol slept? Had anyone been, finally, to see the boy? No sign, if they had. No books or comics or one of those infernal beeping boxes they all carried now. He felt a flurry of curses gathering to fling at their heads, the parents, but what good would it do? He let it pass.

Was the boy cold? Hot? How could you tell? The numbers on

the machine over his head flickered, but didn't change alarmingly, even when something seemed to lodge a moment in his throat.

Sol looked again at the boy's face, in the half-light coming from the hall not so pale, the skin still unmarked with stubble, two tender-looking pimples on the ridge of his nose. The thin lips moving every once in a while under the mask. He had the impulse—no, that wasn't right, he never thought to do anything. It was a picture, really, no more, where Sol put a hand on the boy's head to see if he was warm, brushed back the hair that lay there.

In movies, Sol knew, you talked to people, even when you weren't sure they could hear. What did you say? You cried, you confessed, you made promises. Who, Sol had always wondered suspiciously, was the talking really for?

But maybe he was wrong. The boy was alive still, however sick he might be. You could feel it like a presence, a field around the bed. Maybe he could hear. Maybe he was scared.

What to say?

He looked around for a magazine, wished again they'd brought some books. He knew nothing about the boy, his interests, probably sports, about which Sol had maintained a lifetime's defiant ignorance. Mickey Mantle. The boys had liked him. Was he still big?

It was useless, and Sol, who feared sleep himself, felt a surge of weariness, of loneliness—for the boy more than himself—of consent. Say something.

Words he'd not heard or spoken in half a century came to him, and he let them, too tired to suggest anything better, broken phrases of prayers he'd heard as a boy, gibberish, the only prayers he knew, didn't know really, just the sound of the words, their cadence, carrying absolutely no meaning to him, he didn't even try to understand. *"El molle rachamim shocheyn ba'mromim avinu malkeynu hashkiveynu l'shalom u'phrose aleynu sucat shlomeycha sh'ma yisroel."*

His own bed was cold, he knew, and still wet, and the last thing

he wanted was to get back in it anyway. He should try Nathan
again—where could he be at this hour? Or maybe Sylvia, but it
wouldn't be fair, a call, long distance in the middle of the night—
what kind of news could it be? He stayed where he was, speaking
nonsense words to this stranger, leaning close so no one would hear
what an old fool he'd finally become. When he ran out of words he
began again, if the same or others, or no words at all, just an empty
drone, he couldn't have said. When he grew drowsy and closed his
eyes he was comfortable, he continued, remembering from time to
time to open his eyes and check on the boy, and when, a long time
later, a hand on the shoulder woke him, thin light was pressing
against the windows. He went around to his own bed, which someone had made up for him, sheets dry, a new blanket folded back.

∾ ∾ ∾

They had always walked. As kids it began, for Nathan at least, as a
way of being with Daniel, showing he could keep up, nearly running at his side, answering brightly, making sure he didn't sound
winded. They'd walked all the way to Manhattan a few times, over
the grimy Queensboro, they used to walk to Shea Stadium and the
old Fairgrounds, along the Van Wyck and Grand Central and Inter-
borough. If you could get there by foot, you did. Their walks with
Sol were slower but no less determined, as if the only thing that
mattered was reaching their destination—the Unisphere, the bank
in a replica of Liberty Hall, any of several overpasses where you
could see cars streaming in the night. They stood in silence a few
moments, then turned and went home.

Nathan walked now. He'd been to the hotel, he'd been to the
hospital to find Sol had checked himself out (granted, Nathan was
late, almost two hours), then back to the hotel. No Sol. He'd been
to City Hall, with its plaza of strange, gnarled trees, through it to
where the neighborhood turned rough, back to Union Square,

where the street performer was doing his act again (Louis Armstrong, "What a Wonderful World"), this time with a cane, and
Nathan watched from across the street, half thinking to go over and
ask the man if he'd seen an old guy, big, in a worn gray coat and ill-
fitting slouch hat. He had stopped and stared at a distant radio
tower, red lights dimly flashing against the foggy backdrop like some
message he was too stupefied to receive, or understand. It was even
warmer today, odd-smelling heated gusts coming in from the water.
He walked fast, though there was no one to keep up with, heading,
he thought vaguely, in the direction of Fisherman's Wharf, and several times he had to stop halfway up one of the remarkably sloped
streets to catch his breath, something in him nearing panic.

Was he worried about his father? He couldn't think clearly
enough to tell. The desk clerk at the hotel, with the swollen-eyed,
affectless expression of someone whose sleep is constantly disturbed, hadn't seen him. The nurse, the Jamaican one who'd been
so nice, told him Sol had left, had said he was tired of waiting. He
would see his son later. Nothing in their room looked disturbed.
Nathan called the hospital again, asked for the main lobby, the
ER—maybe Sol, in an uncharacteristic surge of good sense, was
waiting for him there. No one had seen him since he'd signed the
release papers and left.

Was there cause for worry? (Well, of course. Always.) Sol had always been able to take care of himself, physically, at least, and the
antibiotics should have kicked in by now. He was afebrile, and after
his agitated sleep the night before last, Nathan had reminded the
charge nurse to make sure he was given sleep medication. Nathan
said he'd be back, to check on his father, but he hadn't been, and
this realization, for the seventh, eighth, tenth time, sent him nearly
running uphill, and he leaned against the side of a building and
stared up at where the street crested in the odd, flinty haze that
passed for daylight in this city, then down, where he could see water, gray and solid-seeming as the flank of a ship, small whitecaps

skimming its surface. Somewhere behind him a streetcar heaved, rattled its jangly, incongruous bell. You could imagine falling here, rolling, not stopping until you hit the water. Breathe, he told himself. He put a hand under his coat, to his heart, as if to calm it. Where the hell was he? It looked familiar. Clay Street. Between the office towers to the south he could see the Transamerica Building, like a pyramid stretched by a surrealist, last night's compass point. He remembered Daniel telling him it was built on rollers, some kind of earthquake protection, and the locals all had bets about which direction it would topple when the big one hit.

Breathe, he told himself.

Why did simple bodily functions, even the autonomic, seem so difficult out here? Breathe, speak, think, gather yourself, check your rampant pulse. Slow down. Run.

He was in no shape to meet Sol in any case, not yet. He could envision the old man lying motionless on some sidewalk, strangers bent over him. He could see himself looking up too late and smacking right into his father's still-broad chest. Look where you're going! Nathan heard him say. He moved up to where the cement seemed to level off a bit, leaned back against the building and closed his eyes.

∾ ∾ ∾

After two hours Sol was so exasperated he could barely speak. He sat on the bed with his little sack of gauze and ointment and pills, like a fool, like a child waiting for an errant parent to remember where he had been left. Though it was hot in his hat and overcoat, he refused to remove them, sat rigidly still halfway down the bed, not even, after a time, looking at the door.

Aside from him the room was empty now. They had finally taken Brandon to Continuing Care. Not, Clara assured him, because he was worse—if anything he seemed improved over yesterday—

but because that was where he should have been, really, all along. She held soap and a pile of linen. An aide carried a basin of water.

"We clean you up," Clara said to the sleeping boy. "Make you nice for your mama and dad."

"Are they coming?" Sol asked, the thought flitting through that he might stay and get a look at these people.

"Later today." She put a broad arm behind Brandon's back and rolled him, effortlessly it seemed, as if he weighed no more than a handbag. Briskly they replaced the soiled bedding, rolling Brandon side to side. "He look good, you think?" Clara gave Sol a brief, wry smile. "Something maybe cheer this child up."

So it was she who had woken him, made up the bed. He had been too groggy to notice. Sol, embarrassed, looked away. Clara peeled off the boy's hospital gown, taking care to keep his midsection covered with a sheet. She dropped cloths into the basin, swirled them with a finger, then wrung one at a time to gently scrub her patient. "Warm water," she said quietly to the boy. "Now you tell me. Anything in the world better than that?"

That had been nearly three hours ago, and even then Sol was ready. He had reached for the phone and tried the hotel one more time, the last time, he swore to himself, and when there was no answer he left on his hat and coat, put the white paper bag on the unmade bed and sat next to it.

He was not a man used to sitting around. At the factory the workers were accustomed to him leaving his glassed-in, second-floor office and wandering among them, lifting a pump from the finishing table, talking with the machinists, his most temperamental group, listening to their complaints about the flats, which were always breaking down, and the workers he valued most, at the post and lasting machines, where the shoes were actually formed. He remembered to ask after families, kids in school, how the fishing trip had gone, the nephew's wedding, the visit to the doctor. He was, he felt certain, respected and generally liked. When a worker was out

sick, Sol was not above removing his suit jacket and tying on his ancient patched apron to join them on the line.

Well-Built Shoes for Ladies. After old Widlanski had dropped
dead in his Atlantic City cottage, Sol had bought the business out-
right—when, '65? '66? Freda had begged him to change the name,
something more current, catchier and stylish. Why? Sol told her.
That's what we make. (His own grandfather hunched at the bench
in the alcove behind the woodstove, his hammers and pincers and
clasps, the outsize scissors, scraps of pungent leather scattered by his
feet.)

Sol looked around the room, its walls the blandest possible yellow, a faded picture of a hillside in flowers and sunlight, slightly out
of focus (intentionally, he assumed). Someone had pasted purple-
and-blue butterflies to a window for some patient long gone; outlets
for the various machines aligned over the beds, oxygen, suction-
ing, others he didn't know. All these instruments, and more they
wheeled in to hook you onto, to restore you, maintain you, to save
your life, somehow also robbed you of it, even if temporarily.
Hooked into God knew how many of their machines, taking who
could keep track of how many pills (let alone what they were supposed to do), poked and stabbed and prodded by an endless supply
of new hands, you became a piece of the apparatus, reduced to
numbers marked in a chart. And though it was all for you, done for
your good, you couldn't help feeling, if you refused a pill or ran a
temperature, that you were gumming up the works, interfering with
the smooth running of their operation, like the tiny bits of leather
that choked the machines at the factory. You could be tossed aside,
by them, by God. A new part would be brought in, and the hospital's efficient production line would hum along without you.

At the hotel he would tell Nathan (if he ever saw him again) that
he needed to rest. He had slept poorly, if at all, his two nights at the
hospital, and besides, the last thing he wanted to see right now was
his son's sour face, as if it was his duty to stand there and record the

world's failings. He would sleep, tell Nathan to finish up whatever business they had with that girl. Then they could leave. Why, he wondered, growing sleepy in his warm overclothes, had they even come out here? He honestly couldn't remember. Was there anything they learned out here they didn't already know? Was anything, aside from this crazy pushed-up city, the stricken-looking young girl and her wide-eyed, staring son, now somehow part of their collective ruin—was anything even different?

As they washed Brandon, Sol had watched. Again, the paradox about the boy. He was thin, almost sickeningly so, his arms and legs wasted to the point where you couldn't imagine they had ever, or would ever again, carry him through a day. Sol thought he could see from his own bed dim, blue veins trailing through the pasty, opaque skin of Brandon's arms, his hands, his forehead. He looked made of porcelain, broken, beyond hope of repair.

And still, he was alive. Of this there was no doubt. He breathed, his eyes fluttered from time to time (had they flickered open and seen Clara one moment?), and when they shifted him around, there seemed to be movement in his fingers, his head on its spindle of neck. After Clara had buffed him, a faint rosiness lifted in his skin. As close to disappearing as you could be, he was here, present, undeniably so. Still here.

Sol watched until they closed the curtain so they could clean or change whatever tubes they had attached to his privates. His coat grew heavier around him, and though he wanted to be awake to ignore Nathan when he finally arrived, he felt sleep's warm gravity and let his head drop toward his chest. He awoke briefly as they wheeled Brandon out, dressed in clean blue pajamas, not hospital issue, his own, and was aware, distantly, he'd like to say something, get up from the bed, but he was too tired. He had been thinking about something, or dreaming, and he needed to remember what— or was that the dream itself, his needing to remember something? This, also, he was too tired to figure out. As he drifted off he saw himself for a moment in his mind's eye, an old man in a heavy coat, slumped into a posture of overwhelming weariness, or surrender, or grief.

∾ ∾ ∾

With a spasm running through his shoulders and back, Nathan opened his eyes. Had he been asleep standing up? One foot was numb, his jacket half off a shoulder. He took a few long breaths, deep, slow, as he told anxious patients to do, and headed back through Chinatown, to the hotel. If Sol wasn't waiting for him, he could wait for Sol.

A streetcar clattered past on Powell. Nathan pulled his jacket off and held it. Abby. He'd been thinking about her as he dozed. Would he ever, once, leave her presence not flustered, not unsettled and angry and thoroughly confused?

It had begun well enough, with the muffins and coffee, the talk about Daniel and old times. Then something—he still had no idea what—had set her off, something about the caretaker at camp. Could there be a more peripheral, less important character in the world? And it had only gotten worse.

Pat Lesko. Nathan thought he had known the story for years; was what she said true? Could it be?

They were friends at Columbia, Lesko, complexion stark white, peering under a fringe of black hair, long fingernails crusted with dirt. Wore a green army jacket, always, inside and out, winter and summer, its many pockets filled with smokes, paperbacks, assorted pill bottles, articles indignantly torn from newspapers. Rumor was he never showered, just swabbed himself at the tiny corner sink the rooms at Columbia were fitted with. Smoked all the time, literally, cigarettes he rolled himself with tobacco from a soiled yellow pouch. The few times he had seen him, Nathan stood apart, fascinated, watching with a mixture of repulsion and awe. Lesko, the

story went, was the son of a Polish aviator who had flown for England and an Ulsterwoman from a long line of IRA stalwarts. He
had, supposedly, an uncle jailed in London, twenty-five years for
paramilitary activity. They called him Katov, after the insurrection-
ist in Malraux's *Man's Fate* (though not, Nathan noticed, to his
face), and he had no girlfriends, disappeared every few nights, it was
said, to 125th and Lenox, or by the river, where women waited in
doorways underneath the West Side Highway.

There was a large element of theater—even Nathan, still in high
school, recognized this—to much of the protest movement. Rudd
and the others behind their bullhorns, working the crowd with their
ringing phrases, their curses, ending in a chant. The blacks from off
campus in their berets and inscrutable shades, the women who
seemed somehow, in their fatigues or long skirts and Indian blouses,
to wave their heedlessness and sexuality like a flag. Nathan had a
hard-on every minute he was around them. They were serious
about the war, of this he had no doubt, and, though the strains between the whites and blacks were there from the start, about civil
rights, there was the feeling that something unique was happening
in their working together, in their talking to each other in the first
place.

Still, theater pervaded it all. The rallies, the uniforms, the pos-
tures of cynical defiance and knowing better, as if they were sea-
soned veterans of revolution, not nineteen- and twenty-year-olds
who would disperse come summer to their country houses or lousy
jobs or happy or miserable lives at home. They believed in what
they were doing, Nathan thought, but he sensed most of them, if
they managed to come out undamaged, would move on to ordinary
lives of work, acquisition, love, disillusionment, love, if they were
lucky, again. They would have stories to tell.

But not Lesko. He seemed born into his role. You could imagine him dropped anywhere, at any period in history, and he would
know where to go, where to find the people desperate enough to

risk making change. Idealists. Lunatics. He was intense, and he frightened Nathan a little. He believed in what he believed not because someone had argued him into it or he'd read it in a book. Everything about Lesko said he believed what he believed because it was true.

No one knew if he'd ever been a student at the university. He'd been around for several years, lived somewhere north of campus. You could see him at the gates on 116th selling *The Daily Worker*, or across the street at the Chock full o'Nuts drinking mug after mug of coffee, or on South Lawn, with half a dozen newspapers spread around. At the rallies and demonstrations he was in the background, but people kept going over to talk with him, Nathan noticed, and he never spoke into the microphones or moved his hands from his jacket pockets, even when the chanting and fist-pumping began, unless it was to roll and light another cigarette.

Lesko was a funding source for the movement, selling drugs and turning over the profit, a few times, it was rumored, getting involved in smuggling, liquor or stolen stereo equipment to be trucked across the border to Canada. One day, Daniel told him, Lesko showed up with a gun, a blunt gray pistol, and asked if anyone wanted to buy it. There were no takers. Lesko seemed equally at home with the blacks, or equally indifferent to their affections. Nathan had been with Daniel to someone's dorm room one night where music he'd never heard before, all pounding bass and hypnotically repeated rhythms, played through huge speakers, and the air was actually saturated with pot smoke, swirling and deflecting faint light from the windows, from the lamps with red bulbs that were the only illumination in the room. Six guys, plus Lesko, some of them Nathan thought he recognized from the street. They looked up when the brothers came in, a couple nodded. After about half an hour, in which nobody spoke, nobody moved except to pass the bong, they left. On the street Daniel said of Lesko, "He's got the right ideas. But, man, he scares the shit out of me."

That was the story Nathan knew, from Daniel, from seeing it himself, from, three years later, the accounts of Lesko's arrest and trial and subsequent conviction. It all seemed a part of everything going to pieces then—the war now all but officially over, the energy that bound them together scattered in dozens of directions—music, drugs, back to the books. It was around this time, Nathan understood later, that Daniel got into smack. They saw less of each other, and there was a faraway glumness to Daniel, a sleepy nonchalance, not like from a regular hangover or being stoned on weed. Nathan, preparing to head out west to college, consoled himself with visions of his bright future and with the thought he'd finally outgrown his older brother, was free to be his own man.

Now there was another chapter to the story, one that might explain things somewhat, if Nathan could somehow stop and believe it.

Nathan knew, of course, that Daniel had been busted the year after graduation. Not a big deal, they were assured, less than an ounce of weed, intimations to Sol and Freda that it wasn't even his, not really. He was let off, essentially, with a warning. Sol and Daniel by this point were barely speaking anyway, on a direct course to the confrontation at the factory later that year that would sever what was left of their relationship. Freda, from her bastion of worried silence, as if listening every minute for bootsteps in the street, collapsed into tears when Daniel came home—Nathan was back for winter break—to tell them he'd been warned sternly by the judge, given two years' probation, but it was over now. He was alright. He put an arm around Freda and said this: "It's alright now, Ma. It's alright."

And that's what they thought. Till now.

Now, according to Abby, the reason Daniel had gotten off so lightly was he'd conspired with the police to entrap Lesko. The bust had been prearranged, in exchange for the judge's lenience. One thousand hits of windowpane acid for $4,000 in cash behind the

Central Park bandshell at two a.m. one weekday morning. When the hippie who'd sold them the drugs pocketed the money and flashed his badge, Daniel's urge, though he'd been told this was how it would go down, was to run. Lesko just stood there. Two policemen came out of the bushes, one handcuffed Lesko, the other approached Daniel, who, for reasons he still hadn't understood twenty years later, took a swing at the guy. He barely clipped his chin and found himself facedown in the gravelly dirt, the cop's knee hard against his backbone, his arms yanked painfully behind him to be cuffed. He turned his head, once, to look at Lesko, who stood impassively, no expression on his face, as if he'd seen this coming, as if he, not Daniel, had known all along. Daniel didn't look at him again.

"When did he tell you this?" Nathan had asked Abby. He had risen from the table with the carton of milk and gone over to the refrigerator. He stood there, not opening the door.

"About a month ago," Abby said. She was back at the table.

Nathan, feeling anger force itself into his chest, opened the refrigerator door.

"Why?" he said, stiffly, over a shoulder.

Abby sighed. As if she'd been through this before. "Why what?"

"Why all of a sudden? And why'd he tell you?"

"Who was he going to tell? You?"

"He could have."

She expelled a short burst of air from her mouth. Threw her head back as if about to laugh.

"No, really," Nathan said. "Why, all of a sudden, after all these years keeping it to himself, does he decide one night it's time to talk?" He reached into the refrigerator, not seeing what he lifted. "Was it here? In this room?"

Abby blew smoke at the ceiling. "Right here."

"Was he stoned?"

"Little bit. Weed and some scotch."

"And he just started to talk. Just like that, out of the blue."

"I guess." She was angry, gathered into herself, looking straight ahead.

"You guess?" Nathan tightened his hand around the bottle in his hand.

"You gonna do something with that?" Abby said.

He looked down, saw a bottle of ketchup in his right hand, cocked, as if he was ready to throw. He lowered it.

"Okay," he said. "Okay. But tell me, why should I believe you?"

Though she'd only taken a drag or two off the cigarette, Abby leaned forward and stubbed it in the ashtray. She pushed her hair out of her eyes, still looking ahead. "Here's a bulletin, Nathan," she said, and leaned back in the chair. "I don't give a fuck what you believe."

The refrigerator was open behind him, and he felt a little jolt as the compressor came on. He replaced the ketchup and stood to the side, near the Communist flag and the bookcase. He lowered his voice. "Did you believe him?"

Already reaching for another cigarette. She lit it, dropped the match on the table. Still not looking at him. "Yeah. I did."

"Why?" Nathan said again, an odd constriction in his chest, like fear.

"He was haunted by it. He had it with him, all the time. Didn't you see that?" And she shook her head slowly.

"No," Nathan said. "I didn't." He went back to the table and sat.

"You never noticed how unhappy he was?"

Nathan didn't respond.

"I thought it was me, of course, something I should be able to give him but couldn't. And they say women are smarter. Then I thought it was the smack, how it can change your whole personality." She looked at him, finally. He was hoping, he now realized, to find her in tears, but she was clear-eyed and steady. It was Nathan who looked away. She continued. "He was clean, by the way, till that night. Had been for months." She waited, as if giving him an opportunity to challenge her. He didn't. She was looking again at the window. "Finally I just gave up and decided to live with it, whatever it was. Anyway, as long as I could." She lifted the cigarette to her face, stopped, looked at it with disgust and mashed it in the ashtray. The taste of smoke reached his tongue. "But all those years, without talking to anyone—that's what he said, and I believed that, too. To put that on your back and carry it, your whole life. Do you get it?"

Nathan put his elbows on the table, cupped his chin in his hands. He didn't answer.

"Well, what happened to this guy?" Abby said. "I never got the chance to ask."

"Lesko? Jail. A couple of years. When he came out he moved to Brooklyn, became a community activist. I saw his name in the paper. Then he was killed, cops said he'd pulled a gun, members of the Socialist Union said he'd been set up. It was the seventies. Nobody cared."

She swept a hand across the tabletop, sweeping crumbs into her palm. She went to the sink and wet a dishrag.

"Look," she said. "This may not be the best time, but I have something to give you."

He waited while she swabbed the table. As he moved so she could reach the whole surface, the soap she used, or the shampoo, hit his nostrils. She saw him looking at her, he did not turn away, and a light flush colored her skin. He was looking at her, fully, for the first time. Her oval face, her eyes a sea green. The expression he couldn't for the life of him decipher. That hair. She reached into a pocket for the elastic band, gathered her hair into it and finished cleaning the table.

She'd been with Daniel, Nathan realized, been with him, tolerating, maybe even loving, what Nathan had ultimately rejected— his brother's constant need, labile intensity, the way he inhabited your life, drew you to him, the way he could make an ordinary moment seem fuller (or emptier) than any you could experience on your own. She'd been with him through God knew what and she'd lost him. When she collected her thick, dark hair in one fist and twisted the other, holding the white band, around it, Nathan watched intently, as if he had never in his life seen anything like it.

She went to the closet on the far side of the bed and moved some shoes. She came to the table with a bulky envelope and put it before him. It had one word, written in Daniel's distinctive slashing script. *Nathan.*

She went back to the closet and returned with a squat plastic box, red, plain, no markings on it. She held it in two hands. Nathan knew what it was. She put it down and sat across from him.

"He told me this was what he wanted. I had to tell the cops we were married so they'd release them to me. He said he wanted you to have them. And this."

Nathan picked up the envelope. On the front just his name, no jokes, no ironic wordplay. He lifted the red box. It was surprisingly heavy, maybe five pounds, and he was startled both by its weight and by its smallness. A tag read Daniel's name and age, the date, and a long number. He put it back on the table by the envelope.

"Let me know what you plan to do with them," Abby said, her tone softer. "I'd like to be there, if that's alright."

"When did he tell you?"

"What?"

"You said he told you this was what he wanted. When did he tell you?"

"Years ago. He said if he died, have him cremated and give the ashes to Sol. I thought he was joking."

It was impossible, though Nathan tried, not to look at the box. Daniel, all that was left of him, scooped into a box the size of a loaf of bread. Nathan felt the familiar dividing off, part of him sitting there, engaged in conversation, part sequestered, hovering, hiding behind the bookcase or the torn Soviet flag, gripping his hands into fists.

"Why would he do it?" he said, finally.

"Do what?"

"The cops said he went looking for trouble, not around here. He should have known he was in danger."

She shook her head. "I don't know. I don't think he felt he had any choice."

"What does that mean?" Nathan said.

"Just that. What it felt like to me, his life, a narrowing down of choices. Until there were none."

"Do you know what he was thinking? At the end?"

She colored again. "Not really. Or entirely. They'd started coming around Ben's school, dealers. Kids, eight- and nine-year-olds, were being given cash, Gameboys, to deliver packages around the neighborhood."

"Ben?"

"No. I don't think so. The school found out and sent a memo. They had two squad cars by the playgrounds mornings and afternoons."

"Did it help?"

She shrugged.

Nothing he learned out here made any sense. Each bit of information seemed isolated, from a different story, a piece to a different puzzle. They weren't married, not that that counted for anything— he seemed to have loved her, and the boy, too. And yet he walked away. No choices, she'd said. He'd asked her what she meant, and he wanted to know, but in a sense, he already did. Hadn't he felt that way so often himself, understanding as little and as much as maybe Daniel had? He thought of that girl, Monica, of Janet their last night. Being that angry. No way around it. No choice.

"Was he still teaching?" Daniel had been a substitute grade-school teacher, loved it, he had told Nathan one time.

"On and off," Abby said. "When they called."

"And that house, the one Ben was drawing, with the car in front. What was that about?"

First giving him a look as if to say, Really, what business is it of yours? she relented and told him. It was a game they played, Ben and Daniel, the house they'd build when they moved out of the city. Every day they'd add a room, or a tree house, or a swimming pool. The car was Daniel's, he drove them up to see the redwoods sometimes, or down to the aquarium at Monterey. Ben loved the wind, that you had to shout to be heard.

Nathan could see the three of them in Daniel's little red sports car, the one he'd bought cheap when he first came out in '76. He'd come down to Palo Alto sometimes and take Nathan driving. Something shifted outside, softened in the always-changing light. Or was it in himself, a draining of some exhausted rage, finally, a relaxing into the moment. So much lost, so much that made no damn sense, and yet here they were, this woman and he, in this room, on this gray morning. A distant car horn, blocks away, dopplered into silence as Nathan strained to hear. They had both loved him. There must be a part of this they could share.

He looked back to find her staring at him, nearly causing him to wince. The mood, while he was daydreaming, had pivoted again, and again he didn't understand why. She sat erect in her chair, arms protectively across her chest, as if he might jump the table and harm her, her expression imperfectly masking outrage and indictment.

"You hurt him," she said.

He felt his face move, the eyebrows rising, the mouth falling open. But after a moment he said, "I know."

"Do you?" she said. "He tried, you know that? He tried to straighten things out. He was stupid enough, for a while we both were, to think we could do it. Do you know what it's like to get clean, how hard it is to climb out of that hole? He tried. We tried." She brought her hands higher, hugging them under her arms, as if afraid now of what she might do to him. "He was such a fool, your brother, an idiot, always joking, always sounding optimistic, always making excuses for people. When you stopped answering his letters or returning his calls, when you didn't know about his burst appendix that time—of course, how could you? Nobody in your fucking family talks. Except him. He talked about you. 'He's my brother,' he'd tell me. 'I know him.' What a load of shit." She looked away, he could see her teeth working her bottom lip. The tremor in her voice, what he'd earlier been hoping to hear, shook him more than anything she said.

Inside him an answering voice rose indignantly. You think I didn't try? How many times did I get a call in the middle of the night, him waking up in some alley or shooting gallery, whimpering with fear. The calls from jail, not a fucking lawyer, me, three thousand miles away, in Boston for christ's sake—what am I supposed to do? The times I had to wire money—that doesn't count. Money I didn't have, mind you, money I had to lie to Sol about, unexpected med-school bills. He thrust his hands into his pockets, angry. Somebody was going to do something stupid here, he could feel it. His fingers found the small white packet, the one he'd taken from her bathroom. He threw it on the table.

And there it is, he thought.

But there was more, more she couldn't begin to guess at (not that she'd bother trying). What Nathan himself refused to examine too closely, had disguised with resentment and spent patience and his own particular brand of numbed self-importance. He was my brother, he couldn't say. To see him, you don't know what he was like before, to see him fall apart so thoroughly, so miserably. I couldn't do it. I couldn't stop it and I couldn't stand anymore to help it happen. It's not like he didn't do anything to me.

She was crying now, silently, swiping her eyes and nose with a cuff of the sweatshirt. She stared straight ahead, over his shoulder at the window. In Nathan's imagined conversation she stopped long enough to look at him. Tell me, she said. What did he do to you?

Nathan said nothing, the weariness returned, a slowly crushing weight in the shoulders and chest. In Boston, Janet and he would exchange back rubs on the living room rug, some music playing, he going first so that when he fell asleep under her kneading fingers, it would be alright. Waking to see her lying there near him.

He left. He disappeared. He lied to me about what the world was.

Oh yeah, Abby and Janet said in unison. That.

Abby was openly crying, her face lowered, tears running down, no attempt to wipe them with the sleeve, rocking her shoulders. Nathan had no idea what to do. Maybe she hadn't seen him throw the packet at her, maybe he could slip it back in his pocket. But it lay closer to her than to him, and he was afraid of what she might do if he put a hand out.

"I guess," he said, "I guess I'd better go." He checked his watch for the first time. "I'm late to pick up my father." He stood, tried thinking of something else he could say, could he put a gentle hand on her shoulder, but some quality, isolate, durable in her posture, told him to keep away. This wasn't about him, he understood.

He stood in silence, wondering why he had done it, tossed the drugs at her. He was no doctor, that couldn't be more clear. Where there should have been conviction, and the growing capability to help, all Nathan felt, all he had ever felt, was an abject clinging to the basest tenet of the trade—do no harm. Don't leave things worse than you found them. Could there be a more fucked-up reason to be a doctor? He should take it back, open the packet and shake it down the sink. He should sit and talk with her, maybe she didn't want to be alone right now. He'd been trained for this. He'd talked with people about loss. He should offer counsel, expertise, time, concern. She looked up at him, tears brightening her eyes, blurring her expression. He didn't know if she saw him or the packet.

Something in him flinched. For the first time he thought, What are you doing here. You have no right.

He took Daniel's envelope and left the box, then at the doorway turned and went back to get it. He was about to turn again when his eyes caught, inevitably, the small plastic square on the table, about the size of an airmail stamp, a snug red zip-lock at one end. "I didn't know whose this was," he said. "I found it."

She didn't look, in no way acknowledged he had spoken. Was this the best he could do? Give drugs to an addict (was she?).

He left the room. Outside the boy's door a presence, an immanence of calm, of stillness, of sleep. Inside, the boy was alright. How did Nathan know? He didn't. He felt the urge to open the door and check. Instead he made his way up the darkened hallway and let himself out as quietly as he could.

∾ ∾ ∾

The teacher was reading from a book, a story about a girl who gets angry, breaks one of her mother's plates, steals something from her brother, isn't nice to the baby. She's sent to her room to give her time to think. Ben listened, hoping something interesting might happen—she'd climb out the window, or an alien would come visit, or one of her dolls would suddenly start to talk. When instead she lay on her bed and began thinking about what had gotten her mad—so much had changed since they'd brought the new baby home—Ben's spirits flagged. Without even listening, he knew the rest of the story. She'd think for a while, maybe cry a little (she was a girl, after all), give her brother back what she'd taken (Ben had missed what it was, looking out the window), apologize to her mother about the plate. They'd hug and have ice cream or get in the car and go someplace nice and they'd all learn something important that made them feel good and was a big lie anyway and had as much to do with Ben's life as the man in the moon.

He wanted to take out his pad and draw, but Mrs. Downing had already spoken to him once about it, and when Ben and his mom had come in late, really late, Mrs. Downing, who had lots of faces (not all of which Ben believed), had on the one that said she was tired (of Ben being late), or disappointed (with Ben's mom for letting him be). He hadn't looked up as he put his pack in the cubby with his name on it and took his seat between Missy Alexander and Shane Wu.

He had fallen asleep under his blanket at least two times, and when he opened his eyes the last time he was cold, with his feet sticking out and a wet spot near his elbow where his mouth had dripped. There were still voices from the other room, and they didn't seem as happy as before. Ben went to his dresser and pulled out a T-shirt, changed his underwear and socks. He figured yesterday's pants would be good enough. He still wasn't sure if it was a school day (he was beginning to think it wasn't), but just in case he put the blanket on the bed and the dogs in their box (resisting the urge to count). He sat on the bed until he heard the front door open and close, then went out into the other room.

His mother saw him, took something from the table and hid it in her hand. She'd been crying (again), and he stood there. He never knew what to do first thing, say good morning, or go over and crawl into her lap for a kiss, or tell her what he'd been doing or had dreamed. She stood, not looking at him. "We're late," she said. "Go brush your teeth."

When his mom was upset, Ben felt he had to do something, it was his job to do something. But he never knew what, and usually whatever he did wasn't enough. On the way to school he didn't shrug her hand off after they crossed the streets (was that something?). And he looked at her, first openly, then, when she didn't seem to see him, sneaking glances, as if seeing him look, seeing the beginnings of fear he knew he couldn't hide from her, could only make things worse.

At the school they had to check in at the office, then go to Ben's class.

"There you are," Mrs. Downing said, when his mom opened the

classroom door. Her voice didn't match the look on her face. "We're nearly ready for lunch."

"Yes," said his mom. "We're sorry."

"Well, come in, Benjamin. Hang up your jacket and take your seat."

That's when Ben started not looking. He knew his mom stood there for a minute because that's when he heard the door close. Sometimes she and Mrs. Downing stepped out into the hall to talk. Sometimes she was gone before Ben reached his cubby. He didn't know what happened today because he didn't look, and Shane Wu had his feet on Ben's chair, a not unfriendly smirk on his face. Ben pushed them aside and sat.

Last week, when he had missed a bunch of days, Mrs. Downing called him over at lunch and lifted him into her lap. This was so unusual that Ben allowed it, unprepared to resist. She stroked his head and whispered, "I'm so sorry to hear about your mother's friend." Ben had looked at her, confused—was she talking about Danny? His mother's friend? Ben guessed that was right, though it wasn't the word Ben would have used. What word *would* he use? "Everything will be alright," Mrs. Downing whispered. She straightened his hair where she had just messed it up. "You just be a good boy and help your mommy, okay?"

He turned awkwardly to look at her. She was an old lady who wore glasses on a string around her neck and funny dresses covered in flowers and weird shapes. Her hair was mostly gray. When she laughed she didn't open her mouth. Most of the time Ben was scared of her. But though he felt strange sitting there (he had glanced up to see Shane Wu grinning), he also wasn't in a hurry to get down. There was something solid about sitting there, and if the room had been empty maybe he would have stayed, maybe put his head against her just for a minute. She seemed, Mrs. Downing, to come from a different world than Ben's, someplace where people weren't always in a rush, and where, if you woke up in the middle of the night, everyone was asleep, in bed. So much didn't make sense to Ben, and now Danny was gone, Danny who tried to explain things to him sometimes. Maybe if the room were empty and he stayed in her lap awhile they could talk, and Mrs. Downing could tell him about how things were in her life, and he could ask her questions about his. But he looked and Shane Wu's mouth was wide open and he moved his arms on his chest as if rocking a baby, and Ben quickly climbed down.

The girl in the story was now imagining what she would feel like if somebody had broken one of her toys, or been mean to her, or taken something she cared about. Ben looked out the window and saw their house. It had three floors now, about fifty rooms, a swimming pool in front and one on the side and one more in back. This last had a huge slide that was as tall as the house, the others were full of colorful floating animals. There was a roller coaster, a barn for ponies, a stand where they gave you candy, you didn't even have to pay. A pond with leaping fish. He and Danny used to add stuff all the time. One day Danny suggested a tennis court.

"But I don't know tennis," Ben had told him.

"Me neither," Danny had said. "We'll learn."

Around him kids began shuffling, reaching for books under their seats, getting out pencils and erasers. He hadn't heard the story end, or what Mrs. Downing had told them the assignment was. He fought to keep the house in his eyes but he couldn't do it, and he saw, instead, the big rock-covered ledge outside the window, the silver tubes whose tops spun in the wind, the plastic bottles and papers that had blown up against the edge.

He wondered what his mother was doing and then tried not to think about it. He wondered where Danny was now, if he could see Ben, if he felt anything, or even remembered anything from here. He thought about his father, who his mother never talked about, and he knew this could get him really upset, and if he started to cry and Shane Wu saw it Ben would have to hit him and the whole day would change. Stop it, he told himself. He got out a pencil and slowly jammed the point into his thigh. When the pain focused his thoughts he pulled back on the pressure. To his other side Missy Alexander had her journal and was at work, her tongue out, tracing the motion of her pencil on the paper. Ben reached into his desk and got out his journal. He remembered that he didn't know what he was supposed to write. He should raise his hand and ask, but he couldn't. He drew a box and put a triangle over it, then added two more boxes with triangles and began sketching in windows. His leg hurt pretty bad, but soon he forgot about it, working on the climbing tree out back, hearing the sound of horses, and fish moving in water.

The room seemed brighter than Nathan remembered it, the fussy modernist prints on the somber brown walls filled with more color, the tree outside the window—elm? sycamore?—still catching sun. A beautiful, early fall day.

Across the low wood table, Dr. Pendergast struggled with his pipe. He'd done something to his hand. Two fingers were thickly bandaged and he filled the bowl with difficulty, was having an even harder time with the lacquered matchbox, the match, trying to get the thing lit. Nathan watched with what he realized was an uncharitable delight. First Pendergast put the box against the marble base of the clock, but the match just nudged it forward, then he tried wedging the box between his thumb and bandaged fingers, but this sent a match whirling across the table into Nathan's lap. He returned it, smiling. Can I help, he almost offered, but didn't. He hadn't slept in thirty-six hours, his head resonated with a dim metallic whine, his eyes were weighted in their sockets. But this was an unexpected treat. Pendergast, still presence amid all the world's unease, fumbling like a drunk. It made Nathan feel like celebrating. Maybe he'd take Janet out for a drink or two before crashing. Maybe ask her to leave work so they could walk across the river to Cambridge.

"Pardon me," Pendergast said around the pipe stem, pressing the matchbox flat under the injured hand while he struck the match, clumsily, against its side.

"Certainly," Nathan said.

Finally Pendergast got the pipe going, sat back in his chair, trying, it seemed to Nathan, to regain some composure. Here, Nathan thought, have some of mine. He shifted, forced another tiny shriek or two from the red leather couch, spread his arms comfortably on its cool cushioned back.

What had the poor schmuck done? Squash injury? Wandering fingers bent by some hot young neurotic? Or torched himself making waffles, in a hurry to get his two fat kids off to soccer? The possibilities were endless, all pleasant to consider.

Pendergast puffed twice, displayed a polite smile. "Shall we talk about your parents?"

It took the words a few seconds to reach Nathan through his reverie. "Why?" he said.

"We haven't. You never mention them, except in passing."

"Of course I do."

Pendergast was settled now, his pipe billowing away like some happy cartoon tugboat, and Nathan felt his annoyance seeping back, through his hands, which he lowered from the couch, to his shoulders, whose clinching ache reminded him how tired he was. His eyes felt as if two thumbs pressed lightly on the lids.

Pendergast usually let Nathan start their conversation, another elegant trap, Nathan always thought, but today he was prepared. Pendergast must know the old ethical dilemma: If a museum is on fire, which would you save, your grandmother or a Rembrandt? So last week in the ER, a gangbanger, multiple GSWs, they've worked forty-five minutes and he's still bleeding out. The surgery attending finds one bleeder, only to curse that there must be another. The kid's a rare blood type, and when the ER attending asks where the hell the blood is, the nurse says the blood bank wants him to know they're about out of B negative Di—the kid's gone through five units already. They all pause, just a second, to look at her. Lorraine, an old broad, battle-tested, been here twenty years, short gray hair and the arms of a stevedore. "What?" the attending says. "What the fuck?" Meaning

what had she told them at the bank? That the kid was a banger? That
he was bleeding out anyway? That it was not even six on a Friday and
who knew what bloodstorms were coming tonight? And she was a
nurse, no matter how many years she'd been here—what was she doing in the middle of a medical decision? "What the fuck?" the attending said. And Nathan had his ethical dilemma for discussion. It was
interesting, he was sure it was relevant (how, exactly, he couldn't say),
and they could have a good talk, meanwhile steering wide of the type
of conversations they'd been recently having (Marshall Stone, for
christ's sake. His mom and his piggy bank).

Now that plan was a wreck, along with Nathan's buoyant mood.

"That's not . . ." he said. "I really don't see why . . ."

Pendergast, leaning over the bowl with a lit match—in five minutes he'd become ambidextrous—looked up questioningly.

"What do they have to do with my, with our . . . with why I'm here?"

Pendergast sat back, all calm restored, a slight encouraging nod
indicating this was an acceptable response. "Yes," he said. "Yes. And
why are you here?"

Nathan, not for the first time, wondered what manslaughter
would get you in Massachusetts. That pipe was in his dreams. He
woke up smelling it.

"Sex," he said, surprising himself. Lovemaking, he'd meant to say,
but dropped the word as inaccurate. He'd worked hard for weeks keeping them away from the topic; now, exhausted, he was something
close to glad.

"Yes?"

Was Pendergast even aware that using the word as a question was
ridiculous? It was an affirmation, an article, a participle, Nathan
had no idea what it fucking was, but it meant Yeah, I get you, I understand, not What? or What are you hiding? or whatever nasty insinuation Pendergast had in mind. Two stifled squeaks escaped from
under Nathan, and he clamped both hands onto his knees so none of
them would move again.

"Janet. My girlfriend thinks there's a problem."

"And you?"

Nathan shrugged.

Pendergast allowed one of the generous silences that so irritated Nathan. Was he meant to continue? retract? finally give in and blurt the truth? He never had any idea. What he had often thought instead was to ask for an adjusted rate based on time actually spent in therapy. I can sit at home and stare at myself for free, he would say.

"She says I'm angry."

He was startled to hear the words. Now he was in for it.

"Explain?" Pendergast said.

Alright. After all, this was what he was paying for. Even with his medical coverage it came out to about forty dollars a pop, you could still get a meal and a decent bottle of wine for forty dollars, in Somerville if not Cambridge, or a night of beers at the Plough. If Sol had taught him anything, it was the value of a dollar. What was that painting, Miró? Klee? Nebulous blips of color seemed to float free of the canvas.

"She says, Janet, that I use sex. She says when she does something I don't like I take it out on her in bed. When we're in bed, it's like I'm punishing her, she says, and she doesn't know what for." He lifted a hand and dropped it. "Me, either, I guess."

Pendergast shifted only to move the pipe an inch or two from his lips. "Are you?"

"What?"

"Punishing her?"

Nathan looked away. On another wall a Kandinsky, he was pretty sure. He liked art well enough, but Janet was the real connoisseur. When they first met, they used to go to the Museum of Fine Arts on Sundays. Nathan liked the rotunda where they had the Monets, he found the variations of the haystacks soothing, he liked, once Janet pointed it out to him, the way the light moving across them determined what you saw, that without the light, without you to see it, there was no haystack. He liked watching her watch the paintings, and he would stand back a few feet and take them both in, Janet's lovely shape, and beyond, over her shoulder, the quiet allure of the paintings, serene enticements to see. As he stared, another sight slid into view, nothing he could do to stop it—Janet in the doorway while he wakes, lying next to Eleanor. The sick feeling he had too often, of being caught finally, exposed, relief, disgust and a jarring native terror caromed through him. He shuddered it off.

Pendergast, between bowls, put the pipe down and lifted the bandaged fingers to his lap, where he rubbed them with his other hand. Nathan watched him do this.

"We let a kid die the other night."

Pendergast continued the massaging motion, looked at him impassively.

"He would have died anyway. There was nothing we could do. But still, we made a decision and let him die."

The words, draining out of Nathan, seemed to linger unattached in the air around him. Finally, he said, "I don't know."

The doctor nodded.

"Have you anything to punish her for?"

"No."

"There are times, in a relationship . . ."

Nathan pulled his eyes from Pendergast's hands and looked at his face. "No," he said.

In the silence that followed, broken only by Pendergast's fussing with the pipe, the intimate sounds he made with his lips that made Nathan want to gag, Nathan kept his eyes on the prints.

"Why would you need to punish her?" Pendergast wouldn't let it go.

"I wouldn't. I just said I wouldn't."

"You did. I heard you. Humor me a moment."

"Hypothetically? Why would I punish her? Hurt her, you mean?" Pendergast, almost decorously, attended his pipe, giving Nathan time to compose his thoughts.

"I guess I am angry, some of the time. Not at her, there's no reason to be angry at her. It just comes out that way."

"It's something you feel you need to do?"

Where was he taking this? "Yes," Nathan said. "No."

Pendergast finished scraping the pipe, placed it in the ceramic tray.

"What about here? Would you say you're angry here?"

"Here?"

"Here. Angry with me."

Nathan looked at him. He hoped to see malice, or conniving, even the blunt satisfaction of foreknowledge in Pendergast's face, something that would help Nathan deflect the question. But there was nothing behind the mild, patient eyes. "Yes," Nathan admitted. "I am."

"Why do you think that is?"

"I couldn't say."

"Would you care to hear one possibility?"

The urge to say something caustic, to smear that complacent poise from the doctor's face, nearly overwhelmed him. "Sure," he said. "Enlighten me."

"You're not comfortable when people look at you. You're not comfortable when I do it. You don't enjoy these sessions, yet you come back, and once you get here you have trouble talking, looking me in the face."

Nathan opened his mouth to object, but closed it without saying a word.

"There's an interesting cycle of response, we can get into it sometime, if you like. Your anger is intolerable to you so you strike out, make someone else—to put it plainly—feel as bad as you do."

"Why? Why would I do that?"

"Shame. Humiliation."

"I'm not following . . ."

"Why do you keep coming here, Dr. Mirsky?"

Nathan twisted his hands beneath him. This was too much. Some easy sarcasm eluded him and he squirmed without one.

"You need something from me, Dr. Mirsky. From me, from your

partner. That's why you come back. You need something and it's ex-cruciating to need it, worse, to be seen needing it. To be vulnerable. Worst of all, to be faced with the possibility of getting it."

"From you?" Nathan almost spat the words. *"What could I possibly need from you?"*

Pendergast didn't move.

Kandinsky was good, Nathan liked Kandinsky, but if he was going to hang pictures, why not ones that made you feel better, that lady Impressionist, some haystacks, even Renoir's overfed dollies. Nathan had always liked that guy with the blue horses. Why, especially in here, hang the ones that leapt at you, or floated weirdly, or made you keep looking when all you really wanted was to close your eyes. "Alright, then," the attending had said, to himself as much as to anyone else. They kept working on the boy, but the room was altered, no one spoke except for the doctor asking for drugs, suction, clamps. He did what he could and in a few minutes the boy died. The doctor pulled down his mask. He was about fifty, gray speckling his beard and cropped hair, sweat lines across his face. He looked down at the table, shook his head once and walked out. He didn't take off his gloves and left a red hand-print on the glass door, which an aide erased with cleaner as Nathan helped prepare the body. On his way out for coffee, far down the hall he saw the attending talking to a group of people around a lady in a chair.

As he watched the framed print, as he watched the attending lean over the elderly woman who held a handkerchief to her mouth, as he heard Pendergast—could you hear that?—waiting, Nathan split off from the room, a slow-motion dolly shot receding, a man in a space suit come loose from his tether. What he saw then was what he could never—not today, not ever—say to Pendergast.

She was older than most regulars at the Plough, the tavern joke. Eleanor—if she had a last name nobody needed to know it—parked at the first stool every night, there when you arrived, last one to leave if she didn't get lucky. Big, lumpy, a dour hunched grimness in her posture and her too-tight clothing and silly hair, coiffed stylishly like a girl much younger, much sexier, much fuller of promise and allure. She drank steadily for hours, Irish whiskey and water, and most of the time she'd look at her glass or at the cloudy mirror behind the bar or into some indeterminate distance between. Only occasionally she'd turn her gaze into the room, and it was chilling, the hunger, the fending off of disappointment, absurd hope buoyed by liquor welling up through her. She fascinated Nathan, depressed him. He watched her between beers, between chatting up whomever he'd found that night, a reference point, a preposterous compass, she spoke to him relentlessly of something he couldn't begin to understand. She drew him, repelled him, frightened him to look at.

Like any regulars, they'd had a moment or two, Nathan paused at the bar for another black and tan, or, later, Jameson's neat, and if she looked up he'd nod, make some crack about the weather, the music. She was unhappily large, near six feet, skin unhealthy, showing her teeth pathetically in a smile she somehow thought was girlish, lighthearted, inviting.

One night he's drunk, he's wild, he's where he's been so often before. Three times, four, he's told himself to give up and go home. Janet's out with friends; if she was upstairs he would have already left. He's talked to two college girls from BU, Amber and Kellie, but Kellie, the one he'd noticed, was plainly uninterested, kept looking toward the door, and Amber—a clear second fiddle to her livelier, sexier friend—so wide open for attention that he soon lost heart, or interest, and when the guys they knew from school came in, Nathan with relief gave up his seat and went to the bar, a last quick one before the music started and he'd be out of there.

Eleanor at her post, sipping doubles like medicine, shoehorned into a tight green vest, hair slowly coming undone from the pins that held it. Nathan has ordered his second last drink when she looks over, and he's preparing his usual nod of greeting and dismissal when her expression catches at him. She's drunker than he is, a lock of plastery blackened hair slipped forward over an eye, some indeterminate muddy blue or brown, the wiry small whiskers on her chin—polycystic ovarian syndrome; did she know, Nathan wondered, about diabetes, heart risk? drinking wouldn't help—lifted defiantly in his direction. Something else has slipped, pretense, the vanity of expectation. She stares at him with what could be loathing or the last unblinking glower before sinking, and what Nathan sees reflected in her face is peremptory, undeniable kinship. I know you, her merciless undisguised stare tells him.

When Janet finds them it's after midnight, they're asleep at far edges of the bed, a bottle of whiskey nearly empty on the floor. She utters a cry, half-choked revulsion and pain, and she's out the front door without closing it, and Eleanor, moving steadily, without hurry or a glance in his direction, puts on her clothing and goes, also leaving the front door unclosed.

The Plough shuts down at two, the musicians load their van, the bartender empties bottles with a great glassy clatter into the Dumpster out back, people linger for a last joint or pee against the wall. The college kids, especially on a Friday, are just getting warmed up, even louder on the street, as if released finally to the wide free world. Nathan, used to it, dulls his senses against the noise, willing himself into his blank, unresting sleep, but something calls him back. They're below his window, voices, mostly male, a female or two tittering accompaniment, looking up and serenading his apartment, Eleanor, they're chanting, Eleanor, come on down, Eleanor. When Nathan reaches them he only has time for a glimpse to recognize the kids from BU, the girls he'd talked with hours ago, before he's in among them, swinging at whichever face is closest. Landing a half-missed blow on one, then he's belly down in the rubble of the alley and they're kicking him, cursing happily, trying to roll him over for a better angle. And then Janet, who'd gone herself to the Plough in her fury, is there, pulling them off, looking at one boy, who seems ready to take a swing at her, until he, and then all of them, Kellie or Amber, one of them looking with some regret over a shoulder, huddle together and leave. Nathan, on his back now, pain pulsing under one eye, a rib piercing his attempts to breathe. Janet looks at him as if waiting to see what he'll do, but he does noth-

ing, lies there, as if saying, Alright? Now you see. And maybe she does, for after a moment she turns and leaves as well, not for their apartment, but back up toward the avenue and a cab.

Nathan didn't know how long he'd been silent, how long he'd been staring emptily at Pendergast, who hadn't moved or made a motion to interrupt. Nathan looked, something he never allowed himself, at the psychiatrist's impassive, conscientious face. How could I tell you that? Nathan thought. How would I even start? His hands fiercely itched and he dug one into the palm of the other so as not to scratch.

"Your parents." Pendergast had said something. Just now? What had Nathan missed? "They were in the war, yes?"

Nathan looked up.

"And you have the one brother, older."

Nathan didn't respond.

"How did they meet? Your parents."

"In Belgium." He shook himself. Wake up. Now. "Relocation camp."

"Are they living?"

"My father."

Again the pipe, the match, the sucking. Nathan just wanted to lie down. He'd pay the fee if he could just close his eyes for what was left of the hour. When he'd first heard that logical conundrum, in a class somewhere, Nathan, pleased with himself, had piped up, "Depends which Rembrandt." To which some other wag had added, "And which grandmother."

"Growing up," Pendergast said between puffs. "How was that?"

Nathan, actively fighting vertigo—what room was this?—forced himself to answer. "It was . . . I don't . . . It was fine."

Pendergast didn't say anything, and Nathan looked around, with some desperation, for something to focus on. How had he forgotten that he meant to change the time of his appointments to earlier in the day? The way the light outside altered while they sat here was disturbing, and now, while he hadn't noticed, day had drained off, darkness dropping into place like a lid. In the corner of one throbbing eye the Kandinsky seemed to pulse in the room's yellow light, and Nathan

*did everything he could not to see it. At the hospital the attending
had looked up from the dead kid's mother—mourning had begun—
had seen Nathan, but before he could motion him over (though why
ever he would have, Nathan had no idea), Nathan had turned and,
almost in a panic, taken the stairs to the cafeteria.*

"I'm sorry. I don't know how to answer the question."

*"Well," Pendergast said, his voice no louder than before, though
seeming to be in the amplified quiet of the room. "Perhaps tell me a
little about them, would you?"*

Nathan gave him an empty look.

"Were they happy?"

*Nathan brought his face around. "How am I supposed to know
that? What does that mean? Who is happy, for God's sake?" He felt
himself leaning away. "Are you happy?"*

*Without actually moving forward, Pendergast seemed to, a gath-
ering of interest in his eyes. Nathan wearily added this to the
list—when things went south for Nathan, every session, just then
Pendergast started enjoying himself.*

*"They," Nathan said. "My mother." He found he had to stop and
breathe. Pendergast was looking at Nathan's hands. He stuffed them
back between his legs. "My father, you know, did well, owned a factory,
bootstraps kind of guy . . ." Another breath. "American story. Came here
with nothing." Was this what Pendergast wanted? Immobile, even the
pipe for once unmoving. "My mother, she died last year. Never spoke. I
didn't get to know her, you live with someone a whole life, weird . . . I
don't really think she . . ." Another pause, twisting away. As if he were
looking through the wrong end of a telescope, the room drifted, pulled
back, his words took on a dull echo. This was too hard. He wanted to
stop. "My father doesn't say much, either, but with him you know."*

*"You do?" Pendergast put the pipe down in its ceramic tray and
placed both hands, the bandaged one on top, in his lap.*

*Nathan fastened on the first thing he saw. Kandinsky again.
Swirling colors, slashing lines, a face to one side? Magic wand,
maybe, trailing ribbons, Rubik's cube, a flag. Impossible in the throb-*

bing air to make anything of the riot of image. Was he going to be sick? He couldn't regulate his thoughts, he had no idea what to say, what the doctor wanted him to say. Then, careering—when would this stop?—another painting slid into view.

Late seventies, renovated MoMA. As a birthday present to herself, Freda had gotten tickets, and the day they went she dressed up, new dress and a hat, somehow persuaded Sol into a new shirt and slacks. Lines and too many people, and Nathan knew right off this was not Sol's idea of fun. He stayed with his mother, moving slowly through the galleries, cool vibrant Monets, warmer Pissarros, Cézanne's restless gazing, Rousseau's suspended dreams, waiting until the crowd before them made room, while Sol distractedly plowed ahead. Nathan looked over once to see him staring at a Picasso as if it had just insulted him, another time sitting with two other overdressed men on a bench, all three looking like they might have to sit there forever. Then he disappeared.

After two hours he and Freda needed a break. He'd enjoyed walking the galleries with her, was surprised when she pointed out things he didn't see in the paintings (where had she learned about African masks?), and Nathan left her, flushed and weary (and yes, for the moment, happy), over an iced coffee in the cafeteria while he went to see what had become of Sol.

It took a while to find him. Nathan walked through the photography exhibits, the furniture, past a huge, stuffed Oldenburg ice-cream cone (he'd have paid money to see Sol's reaction to that one), then, beginning to wonder if the old man had given up and taken the subway home, he found him in a gallery upstairs, off to one side, motionless in front of a large painting. Something in his posture made Nathan pause, and he stood a few moments watching, obscurely afraid to interrupt, and when his father did finally begin to walk away, Nathan turned so the old man wouldn't notice him. Then he approached the painting himself.

What he saw made him take a step back. A landscape of war or its aftermath, gray and brown, nothing moving or alive, shattered objects, masonry, pipes, twisted metal bars. In the middle, a figure,

*maybe a boy, howling, not of this world, huge head impossible to sup-
port on that spindly useless frame, arms and legs warped, skin ribbed,
glistening, wearing only a gashed-red drape of cloth, the picture's
only color.* And behind his enormous, weighted head, another, even
larger, disembodied, floating, its mouth an identical mute echo of the
child's, or maybe its source. *Child born of a nightmare so intricate
and visceral and authentic it admitted of no denial, no escape, a
silent howl on this blasted piece of land all there was, from now ever
would be.* Someone standing right by Nathan let out a soft moan, but
when he turned whoever it was had moved off. How long he stayed he
couldn't say. When he finally found Sol and Freda in the gift shop
(Freda had bought a small poster of Picasso's wildflowers), Sol looked
the same, and Nathan, who had thought he must say something to
his father, realized he would not be allowed, and was grateful.

He shook himself. "What's that called?" he asked Pendergast.

Pendergast turned to look at the print. "Yellow-Red-Blue," he
said, and Nathan was too sapped to examine whether this could really be the name of the painting or if Pendergast was being ironic. As
if it made any difference.

"You asked were they happy. I don't know how to say." He forced
his head around to face Pendergast. "What I mean is, what they went
through. The war. I don't think being happy was the point."

Pendergast, lips compressed, raised his eyebrows.

"Happiness?" Nathan shook his head quickly, felt his hands
clenched in his lap. "How do you even . . . Being safe, yes. That mattered.
Being here. You see? Don't you ever forget . . ." He trailed off again.

Finally Pendergast spoke. "Did they tell you this?"

That day at the factory, the shoes, the men in a mob by the wall.
The smell—was that what Pendergast's pipe recalled to him? Daniel
and that laugh. "No," he said.

"They didn't have to."

Nathan didn't respond. The room was draining of light, of sound,
like a set when the play is over, soon they'd come for the furniture,
cart it off, carry him to the darkened wings.

"*Parents love their children.*"

Pendergast, drifting in mild shadow, full night now, Nathan and this stranger, his unfathomable, unwanted Virgil. "Go on," *he said.*

"*How could you, how could you be happy? It would be . . . dis-loyal. Like turning your back, you know? I mean, hope? Faith? Trust? Come on.*" *He closed his eyes.* "*They didn't need to tell us.*" *The sensation, oddly welcome, that it was not him saying these words, but someone else, he and Pendergast could just listen together.* "*But they loved us. Of course they loved us, they wanted us to be happy, that was the whole point. So my brother and I could have everything, all that had been taken. Otherwise . . .*"

He stopped. It was exhaustion. He knew the physiology. Exhaustion that made the lamplit room seem an island in the dark outside, made its raw panels of color and loony tunes couch seem real, when they weren't, obviously, they weren't. Cut, somebody should shout. That's a wrap. Pendergast, on cue, "*Otherwise?*"

Nathan, confusion and nameless fear becoming palpable, a presence he was afloat in, looked up at the doctor. Pendergast had just said something else.

"What?" *Nathan said.*

"Your brother."

"I'm sorry?"

"I was asking about your brother."

"My . . . He's in California. We're not in touch."

Nathan stopped again, realizing he had been staring the whole time at Pendergast's hand, the outsize fingers, muffled white. The boy in the MoMA painting, one arm limp and oddly hanging, the other ending where fingers should have been, hands that would never again do anything.

"He hated him."

Pendergast leaned forward. Nathan kept looking at his hand. "Who?"

"My father. He hated my brother."

Pendergast, who so rarely moved, was now somehow even stiller, leaning just slightly from the upper body, giving Nathan time. The pipe, gone out, rested in the ceramic tray.

"Or. Or he was scared of him, of Daniel. And that's what he hated . . ." He trailed off, his words tinny and refracted and barely audible. Someone else could have been saying them, anyone else. Let them finish for him.

"How did you know?" Pendergast was quiet, too.

"You could tell. You just had to see."

Pendergast reached for the pipe but instead of loading it, turned it by its stem so the bowl faced down. He slid the box of matches so that it aligned with the ceramic tray. Nathan watched these movements as if they made any sense.

"My mother said something once. I never got it." Pendergast had sat back in his chair, hands folded in his lap. "That Sol told her once, when he looked at Daniel he had to shake his head not to see Chaim, his brother. He died in the war, I think they were together. Daniel was named after him. I don't know, I never saw the guy."

Finally, after another moment in which Nathan said nothing, Pendergast gestured down at his hands, which Nathan only then realized he had been staring at again.

"Squamous cell," Pendergast said. "Recurring." He held them up. "My father had it, too." Nathan, amazed to see it, noticed for the first time the man's hands, the hard, cooked-looking scars along the fingers. "It's under control," Pendergast said.

"It is?" Nathan said.

And as he'd done in their other sessions, to Nathan's fury, though not this time, Pendergast raised both palms to the sides of his shoulders, the universal gesture of unknowing, of acquiescence to fate's hidden design. How, he was telling Nathan, could you possibly know? Time was up, and Nathan, unsteady trying to stand, mumbling goodbye, thanks, next week, made for the door, the stairway, and night outside.

7

Back at the hotel Nathan replayed the messages from Sol, a new one from Sylvia Grossman. He listened, first disappointed, then relieved, there was no call from Janet. His father sounded disoriented. "Nathan," he said. "Nathan, are you there?" The second message was almost eerie, he couldn't say for certain it was his father, but it was, somehow he knew. Just silence, maybe the sound of breathing behind the scattered background hiss of the phone line. Fumbling sounds, the receiver dropped, a dial tone. Then Sylvia Grossman's nervous amiable voice.

"Hello? Hello, Nathan? This is Sylvia Grossman, calling from New York. We met one time, last year, maybe you remember. I'm a friend of your father's. From the building. Is it too early? I hope I'm not disturbing anyone. I spoke with your father on the phone. I'm so glad they're releasing him."

Here she paused, and Nathan could see her, neat gray hair and kind, worried face, gathering herself.

"Also, and I hate to bother you—would you call me, Nathan? Just for a moment? Your father isn't so easy to pry information from. Is he alright? What's going on out there? It's so hard to tell with him, everything's a joke. I'd be so grateful to hear it from you, a doctor. I promise not to keep you. Here is my number."

Nathan realized he wasn't listening and played the messages

again. When had Sol called? Didn't he know messages didn't play aloud in hotels?

His father's had come in at 3:26 and 3:29 a.m. Nathan forgot about Sylvia Grossman's request and had had to pull a piece of paper from his pocket to quickly jot down her number. He stared stupidly at the square light on the console, as if Janet might have phoned in the five minutes he was on the line. Shelby's cluttered living room flashed through his mind. Janet had said not to call. She'd moved out. She'd been to the hospital. His, he wondered? It was closest. If he'd been there . . . But she never would have gone in. Never would have had to. And why did that matter now, he thought angrily. It seemed impossible they'd had pasta and red sauce in their Cambridge apartment just three nights ago.

His head felt swollen from drink, his neck and shoulders torqued from sleeping on her couch. Why couldn't he say her name, he wondered? Say her name.

"Abby," he said out loud. "Abby's couch."

After a few minutes he stood and picked up the paper from near his bed. "Janet," it read, in his writing. "I'm sorry." He crumpled it again and let it drop. For some reason he went to his father's bed and lifted the pillows tightly wrapped in the spread. There they were, as somehow he'd known, the lightweight blue pajamas with a thin red stripe, the tops folded over the bottoms. Nathan closed his eyes, his head actually ringing with exhaustion. Where the hell was Sol? He could call the hospital again, then what, the cops? He glanced up and saw himself in Daniel's shirt, then looked to the back of the closet where he'd put the red box, behind the suitcases, so Sol, should he wander back here, wouldn't see it. That's why the door was open, the light on. The box was gone.

∾ ∾ ∾

Soldiers, camp inmates, victims of repeated abuse described the phenomenon, depersonalization, retreat of mind from limb. Disintegration of behavior and consciousness, the body left to its own devices: march, eat, endure. Nathan had seen it in the grief-stricken, who sat there sipping the coffee they were given, or signing papers, struck, as if by some overwhelming force, eyes vacant and dilatory, expressionless. If you touched them, as he'd done a couple of times early on, they either didn't feel you or else flinched, as if any impulse from the world outside could only be cause for more alarm.

He was nearing that stage himself, he understood. The waves of nausea that rode through him every so often, hoisting smoke and liquor onto his tongue, were almost welcome, preferable to the thick imprecision of his senses, the thudding incompletion of his thoughts.

He had called because, literally, he could think of nothing else to do. Rivera, who came on the line much faster than Nathan expected, listened a moment, then said, "Where are you?"

"Why?"

"It's lunch hour. I'll swing by."

Now Nathan stood on the street, in front of the bodega next to the hotel. It had grown still hotter, a slow breeze carrying used city smells from the bay. For a while a man stood near him, sipping a forty-ouncer from a paper bag. In between sips he replaced the cap and looked out at the street. He was trim, fifties, in a porkpie hat and striped green shirt. When he was done he neatly screwed the cap back on the bottle, wiped his mouth with a flannel handkerchief, deposited the bag in a trash can chained to a light pole, waited for the traffic signal, and walked away. Nathan watched him step into a doorway. Bits of paper and debris collected and blew off in the heated wind, several advertising a strip club nearby. Nathan stopped one with his shoe. "XXX XXX XXX. Two drink minimum, third one free." Another skittered by and he caught a glimpse of

"Raven, Mistress of the . . ." He looked up the avenue at where the lines of buildings and traffic converged, down toward the Financial District and Union Square. The streets of an alien city. Daniel had walked on them that last day. His father was out there somewhere now (in his winter coat and laborer's cap). Each of them on separate tracks, coming no closer no matter how anyone moved. A green, late-model sedan pulled up and Nathan got in.

"You look like shit," Rivera said.

"Nice to see you, too."

Rivera pulled into traffic without signaling, shifted lanes smoothly. Nathan, an aggressive city driver, given to sudden accelerations and lane changes, was impressed by how calmly Rivera maneuvered the big car through traffic. He wore sunglasses and a different suit, was otherwise exactly as he'd been the day before yesterday, and Nathan, who'd had enough surprises, found this a welcome quality. He was almost glad to see him.

"So what's your best guess?" Rivera said.

"Mine? I don't know this place."

"Not the place, your father. Where would he go?"

Nathan thought. The image of Sol, hulking, overdressed, lugging a box of ashes through the streets, came to him, but what street, heading where, he couldn't say.

"I don't know. A cemetery? A park?"

"How about a synagogue?"

"Not my father."

They were weaving up and down the avenues, Leavenworth, Taylor, Jones, cruising several blocks on Geary, O'Farrell, Turk, before turning a corner and trying another. Rivera didn't actively look around, though Nathan guessed he was trained to see what was there. Nathan himself felt compelled to twist every which way to see down alleys, into storefronts, the sit-down counters of restaurants. Occasionally a street person, some gray-headed old guy in a dark coat or slouch cap, caught his eye, but no one close to Sol.

"What did your father know of the circumstances?"

"You mean did I tell him what you told me?"

"Which was a mistake, by the way. A total breach. I've regretted it ever since."

Nathan looked over at him. Rivera kept his eyes on the street, one hand easily moving the wheel. Nathan glanced around the car. Was this a department vehicle? Family car? Immaculate, like Rivera's desk, no traces of home or family, no telltale signs of police usage, either, fast-food wrappers, or paper coffee cups. Nathan remembered all the sports photos and posters over the inspectors' desks, and Rivera's corner walls, bare, the D.A.R.E. poster, probably somebody else's idea, on the filing cabinet nearby.

"I appreciate it," Nathan said.

Rivera turned toward him a moment, looked back at the road. Nathan did as well.

"Yeah, I told him. Briefly."

He had been on his way out of the hospital room. Sol was too tired to talk to him, though he didn't look it, had told him to come back. When Nathan had walked in he'd been appalled to see the curtain between the beds drawn back, a pale, unconscious boy exposed in the other bed, an upsetting sight to anyone, and he'd had half a mind to complain to the nurse. He'd been rebuffed. He'd run up the stairs with news, and Sol didn't want to hear it. Annoyed, Nathan had muttered, taking his jacket, "He was out looking for drugs. Got himself killed." Whatever reaction he'd hoped to incite by saying this—interest, anger, surprise—he was too annoyed by Sol's self-involvement to wait around and see it.

Having driven up and down the streets in a crosshatch movement, Rivera crossed Market and began the same prowl up Howard to Seventh, down Folsom to Third. The neighborhood was a confusing mix, boutiques and upscale businesses on one block, squalid apartments and empty lots on the next. In his weary, unfocused state, Nathan thought he saw people throwing things from a build-

ing. There must be a fire, tables, a bed being heaved from a
window. But Rivera didn't notice, and Nathan realized it was some
gigantic piece of urban art, the entire building—tables and chairs, a
bathtub, a reading lamp, all suspended in midair, attached by wires.
Messages he didn't read scrawled on the ground floor.

"You think Sol went looking . . . How would he know where to
go? I wouldn't have a clue, how would he?"

Rivera shrugged. "Let's keep driving."

Rivera got on the radio twice and asked someone if there were
any reports. The radio blared twice back, absolute gibberish to
Nathan, and once Rivera spoke on his cell, about another case entirely, as far as Nathan could deduce.

Outside, the medley you'd expect on the fringes of a city,
perhaps varied more than usual by the encroachment of renewal.
Office types entered a warehouse, revamped into a tony athletic
club. An antiques dealer moved statuary onto the sidewalk and latte
drinkers sat at delicate wire tables outside a Starbucks. Alongside
these, street people pushed shopping carts, stood off to the side in
groups, slept in doorways under cardboard or filthy blankets. It was
preposterous, Sol carrying the box through these streets, looking for
what? Where it happened? His son's killer? It made no sense. At a
vacant lot, Rivera pulled over. Nathan saw nothing in the lot but
rubble, the distinctive urban ruin of bricks and bent rebar, weeds,
tires, dirt piled to one side, a shopping cart upended, wheels in the
air. Nathan had no idea why Rivera had stopped, then saw, at the far
end, near the base of an apartment building, a body low against the
wall. Nathan's chest clenched and he had started to open the door
and stand when the body moved, and a face, black, and a coat not
near the color of Sol's came into view. Elaborate and artful graffiti,
puffy silver loops and darting blue angles, covered the wall behind
the man. Nathan stared but couldn't make out a word.

"Okay," Rivera said.

After an hour, going as far west as the Civic Center, east into the

Financial District, around the edges of Chinatown, Rivera pulled up again in front of Nathan's hotel. He took off his sunglasses, checked his watch, picked up the cell phone from the console and hit a button.

"It's me," he said. "Still nothing?"

He waited, listening, then said, "What about the outlying districts? He could have taken a bus."

Rivera nodded some more, listening. "The airport? Okay," he said, "thanks," and closed the phone.

He shook his head at Nathan. "Nothing. We sent a description around, no one's seen him. That doesn't mean anything, in fact, it's good, probably. If he'd been hurt, run down, someone would have been called. He's probably out walking. I suggest you just wait until he decides to call or come back." He looked Nathan up and down, Daniel's ill-fitting clothes. "A little sleep wouldn't kill you either."

Nathan looked at him. He was handsome, his neat features and cleft chin and dark eyes, his perfectly combed hair. Altogether he seemed a genuinely nice guy, competent, someone whom Nathan normally would have admired, envied his assurance and easy diligence. Rivera, Nathan sensed, would never allow his life to get as painfully muddled as Nathan's was. Rivera, looking back up the street, rubbed his eyes with two fingers, and Nathan thought maybe he hadn't gotten much sleep himself. Too tired to think of a preamble, Nathan put a hand on the door to get out and said, "Any news?"

Rivera had a hand up to his chin and rubbed first one side then the other with the backs of his fingers, as if checking for stubble. "We're not going down that road again, are we?" he said.

"No," Nathan promised. He held up both hands. "Look, no pencils." He put them down. "I'm just asking."

Rivera checked his watch, looked in the rearview mirror. "We may have some new information." A huge SUV cruised slowly by, hoisted high over its wheels, chrome additions to the fenders and hood. The driver, a young Latino in sunglasses, gazed impassively out the window. Nathan thought he saw Rivera flick his chin up in disgust. "There were three other shootings that day, two in the same general area. We're looking to see if they were in any way related."

Nathan remembered something about the shootings in the papers when they'd arrived. "Gang Spree Kills Two, Several Wounded." He'd connected the date but it hadn't occurred to him one of those might be Daniel.

"But the other day you said he went out looking . . ."

"I know what I said, and I shouldn't have said it." He looked back at Nathan, unfriendly now. "You pissed me off, Doctor. You got under my skin, which, I also shouldn't tell you, isn't easy to do. I said a lot I shouldn't have."

Nathan waited.

"In our interview with Miss Morris she said some things about the victim being troubled about drug activity at her son's school. He made some remarks to her on the phone that led her, then us, to believe he might have set out with a specific intention."

"And now?"

Rivera ran a hand across his chin, again the backs of the fingers. "Now we don't know."

"And the gun?"

"No bullets. Never fired."

Nathan closed his eyes, opened them, as if trying to wake himself.

"You said he went out of his own neighborhood. Why would he do that?"

"Miss Morris now indicates your brother was living nearby at the time. Apparently had been for some weeks."

"I don't understand."

Rivera lifted a hand to the wheel, moved it as if he were already driving. "That's all I know. Apparently he moved out prior to the night of the incident."

Sylvia Grossman. Janet. Abby—could he find the number? Sol. Check the messages. All the things he needed to do crowded in on Nathan along with the simultaneous knowledge he was too drained and weary to choose which first. At least upstairs he could wait by the phone.

"Thank you," he said.

Rivera, his sunglasses back on, made a quick motion with his chin. As he got out, Nathan couldn't tell if it was acknowledgment or the same derisive gesture he'd directed at the kid in the SUV.

∾ ∾ ∾

They'd taken Ben to an amusement park up the coast one time, a charming decrepit facility in the redwoods, organized around fairy tales. It had a slide coming out of the Old Woman's shoe, a tunnel emerging in Alice's underworld. Humpty Dumpty forever tottering on his wall, Snow White asleep in their hut while nearby the Dwarfs mined Day-Glo ore and glittering gems strewn on a cave floor. The Crooked Man's house was at crazy angles, smaller at one end, though you couldn't tell this until you walked through and the ceiling and walls pressed in. Abby sat at the table in her apartment and had a similar sensation now, the room looming and falling back. As in some trick focus shot in a movie, she, in the middle of it, didn't move at all, watched Ben's red cereal bowl, its spoon at an angle, two green Froot Loops in a splash of milk to one side.

When she was little, her mother had loved telling her stories of her own life, how she'd met her dad, how they'd found this perfect house while out driving, how Abby herself had emerged from a magical trip east to Chicago, where her father's family lived, a Christmas Eve celebration, champagne glasses in the snow, which Louisa was seeing for the first time in her life. As a small girl, Abby was delighted by these tales, nestled warmly in their narrative weave, each event in her family's life charmed, ordained, predisposed toward the happiness they all now shared.

Her own life hadn't played out this way, and even when she was younger, hadn't left home but was preparing to, she had been nagged by certain insistent questions. What if Dad hadn't decided, at the last minute, to come to that dance with his cousin? What if driving that day they'd turned down a different street? What if Dad's family didn't live in Chicago, or it didn't snow that night, or instead of taking the champagne out to the backyard they'd drunk it instead and passed out on Grandmother Morris's couch, watching that awful Jimmy-Stewart-on-the-bridge movie? Who got to choose these tidy little homilies with their ever-after endings, who got to pick the cast and settings and the arc of gratifying event? Not Abby. How did you join them, her mother's crew—the allotted, the willfully blind, the contented? Abby had dreams sometimes of breaking into her own parents' home, not taking anything, just walking through the rooms and looking.

The expression in that woman's face, Ben's teacher, the smug, entreating kindliness—we all wish you so well, Abigail. Why must you disappoint us? And Ben, afraid, or too angry—she couldn't tell which anymore—to look at her as she left.

It sat there in the middle of the table, right where he'd tossed it, glassine dull in the light, its red edge vibrating in her vision against the worn grain of the wood. That druggie friend of Daniel's, Medium, had brought some white powder from New York, Abby still remembered the gleeful chuckling, like two boys over a porno magazine. Daniel must have hidden it for later, forgotten. Now here it was, Abby's own looking glass, her own well to fall into.

Of course she would have taken him back. Wasn't it clear she loved him—could anything be clear if that wasn't? But it wasn't Daniel anymore, he was back on the stuff, he'd made his decision. She couldn't go through it again, the nodding distance, the shambling movements, the middle-of-the-night sweats, water pouring off him, waking to find him gone. Everything directed at himself and his pain—getting well, he called it, just gotta get well. By leaving them? Running back to the shit? She laughed in his face, in its strain of sickness and despair, a rebuke to anything she might say. Go, then, she'd thought, get fucking well. It was insane—how did staying with them turn into being sick? What was so bad here he needed to escape, recover from? Though she knew, knew for herself looking around the room and its dingy clutter, cleaning had only made it worse, and she knew from Daniel, from looking at him shouldering the heavier and heavier load through the years. Who was finally kidding who?

But you didn't give me a chance. I would have taken you back, you idiot, I would have held you and cleaned you up and I would have loved you. I would have taken you back.

And his brother, who was he to accuse? In honesty, had he? It seemed they'd talked for hours but she hadn't any real sense of what was said. She'd accused *him*, the brother, hearing the words, though it was the last thing she wanted, directed at herself. You hurt him. You let him down. When he needed you, you told him not to come back, you'd had enough, everyone had finally had enough. Does the boy miss me? What about Ben? Miss what, she'd said, how do you miss a ghost? Daniel had said nothing, and a few moments later he'd hung up, these were the last words they'd spoken. There's nothing for you here, she had told him, and those words, too, in the funhouse her brain had become, ricocheted back at her—nothing for you here, Miss Abigail Morris, not widowed, not orphaned, not penitent, not free. Not here. How do you miss a ghost? Who else is there?

And the ache, which never strayed far, hovering, a nimbus of dark hurt, moved closer now, enveloping her, hard as a shell with the sharp points inside, pressing until the walls and floor and ceiling crowded in, until her breath wouldn't come and all she could see was the packet on the table, prescription the nice doctor had left her.

∾ ∾ ∾

In Jerusalem, their last trip together, Sol and Freda had seen a holy man's funeral. They had been walking, the day was hot, and, becoming aware of some commotion on the street approaching theirs, had stopped gratefully against a wall and watched. The body was on some kind of stretcher, wrapped in white cloth, so you could almost make out the features. He was carried by bearded young men in dark suits and followed by a throng of the faithful, and the intensity of their grief almost colored the air around them. There were few sounds, the hushed shuffling of feet, an occasional word exclaimed in lamentation. Every mouth was busy in prayer. The people on the full street—day laborers, students, tourists, young soldiers with rifles at their hips—all stood back. Some even began praying themselves. Sol, who didn't realize he was so winded, caught his breath with difficulty. The city's famous light, the way it fell just so on the whitened stones and arches, the far-off hills, had not softened this day, and if he could not see the sun he could feel it, swelling, gathering even more strength. He watched the bier and the attending crowd, brought up in the rear by a ragtag group of children whose skipping to keep pace contended with the solemn looks they felt obliged to wear. He was overcome by the heat.

The gall of these religious, hoisting a body through the streets. From the back, they could have been pushing forward to see a ball game, a parade. He could feel the acid taste of contempt on his tongue.

It was a mistake to choose this time for a walk. Freda, whose heart could not be taxed so, should not be out in midday. When the procession had passed—a lone boy in sidelocks and a huge dark yarmulke looking back just before he disappeared around the corner— Sol took Freda's hand and prepared a knowing remark or two before guiding her back to their room. In New York there were religious, but they didn't get to Sol the way these people did, and while at home he kept most of his comments to himself, in part because he knew they upset Freda, here it was a different matter. They acted as if they owned the place, as if their sloppy grieving was everyone's, as if it wasn't obvious to anyone with a clear, rational view . . .

He had turned and opened his mouth to speak, but stopped, astonished, to see Freda's face wet with crying, her lips moving around silent words. He stopped, stunned, and waited quietly till she was done, his head filled with a confused buzzing and the pressure in his chest—he had no idea why—gradually easing as he watched. When she was ready, which she let him know by a single glance, in the shorthand communication they'd developed over forty years together, he walked her back, forgetting entirely the cutting remark about the ostentatious and vulgar religious. He kept hold of her hand and did not let go until they were in the chilled dark well of the hotel lobby.

By now Sol should have been used to the crazy streets here, at least no longer surprised at the startling inclines and dizzying views. But he was. He had to pause every few steps, and when he looked around to find his bearings, the opposite happened—he was disoriented, sometimes a bit sick, the thinnest edge of panic (what if he got lost, really lost?) wedging into his chest. The box was unwieldy, too big, too heavy to carry in one hand, though not big enough to hold up to your chest. Sol bore it in front of him like a waiter presenting a dish, or a participant in some obscure rite. The red plastic warmed and grew slippery with sweat, and he had queasy presentiments he might fall, he and the open box rolling down one of these ridiculous streets until a trolley smashed them, a car sent them flying, until they sank into the cold, churning water.

At one point he sat in the park they had passed two days ago, looking for the crooning *shvartzer* in the white suit. He paused to get his breath on an overpass and stared at the dark street below— Pete's Cleaner, Taqueria, Foreign Exchange. Green Door Massage: Incall, Outcall. He passed a playground with signs in Chinese and English, children scrambling on an elaborate green-and-yellow climbing fort, a mural on a brick wall of a boy riding a dragon,

his expression—whether exultant or terrified—unreadable to Sol.
At the bottom of the plunging streets, far below, a bridge, not the
red one but blockier, gray, tacked across the horizon like a backdrop, and he looked up to see the white spire of the triangle-shaped
building, the one he'd seen Nathan, who could get lost finding his
keys, looking at as they walked.

Finally he was exhausted. He'd walked an hour, maybe two. For
some reason all the streets were uphill, unless he turned around,
which he stubbornly refused to consider, and his breath was raw in
his throat, his pulse pounding uncomfortably loud in his ears.
Thick air blew from the water, hard to grab into your lungs. He
stretched his shoulder and neck. It was hot. Better find a place to sit.
Better eat the crackers they'd given him and the pills he had in his
pocket. The red box slipped several inches and he barely caught it
before it fell from his hands.

He had left the room quickly, resolutely, as if he knew exactly
what to do. Now, after walking through half the city, reaching clumsily up with a coat sleeve to wipe sweat from his dripping face, he
had no idea.

He had found his way from the hospital, only a few blocks to the
hotel, and by the time he opened the door, expecting to find
Nathan passed out in his bed—he'd had liquor on his breath when
he'd run into Sol's room the day before—his rage was so strong it
tinted his vision. He thought he might strike his son for the first
time in years—leave an old man like a fool for everyone to stare at,
every nurse and orderly and cleaning person in the place poking a
head in to ask was he okay, could they get him anything, was there
a number to call. I'm waiting for my son, Sol told them at first,
then, No, thank you. By the end, when he'd shuddered awake from
a heated, uncomfortable nap to find himself still on the hospital
bed, no sign of Nathan, he'd simply risen, grabbed the small bag
they'd given him, and, without a word to anybody, walked out the
door. Had Nathan been asleep, Sol might actually have done it,

gone over and beat him with a fist—he could see it, could see himself walking over and pummeling the boy's smug cantankerous face. He was ready for it. And God knows, the sonofabitch deserved it.

But the room was empty, Nathan not there. Both beds were still made, as if neither had been slept in last night, and Sol was taken briefly with the odd notion that he had somehow let himself in the wrong door, when he saw, under the small table with the phone, a piece of paper. Stooping to grab it brought back the pain in his shoulder, and he sat on the edge of Nathan's bed, rubbing as close to the spot as he could reach. "Janet, I'm sorry," he read, in Nathan's heedless scrawl. Janet who? He didn't remember any Janet. Sol pressed the shoulder, then the side of his neck, which had stiffened in the hospital. He read the words again, shaking his head. Nathan might never finish any other part of his doctor's training, but the handwriting he had mastered. He was about to put the paper on Nathan's side of the night table, lie back, and turn on CNN, maybe get his first real rest since leaving New York, when the light in the partially opened closet caught his eye. Something inside had shifted, forcing open the door. Their two bags, stacked on the metal rack, Sol's extra clothes. But something was different, the suitcases at an angle. They'd been moved. The piece of paper fell to the floor as Sol got up to take a closer look.

ↀ ↀ ↀ

It wasn't like he'd never done it before, and he thought about it almost every day. Well, he'd done it only once and had gotten in big trouble, the only time his mom and Mrs. Downing were both mad at him together. You need to promise me, his mom kept saying, making him look at her, and Mrs. Downing stood there like she wouldn't believe him no matter what he said, so he said it, I promise, and his mom shook him by the shoulder and said, Do you? Do

you understand this is serious? and Ben said, Yes and I promise and
I'm sorry, and Mrs. Downing looked like she thought he was lying,
and he couldn't believe he had ever thought she was nice. His
mother let go of his shoulder and when he looked at her again he
could see she was scared and Ben was worried she would start to cry
and then that was all he could think about—getting her out of the
schoolyard, where she'd dragged him when she'd found him a block
away, running, late as usual to pick him up.

So, today, when she was late again, he prepared himself, just in
case. A group of boys, mostly bigger kids, but including Shane Wu
and another boy from his grade whose name Ben didn't know, were
allowed to walk home together. Ben didn't understand why he
wasn't allowed, since he couldn't live farther than they did, but he
guessed no one lived on his block, he'd never seen anybody from
school there. And when he asked his mom about it one time—
Could he walk home with some other kids?—she'd gotten that
funny look in her eyes, like he was saying something he didn't
mean to say at all, and she said, No, honey, Mommy will pick you
up. But she didn't. Half the time he was the last one here, except for
Phoebe Alvarez and her ugly sister, whose mom worked in the library and who sat on the school steps, reading, and wouldn't talk to
him anyway. Today even they weren't here. He didn't notice until
the file of cars in front of the fence thinned out and the parents
(never his mom) who stopped to talk while their kids played tag or
kickball had called them over and left. Then he saw that the steps
were empty, and when the janitor carried out the black garbage
bags he didn't stop to pull candy from his pockets for Phoebe and
her sister with a finger raised to his lips, meaning, Don't tell, It's our
secret, and Phoebe's sister, who already had hair on her lip, would
let out a giggle you could hear all the way across the yard. Well, today even they weren't here, and the janitor heaved the bags into the
Dumpster like he was angry and went back inside, slamming the
big green door. A group of teachers, Mrs. Downing was one, stood

by the school entrance, talking, and besides Ben there were only
about six kids left. He didn't enjoy soccer, wasn't much good at it,
but that was what they were doing, Shane Wu and the rest, and
when Shane Wu chased the ball nearby, Ben ran over and joined
in, just in case.

One time he and Danny and his mom had driven to the beach.
It wasn't a holiday that he knew of, or anybody's birthday, but that
morning his mom had woken him with a smile and said, Hey,
sleepyhead, you don't want to miss the beach, do you? and for a
minute he thought he'd forgotten they had planned a trip and he
wondered how that could happen, but then he saw her smiling and
she reached out to his hair and he knew she was joking with him.
Come on, she said, wash up and we'll go.

It was Ben's favorite beach, smaller than the one near the
bridge, though you could see the bridge from here, too, burnt-
looking red, strong between the high green rocks. One time he'd
seen the whole thing disappear in clouds and he couldn't believe it.
All you could see was the red tower at one end, not at the other, and
the whole bridge was gone, like magic. Ben had stared at the fog for
he didn't know how long, till his ears stung and his nose ran and finally his mom came and nudged him to head up the beach toward
the cable car and home. He couldn't believe it, amazing that something so big could be erased like it was never there at all. He
couldn't wait to tell Danny. He couldn't remember where Danny
was that time.

But this day wasn't foggy and the bridge was bright in the blue
sky and Ben could see the tops of cars skimming along. They'd
brought Frisbees and his baseball glove. He wasn't good at sports,
but it seemed important to Danny and his mom that he enjoy playing, so he tried, and when he missed, he chased the ball into the
cold foamy surf, and that was fun. They ate fried chicken and potato salad and baked beans, and Danny and his mom had beer and
Danny made a game about drinking his bottle and switching it with

his mom's, as if she'd finished first, but she knew what he was doing and finally she got on top of him and held him down and called Ben over and they had Danny nearly covered in sand, his legs and one arm and most of his body, when he opened his eyes and growled, grabbed Ben and lifted him high in the air.

Ben was climbing at the far end of the beach, where weird crabs with one big claw ran under wet rocks and orange starfish almost the color of his own palms stuck to the sides of the freezing pools. He tried feeding a piece of seaweed to a crab, but it wasn't interested, and he tried setting a small crab on a starfish, just to see what would happen, but it scuttled off. He began carefully peeling the starfish from the rock, working gently from the tips in, delighted and a little scared at the feel of the cold live thing in his hand. He had it ready to show them, held it in both hands, which made climbing off the rocks pretty hard, but he managed.

He didn't need to get very close to know everything had changed. They weren't lying together like when he'd left and they were talking but not looking at each other, his mom on a towel facing the water, Danny throwing things in the bag, and if Ben couldn't hear any words he didn't need to and he stopped where they didn't see him and waited.

Sometimes when he waited, in his room, or at the table, they would remember him, and Danny would make a joke out of it and his mom would pull him into her lap and they would all make a game of pretending nothing had happened, which was a silly game but alright with Ben. But other times, like today, they kept going, and Ben thought of what he could do (he was too big to cry, though that was the need he felt hardening in his chest), but nothing he did ever worked anyway, so he watched until he was certain they would not stop—his mom had the towel wrapped tight around her legs now and was not talking anymore, Danny still throwing things, books, bags of food, Ben's glove, at the beach bag, shaking out towels like he was hitting something in the wind. Ben looked around,

at the water, at the rocks, at the trees that led from the parking lot
where they had left the red car. It was these he made for, as angry as
they were, forgetting the starfish he had brought to show them until
its gritty pulp mashed in his fingers and without looking he let it
drop into the sand.

∾ ∾ ∾

The phone rang four times, twelve, eighteen, twenty-five times. Listening to its rasping cry, Nathan imagined the sound in each of the
apartment's three rooms, not as they were now (emptied, stuff scattered like trash), but as he'd left them. The living room with its sagging bookshelves, CDs haphazardly on the floor in front of the
stereo, the throw rug near the sealed fireplace. Janet's novel on the
couch, P. D. James or Ruth Rendell, the lacy bookmark her sister
had made for her when she left for school holding her place. His
pile of journals, books. In the kitchen, two coffee mugs on the
round table, Sunday's paper, mostly unread, on the windowsill. In
the dishrack, wineglasses and plates from last night's meal, in the refrigerator leftover Chinese they'd figured to eat sometime the following week; above, in the freezer, vodka and pints of Cherry
Garcia, Janet's late-night vice and sleep aid. Their bedroom.
Through the window, Nathan imagined the fat man across the
street, still happy with his new hat and jacket, climbing slowly down
his steps.

Nathan wondered, if he stood here forever, or just left the receiver dangling, how long would the phone in Boston ring? How
long before some operator somewhere between here and there cut
in and requested that he hang up or redial? How long before a computer someplace decided he was taking up valuable line? Or till Angelo, their super, came in with his key and angrily slammed down
the phone? Maybe it would just go on, hours, days, weeks. Maybe
right now across America there were hundreds of phones ringing in
empty rooms where no one lived anymore and where no one would

be hurrying back to pick them up and say, Hello, sorry, are you still there?

At thirty-six rings Nathan roused himself with a shudder. The hotel faced another dingy apartment house, the color of dirty talc. In one window, a small boy in a striped T-shirt, elbows propped, looked down at the street, occasionally aiming a spitball at passersby. Two floors higher an elderly woman in a flowered housedress positioned a parakeet in its cage and a single stalky geranium on the sill of one window—it was growing even hotter—and sat with a drugstore box of chocolates in the other. He had Shelby's number, he could call Janet there, even if she'd asked him not to. The wallowing music, the tea and starcharts. Hi. Just wanted to check in. Miss you.

The crumpled paper he had picked up from the floor was on the table in front of him. He closed his eyes. If he could just smooth his mind, get clear one single moment, maybe he could lie down, clean sheets around him, the traffic and the cable-car bells far off in the street. If he could only sleep. The edges of his vision shimmered with a brightness, the aura of hallucination. He'd been exhausted many times, but not like this. He'd sat with patients experiencing panic attacks and they told him the first sign was movement at the edges of everything, colors slightly too vivid, the sense of the world shifting on its own around you. He turned the paper over and read the number. This time the phone was answered after one crisp ring.

"Mrs. Grossman?"

"Yes?"

"Nathan Mirsky."

"From Los Angeles?"

"San Francisco, yes. How are you?"

"Oh, Nathan, thank you for calling. I didn't expect . . ."

There was a silence over the line, as if, even talking to him on the phone, she was pausing to arrange her hair, straighten her clothes.

"Yes, Mrs. Grossman, I just wanted to assure you." His measured professional voice, intact, surprised him. "Everything is alright."

"Is it? I'm so glad." Her voice lifted, he heard her smile. "And Sol? Have they let him out of the hospital?"

"He's fine. He's napping right now or I'm sure he would tell you himself."

"Oh, don't wake him."

Nathan had only been in one apartment in the building, his parents', yet he could see, as if he'd been there a dozen times, Sylvia Grossman's rooms, the deep-backed old-fashioned sofa with its crocheted afghan folded over an arm, the low table with a glass bowl of fruit. The bookshelves full of Herman Wouk, Harry Levin, works on Israeli archeology and heroism, the nest of framed photographs on the table by the door. The bathrooms immaculate, in case anybody should drop by; the kitchen stocked, though she fed only one these days, and the big bed in the bedroom made up each morning, both sides, as if both sides had been warmed and rumpled with use during the night. Her husband had had cancer, long terrible stages of decline. Nathan's mother, who litanized the health of everyone she knew, had shared it with her son, the doctor.

"Good idea," Nathan said. "I'll let him sleep."

Again a quiet shuffling, and Nathan, without even trying, or not trying hard enough to evade it, saw her pat the front of her blouse for wrinkles, check that her hair was contained in its bun. "And the other?" she said.

The other. Other what? Other day, other time, otherwise. But he knew what she meant. Daniel.

"Oh, that's been straightened out, Mrs. Grossman. Not to worry. Sol can tell you about it when he gets home."

A new tone in her voice, melodious, cheerful. "Maybe you could come to a small meal, Nathan, nothing fancy, when you get back. I'd like to invite you and your father. Will you be staying in New York any time? You'll be hungry after your trip."

Dear old lady. As if they didn't have food in California. Come to think of it, besides the bagel and muffin earlier at Abby's, he'd barely eaten since he got off the plane. "Of course," he said. "It would be a pleasure." And he was almost ready to shake himself of her image, a neatly dressed, gray-haired woman standing by the window of an apartment house off Queens Boulevard, in Forest Hills, New York City. But she went on.

"So what shall I make? Tell me what you like best."

"What's your specialty?"

"People enjoy my roasts."

"There you go." His head was wobbly under its own weight. He forced himself to keep his eyes open, as if, at any moment on the street below, he'd see Sol in his brown coat moving forward, holding a red box before him.

She was still talking. "I'll get beer. You young people like beer, don't you?"

He loved beer, Nathan told her, beer and one of her roasts would be terrific, and after another question or two she was satisfied and made him promise to take care of himself. And his father. He hung up. In the street below, a small black man rubbed the back of his neck and looked up at the building opposite, toward the empty window where the boy had been, a filthy curtain hanging motionless. The parakeet, charged by the view, as if he'd seen it all, called hysterically and flapped in its cage, but the man didn't look at him, just kept rubbing his neck as he walked away. The woman reached over and gave the cage a slap, which silenced the bird, and she sat back with the box of chocolates angled toward the light, as if showing Nathan her selection. She chose one, held it daintily in two fingers, and brought it to her open mouth.

The boy, smirking nearby (why no school?), would be back. The woman was here every day, the parakeet and the spindled red flower. The same man would walk here tomorrow, feel the warm splat on his neck, look up and wonder, give it up and walk away. This was their dance. One more vision to shake himself free of.

Nathan stood quietly, unmoving except to breathe. The world

around him had grown sheer, brittle, a complicated balance miraculously poised against chaos. One wrong move and he would topple, taking it all with him. To see what came next he didn't need to
close his eyes, but he did.

The stairway would be the same, badly lit, musty, and though
Angelo painted the banisters and walls every other year, it retained
the smell of old newspaper and reheated food. The obese tabby,
hard to call it a stray, would be asleep on the mat outside 2F, front
paws curled complacently about some treasure from the street.
Nathan would drag his suitcase up three flights, so tired—drove all
night to get here—he wanted to drop it anywhere and sleep, but
he'd keep going till he reached their floor, their door the last on the
left, the sprig of dried flowers she hung when they moved in still
holding its shape below the painted apartment number. Inside,
she'd be waiting. Just showered, in his worn college robe, the faded
red plaid, hair tucked in a turban of blue towel, face scrubbed fresh
and gleaming. Finally, he'd made the right choice. He barely made
it, but he was here now and he could hardly restrain himself from
running over to her and taking her in his arms. Jesus, Janet, oh jesus, I'm so sorry, there's so much I want to say.

But here Nathan's vision flags, and as Janet without expression
stands there, arms at her sides, he drops the heavy suitcase to the
floor and stops, hardly inside the doorway. She looks at him, he
pauses, then looks away. He can think of nothing to say to her.
Nothing at all.

∾ ∾ ∾

"You lost?" Shane Wu asked.

They were barely out of the schoolyard. All Mrs. Downing had
to do was look over and she'd see them. Ben shook his head. When
Shane didn't respond he shook it again and said, "No," and another
boy put a shoulder into Shane, who almost dropped his book bag.

"Whatever, man," Shane Wu said, flicking the black hair from his eyes. "Let's go." Ben followed at a short distance, willing himself not to look back at the school.

That day at the beach he hadn't been lost, either. There was a tree by the parking lot Ben had seen, a branch going out and up like a signal. The sun came in through thick piney leaves, and the smell was good, a little like the water, a little like the shade. The sand was soft, and from behind the tree he could see the whole parking lot and some of the beach, and no one, he was certain, could see him.

Cars pulled in, people climbed from the beach, loaded up and drove away. It was maybe half an hour before Ben saw his mom, a hand over her sunglasses and looking around at the cars. He could tell she was calling because he recognized the way she moved her mouth, but wind blew her voice back toward the water, and it was like she was in a dream or a movie where you try to talk but no sound comes out. She left but was back soon, with Danny this time, and then other people were looking too, calling out Ben, Benjamin, which nobody but his teacher ever called him, and Ben was just about ready to come out. The sun had moved and the sand was cold under his feet. His mom, when she passed the last time, was crying, and Danny looked like he might start, too. Good, Ben thought. They stood near the red car and Danny put his arms on her shoulders, but she shook them off, angry, and they went back to calling him and walking toward the beach. Ben had had visions of staying all night (except he hadn't brought any food), of digging a hole to sleep in (except the sand was packed down harder than he expected). He didn't have any toys, which was a little-kid thing to think about but he couldn't help it. He was cold and hungry, and making his mom scared was never as much fun as he planned for it to be. An old couple was looking now, the man's bony legs in striped shorts, the lady in pants and a jacket the color of cotton candy, taking small, old-people steps back and forth in the parking lot.

He would come out, but not yet. He wasn't ready. He had a feeling the longer he stayed the bigger the chances something might change—he didn't know what—and if this idea scared him, it excited him, too. He imagined he could live here if he chose to, in these trees, he'd find some water, he could steal food from the baskets. He imagined the police coming, and the army, angry-sounding soldiers in trucks shining big lights and helicopters overhead, broadcasting his name. The old man was saying in a weak, twisty voice, "Benjamin, Benjamin," which nobody ever called him, and the lady stopped and looked right at him but didn't see a thing. He could stay here forever. Soon the fog would come in, huge pillows of it, and Ben imagined people would come to this spot and say, It was here, right here where he disappeared. The lady turned when her husband toddled over, and he heard her old-lady worried voice. "Howard, where is that boy?" she said, and Ben, hunkering down behind the signaling tree, whispered, He's gone, lady. You'll never find him.

∿ ∿ ∿

Abby thought it was lost, but she lay facedown on the floor and pushed her hand under the bed and there it was, deep in the dust and fallen paper. The chipped gilded mirror, razor blade tucked behind it, a still-familiar weight in her lap. She tapped out the packet, chopped four thick lines, plenty, more than she would need, and tightly rolled a dollar bill. She bent toward the mirror, the first line hitting like a warm memory. Right, she said out loud. Right. The second settled where the first had gone, in her shoulders and the back of her neck, below the skull, in a soothing, flooding surge through her chest and arms, in the muscles of her face which she hadn't realized were clenched until they yielded as the world pulled back, softening, her breathing from far off and from close by in some obscure cadence with the shimmering light outside, and

sounds—water? birds?—lifting from the street. When she stood she
was entirely weightless, her clothing slipped to the floor and her
arms out at the shoulders as if she would indeed float free of the
ground. The third line she didn't remember doing, so she did the
fourth, and now where she was there were no ghosts, no questions
without answers, head swaying deliciously on a bolster of light,
empty, empty, mouth in joy and forgetfulness dropped open, the
face in the mirror smiling tenderly, and all she had to do was let go
and tumble, any minute now she would. Let go. Fall.

∽ ∽ ∽

He couldn't walk another step. He'd stumbled once already, a
young woman rushing over with a concerned look, holding him by
the arm (the good one, thank God), saying, Are you alright? Maybe
you should sit down. No, Sol told her, restraining the urge to shake
her roughly off, I'm fine. He thanked her and got to his feet. Somehow he hadn't dropped the box, which had somehow lost the white
tag on its lid, and when he turned the corner away from the
woman, vision swarming in reds and yellows, angry black dots, there
it was, towering white walls and stony cross in the air. He needed to
sit down, that was all. He made his way up two side steps and, unsure if he had the strength, pulled open the carved wooden door.

A hush in the huge chamber, dim vaulted arches receding, windows throbbing blue and red, whites shimmering painfully with
sun. Sol had never been in a church in his life, would have preferred a restaurant, a gas station, a deli where he could sit a minute
in front of a fan. In here it was like nothing so much as a tomb, thin
voices from the few people ahead of him swallowed in the vast
space, two men in dark robes arranging a white table in a practiced
pantomime, stopping to kneel in prayer.

This was no place for him. Just let him sit a minute and he
would get out. At least in here a person could breathe, and he

thought he might close his eyes, rest them a quiet moment. The organ surprised him, long silver pipes arrayed like faceless men in armor, lifting breathily light trills of melody, trickling like water across Sol's burning face and neck. Maybe just one minute to close his eyes. In the empty last pew he would put down the box and take off his coat, which swayed with perspiration.

But before he could sit the music changed, took on a different cast. First a high note held like an intake of breath, then falling in a tumble it swelled, grew louder, sprouting chords piled on each other, climbing, weaving without pause in a clamor of chaos and deafening confusion that had Sol clenching his jaw and fighting the urge to cover his ears. Every few moments the chaos abated, held place like a wave at its crest, before collapsing again in a braided flurry of notes that made his head spin, ringed his closed eyes with visions of yellow light. He forced his eyes open to see if anyone else was so affected, but ahead three ladies chatted amiably and the priests were at their work, preparing the shrouded table, as if there were no sound, no music at all. It's me, then, Sol thought, fingering the bottle of pills. I need to get out. But he was rooted to the floor, held, if that was possible, by the sheer scale of the noise. Never had Sol heard a sound like this, his breath lodged solid in his chest and his eyes not knowing what they saw (see this music, he understood, and you would go mad), until the roof must fly off and the windows explode. He had not put the box down or taken off the coat, and anxious now for his next breath, which seemed delivered awkwardly from someplace near his back, he held himself in bated fear. And still it grew, chords scaling one another demonically, ringing off the walls, the silver, faceless regiment, black slashes for mouths, trembling just slightly in their righteous, blistering roar.

Then, abruptly as it had begun, it was over, a shuddering echo making its way through the gloom, then tolling silence. The ladies got up and made their sign, gathered bags, and walked past him in the aisle. One priest spoke to the other, and their voices, after the upheaval, seemed remote. From behind a small platform to one side of the altar a head appeared, and both priests turned to chat until, first stretching a neck stiffened with hunching over the keyboard, the figure sat back down. Like small quick-footed creatures scuttling the high walls, the music started again. The priests were finishing their preparations, laying out last a goblet, neat folded cloths, a silver container on a stand. In a wild moment Sol thought to run up and hand them the box, grimy and streaked with dust. "Take it," he'd say, in Yiddish, knowing they wouldn't understand a word. "Take it. I'm done."

Instead he turned, panic leaping inside him as his feet scuffed gray flagstone, and got one hand on the door. He fumbled with the huge wrought handle as the music gathered force, glanced for the first time beyond the altar at the nave's front wall, where under the glittering window on a red curtain, illuminated, their tortured boy writhed on his cross. Stung, he looked away, foolishly forced the door with his hurt shoulder, and, muttering words he did not recognize, stumbled into the coiled, blinding heat of the city at midday.

My Dear Mrs. Koenig,

First must I apologize for the lengthy delay it has taken me to respond. I am not habitually this way, which I tell you only to express how much your letters touched my emotions, so much so, Mrs. Koenig, that for many days I have been unsure what to write in reply, or how.

I ask myself will it be a comfort to hear that so many, like yourself, have similar such stories? In my heart I am guessing not. I myself have a story not so unlike, Mrs. Koenig, that I too have been unable to speak of to no one but my Freda, and now she's gone, to no living person at all. And yes, it is not a thing you can put down a second, even should we live, you and I, Mrs. Koenig, a hundred years.

What can I say to you? Nothing that would ease the heartbreak for your Nechama Raisa, and I understand, believe me I do, that to ease even a little the pain would be more unbearable for all we have is what to remember and what loss to feel. She sounds, Mrs. Koenig, a brave resourceful young girl. And No, Not For One Minute do I think it foolish to suppose maybe she made it out, is alive, who can say, happy somewhere and safe. Of course, Mrs. Koenig, think of her so, think of your neshomaleh *as free*.

Nobody can understand the chances we took, the circum-

stances we faced. In all the words in all the books I read this comes through the loudest—no one who wasn't there can understand. And what choice was there, Mrs. Koenig? Please, the one thing I am certain of is you can't go on blaming yourself. A roundup is a roundup and you were not wrong in fearing it for what it was. And maybe she did make it, your Nechama Raisa. You did what only a loving mother could do, leaving her with the neighbors was the only blessing you had to give. Never forget this. I would not dare, never, to tell you how to feel, only to blame yourself for loving and doing the best you could by your child—it's hard enough, no, without that?

Perhaps I have said already too much. Words meant only in friendship, and you did write, Mrs. Koenig, asking me.

We have not met face-to-face, and as I am retired from my work and traveling very little it is unlikely we shall have that opportunity. So, if it is not too bold, Mrs. Koenig, I offer my hand, as someone who also has known something like your sorrow. And it is my dearest hope that the memory of your beautiful daughter will bring to you peace, and if not happiness, Mrs. Koenig, then rest.

If there was more I could say, how gladly would I say it.

In comradeship and warm regards,

Solomon I. Mirsky

Then there is that time of night when, long sleepless, the body cedes at last and the mind, released as in sleep to wander, pays no attention to your starved and weak admonitions, No, Not now. His bed in the other room is waiting but he will not sleep tonight. To the north, new and meaningless constellations form and shift, planes in their holding patterns stacked over LaGuardia. Below in the street buses heave up the boulevard and the forsaken sound of garbage-truck brakes signals that this night, too, is passing. Could he forestall it, he would. In his dry mouth the taste of metal. He folds the letter in his lap and without closing his eyes, sits back and dreams.

———

To the young, life is unassailable, fixed. It seems obvious everything will be the way it is forever. The gray room he lives in, the yard with its spiny tree where his mother hangs clothes to dry; the dirt road leading always to town one way, past Kleinot's farm the other. His father at the shop, stooped, dreaming behind the counter while the customer examines yet another bolt of cloth, a third identical packet of pins, every felt hat for winter; in shul disappearing into the yellow tallis, whispering, keening in prayer. His mother, streaked pink from the steaming pot, fishing out some bit for him to taste, falling asleep over her darning by the stove, after all have gone to bed combing out her long hair by the candle while Sol, who she assumes is asleep also, watches from his pallet on the floor. The hook-nosed failed rabbi who teaches cheyder, fingers tormenting his inadequate beard, dead book-blinded eyes alive in sudden rage as he lunges across the table to slap the head of a joking or nodding child. The stable, the tavern for the goyim, the church looming in the square, the pump where ladies stop to rest and men for a smoke. Evenings, Kleinot's outraged geese waddling stiff-necked into the road, distant howling dogs, the wind in the lone oak, the uncountable stars, all night the white-faced moon rolling above his head—these, once as fixed and permanent as they now seemed unlikely, impossibly remote. All had been monumental to Sol, unchangeable, as undeniable as he was to himself in his own skin, his own brain, peering from the eyes in his head.

And primary, most convincing of nature's predominant law, was Chaim: lean, assessing, four years older and still a head taller when Sol stopped growing; startling gray eyes and wild shock of hair, a chance inheritance from the Lublin side of their mother's clan, the fire-eaters, Bundists, musicians, Zionists already in Palestine. (Sol's own sallow Mirsky eyes drawing notice from only his mother, limp straight hair thinning even before the camp.) Chaim, whom even the goyim seemed to know, and approve, who left home at sixteen to join the army, reappeared four months later with money and miraculous stories to tell, who drank vodka with friends he met in town, who argued politics with strangers, who somehow, despite the daily weight of evidence, believed in the Jewish God, a deity of provenance and mercy and alert resourceful care. "Talk to Him," he would tell Sol, some childhood disaster imminent. "Pray. Let Him help." Chaim: taunting, fickle, generous, quick-tempered, sinking for days in a gloom so thick only their mother could approach, and even she did not often try.

Then the day the world stopped. Soldiers in gray trucks and they were pulled from school, dread, not yet taking form, circling in the air above them. Marched to the village square where Lubya, the rabbi's son, had to choose in front of everyone—leave his sisters to the soldiers swilling vodka and singing, or beat his father with a weighted club, his choice, swinging blindly through tears and snot until blood seeped, then poured, from the matted beard, the old man in Yiddish saying, "Good, my good boy, Father loves you." The Jews in rows at the side of the square, no sound but the soldiers' happy cursing and coarse remarks, the weight of the wood on the rabbi's head—it was to Chaim Sol looked in faithfulness of habit, what is this, what was to be done? But Chaim, Adam's apple working and eyes fixed, did not look back. The two long train rides, night in the locked barn when rumor started they would be burned alive, in the morning six people crushed against stable posts in the blind panic. Even at the camp, long past the most unreasoning hope, there was Chaim to look to those unending months when the truth, finally revealed in its crushing reality, made Sol grieve and then despair and then pray for death. Finally, after that night he did more than pray for it, he chose it for himself, turning his tin bowl aside when the Greek approached with the spotted ladle, straggling late for roll call, knowing what that could mean, slow to follow orders, looking with halfhearted longing at the electric fence where others who had thrown themselves were frozen like stumps in the wire. But he did not die, Chaim's own vigilant God would not permit it, and after a while Sol stopped praying and, emptied of everything else, knew his fate. To live, despite his *wishes, despite everything he desired. To take memory in the body and carry it, forever.*

The barrack, originally a stable, was long and unlit, and even had the two small stoves given any real heat, Sol doubted it could ever be warmed. Lying between Chaim and, first, the Litvak who managed, somehow, to keep his heaviness, the sour smells off his body negligible, to Sol, for the presence of all that warmth nearby (then the weight had fallen off, as if hacked away, and the Litvak sat up with a cough and a startled expression till one morning he was dragged to the infirmary and was gone). Then, after the Litvak, the quaking postal worker from Kishinev, who prayed all night and slowly wedged his bony back into Sol until his dreams were about being smothered (until they were about looking for food, frenzied as a dog, and then no dreams at all), Sol would imagine, or try to, Kleinot's horses in their stalls, the quiet nickering, smooth haunches shifting against wooden slats, nuzzling hay still warm in his hand from the day's slow heat. What never left him, still fifty years later, like a lid closing over him, first thing his eyes met when the door slammed open before light, last thing at night when all he prayed for was an end to the cold in his feet, the ache in his belly and bones, the wooden planking above his head, where five Poles huddled in the top tier, wood so stained and effaced, as if with smoke or grease or the rank exhalations of hundreds of men trying to sleep, the grain vanished, impossible to tell any longer what it was.

There he lay, wishing for emptiness while the others slopped food from tin cups, ate or hoarded their scrap of bread. No one ever knew how news spread in the camp, but it did, and by noon, returning from the field where they were digging a new foundation in the frozen mud, Sol knew, and now, his detail returned from the tool shop, Chaim was finding out. The Greek took him to one side and with his cronies, two Russians with faces like axes, spoke to him quietly.

When you have been hit enough times, hard enough, you don't

register any more the power or even the source, one hit doesn't hurt in
any particular way different from the next or the one before, one
doesn't surprise you with its lenience, another announce it is the
killing blow (though you fully expect one will be). Sol had seen, years
ago, two men fighting on the side of the road near home, and it was
like this, methodical, ordained, as if there never was a time before the
blows or would be after and you were mad even to think so. It was like
this now: his mother and sister hung in the yard of Barrack Eleven,
with six others, reprisal for some thieving in Canada II by a group of
Slavs. Only their mother, Sol later learned, had been selected by the
kapo, but Chana had refused to be separated from her, even in the
barracks yard when their fates were clear, and the SS had been only
too happy to add another rope and wooden box to the long iron rod
on the wall. They were hanging there still, the twitchy Italian who
brought the news said, not to Sol, to the Greek and to the Russians,
unable though to stop looking over at the boy, who left his food on the
wooden bench, found his tier of bunks and silently climbed in. Their
faces, his mother's never free of weariness, his sister's before the evacu-
ation clean, untroubled, and the others he hadn't thought about
recently, none of whom he'd seen since they left the last train—
his father, his grandparents, his cousins Malke and Lazar, now they
swarmed in the depthless scoured wood and Sol, not yet sixteen, alone
in the bunk, tried no longer to see or hear or feel and, as if any of
these were possible, closed his eyes.

But he heard Chaim. The scream itself was a shock to the whole
room, where no one ever spoke above a whisper, where cries that came
from the dark, sometimes his own, Sol feared, were weak with despair
and illness. But Chaim's rang out, full-throated, fierce, and when he
upset the food pot and stools, when he tried to push back into the
yard and had to be held down, when he was muzzled finally with
some piece of cloth (Sol, still with his eyes closed, trying not to hear),
the Greek stood over him while the Russians sat on his chest. In his
terrible Yiddish the Greek said, "Boy, there is nothing you can do," at

which Chaim, half throttled by the gag and the weight on his chest, writhed and struggled again, until someone hit him and he lay still. The Greek said to someone, "He would kill us all."

No one knew where the Greek had come from, he had just appeared a few months before. Everyone knew him now, knew about clothing stolen from the Canada warehouse, the Russian pistol buried under the plank walls. Chaim knew. And he knew, they all did, that for a piece of iron lifted against a guard a month ago the SS had wiped out an entire barrack in reprisal, as entire towns had vanished after Heydrich's death. When they let Chaim go, the Greek walked him to where Sol was lying and told him to get in, to sleep, to remember the six hundred living souls in the bunks with him.

Later, when Chaim climbed out, as silently as he could, and when he went to the loose board in the wall for the pistol, Sol knew what he was doing. He thought to say something, to reach out and hold his brother back, but he didn't. He thought to rise with Chaim and follow along, but he didn't do that, either. He would always wonder why. The sounds Chaim made, moving the panel, digging in the dirt, fumbling in the cold, were as clear and vivid as if a light were trained on him, and Sol knew exactly what was happening when the Greek, slowly, as if with regret (but without hesitation) approached him from behind. The scuffle, the sound of a body hitting the wall, a head against a bunk post, twice, again, Sol heard all this, and the silence, except for the grunting of the Russians as they heaved Chaim into the snow, all of it he heard, begging not to (if he could no longer get any breath, why could he hear and see?), above him the blotted wood, no prayers come to him, no faces any longer, somewhere out in the fields horses shouldering together, hooves tamping, and wet breaths disappearing in plumes under a blank pit of sky.

8

As Nathan read the letters one by one, the torn half pages from legal pads, the Post-its and napkins and backs of envelopes, the occasional quote carefully written on an index card, he finally heard the voice. Daniel's letters had been this way, so entertaining, immediate, it was like hearing him speak. The big envelope was stuffed with paper gathered for weeks, maybe months, into the world's messiest suicide note—gossip, parable, reports from daily life, pages indecipherably scrawled when Daniel was too high to think straight. A grade sheet from the school he subbed at. A box score from Barry Bonds' first Giants game. Two-sentence critiques of foreign movies Nathan had never heard of. Slowly, it seemed they were in the room together, and Nathan, who would have his own say soon enough, soon enough might find himself shouting at the top of his lungs and flailing at ghosts, let Daniel talk for now. He was good at it, and it had been so long.

From time to time he paused to look out the window. The lady had collected the bird, grown hysterical in the heat and street noise, and gone inside her apartment. The spitball kid was gone, too. Occasionally, the muffled thump of rap reached him from passing cars. The man drinking beer was back with another, wiping a satisfied hand across his face before dropping his bag in the trash can where he'd dumped the first. Crossing the street, he was surprisingly nimble, picking his way through traffic. He skipped onto the sidewalk and Nathan caught the buckles flashing on his high-top boots.

He found the photo under some fallen notes, the one he couldn't identify earlier, Daniel's arm around him, both smiling. Of course. The shoes. It was just a party, they'd thought, another no-cost gesture for the common good. The union had called, to have management's sons present would make a powerful statement for the papers. No confrontation planned, just peaceful pickets, a chant or two, an orderly exercise in civil protest. Sure, why not. Nathan remembered even when Sol saw them there, a minute or two after someone, a friendly woman from the factory, had snapped the photo, it had all seemed that simple, the old man's stiff, grave outrage silly, out of date. Seemed that way until Sol saw them at the dock's far end, laughing, and they saw the look on his face.

How was it possible? he had been asked, Janet had asked, he'd asked himself. Everyone had seen them, the pictures of shoes, the hair in bales, mountains of eyeglasses, teeth. Janet, back in Cleveland, had seen them.

Not Nathan. Who would have shown him?

The brothers smile, looking out of the frame, Daniel's tasseled hat, Nathan's blousy Indian shirt, they're thinking of beer, weed, music, girls, they're thinking they've made their point, will be back in the Village by happy hour. A good day's activist fun. Then he sees them, the older boy draped affectionately over the younger. Nathan, years too late, shuddered. Only kids get to be that casually cruel, murderously stupidly blind. What in the world did they think they were smiling at?

The answering machine picked up. The swooning music wasn't any less annoying than before, but he could almost ignore it. "Shelby, this is for Janet," he said, and paused, as if she would hand over the phone. "J, look, hi, how are you? Look, I haven't been straight, I haven't been able to be. I don't know what I'm saying anymore, I don't trust it anymore and I can't think clearly . . . and I don't know, Janet, what I can say, to you." He looked out the window, nothing—people waiting for the lights, taxis in traffic, store-front doors opening and closing. "I had no right, you see, to hurt you. Ever. I didn't want to hurt you, I don't think I did. Did I? I loved you, I thought. I tried to do it right. Ridiculous, huh? Too long in coming, too little, too late. Maybe I did mean to hurt you, Janet, but I swear to God I don't know why." He took the phone and pressed the receiver hard to his forehead, then brought it back to his mouth. "I'm really tired. Sol's somewhere on the street. He took the fucking box, he took Daniel and he's wandering. I can't find him." He wasn't making sense. He started to put the phone down, then lifted it again. "Janet, I wish I could have done better. I wish I could have." A cable car on Powell heaved uphill, bells and the ceaseless sawing of the tow line. Behind closed eyes Nathan saw children chasing a circus wagon. He waited until Shelby's machine cut him off. He went to the window. Another cable car crested the avenue, tourists antic like monkeys, hanging from the sides, craning faces pulled shapeless by delight. Where in God's name was that old man?

∽ ∽ ∽

Of course he loved them, it was a ridiculous question even to ask. A father loves his children. Yet to the day she died Sol could not explain himself to his wife.

Sol was not—he would have said this of himself—an introspective man. He had once met a grandfather in Lublin, otherworldly blue eyes drifting over a white beard, the sort of man who looked like he could spend all day whispering to God, planning his course to Paradise. Not for Sol, this woolly option. The portion life had handed him demanded action, no thought that did not require a result. He'd like to see anyone do better. Let his sons, should they choose, pick at philosophy or religion. For him it was duty, which meant someone had to get things done, and responsibility, which meant doing it right. It was the factory and the workers at the machines and tables, invoices and arguing with distributors, keeping a watchful eye on shipping costs, the price of quality leather— everything that went into something as simple as making a shoe (and in this big country, how many could do even that?). It was the shoes themselves in their simple brown boxes with "W-B" stamped on the side, rows two hundred feet long waiting for shipment to twenty-seven states, Brazil, Canada, Europe. It was sitting down every single night before a table to which he, Sol Mirsky, had brought the food, in rooms to which he brought the electricity and heat, to rest a little and to eat, to hear about Freda's day and look at her shining face, to wonder through his tired eyes at his weedy, clamorous boys, their tumbling world of sports and adventure and contention.

Still, love is what you share, so he'd been told. And what he shared with Freda they had long ago decided would not be shared, could never be (were it even possible), with the boys. Let them look forward; wasn't this what a parent gave a child, a ground from which to look out at life? And he and Freda, also, looking to see what the boys saw, over their shoulders, in this way could they maybe leave behind some of what could be left? Wasn't that love?

The heat had drawn back somewhat as Sol walked through the streets now. In Chinatown he stopped to stare at vegetables he had never seen before, bulbous and thorny, shapes you would never think were food. Turtles flapped uselessly against the walls of plastic buckets, huge slime-green frogs lay panting in a shallow pool. Children skittered past, shopkeepers with eyes that didn't move looked out at the street. When an old woman on two canes approached in front of a souvenir shop, racks of cards and toys and clothing for dolls out on the street, there was not enough room to pass. Sol moved aside, but that was not sufficient. The woman, with skin like a walnut, looked at him as if she could wait till doomsday, and Sol, worried about falling, stepped over the curb, one foot splashing in a runnel of soapy water. Without giving him so much as a look, the old woman on her two sticks passed. He needed to get home.

He walked on, hoisting the red box awkwardly every few steps, stopping often. At the end of one tipped street he looked down, something he had not been able to do before. Hills in one direction, slanting into mist, the bridge in another, the only thing unmoving in a weave of gray water and sky. The stack and rough abutment of a factory, a sight first familiar, then, dizziness swarming, frightening (not his city). He had to rest soon, had to locate where he was, find their hotel. But Sol had never once in his life asked directions of anyone. He brought the box, heavy now, to his chest and walked.

That day at his factory, almost thirty years ago. Was that what made him shudder, looking down the hill? The union breaking in, workers looking at him suddenly like he was a jailer, a *Kommandant*. Sol wasn't opposed, not really, to the union. He had always thought someone should look out for the workers—he had tried to himself; overall, he thought, he had done a reasonable job. And he could understand the need for a group of your own, a bulwark to protect and defend. Fair enough. But their tactics made him livid. Posters denouncing him all over the walls. Cutters, stitchers, loudly leaving their worktables, announcing it was time for their mandated break (who had ever argued?). Whispered meetings in the coffee room, strangers with signs outside the factory doors, his car pelted with eggs one morning—men he didn't know had thrown them, to this day he'd swear that—the union representative, better dressed than Sol, than any of them, haranguing them morning and night: No Old Country here, this was America, workers had built this land. What do you have to show for it? the man screamed. (Plenty, Sol thought, growing angry.) Think of the future. Your children are counting on you.

And though Sol had offered to talk, to negotiate, still the man with the new coat and megaphone and the shadows who drifted in the parking lot all day kept going, calling Strike, Strike, Shut It Down. It was the summer the whole country had gone crazy: the Kennedy brother, that Reverend King, riots all over, Newark, just up the road, in flames. Daniel, one of Sol's own boys, arrested on his school campus.

Had he ever denied anyone a fair living? He tried to tell them, but something was in the air, something Sol recognized—nobody wanted to listen, they looked past him, faces set with righteous purpose, breathing the air of a higher cause—this he recognized. He went to work every day, doing his duty, though the feeling restored in his gut, stone-cold, like hunger, was terrifying, and the posture he had never forgotten, stiffly erect, seeing and not seeing at once.

At home, he told them nothing.

Friday, the last day of a difficult week. He would take Freda to a movie, maybe, or a restaurant in the city. (On Monday he would call, they would sit down finally, Sol with the men in suits, and he would concede nearly all they asked, and, rigid nerves at last fraying, demand a meager concession or two, which the men in suits would serenely, expansively allow.) It was not even eleven when somebody, not a foreman with a key, got into the booth and sounded the work horn. Three short bursts, like the end of the day, not the long one Finkel gave for lunch. From his glassed-in office on the second floor Sol watched as men, even some of the women, dozens, probably half his 120 employees, rose at the signal and lined up at the loading-dock bay. He was frozen at the dim window a moment, remembered the wooden club behind his desk (for what? As if he would lift it against anyone), and after what seemed like many cowardly minutes, he took the metal stairs, empty-handed, to see what was happening.

Each worker was handed a stack of boxes, as many as he could carry. Outside, at the dock, they opened the boxes and threw the shoes. When Sol came out the pile was just beginning. When they were done it was as high as the loading platform, hundreds of Well-Built shoes, glistening new with polish, some still trailing blue tissue paper; shoes for people to wear, now a pile of garbage. It made him sick, physically sick, to watch. He had come down to see who

was causing the trouble, look some people in the face. But it was all
he could do now not to fall to his knees and heave the bile that
swam in his mouth. What were they doing? The ones at the pile
were absolutely silent. Behind him a few women, the older ones,
probably, who filled the boxes (some of them had seen things), were
crying, and somewhere Finkel was shouting into a phone.

Then he saw them, his sons, and the shock made him stagger,
like a blow from behind. He was close to the lip of the dock, could
have fallen and broken his neck. Somebody caught him under the
shoulders, straightened him and let go. Before he fell again, before
he went blind with the cold sun off the high windows and retched
at the fumes he had always claimed not to notice, before he went
insane at the small sounds the shoes made hitting the pile, he stumbled back upstairs and locked his office, where he remained till the
end of the day. Before he turned his back on the shoes, the workers
he'd considered to be friends, and found no one resisted him, before he could sense they had stopped out on the dock and everyone
was watching him, before any of this, he had looked up and seen
them, his two boys standing in the sun and smiling.

Even the week she died, Freda told him. Not over and over,
which wasn't her way, not even in words. Just in the flagging look
she gave, the worry that didn't need expression to hit home, that let
him know what was on her mind. Only once had she said the
words, the first night at the hospital.

It was quiet. The doctors, having made their hurried, concilia-
tory exam, had hurried off, as if embarrassed they couldn't do more,
as if nothing would ever change (and it wouldn't) no matter whose
wife, whose mother or daughter, died this week. From the window
where Sol stood you could see the Parkway looping toward the
Island. From other rooms, he bet, you could see Flushing Meadow,
the shining steel globe the boys had loved so much. It was fall,
leaves were blowing past the window. One of the last still moments
they would have together, before the pain, as predicted, got worse,

before the medicine closed around her and when she opened her eyes all he saw was the glint of its ebbing or a fixed vacancy that scared him, as if she'd already gone.

Freda was propped up in bed. She'd had a bath and her hair done in the afternoon. There were fresh flowers Sol had brought (not from the crummy stand in the lobby but from the shop on Queens Boulevard, a whole armload of blues and reds). As the light thinned over the highway he didn't turn on the lamp. Let her sleep. He watched her, his mind thankfully emptied of anything but watching her, his Freda, head to one side, pretty in the blue sleeping jacket the boys had sent, with her hair all nice, one arm on the blanket curled back toward her face. His beauty. He had always watched her sleep, enjoyed it even now, even as he understood she was leaving him, each slumber a rehearsal for the final leave-taking. How often had he spilled over with rage, so many times, heading out when he couldn't stand it, pacing the lobby downstairs where the music and the blind, worried faces would drive a happy man mad, cursing the efficient bustle of the hospital all around. That, too, tonight, was past. He was empty, glad to be, weightless just looking at her, the room dark now, his wife sleeping just a few feet away, their breathing the only sound. Sol watched her, grateful, amazed.

When she spoke and woke him in the chair, he didn't understand. Had he fallen asleep? "I didn't hear."

"You have to tell them," she said.

Again he didn't understand. He shook himself, as if hearing was the problem. Tell who? Tell what?

"Before you miss the chance."

There was, for once, no movement in the hall, no one, as far as Sol could see, rushing about. He could barely hear laughter from the TV, muted now the hour was late. He looked at Freda. He knew.

"The boys," she said.

Once, before you miss the chance—and that could be any mo-

ment, it could be any day, you know that, Sollie. You have two sons.
Tell your sons you love them.

And when she slept again, her head drifting, he sat immobile in
the chair. He could not explain, had not even tried. He would do
anything, he would walk through fire for this woman. And he would
do this, too, if it was in his power. But he knew, three days before she
died, he could never explain. While her head was filled (he hoped
so) with visions of shouting at the lake in summer, diving from the
floating dock, dinner, laughing at something the parents could never
follow, playing ball in the street out front, the sounds of sneakers and
bats dropped on the asphalt—anything, Sol hoped, that would
soothe the time for her, he saw the factory: shoes glinting, small popping sounds as new ones hit, rolled, his own yard a mound of
corpses, and beyond it, his own sons in a casual embrace, laughing.

The phone kept barking for more change. Luckily, Sol never
went anywhere without a pocketful. He fed it once to get the number, then blindly fed it again after he'd dialed, balancing the red box
before him on the tiny shelf, waiting to be connected. When the
gruff voice, not unfriendly (Clara? Could it be?) asked what was his
relation, he fumbled the words. Finally he muttered, "Uncle. I'm
the boy's uncle," and the woman told him to hold.

"Hello?" a voice said, and sinking, he immediately regretted the
call.

"Hello," the woman said again. "Who is this?"

Sol roused himself.

"A friend. Calling to see how he is doing. Brandon."

"Who is this?" the woman said again, loud now, and she spoke
to somebody in the room.

"We were in the same room. A friend. I just wanted to see was
he doing better."

A pause, Sol could hear arguing. "Don't take a tone with me,"
the woman said. "I have no idea." Then another voice, a man's,
came on the line.

"Hello. Who is this?" Sol didn't speak. "Look, who *are* you? You have no right to be calling here. I *know*," the man said angrily into the room. "That's what I'm doing." He came back on the line.

"We have a sick child here. Very sick. Do you realize that? I don't know who you are, what you think you're doing—I'm *coming*," he said, away from the phone.

Sol could hear him breathing. The man coughed. "Listen to me," he said, biting off the words. "How dare you . . ." The line went dead.

Sol stared a long moment before remembering to hang up the phone.

He took the box from the shelf and began walking, too dazed or tired to think straight. Images circled him: Brandon, Freda, Sylvia in New York, the boys. "Before you lose the chance." Had he the energy, he would have banished them all. He looked, from habit, at the street signs, as if to decide on a direction, but looked away, not registering what he saw. In his head thought skittered raggedly around the one unshakable notion, the one that never left, feeling to match the taste of metal and blood in his mouth. Was it such a big thing his wife had asked? Was it too much to make her that promise? Yet he had failed her, even in this, the truth being there was no one in his long life he had not betrayed.

ༀ ༀ ༀ

Ben thought he would have to ask Mr. Li, the way he had to one time when his mom went to the store and locked him out by accident. Mr. Li had invited Ben in and offered him tea, which was weird, in his dark apartment, but Ben hadn't known what to do so he took a sip. It wasn't like tea at all, sweet and just warm enough to wake up your tongue. Mr. Li had books and a small TV, and on one wall a cool kite in the shape of a bird, though Ben was too shy to ask if he ever flew it.

But he didn't need Mr. Li this time. The door was unlocked and, opening it, Ben began moving fast, as if this were rehearsed, dread sifting through to settle in his stomach and fingers. Maybe this was the time.

There was his mother, half off the bed, no clothes on. The streaked mirror he'd tried to hide was on the floor by her underwear, a rolled-up bill nearby. Dull window light hit across her stomach, her boobies, one arm. He couldn't tell if she was breathing, and he thought maybe if he hit her really hard he could find out.

He didn't look at her again.

Under his own bed was the cigar box Tommy had given him. He checked every night to make sure it was wedged exactly where he'd put it, between the wheel of the bed and the wall. He took it out and sat on the floor. Inside the box, his two-dollar bill with a president Ben couldn't remember in the picture, a funny screaming little pink alien man, smaller than his finger, that Danny had brought home one day. A penny stretched and flattened with "Benjamin" stamped on its blank face. Six ticket stubs from Candlestick Park. Rocks and a round piece of wood Ben had found fascinating at one time and which he tossed aside now. Some drawings. A creased photograph in a dirty paper frame—"You Made The Break!" along the top, "Alcatraz, San Francisco, USA, 1988" along the bottom. His mom and a man in a uniform giggling, arms around each other, stepping off a boat. As he did every time, Ben studied the man's face before putting the photo down. Last, the knife with the spring release, and small hacked pieces of gold and brown and white rubber, number thirty-six, what was left of him after Ben had cut him up the night she told him Danny died.

He looked in a few drawers, threw some clothes on the floor, didn't take anything, just the cigar box. He decided to cover her up, see if she was breathing, but then was afraid to get too close. What if this was the time? He didn't like the words in his head, and it was not okay to cry. He dug a fingernail hard in the soft part under each eye and didn't look in the other room. He was halfway down the flight of stairs, running, when the door clicked shut far above him.

She would tell no one.

And what was there to say about a confirmation, long pending, the end to a sentence begun so long ago she could have forgotten (though she never did) its all-along intent, the meaning inscribed in her bones and eyes and memory, and now, belatedly, her heart.

The doctor, a kindly man, soft-voiced, big in the back and shoulders, slumped a little as if under the weight of all he'd seen, or the news he bore, had come into his office, where the secretary had told Freda to wait. He didn't say a word. He walked up behind her, then to her side, he reached out and put a hand on her shoulder. There was nothing to say, no need. Later, test results, X-rays, recap of her history, possible treatment options, a new word to Freda, "palliative," and then the last question, how long, and bless him he didn't flinch, didn't look away, didn't leave her yet in the solitude maybe even he sensed she would be occupying hereafter. Months, four, maybe six.

As she walked through the rooms of the light, airy apartment, arranging things there was no need to arrange, tidying what was already neat, Freda Mirsky realized two things. That silence was her ambience. And that she had been saying goodbye for years. The two of them in Jerusalem: she'd broken down as they carried the dead holy man past her in the street, Sol abashed, tormented, clumsy in his attentions, and of course she couldn't tell him why she cried, couldn't even understand it herself, not fully, the clawing ache in her chest—her own family never attended, never borne to their graves or consecrated in farewell. The Hebrew word for burial means "accompaniment."

Her mother, in the second camp, she never thought to say good-bye. It was a regular work detail, Freda at the laundry, her mother with a group of Russians in the Kommandant's garden. A hot day, cloudless, airless, they'd been on half rations (half of what?) for some infraction nobody had bothered to explain. They were wearing down to nothingness, but no one, not Freda, not the Russian woman who told her in a foreign Yiddish, not, as far as she could imagine, her mother herself, could believe it when Rose Adler lay on the ground by the far gate, where there would be beans on fancy trellises imported from Bremen, that she would not rise, that she would lie there, staring as the Russian ladies whispered around her (Get up, they'll see), then tried bodily hauling her to her feet, then, unsuccessfully, of course, to hide her from the kapo's eyes. (This woman, a Romanian with one silver tooth in her mouth and arms like a man's, with a man's, a certain type of man's, hard pleasure in others' distress, had seen Freda in the washing area outside the barracks next morning. A moment's recognition, the brief raising of the lips, a sneer, a warning, a convulsion of loathing and pride. Fifty years and more later, Freda had never forgotten.) No one believed this was the moment that she would lie unmoving under the kapo's whip and heavy boots, wordless, that when they finally dragged her out beyond the fence and left her she would still have made no sound.

Freda's brothers, her father, she'd lost sight of as they were emptying the first train. She was helping her mother, who was helping an old woman with a baby on her shoulder, and when she turned back to see where they were in the men's line it had moved and it did not occur to her—too tired, too hungry, too numbed from the marrow outward by fear's relentless pulse—that she would not see them again.

Freda walked through the rooms. On the patio her plants swayed in the afternoon breeze, she'd carried them out to wash them this morning before her appointment. Maybe Sol would bring them back in for her. On the kitchen counter their breakfast dishes, the marmalade he loved, the toast she hadn't been able to eat. She walked.

On the round table, pictures—the boys, weddings, and the others—some names Freda knew, many she didn't, a few she couldn't even swear were family (someone's, yes), but she hung them on her wall, arranged them in the nesting of frames on the whitened wood, and every Friday night she lit the candles there, first her boys and Sol, later just Sol in glum acquiescence to her melancholy rite, watching her wave her fingers three times before closing her eyes, praying mutely to these pale witnesses who floated in and out of her dreams.

Shall we call your husband? The first words the doctor spoke after they'd stayed there, bound in the moment before she became again patient, dying, he doctor, beyond his powers. No, she had shaken her head. She had told Sol it was just a regular checkup when he'd offered to come along. Nothing, Freda told him, I won't need you, you'll be bored. Go swim.

Sol, her husband. Almost fifty years of life with him, and their parlance, their most secret and intimate attachment, was itself silent, loyal, abiding, in its own way thankful, but unyielding, isolate. And if inadequate (especially in this country, where everything, they told you, was easy, or should be), all the more precious because it was the best they could do, and because they were together at all.

And nothing was more painful than trying to talk, witnessing his rare outbursts of need. The last time, right before he sold the factory, staying on as manager so he could draw a salary and have somewhere to go in the mornings, but ceding the rights to a firm in Chicago. Came home in a rage so violent he was still flushed with it, his breathing still altered, the scowl of insult and betrayal so marked on his face it would have been, in another man, another circumstance, comical. She had brought them tea, let him sit as long as he needed, watching with sympathy the feelings twisting through him. And when he told her, in spasms of broken words, for once she too was appalled, though not, as Sol was, entirely at their boys, for them as well, for their brashly stupid belief in privilege, their own and others', their avid heedless plunging into a world they were sure would accept them, protect them, forgive them if necessary. A world of constant second chances. They, especially the older, seemed born into this certainty and Freda, who knew better about the world, never stopped fearing for them.

Slowly, he told her. Doogan and the union. Protest marchers out front, strangers with stupid signs on sticks. They hadn't let his car pass for a good five minutes, Hirsch, Eisenberg, Welther—how long had he known them, twenty years? Yardlovker, who should live long enough to know every misery, leading them out in line. Then—and here he upset his tea; again, in another man, another history, she might find it funny that this, the abuse of honestly made manufactured goods, seemed to outrage him most—then they'd taken, each and every last sonofabitch who should get boils on his shingles, the new shoes from the loading dock, thrown them, one by one, like some goddamned parade, into the truck bay. The sound, he said, I can't tell you. The smell. The light on them, the way they piled up. Some of these men had been over there—hadn't they seen, any of them? Shoes, eyeglasses, piles of human hair. To see this again . . .

Here he broke off, stared at the high windows, a woman across 108th Street beating a carpet against the rail of her patio. And Freda thought he was done. And she thought of what she might make him to eat, a brisket, though that would mean another trip to the butcher, maybe he would walk with her, maybe they would sit on the boulevard before it got dark and feed the pigeons.

But he wasn't done. Freda could tell from the way his body, instead of relaxing, grew rigid all over again, and his face, which had released some of its contortion in speaking, regained it, with a new trembling quality to the anger, as if he might cry. And she grew afraid.

"I went out," he said quietly. "I don't know to do what. Talk some sense, throw a few off the loading dock. Get in the car and leave the *miserable traitors for good. Forty years, forty years' honest wages . . . Doogan, the bastard, we talked in my office the day before." He looked up at Freda, thick fingers working each other in front of his chest. "Then I saw them . . ."*

And Freda, not pleased to recognize it in herself, realized she didn't want to hear, didn't want to look at him. Back across the street the woman had dragged out another carpet, bigger, bulkier than the first, purple with red and orange slashes in the low light. She hauled it in several tugs over the railing, she whacked it with a beefy forearm. Even from here Freda could see little detonations of dust. Some of her earliest memories, from their living room in Bremerhaven, watching Lilja the maid, with arms just like this lady, beating their Persian rugs out the courtyard window. Lilja would call her into the kitchen to taste the soups, the strudel, the apple dumplings that were her specialty. Lilja would walk them to the synagogue on Saturday mornings, hustling Freda and Johann and little Martin along, then go home while they prayed, to rest and be with her family, and sometimes, when they went on an outing, Lilja returned on Monday with a present for Freda, her favorite, a cheap but lovely hairclip, a flower pressed for drying . . .

". . . laughing," Sol said. "Over by the gate. The older one laughing and his arm around the younger, having a party. I swear to you, if I had the strength, if I wasn't ready to fall over, I would have killed them both."

Lilja had a daughter, too, Freda remembered, some outlandish name, Brunhilda, Bronshweg, something. In the Adlers' kitchen she would always climb into her mother's lap, staring at Freda, defiantly reclaiming sovereignty.

"I said something."

And now Freda was forced to listen. He spoke so quietly she had to repeat what he said to herself to make certain she understood. He was moving his mouth as if he wanted to spit.

"What."

"I could have killed them, you understand?" He swallowed and now pure misery filled his face. "I would have, I'm telling you. All we went through, and this, so they can make a joke, a parade? They were handing papers through the gate. They saw me. The younger, he was afraid, but the older was ready for a fight."

They have names, Freda thought, angry suddenly at them all. Daniel. Nathaniel. They have names.

"To him I said it."

"Said what?" And an edge had crept into her voice, though she doubted Sol heard it, looking at this man, her husband, his brawny neck and head, his eyes refusing to roam behind the glasses, as if it were his only purpose to stare life down every minute, never look away.

"To me you're dead."

"You said?" and he nodded, then looked past her to the window, and her careening brain, which had relinquished the warm kitchen on Ludwigstrasse for the grim, dusty yard in front of his factory, a pile of glistening shoes, now saw the three of them, her family, in some indistinct distance, at the factory and not, real and vanished. "Sol. You said what?"

"I didn't mean it." And when he turned away she realized it was in shame as much as despair.

"So why? Why did you?" Even he, she was sure, could hear the dismissal, the disgust, in her voice. They have names, she found herself repeating. Daniel. Nathaniel. Names.

And the look he turned on her, mouth working again, eyes straight ahead, like the doctor's face today, like her mother's exhausted waving as she tramped off with her detail, like the little boy glancing back from the funeral procession in Jerusalem, his face full of mischief, somehow Freda knew this would be one of the last images she saw on this earth.

"Why?" she said again.

"Why?" Something rising in his voice, beyond anger, beyond re-

gret, an old sound, though she hadn't heard it from him before. "Because I did mean it. For one minute I meant what I said."

And that was all. Her unruly, reluctant mind finally locked into focus and she could see it, the factory with its greenish-brown walls, the high windows that seemed too dirty to admit either air or light, the chanting mob, men Sol thought of as friends, the shoes in their pile, discarded, trash. And her boys, Daniel like an Indian with black hair and beads and leather hat, his constant grin hiding from everyone else, maybe, but not Freda, his deeper uncertainty. And Nathan, to whom his brother was a deity, a household god to worship and emulate and defend and secretly resent. Her boys. Nathan. Daniel. Didn't they know anything? Didn't they understand the only sins you will never be forgiven are the ones you commit against yourself?

She had taken Sol out, forced him into his coat and hat, and when they passed Pastrami King after sitting in the park a half hour (no bread for the birds), she pulled him through the steamy double doors, the air thick with brine and the sweet, pungent smell of cured meat and heated potatoes. She hadn't allowed him here in years (though she wondered if he didn't sneak in himself sometimes, after his morning swim). She'd ordered for them both, just a bowl of soup for her, for him pastrami and corned beef on seeded rye, sour tomatoes, side dishes of creamy potato salad and coleslaw, both. And when he didn't eat more than a few bites she had tried to enjoy her chicken soup (too salty), and when he seemed ready she took him home, let him soak in a bath for an hour (water his only soothing), and when she saw he was safely in his study with the maps and data sheets and letters spread on the desk, she cleaned up the counter in the kitchen, separated the laundry into whites and colors for tomorrow, checked the milk and eggs for their expiration dates, walked a final time through the apartment, piling the pages of the Post neatly on the round wooden table, and only then, with Sol's grunts and shufflings barely audible, did she lie in their darkened bedroom under the thin spring blanket with eyes open, hearing everything, the tears warm on her face, running past her ears onto the pillow.

When he comes home today, a little less than a year from when she will be put in the ground (and will they be there, all of them, to attend, say goodbye?), he asks, What did the doctor say?

He is flushed and disheveled, his gray flapping hair in every direction, his Mets gym bag stained wet at the bottom. He drops it where he stands and waits to take off his jacket, frightened, that anxious wary smile, wanting from her only good news.

Is there anything I can do? the doctor had said, a gentle man, humbled by how little, finally, there was. And for a moment, brief but searing, she had almost told him of her plan, to bring her boys back, gather her family, have them sit around the old table again, and talk.

Now Sol is waiting for an answer. "Nothing," Freda tells him, "everything's fine." And grunting, at the intrusive bossiness of doctors, at his own weak worry, at his urgent need, after the eight-block walk, to use the bathroom, he leaves her and she hears him fussing in there. In the kitchen she gets out cups and lemon for their tea, a poppy cake she bought near the subway to treat them both, its pulpy sweet seeds oozing as she cuts two small slices. She sits. It's an illusion, she knows, that the day lasts longer up here, it's just that from this elevation you can see into the city, or over the bay where darkness has already sketched in the lower portions of sky. It is a sad time of day, a quiet time, and perhaps Freda's favorite hour, earth and sky making their silent, inevitable turns toward night, a softer moment than dawn with its colors and brightening lights, its clamor of hope and desire. Here a moment when nothing, briefly, need be done. Soon dinner, the round of cleaning and listening to Sol recount the day's triumphs and defeats, part of her listening, trying to help, part of her withdrawing as it always has. Soon. For now, in her darkening kitchen two cups, lemon sliced, cake on plates, blue evening filling her windows, it is enough to sit here and wait for her husband to join her. It is enough.

9

Maybe he should call Rivera again.

Nathan was downstairs now, in the open doorway of their hotel, where the young clerk with the Arab accent nodded over some big text and the cool air of the lobby pushed him forward, while from the street undulating waves of thick heat seemed to push him back. He leaned against the cool glass of the unopened door to the side.

One thing Nathan enjoyed about the medical training, endless as it might be, was the opportunity to do something. There were tests, procedures, consults, medications—a battery of possible actions. And it had occurred to him that his hesitancy in selecting a specialty, finally, lay somewhere in this paradox: the higher up the ladder you crawled, the less certainty you found. Yes, there was power. Pick up the phone and people all over the hospital began moving. When a decision needed to be made, everyone looked to you, went silent—you, the hub about which all the intricate machinery spun. There was that. But quickly Nathan had learned the flip side of power was its own limit—how often, simply, there was nothing to be done. And if everyone, aides on up, shared in the moment's tense foreboding, the decision was yours, the doctor in charge, your responsibility, your call. How often had he seen even the best, most confident and powerful doctors come up against this limit. Patients thought of doctors as a cross between mechanics and conjurers—there must always be a solution, some pill, some surgery, some experimental drug. But there wasn't, sometimes, and sometimes these things didn't work, and even interns came to see the truth about medical practice: that for all that was known, which was a good deal, more every year, it was a small bulwark against all that wasn't—the intractable, mysterious counterprocess of a body in retreat. While other residents bristled under the constraints of their position, the menialities of charting histories, orders from above, Nathan didn't. It had taken months to master the simple stitch, and he appreciated the efficiency, the result. A well-set cast, a splint that relieved pain, even a prescription he had reason to believe would succeed, filled him with a sureness of accomplishment he realized he had been looking for, always.

One night in the ER a woman presented with severe stomach pain, cramping in the legs, a mysteriously high fever, and Kellogg, desperate for publication before his residency ended, ran off to the texts, saying, Nobody touch her. Don't do anything to mask the symptoms—this might be one for the journals! Nathan had gone in and assessed the woman, in such pain she had writhed off the exam table onto the floor, a stocky Latina mother in her forties. Her worried daughter, high school age, was kneeling and stroking her hand. The woman was wincing so hard her eyes did not open until he slipped the needle into her arm. She looked right at him then, her rich cocoa skin blanched gray, just pooling some color as her muscles let go. Looked at him until she closed her eyes again.

Kellogg went apeshit. He'd phoned the infectious diseases doc (the woman had been to Santo Domingo), who was willing to hear him out after he'd finished his exam. Nathan looked at Kellogg, five years younger but with middle age already grinding at him, a way he had of pinching his upper lip, hair slicked anxiously over a thinning strip where pink scalp shone, at once pompous and pathetic.

"Oh, well," Nathan said unkindly, "I guess *JAMA* will have to wait." Kellogg touched his lip and stomped off to take it out on the nurses, leaving Nathan quietly buoyant for the rest of his shift. From time to time he went in to check on his patient. She slept.

That was a good night. But medicine, like the various lives he'd contemplated for himself, most often confirmed how little could be done in the face of history, fate, the odds. A blood vessel deep in the brain bursts, as it has been waiting to do for years. Countering gravity, cigarettes, a killing diet, a heart finally gives out. A child (nine, was he? ten?) dumped by chance's whim into a world overrun by guns and a swaggering indifference to mortality, shot five times (five!), no one knew by whom (some other kid stalking his own bullet). In the middle of the night, a woman unable to sleep discovers her mind unhinged. After a life of dormant quietude, a signal goes off and cancer cells awaken, begin their steady tramp in the blood. Some are aborted, some spared, some are doomed.

Then you stumble in, with your plans, your specialness, your wild dreams of a future. Who are you? A bit actor who thinks he's written the play. (Bloody handprints on an ER door, a girl's exhausted thanks when you bring her mother a blanket. Stubby finger cocked like a six-shooter, dark eyes over delighted grin: *Yo!*)

Every move he'd made since dropping by to check on his father in New York (no, before that, Janet), his talks with Rivera and Abby, his wanderings last night, everything, looking back, was foolish, useless, and unaccountably destructive. It would be enough, Nathan thought, simply to stop. What had he accomplished? His father out on the streets, twenty-four hours ago delirious with fever and pain. What were the chances he was taking his pills? Janet, if she was okay in Boston, was so only because he was gone. Abby, since they'd arrived, was, if anything, worse. We tread isolated rounds of misery, Nathan was thinking, wildly—where was this language from?—and all we can ask is to be left alone, when a cab door opened and he heard Dr. Laura mocking: "You lie lousy, you know that? You're a lousy liar. Try another one." And her corrosive, humorless laugh. He was losing it, big time. The driver looked through the cab window at Nathan. Nathan closed his eyes.

And the purpose of this whole trip—to learn what happened to his brother—look how far he had succeeded there.

He heard the cab drive off. He saw himself now, how he had careened out here, blind, aching, angry, desperate for answers. *Tell me*, he wanted to grab hold and demand of Rivera, Abby, the guy drinking beer from a paper bag, anybody on the street. *Will somebody please just fucking explain?* Something in all this mess had to come clear, for him, for his father, for Abby. He'd turned for clues to Rivera; hoped speaking with Abby would set things straight. He'd hoped, weakly, groping at the tumble of papers Daniel had bequeathed him, to find this truth: that his brother, whatever his late failings, had fashioned a coherent, purposeful exit. Daniel had died to save lives, to call attention to the terrible plight of the city's children. That's what had risen in Nathan when Rivera first told him about the gun—Daniel had died for principle, to leave a message. It was not, therefore, a fumbling halt, a final misstep in a life of too many. There was resolve, an idea. He had died a hero.

It was not Nathan's fault.

He moved to the bodega near the hotel, standing where the beer drinker had stood. Kids slumped by (how did they manage to look angry simply walking?) wrapped in do-rags and shades, plugged into headphones. A couple hurrying out of a hotel across Post, he still pulling on his jacket, parted, without saying goodbye, in separate directions. A guy in a battered delivery truck pulled into a no-parking zone, shut off his engine, arranged a small tiger-striped pillow behind his head, lay back to sleep. A man looked at a folded newspaper while his dog, a big shepherd-collie mix, took a leisurely dump by a mailbox. People talked into cell phones, eyes looking ahead at nothing, as if this moment, just walking down the street, was unbearable on its own. Under Nathan's feet the cable ground away. The city hummed. He looked up for the spitball king, the lady and her bird, but they had vanished, only the washed-out geranium remained, anchored stiffly in its pot.

Was it really so much to expect a message? Nathan supposed it was. He had read the notes with excitement, fear, some cowering faith, but they delivered only more bafflement. Daniel to the last:

funny, volatile; wonderment and insight and irreverence, towering self-pity, but no answers for Nathan in the spill of words, no tying up of plot as any self-respecting suicide note should be expected to manage. What could Rivera tell him that his brother wouldn't?

He let go of the idea, too exhausted by his brain's loops and car-omings to persist. The delivery driver yawned like a cat while a cop stood behind his van, writing a ticket. His dog satisfied, the man with the paper walked off, still reading. Above Nathan a window slammed shut, another opened, a radio played. He let go, thinking he might collapse, sit down right here on the filthy pavement and rest, when slowly, sifting through him on the corner of Post and Jones in the brewing heat of a San Francisco day, came the true and numbing recognition—that his brother, probably, had died for no reason at all. He died because he was an aging addict who'd made too many mistakes, who understood there was no hope he would stop making them. Who'd given up. And maybe not even that—who'd simply been looking for his day's fix, scared, addled enough to think an empty gun would protect him, confused and alone. And gone.

Maybe Nathan would call Rivera anyway. Buy him a beer. Something about the guy, something Nathan didn't understand. Movie-star good-looking—why be a cop? The walls around his desk, empty, the others cluttered with posters, photos from hunting trips, uniformed award ceremonies. Who'd put the D.A.R.E. sticker up? There was one picture frame, facing away from Nathan—kids, a wife? He looked like he'd seen a lot. What, Nathan wanted to know, was behind the reserve, the handsome calm (some line in Daniel's notes about beauty being a pledge, what did that mean?)— why did Rivera seem to understand something Nathan needed to know?

He shook himself away from the plate-glass window of the bodega. Ridiculous, all of it. Rivera was a cop. He had no more to say to Nathan than a barber would, a politician. Pendergast. Next he would be stopping people as they passed, panhandling for advice.

He turned east, west, toward the water and away. He waited for sensation to ease back into his limbs. Finally, he turned down Post, into the heat. Beauty is a pledge, he couldn't remember the rest. The street buzzed, droned, the cable rasped its song under his feet; he thought he might fall over if he didn't rest, on the street salsa, rap, someone arguing in Chinese, someone laughing hard. But he couldn't wait any longer. Sol, as stubborn as he was stupid, was out here somewhere. God, it was hot. The early mist lifted, the city's peculiar liquid light blazed through, every face, every building and storefront, the shoes on people's feet and the clothing they wore, everything, the misty hills to the south, gray water ahead, all spotlit, highlighted, as if mocking Nathan, whispering to his swooning brain, Look here, here's what you want.

It was hot. Nathan walked.

As he did, a new image came to him, as if measured out in cadence with his feet on the pavement, an image as baffling in its way as any of the others, and he saw his brother that last morning, not far from here, walking these streets, as Nathan was now. Going wherever. Thinking whatever. Out walking. Nathan looked up at the web of trolley wires. Up the hill, the spiky tower of a church. He stopped, and here, in the alien clash of a distant city, its bruising light, its woozy, unfathomable views, Nathan loved his brother. And the loss, the misery suffered mostly alone (gratitude toward Abby and the boy), settled over Nathan as a new weight, different, not entirely unwelcome. Nathan loved his brother, and how hard it would be now, knowing he'd never be able to tell him so.

∾ ∾ ∾

The dog saw him first, charged the length of the crowded sidewalk, got its dusty paws on his shoulders and its muzzle, wet and stinking, in his face. "Hi, boy," Ben said, smiling, pushing him gently down. "Hi." The dog, turning eager circles, swept against his legs.

Tommy, who never said much, looked over. It was afternoon,

still getting hotter, and Tommy had moved from the sidewalk into
the entrance of a closed-up store (Rx Rx Rx in chipped green letters
in the window), his body in shadow, his feet in the gray sneakers
without socks sticking into the light. Against the storefront his cardboard sign, coffee cup.

It was the dog who attracted Ben that first day. Then, and every
day since, Dog (Ben's name for him—he never heard Tommy call
him anything at all) had come loping up, tail joyfully whipping, circling Ben as if he'd been gone weeks but was back now and surely
had a treat in his pocket. He was a funny-looking kind of dog,
brown with curly fur and a long nose, white spots all around. He
had a funny face, and he'd look at you as if he'd just asked a question and was waiting for you to answer. Ben could tell his mom was
worried, the way she kept looking at Tommy (they didn't know his
name yet, or Dog's), sitting on his cardboard close to the coffee
store where she worked, then back at Ben, who was by now on his
knees, laughing as the smelly dog tried to lick his face. Ben didn't
remember what kind of day that was for his mom, angry or sleepy or
sad (she was usually better in the afternoons), but she saw him
laughing, and looked over at Tommy again, and let him be until
she said, C'mon, we don't want to get Mrs. Downing mad. As they
walked off, she let Ben drop some money into the paper cup.

After that, whenever they saw Tommy and Dog, she had money
for the cup, sometimes a sandwich or leftovers in a paper sack, and
when they turned the corner, Ben had to let her wipe his hands and
face in front of everybody with cold hard little towels that smelled
like soapy lemons. That was the deal. Sometimes she let Ben bring
a treat for Dog, like a hot dog he didn't finish, or a carrot that had
started to go soft. This was if Ben was good and went to bed, or took
a bath by himself, or ate some of the gross vegetables she put on his
plate, weedy, lumpy stuff that would fold up on his tongue and stay
there if he didn't chew and swallow fast.

Tommy kept looking as Ben walked over between the people,

holding his cigar box, Dog's curved tail swatting his legs. In the beginning Ben thought Tommy couldn't talk, but he could. He said
words to himself, mostly so quiet you couldn't hear, and sometimes
he got upset and said strange words to Dog, who lay there looking at
him as if he was interested. Ben was used to Tommy not talking. It
didn't bother Ben anymore, and he talked to Tommy all the time,
sometimes in his head, sometimes with his voice, and when
Tommy looked at Ben it was like he'd heard everything and it was
okay, whatever Ben said, so he talked to Tommy a lot. I left, he said
to Tommy now, in his head. I didn't say goodbye.

There was room in the store entrance, though it smelled. He sat
by Tommy, put the cigar box between his feet and opened it, tore a
sandwich he'd found in the refrigerator into three pieces. Dog ate
his in one jumping bite, then waited around for someone else's.
Tommy held his in his hand, and Ben took a nibble of the peanut
butter and jelly and wrapped the rest for later. There was an apple,
too, and a granola bar, and he put these on the mat next to Tommy.

Out in the light, people walked by. Most didn't stop or look,
some looked and didn't stop. Every once in a while someone
stopped and looked and dropped a coin in the cup. They read
Tommy's sign. A woman sweating in a fancy coat walked by, then
turned around, staring right at Ben. She came back and folded a
bill into the cup (Ben couldn't see the president), still looking at
him walking away, as if she wanted to say something. Once when
he was sitting with Tommy and Dog a lady in a beat-up coat and a
funny sliding purple hat stopped and wouldn't move away, even
when Tommy stared out into space and Ben, who'd watched him,
did the same. "Are you alright?" the lady asked, tilting her head so
the big hat slid. "Do you need any help?" She was a nice-looking
old lady, chins all over the place, kind of fat, which Ben liked, and
her dark face, except for now when it was all twisted up looking at
him, seemed like it was usually happy. Ben, who watched faces a
lot, could tell.

She stood there, and Ben was uncomfortable. In another situation he would have answered, just to be polite, Thank you, or, I'm okay. In a really different situation he might have looked back at her and said, No, I guess not. Behind this lady's face was a nice room with a table near a window, pictures in frames on the walls, a plate with cookies on the table and a cup with something to drink. He could almost smell the cookies.

But Ben did as Tommy did, stared out as if something in the air was moving, or something far off was just about to come into view. Soon the lady in the big hat walked off. For a couple of days Ben wondered about her and her room, then stopped thinking about her, which he told himself was like forgetting but he knew it wasn't.

In the street, cars lined up, waiting for the light, two blue, a red, another blue. When the light changed they moved and a new line formed, a green, a black, two taxicabs—orange with yellow stripes. Ben liked to look at the drivers who sat waiting and see if he could make them turn their heads. Usually the light changed and they drove off, but sometimes they turned, like someone had said their name. This was exciting, and a little scary. One time a guy in a truck had stuck his middle finger up, which Ben knew wasn't friendly, and two boys in a car, who looked over one at a time, threw a McDonald's bag full of trash out the window as they left. But once a little girl pressed her face to the window and blew out her cheeks, which made Ben laugh, and a couple of times people smiled or waved. Today nobody turned, and when Ben got tired doing it, he looked at Tommy.

Of all the faces Ben had ever seen, Tommy's was the most amazing. On a person. At the zoo tigers had amazing faces, they stared with orange eyes that didn't blink and seemed a lot smarter than you would've guessed. They looked like they were thinking about how you'd taste. At Caitlin Goldman's birthday, he'd looked a long time at this dog's face, a pug it was called, which was a good name, better than what Caitlin Goldman called it, Phyllis. This dog looked like it had eaten something so sour it had pulled its whole face in. But its eyes were big and wet and its nose not too cold, and it let Ben pet it as long as he liked.

Tommy's face, one side was normal, though you could tell he spent a lot of time outdoors. It was covered with gray and white hairs, not a beard exactly, and had red spots, especially on the nose. His mouth sometimes moved, even when he wasn't talking, but Gerald Lombrano, who sat near Ben in Mrs. Downing's room, did the same thing, and he ate his own boogers, which Tommy never did, at least Ben hadn't seen him do it. The other side of Tommy's face was the amazing part. It had shiny patches, like tiny coins, like the skin had been rubbed off, and there was a part under his nose that didn't look like skin at all, stretched and pink, and a crooked line ran from his mouth to under his eye and into his hair. This side was where the funny moving was, like the muscles didn't work. Ben asked his mom once and she told him Tommy had been burned, Tommy was a veteran. She told him what that meant. When Ben slipped behind Tommy's face he saw him on a stage in front of a castle, where he turned slowly so everybody in the audience could see. The king put a medal around his neck and everybody clapped. One time Tommy pulled two metal tags on a chain from his shirt and let Ben look at them. That was the day Ben decided he would show Tommy the picture, the day Ben decided they were friends.

He had no plans. He thought he had, when he ran out of the apartment, plenty of them. He'd come back and set the building on fire, his mom and Mr. Li and everyone inside. He'd prop open the front door—which Mr. Li said never to do—so anyone could come in and do whatever they liked, Ben didn't care. He'd find a group of gypsies and become their leader. He'd get on a boat. He'd do something that would make him famous, make them sorry, make them wonder if that was the same Ben they knew before.

Or he'd flag down a car—people did it on TV—and say, Take me to the beach, please. But he didn't know which beach, and he had forgotten blankets or a pillow (and he'd given away his food), and even if he could burn the whole house down with her inside it, he still couldn't get into somebody's car without asking his mom. When he saw the dog charging toward him and Tommy on his cardboard mat, Ben knew that was as far as he'd figured, and now he took two slices of the apple Tommy was cutting with his knife. People walked by in the sun, and Dog, seeing there was no more food after the apple, turned a few times and rested with his jaw on Tommy's knee. He had no plans.

After a while he opened the cigar box and began emptying it between his legs. He took out a metal screw and told Tommy it was from a place he'd visited it with his class last year. Mrs. Downing had told them not to touch anything, so Ben got as many pieces as he could. He'd thrown them away when he found this. It's from a World War II submarine that's in the water down by the gray bridge. Tommy could go see it if he wanted. It was a fat screw painted black, and Ben had felt guilty taking it because maybe they would need it for the submarine, but there it was, just lying on the floor, and he couldn't help himself and put it in his pocket. That day he was all excited because after the submarine they were going to Alcatraz, which was kind of cool and a little scary (they closed the lights and the door of a cell, like they were locking you in, which everyone knew was a joke but Ben held his mom's hand anyway). When they came off the boat ramp, just like in the picture, Ben looked all over for someone with a camera, for men in white uniforms. He looked at every face he saw and was so excited his mother felt his head but Ben shook her off.

He knew who the man in the sailor uniform was, he told Tommy. His mom didn't talk about him but Ben knew. He didn't like to think about it.

He continued emptying the box. This is Thomas Jefferson, he remembered, and told Tommy, showing the two-dollar bill, then turning it over to show the serious men in strange clothes holding pieces of paper. They had lines all over them that made them look electric.

And this is a penny, when it's all stretched out. Then he took out some drawings of his and Danny's house, the pools and the rides and the fishing pond, the garage with seven red cars. There's plenty of room, he almost told Tommy, you and Dog could come live there, but something made him not say it. Then, even if it made him sad, he laid out the pieces of number thirty-six. Tommy should see this, too. You could see two feet in one piece and a section of the tummy in another. You couldn't see much of the face or head because Ben had made sure of that with the knife, and he felt sorry about that, every day he felt sorry and tried to make believe the dog was just lost, but he knew better, and he tried not to think about it.

Number thirty-six, he told Tommy.

Last was the picture, not black-and-white but with the colors gone funny, some too bright and others fading away. Another sunny day—you could tell from the sunglasses, people's clothes. His mom, younger, in a short dress with blue and white lines on it, flipping up as she walked, was looking at the man. The man, in a sailor suit (actual, all white, with that round hat and a black ribbon on his neck), had his arm around Ben's mom, and he was big, he looked like he could lift her and swing her around. They were laughing like it was a good day, like there would be lots of good days and having your picture taken was no big deal. They didn't even look at the camera. Tommy looked at the picture a long time and Ben didn't say anything, and when he put it back into the box, dumping everything else on top, he knew it was too late, the bad feelings were here.

He'd hoped to leave them back in the apartment, or lose them walking between people on the street. He knew opening the box was risky but he wanted to show Tommy the picture (Tommy had shown Ben his tags), and anyway, Ben, who was an expert, knew there was only so much not thinking about something you could do—you were really thinking about it all the time.

But he would not cry. They were here and there was nothing he could do. His mom half off the bed, wearing no clothes. Mrs. Downing, writing in her book. Danny, waking up on the couch and smiling stupidly when Ben went to the refrigerator, happy to see him. His father in the sailor suit saluting from the deck of the submarine. The Alvarez girls—why weren't they on the steps today? He took the soft skin under his arm between two fingernails, testing.

Ben liked the idea of people out looking for him, but it was never as much fun as he hoped. Once, when he was little, he hid from his mom in a grocery store, which was fun at first, but when the manager found him behind the stack of soda bottles and pulled him out by his shirt, he saw his mom's face and it wasn't fun anymore. He didn't want everyone mad at him, and he knew what it felt like to be worried, and he didn't really want to make everybody feel like that.

The Alvarez girls, the pretty little one and the older one with dark eyes and a mustache on her lip, who scared him. Maybe they had gone on a family trip, Ben thought. Or maybe they were out sick. But he didn't believe it. Sometimes bad things happened, and you didn't even know they were happening at the time or maybe you would have done something, but afterward you knew and then it was too late. He couldn't remember another day the Alvarez girls weren't on the steps. He took the skin and rolled it, softly at first, then harder, using his nails.

Next to him Tommy was talking, and Dog, who'd woken up, was listening. Ben tried, too, but he couldn't understand. Tommy was upset, maybe he had heard Ben's thinking. He had his legs pulled up and his hands around his knees and he was rocking, faster, then slowing down. Dog was watching, ears twitching, looking hard. Ben tried to hear. Zafiel, Tommy said, whispering. Metatron, Rachmiel, Eluziel.

He wouldn't cry. Danny was gone and Ben had no idea why. Danny made him laugh. Ben always knew there would be no house, but now there would be no more rides in the car with the top down and everyone yelling into the wind, and no more trips to the big trees or the beach. His mom cried all the time, and what was he supposed to do, he tried all day to think of something to do but he couldn't find anything. Missy Alexander cried sometimes and Ben could make her laugh, make funny faces or stick a crayon in his nose, but this didn't work with his mom. Out in the street a truck blasted its brakes and somebody cursed and the horns began honking. He got the skin under each eye between his thumbnail and the other fingers and soon his hands started shaking from pinching so hard, he wouldn't cry, little green lights exploding in his head, Tommy still talking crazy, Sidrach, Misach, Abednego, they were everywhere now, Danny in his car, his father on the submarine, the Alvarez girls, his dogs in two lines, his mom walking with Mrs. Downing, everywhere, and right before Ben closed his eyes a shadow moved into the hot light, blocking them but only for a moment, all there, everyone he had ever loved and lost and driven away.

∾ ∾ ∾

The cars were honking, and Sol was still in the middle of the street. He gripped the red box tighter and kept walking, looking straight ahead.

He had remembered the pills in his pocket (in his ears Nathan's scolding voice) and bought a cold drink from one of those little stores, the woman behind the counter staring at him and the grubby box he'd set down. So look, Sol thought.

If he were younger, or less tired, or, he even admitted, a little less stubborn, he would have taken the coat off, the hat, which sent hot drips of sweat into his eyes every few steps. Maybe he had a fever. Maybe he was lost. He had assumed (why, he didn't know) he would recognize something, out walking in a city he'd never been to before. He didn't. He had assumed sooner or later he'd bump into his son, though what he'd do then, if he'd turn and walk away, he hadn't quite decided. But every street, away from the water if he could manage the steep ones, was new to him, he could swear he'd never seen it before, and after a while he gave up trying to figure out where he was, just put his head down and walked.

As a young father, though he hadn't said as much to anybody (not even Freda, who didn't need telling), he had been proud of his boys. Daniel they all called a prodigy, from the start he was something special. Nobody believed it who wasn't there, but he talked at eight months, whole sentences by a year. He could sing (like Sol's grandfather, the shoemaker) in a high, sweet voice, and at three, just to see what happened, Sol taught him to play chess. By six he was beating Sol and he had his head in books all day. He decided to read the Bible, all of it, and every morning he would recite to them the stories he'd read, the flood, the ten plagues, the pillar of salt. Sol remembered a happy child. He could still hear the two of them playing in another room.

The younger boy, Nathan, didn't have it so simple. Not easy, being brother to a person so gifted, so admired (this Sol knew from Chaim). But he was a happy kid, too, Sol thought. He loved sports and animals and following his brother around all day. Daniel taught him big words, which sounded funny coming out of his little mouth. ("That's ironic," he said for a week, about everything. He was five, maybe.) Sol's memory of the boy centered on wide eyes locked onto whatever was happening, as if that was life, to see and absorb everything around you. A strange child, also, in his way, this watching, this holding apart. But they were happy, healthy, loud running boys (he liked to feel them, the solid flesh and working muscles, the feet and arms pumping). Both got good grades (Daniel always in trouble for some prank), and everybody went out of their way to tell them (mostly Freda, who would listen) what wonderful boys they had, what a future. The king and queen of *naches*. If Sol could see them now, the know-nothings.

A sudden metallic clatter, wheels and bells and the glitter of glass, one of those cockamamie trolleys nearly knocking him down, people hanging off and grinning like from a merry-go-round. Sol, frightened, nearly dropped the box, took a quick step back. Two trickles of sweat snaked from under his cap, one into his eye, the other swaying fatly at the end of his nose. He shook them off angrily, looked the trolley two blocks up the hill until some idiot's waving at everyone from the back step made him turn away. How did people live in this place?

He waited another minute, managed to swipe his face with a sleeve, then started across again.

What was a man supposed to tell his children? Everything? Did he have to say to them, every day, how he felt?

Maybe he did. (Freda thought so.) But nobody ever told Sol anything, and by the time he might have wanted to ask, by then nobody was left. And what could he say? Listen, I saw things I can't explain, even tell. I got changed, you understand? Parts of me killed off—how do I know they weren't the best parts? Was this what you said to children? Once I had a family, like this one, two beautiful sisters, I watched all the boys stare. Once we were hoodlums and tied a dead cat to a crazy man's coat and chased him through the village. Once I thought I would go to the city (not even a city, a provincial town, but with a college) and study law. Once, once, once—what was the point, what could be gained?

Once there was a pond so full of human ash it was muddy gray and the wind was full of it like snow. Once people died around me every day and I couldn't have cared less about flies on a windowsill.

This? This to small boys with their big eyes and shining dreams and their Mickey Mantle and Pete Marinovich and their astronauts and Beatles and Someday I'll play for the Knicks, Daddy, you'll come see me, and Someday, Dad, I'll be president of the United States.

Once I lay in a wooden box and listened as they beat my brother to death.

Once over a pile of shoes I watched my two boys laughing at my life, my memory, all I ever had, and I prayed to the god I knew wasn't there to blast us all dead on the spot.

So Sol said nothing. He felt his sons, their strengthening bones, their faces intense with whatever passing emotion, when they were little he put his own face into their hair which smelled like warm leaves. He marked their heights on the side of the kitchen door, and when he and Freda sat in the living room in front of Ed Sullivan, the cowboy shows (what was that magic American place? the Ponderosa?), from their room came the sounds of laughing, ambush, ridiculous stories of pirates and desperados, and Sol felt something he never could express (something that never lasted), that pulled through him like a cable and made him strong, and he wanted to go out in the middle of the street and wave his fists at the empty sky: This, you sonofabitch. This.

The box in his hands, spattered with sweat and streaked gray, was hauling him downward, heavier every step. Soon he would have to stop. He paused before a parked police car, a black officer (hard-looking, nothing like Clara) stared at him silently. Nothing special, a tired old man with a box, in all this noise and tumble. He walked on.

But there was something, Sol thought, emotion pooling up through the exhaustion, the store of gruff resentment he wore like another coat. This is not what a father should do. A father shouldn't be carrying his dead son deeper and deeper into a place he didn't know, all that was left of him in a plastic box. Surely, if there was any reason, an order to anything at all, this was wrong. Daniel, he found himself saying.

This Sol understood: Once you are cast out there is no getting back in, you can live a thousand years. He clutched the box to him one last time and turned up another hill.

The street, like all the others, was teeming, stores and cars and trucks unloading, people shouting, taxis blocking traffic, people stopped right in the middle of everything, like nobody had to get by. He had almost walked past them, a man and a boy on a filthy mat, a spotted, mangy dog with its tongue out in the heat. The boy, holding a cigar box in his lap, his face smudged with jelly, asleep against the man's shoulder. The man stared into the street, not moving, even when Sol stopped before them. Then the boy opened his eyes, looked up at Sol. He rubbed his face. "You run away, too?" he said.

ᐁ ᐁ ᐁ

He couldn't wait any longer. Nathan had seen the effects of complete exhaustion, seen otherwise reasonable people break down, mothers slapping children in the ER, cursing family in ways none of them would forget. A resident he had liked, De Stefano, so drained after a sixteen-hour shift he had just put his head down in the cubbyhole where the docs wrote their notes and slept, right there, with the on-call room and bed just up the hall. The charge nurse said to leave him be. One time, he had watched a woman, anxious, intractable, unable to sleep, pull an IV from her arm with such force that her gown, and almost immediately the whole side of her bed, were covered in blood. All she did, with a look of unmistakable relief, was lie back and close her eyes.

There was nowhere else to go. From a phone booth he had finally called Rivera, but the receptionist told him he was out on assignment, and when she connected him to voice mail, Nathan had nothing to say. He'd been back to the hospital, called the hotel. He'd stopped in Union Square, in front of a howling troop of skateboarders, as if, in the unending surge of shoppers and tourists and people out wandering, Sol would come to him. His mind had locked down. There was nowhere else to go.

And, of course, there they were, in front of the grubby yellow building, on metal folding chairs, each a different color. Sol, Ben, and Mr. Li, the landlord, the boy with an ice cream, the men drinking out of white mugs, like the geezers back in New York, out cooling themselves on a hot day, the ball game playing on a radio in the window. He walked over to Sol.

"Where have you been?"

His tone, even in his own ears, was so harsh he didn't say any-thing else, not even when Sol looked at him but did not answer the question. The boy, his face remarkably filthy, streaked with food and sweat and maybe tears, now ringed around the mouth in sticky chocolate, had a battered cigar box between his legs, and Nathan saw, by the chair Sol was in, the red box of ashes, looking like it had been rolled through the street. From a window behind the soiled shade, the announcers announced, and intermittently you could hear the sounds of the crowd at the park, tinny, distant, a sound from Nathan's childhood, immediate consolation. Mr. Li, after a couple of breathy sips from his mug, said to him, "More chair in-side."

That sounded to Nathan like a delicious possibility, just to sit, have a cup of whatever they were drinking, listen to the ball game, as he used to with the old men in front of their apartment building when he was little, or with a transistor hidden under his pillow late at night when the Yankees were here, on the far coast; summer nights when it never got really cool or dark, his head filling with the sounds of the bat, the faces and calls from the crowd, his own silent heroes moving on a green field three thousand miles away. He nod-ded at Mr. Li, climbed a step to go and find a chair for himself.

"How's your mom?" he asked the boy, who, having bitten the tip off his sugar cone, now held it over his face to suck melted ice cream out the end. While he paused to answer, three creamy drops, one after another, fell onto his shirt.

"She's sleeping," Ben said. "She took something."

Nathan was up two or three flights before he remembered he hadn't asked if the door was unlocked. It was and he threw it back against the pile of coats and ran inside. He hadn't asked what she took; he knew. She was on the floor, naked, and from the odd angle of her body, hips twisted, an arm pinned under her head, hair splayed over her face, he thought she was gone. Something gathered in his chest and he thought he would scream. But when he turned Abby to feel her pulse she moaned, opened her eyes at him a moment, and though she was clammy and a little chill (he saw the smudged mirror, the empty packet and dollar bill), he knew she was alright, and lucky to be. He rolled her over and checked her pulse, did it again. He pried open one eye and she opened the other, then dreamily closed them. She made as if to roll on her side and Nathan heard himself breathe.

When he laid her on the bed, pulled the twisted blankets free to cover her, she opened her eyes again, stoned, dreamy, and in them Nathan saw too many things: recognition, relief, invitation (he still had on Daniel's shirt), and she was beautiful, he realized, breasts rising with her breath, her body slim and open and relaxed on the sheets, those green eyes when she looked at him. For an instant, he saw it all playing out. But a roar went through his head, a resounding No, the first thing heard clearly in days, and he got a glass of water and put it near her, cracked the window for a breeze. He found a pillow, covered Abby with a blanket, dragged a chair over so he could hear if she called out or needed anything, and waited till she closed her eyes. He looked once around the room, the books, the flag, the photos, and with a Giants blanket he had found on the floor over his shoulders, in the hard-backed and lumpy kitchen chair, waiting for the EMTs to arrive, he watched her breathe fluidly, adjusted her covers, then let his own eyes close. And for the first time in more days than he could remember, Nathan slept.

guy who caught Barry Bonds' 400th wants fifty thousand for it. probably get it, huh? caught homerun off Norm Cash, remember?, 65, 66?, dragged old man to the Stadium, he brought a newspaper. wonder who has that ball.

it's the middle names that get you, the ones for the parents. the dull, smirking lunk they call Toro was christened Edgar; glum, dowdy, gum-smacking Tiffany is somebody's Rose. all your best dreams and wishes for the future loaded on their little backs. this one, Luis Otavio Hernandez, not much to notice in a group of thirty bored and restless and preoccupied souls clamoring for anything to hold their attention. embarrassed, when I heard he was the one, it took a minute to locate which kid, which gangly thirteen year old sprouting pimples and Scooby-doo whiskers they pridefully don't shave, all of them trying for that fuck you first look, dead in the eyes, but they drop it, some of them, when an idea catches. beautiful to see. not the most motivated kid, one I wondered was he getting enough sleep, to eat, what was the deal at home, had his macho hormone machine pumped him toward the irrevocable bad choices so many make. But I couldn't separate him from the hooded crowd till I saw the picture in the paper, his Mom

crying and a little sister in their living room, and there over a
shoulder, Luis's oak tag map of Ecuador with the cutouts of
jaguars and mountains and mestizos, my assignment last
spring, and then I remembered the one conversation we'd had,
Ecuador had already been assigned but Luis came up and
said his moms was from Quito, he hoped to visit maybe this
summer, family, you know, so could he do Ecuador too? And
he did a pretty good job, I remembered. Luis Otavio Hernan-
dez, now in a box with the back of his head gone from a stray
bullet, meant for another child.

this is what they say: wrong place wrong time. what other
place what other time was there for Luis who wanted to go
fishing with his abuelo in Ecuador this summer, his whole life
leading to the moment he was standing with his homeys, look-
ing tough, looking cool. wrong place wrong time, like an acci-
dent of geography or scheduling. what good that little wave of
dismissal, consolation to the indifferent, to his mother in her
living room, to anyone who cared?

As Nathan wrestled with the bulky, clumsily taped envelope, it
came apart in his hands, showering the carpet with Post-its, newspaper clippings, scrawled napkins and the backs of takeout menus,
crimped yellow pages from legal pads. Nathan, who only now wondered if there might have been a chronology to the stack, looked at
the scatter of paper and doubted it. He stared a long moment at the
windows, the thin gray hotel drapes absolutely still, then gathered a
handful from the floor and began to read.

Abby, late at night, the boy's sleeping, windows open to the
breeze, burnt cheese on toast, a pot of tea, Trane or Prez or
Ella or Evans. The only thing in the world—watch you put up
your hair, paint your toes, hum along the way you do when
you think nobody's listening.

Kafka: It is conceivable that Alexander the Great, in spite of the martial success of his early days, in spite of the excellent army that he had trained, in spite of the power he felt within him to change the world, might have remained standing on the bank of the Hellespont and never have crossed it, and not out of fear, not out of indecision, not out of infirmity of will, but because of the mere weight of his own body.

That picture, the moment in time, me and you stoned, laughing, arms around each other, looking into the sun. I should send it to you, or send it to Sol, or burn it, our family Zapruder before all hell blows loose. I swear, I was too high, too full of the bright, stupid, unheeding day to even think about the shoes. we were striking a blow for the workers, right?, taking our convictions home. of course he would be mad, the silent man, lord of absence and restraint, but who saw Sol, who saw the shoes piling up in the loading bay, who saw anything till he came over, and that's what you can never forgive—who saw? And when he told me he wished I was dead for what I'd done to him, that I never was born to begin with, I looked at him then, I certainly did, and not for the first time, my righteous, unappeasable, unanswerable dad, not for the first time I opened my eyes and agreed.

so Stengel benches Mantle because he's so hungover he stinks from it, Mantle at the end of the dugout 8 innings with a cold towel around his head. bottom of the ninth, Stengel sends him in, Mick hits a three-run shot to win the game. Somebody (Johnny Ellis, Hector Lopez) says Mick, How the fuck? Saw three balls coming, Mick says, swung hard as I could at the one in the middle. choice.

At the outskirts of the camp was a pond where they dumped the ashes. The Kommandant, an engineer by

*trade, knew this solution wouldn't hold—even a pond this
size would fill up sooner or later, and another plan would
need to be found. Proposals were made. But the pond
never filled. The remains of thousands of bodies, an SS
Lieutenant assigned to monitor the situation. Yet even after months of monitoring, the pond, as if it had no bottom,
continued to admit more ashes.*

ever read the symbolists, Dr. M? probably too late now, important, could be, certain age, time, afternoon. maybe you have
read. I'll ask at our next heartfelt reunion.

images, they say, are all that last. Mallarme (Valery?) catching glimpse of a girl from a train, she on the platform, he pulling
out, never see her before or again, never forget. Genet (later): love
is walking the street and seeing, through a darkened house, a
back garden in sunlight. Rimbaud, battered by everything.

it is late but it doesn't matter maybe—this girl, how even tell
you, high school, before your time, ill, dying matter of fact, delicate and beautiful and before you even knew you sensed it, her
difference, she knew it, though all she wanted, ALL she wanted
was be the same. spoke to her two times, three, then sick again
and gone. some reason past days won't out of my head, we sit on
synagogue steps we talk she has to go can I see you tomorrow
sure okay tomorrow but once it's too late it's too late forever and
I don't know this know anything yet. Corey her name. Fifteen.

*Today a representative of the Mayor's Task Force on
Narcotics said the city is fully aware of increased illegal
activity around schools, specifically the use of children as
couriers in the trafficking of narcotics. Several plans are already in operation, some of them undercover, and further
measures will be taken. "The safety of our children," he
said, "is our greatest concern."*

how do you get a name? Medium got his in a drug deal gone
bad. things go rough, somebody pulls a gun, story goes, shoves
it in his neck. Think you're big stuff, fucker, guy says. No,
Medium tells him, just medium.

A man is receptive to counsel only to the extent that he allows
his situation to speak. —Walter Benjamin

the pictures of the roundups disturb most, in Hillesum diary
Jews gathering in Amsterdam for the trains—little boy in
shorts and black shoes. Sol somewhere, not much older.

In the barracks, horror—starving, huge eyes emptied even
of suffering stare from skulls, heaps of limbs barely human,
midden of the slaughterhouse—arms, heads, knees, a crotch, a
collapsed breast. but these somehow are beyond comprehen-
sion, severed from us living, startling in their familiarity but
crossed over, like bloated dead at Gettysburg or inmates star-
ing on death row—terrible, fascinating, but removed, artifacts
of a different world.

But these pictures, families with luggage, civilized people
waiting in line, the unknowing translation begun, faces and
clothing and belongings showing still the various definers
of wealth, beauty, dignity, grace or its lack. Strain on their
faces, worry, but no terror yet as they march toward extinc-
tion. "Hard times, surely," they say, "but there's a war on and
everything, after all, is hard. And anyway, people are not
monsters." These photographs are unbearable.

What these people want, what everyone does, what you fig-
ure's coming to you, is your own story, your life. It's your own
history you're trying to make. And you don't realize yet that's
over. You don't want this other, this one you never chose. But
here it is. And soon enough it is yours. Soon enough you come
to see it always was.

They love to say it, like sheep, they went like sheep to the slaughterhouse. What real alternative? Only one — rage, every minute. Like the guy on the highway who will kill you, really kill you, because by accident you cut him off. Like those men in the woods, waiting for years, stockpiling lunatic angers and resentments along with ordnance, and then one day, as they foresaw all along, it's true, the enemies gathering at the gate.

But if you don't live that way. If you live somewhere uncomfortably between the delusional margins of terror and idiot bliss, if you accept some are good, some are evil, most a confused mix, greedy, at most cowardly. Even some genuinely kind. You walk down the street in the middle of the day and you figure the odds are pretty good you'll make it home. How, then, how are you supposed to be prepared to see murder in your neighbor's face?

The prospect of prayer itself becomes intolerable, the words unspeakable because of need unspeakable, desperate wish they'll be heard. This rabbi, young guy, ambitious in grandfather pants and exhorting pose, still hoping to change lives, gave me one in rehab: "Lay us down oh Lord in peace and awaken us to life." Pretty good, Nathaniel, save it for a shaky night.

But here, the saddest most beautiful prayer I know: "Beauty is a pledge of the possible conformity between the soul and nature, and consequently a ground of faith in the supremacy of the good."

Try carrying that around without breaking your heart.

Heeneh ba hayom boer k'esh tanur

Basho: *Even in Kyoto —*
                hearing the cuckoo cry —
                I long for Kyoto.

10

And there it was.

Later, Ben would forget this particular day, who he had been with, even (though it would return to him eventually, when he was older) why they had come. What he would always remember was first seeing the water from the car, then the bridge, then the beach from the sloping path, and the green-blue ocean rolling in waves onto the sand. It had been a bad couple of weeks, he'd been scared all the time. There was a lot he didn't understand (a lot he didn't want to know), but he knew getting back to this beach was the first thing that felt right. A group of fat seagulls gathered by the edge of the foam, and as he walked, Ben kept his eyes on them.

Abruptly Ben dropped her hand, ran on ahead, and Abby, wearing sunglasses against the suddenly vibrant sun (it had rained overnight, scrubbing the air blue), feeling the small thud in her head and guts, let him go. The path was angular and full of shale, and she worried Ben would trip over the side but he was surefooted, legs and arms pumping as he reached the sand and tore after some unsuspecting birds. The air was finally eased from its cloying heat, she could breathe a little, and part of her wanted to run after the boy, but Nathan and his father behind her were moving slowly and she stayed back with them.

Over the girl's head Sol could see the red bridge slide into view, the one he'd been looking for since he'd arrived. He had seen bridges, of course. The webbed, Old World Brooklyn, the Verrazano, the George Washington, the hideous, clogged Queensboro with the tram gliding by in the air like an insult to you stuck in traffic. But this was different, and a confused emotion began working its way into Sol's chest. Its color against the sky, the way it jutted from the headlands to the north, the water slamming in foamy bursts against the tower footings—it was a beautiful thing to see, and Sol was unprepared for beauty this day, and it set some odd things moving in his head, behind the eyes, and Nathan, who could be called a lot of things, but unobservant wasn't one of them, noticed something immediately and took hold of Sol's arm as they made the final turn down to the beach where Sol, who felt he'd been carrying the red box most of his life, hefted it in preparation for shrugging Nathan off, then put a foot in the dense, unstable sand and let his son's arm stay where it was.

Nathan, who had been keeping his eyes on his father's heavy, unyielding gait down the scrappy path (he could see him hurtling, box over coat over stubborn cap, onto the rocks below), glanced up for no reason, and suddenly there was the bridge, its burnt orange almost painful against the backdrop of clear sky, the water tossing below. He was startled; though he'd known, of course, it was there, seeing it was a shock, and for a minute he thought he'd lose his own balance and stretched out a hand for his father's arm.

Down on the beach the boy, who'd shot out of the car like an animal finally uncaged, was running; Abby was by the foot of the path, waiting. When Nathan had opened his eyes yesterday evening, slumped painfully in the flat chair, yet rested, miraculously, she was at the stove, dressed, making coffee, and she gave him a quick look, open, friendly, as if she was used to seeing him there. For the first time since he'd left Janet in Boston, Nathan felt nothing he needed to question, the clamor in him subsided, and he watched Abby move from stove to sink to table without saying a word, grateful, sad, and still.

Freda would enjoy this, Sol thought. Sylvia, too, maybe he

would bring her. She was no great hiker since the accident with her hip, but she was willing (her walks on the boulevard every afternoon), and Sol allowed himself the picture of returning with her one day, walking on this beach and looking at the water. Ahead the boy dug his hands in his pockets. He was approaching the birds, whose wings fluttered in nervous anticipation, and Sol, who allowed this, too, saw his own boys, both, running toward him and Freda on the beach in Rockaway, sand and salt on their skin and hair, then Daniel in the middle of the night reading a book in the big chair when Sol gets up for a drink, Nathan driving them crazy dribbling that basketball through the house until they all thought they'd strangle him. They hurt, these memories, but Sol allowed them. Then another, even more distant: he, in his stiff wool suit, holding his ancient grandmother's hand as they walk to the stream in Dubossar, New Year's Day, Chaim, already at the grassy bank, tossing bits of bread into the water as the wheezy rabbi chanted, in Sol's pockets more bits of bread, his turn next.

Beside him Nathan had stopped, was looking past Sol at the view, and after a moment Sol handed him the red box. "Here," he said. "I don't want to fall."

Ben took handfuls of the crumbs the old man had given him and tossed them high to the birds, somehow got in their middle and it was amazing, the whole world exploding in wings and beaks and bright sharp eyes, air sliced through with their raucous, toneless cries, and Ben in the middle of it, screaming and turning himself, turning in delight as his mother, who realized she hadn't done this in days, and the two men approaching her on the sand, stopped to watch.

Out in the steely-green breakers, and he knew it wasn't real, didn't bother to shake it off, Nathan saw a head, a hand. He watched a minute or two and it was gone.

"What's out there?" his father said, as Abby came over. "Nothing," Nathan said, "Japan," and they walked across the sand to where the boy, having emptied his pockets, had already reached the water.

ACKNOWLEDGMENTS

This book was a long time in coming and I have many people to thank.

The works of Lawrence L. Langer gave me insights vital to my understanding of these characters. Roger Jacobson, M.D., discussed with me some of the emotional difficulties families such as the Mirskys might encounter.

Sergeant Evan Fieman of the Corvallis (Oregon) Police Department, Inspector Thomas P. Walsh of the San Francisco Police Department, and Investigator Charles L. Cecil of the Medical Examiner's Office in San Francisco all were generous with their time and patient with my many questions.

Professor Mary Jager helped me with Latin, Rabbi Meir Havazelet with Yiddish. Charlotte Jacobs and Brandon Brown generously gave of their time and knowledge. Tina Eskes gathered many necessary documents. Gustav Davidson's singular *Dictionary of Angels* (where my father is acknowledged on page xxvii) was a delightful resource. Allyson Wolfe, from the Museum of Modern Art's Registrar's Office, was very helpful in reconstructing the museum's displays in the late 1970s.

Without the intelligent and warmhearted readings of many close friends, the book would not have been possible. I'd especially like to thank: John Daniel, Tom and Laura MacNeal, Joe Millar,

Gavin O'Neill, Karen Ford, and Molly Brown. For their friendship, stewardship, and long faith, my deepest gratitude to Tracy Daugherty, John Glusman, and Ted Solotaroff.

My family—my boys, my wife, Molly—anchored me through some difficult times. My unending love.

Last, I would like to acknowledge the support of the following institutions that gave me time, the hardest resource to acquire: The Mrs. Giles Whiting Foundation; the Solomon R. Guggenheim Foundation; the Program in Creative Writing at the University of Oregon; the Rockefeller Foundation, and Gianna Celli and her staff at the Bellagio Study Center, where this book was begun.